WANTED: DEAD OR IN LOVE

Kym Brunner

MeritPress

F+W Media, Inc.

Published by
Merit Press
an imprint of F+W Media, Inc.
10151 Carver Road, Suite 200
Blue Ash, OH 45242. U.S.A.
www.meritpressbooks.com

ISBN 10: 1-4405-7057-4
ISBN 13: 978-1-4405-7057-5
eISBN 10: 1-4405-7058-2
eISBN 13: 978-1-4405-7058-2

Printed in the United States of America.

10 9 8 7 6 5 4 3 2 1

Library of Congress Cataloging-in-Publication Data
Brunner, Kym.
    Wanted : dead or in love / Kym Brunner.
        pages cm
    Summary: Teens Monroe and Jack are possessed by the spirits of the outlaw lovers Bonnie and
Clyde.
        ISBN 978-1-4405-7057-5 (hc) -- ISBN 1-4405-7057-4 (hc) -- ISBN 978-1-4405-7058-2
(ebook) -- ISBN 1-4405-7058-2 (ebook)
    [1. Love--Fiction. 2. Spirit possession--Fiction. 3. Adventure and adventurers--Fiction. 4. Parker,
Bonnie, 1910-1934--Fiction. 5. Barrow, Clyde, 1909-1934--Fiction.] I. Title.
    PZ7.B828453Wan 2014
    [Fic]--dc23
                        2014001601

Cover design by Frank Rivera.
Cover image © iStockphoto.com/iconogenic.

This book is available at quantity discounts for bulk purchases.
For information, please call 1-800-289-0963.

DEDICATION

To God: You make all things possible. Thanks for always having my back.

CHAPTER 1

Friday, May 20th // 8:42 P.M.

Monroe

I deliver a third Bugsy Malone to the old guy at table seven, whose unnaturally dark hair against his wrinkly skin makes him look ridiculous, not younger. He watches me as I lean forward to place his drink next to him, making no effort to hide the fact that he's staring at my cleavage. He rests his age-spot-riddled hand on top of mine, his diamond pinky ring glistening off the stage lights. "What time you get off tonight? I'd like to buy you a drink."

He strokes my hand twice, making a river of disgust rise up my arm. One look at his smarmy smile and I know he's a rich jerk who's too full of himself to realize I'm only acting like a promiscuous flapper. I'm a breath away from saying that I'd rather stab myself in the eye with his butter knife than have a drink with him, when I stop myself.

Insulting the customers is definitely *not* on the list of good business practices.

I chomp on my gum a few times, pull myself back into character, and break out the stereotypical Jersey accent we're all supposed to use, "Sorry busta, but we ain't allowed to date the customers." I slide my hand out from under his, walking away before he sees me grimace.

Luckily, there are only three songs left in tonight's performance of *Gangsters of Love*, our musical dinner show set in the back alleys of Chicago during Prohibition. Once you walk through the doors of The Clip Joint, you'd swear you're in a bustling, noisy gin mill swarming with flappers and mob bosses. Dad's owned the place sixteen years now, making this boozy jazz scene such a big part of my life that if there were a time machine, I would fit right in during the 1920s. An era filled with people who live for the moment appeals to me.

Clarissa, one of six servers on tonight, hustles down the aisle in a yellow Charleston dress with layers of fringe. It's one of the cheap flapper dresses Dad buys in bulk from an online Halloween shop for our waitresses, along with strings of fake pearls and brimless hats. I brush my hand through the beaded fringe on my own dress, a black silk, drop-waist beauty I purchased from a local vintage shop. I just hope these beads don't fall off as quickly as the last one.

"Psst—meet me in back!" Clarissa whispers, before doing a double-take. "Whoa! Love your hair!" She reaches up and strums my shoulder length bob, her eyes wide with admiration.

"Thanks, Clarissa," I say, relieved that someone likes it as much as I do. I'll admit that getting my boring brown locks chopped and dyed into a flapper-inspired black bob three days ago was impulsive. But just like the original rebels, I didn't want to look the same as every other girl my age—long hair, straightened or curled, or else pulled up into a messy bun. Like my mom used to say, why be a sheep when you can be the shepherd?

Thinking of her makes me send a quick mental message: *Hey, Mom. I followed your advice.* I smirk at her imagined response, "For once."

I gather a few dirty plates before heading toward the busser station, curious to see what Clarissa wants. We're work friends, but we don't hang out. She's a senior too, but she goes to the huge, laid-back public high school in the city, while I attend the small, uptight, busybody factory known as Chicago Preparatory Academy. Not for much longer, thankfully. Only one week until graduation, I think with relief. I can make it.

The second I lay my empty drink tray on the counter, Clarissa gushes, "Guess what? I just counted and there's only eighteen more days until L.A.!"

"Nice!" I give her an enthusiastic high-five, although secretly, I'm worried for her. Clarissa's super pretty and genuinely nice, but a few weeks ago when Dad gave her a chance to fill in for the small role of the bootlegger named Thelma May, she forgot three of her six lines.

In any case, she's off to Los Angeles hoping to be discovered, whereas I'm only hoping to discover that my roommate isn't mean or crazy when I start college in the fall.

If NYU doesn't rescind my admission before then, that is.

The "I'm baaacck!" deluge of doubt floods into my mind, so I shove it to the side and look onstage. Vinny, our best singer, is crooning Al Capone's crude love song, "Getting Hard Time for You," to his sweetheart, a machine gun resting across his waist in a very suggestive pose. It's a crowd pleaser, but it's also the second to last number and our sign to wrap things up.

Clarissa doesn't waste any time. She taps a few buttons on the touch screen and the printer spits out receipts. I wait for her to tell me whatever it is she called me back here for, but when she doesn't, curiosity gets the better of me. "So . . . was that what you needed to talk to me about? That you only have eighteen days until L.A.?"

She giggles, rolling her eyes. "Whoops, I forgot! Hank texted me about a party at his friend Kyle's house." She glances my way as she grabs the receipts. "Want to come with?"

I almost blurt out that I'd love to when I remember the warning the judge gave me. I nudge her over and start printing my receipts. "I don't know, I uh . . ."

"There'll be a lot of hot guys there," she coos, elbowing me.

A party full of hot guys sounds amazing, but given that Clarissa is the bubbly actress type, I doubt our definitions of hot guys are anywhere close. She's probably into buff show-offs who can make their pecs dance, while I only want to meet a guy who is interesting, intelligent, and into me—what I call my three "in"variables. Insanely handsome would be nice of course, too, but that's not a deal breaker. I keep telling myself he's out there somewhere. Maybe even at this guy Kyle's house. Sadly, a girl on probation has no business going to a party.

Not wanting to talk about my recent stupid mistakes, I blurt out the first excuse I can think of. "That's sweet of you to ask, but I'm super tired tonight." I sigh loudly for effect.

She stares at me as if I just admitted to killing a puppy. "Tired? It's Friday night, Monroe. You can't go home!" She puts her hand on my arm. "Besides, you'd be doing me a big favor if you came. Hank said the football team showed up and there's hardly any girls at the party, so *please* come?" She looks at me all doe-eyed, like she really wants me to go.

Being asked to a party because I'm female is only marginally better than being asked so I can be the designated driver. Not to mention that football players are only a hair above stoners on the evolution chart. On the other hand, my entire high school is out dancing their butts off at prom at this very moment, while I'm stuck here at work because the dean, a.k.a. Dickhead, revoked all of my Senior Weekend privileges. So heading to any kind of party sounds better than going home to watch *Intervention* reruns until I fall asleep on the couch.

Still. I'm sure I shouldn't go. Definitely not a good decision.

"Okay, I'll go," I hear myself say. As soon as the words leave my mouth, the familiar fingers of regret crawl up my spine. What are you doing? Take it back!

Clarissa claps excitedly. "Great! Meet me at the door at 9:30." She tucks the last receipt into the black bill holder and slaps it shut, hurrying off to distribute the checks before I can tell her I changed my mind.

As the cast performs its last number, I place the bills next to my customers, ambivalent about what to do. There'll be alcohol at the party—a liquid grenade that has gotten me into trouble in the past. But as long as I don't reach for that pin, I'll be fine. And what are the chances *another* party I was at would get busted? Normally I'd say between slim and none, but given my shitty luck, the SWAT team is probably getting dressed in full combat gear right now, waiting to bust me. I laugh at my own joke. Okay, okay. Even I recognize that's not true.

As I walk from table to table getting signatures and collecting my tips, I let a sliver of hope break through the sludge of the past few weeks. It'll be nice being with kids who don't know me, who won't ask a million questions about *that* day at school. If Mom were still alive, she would have given me a hug and reminded me that what didn't kill me would only make me stronger. Turns out her death two years ago didn't make me stronger, but it did almost kill me. I chase the pity party away with a brisk walk to the register. No time for that.

When the customers have cleared out, I wipe down my tables in a hurry, hoping I'll have time to freshen up. Halfway through my routine, I find a man's wallet. I look inside and smile. Looks like Creepy Old Dude's going to have a hard time buying drinks for any girls tonight. I slip his wallet into my pocket and make my way to the kitchen with my dish cart.

On the way, I pass Dad's pride and joy, a display case filled with Lucky Luciano's gray flannel pinstriped suit and black hat. Even though Dad already has six glass cabinets full of cool gangster stuff like Al Capone's cigar cutter, John Dillinger's hat, Pretty Boy Floyd's bulletproof vest, and Carlo Gambino's blood-stained shoes, he's always on the lookout for more. I'm excited to find out if he bought anything at the gangster memorabilia auction he went to this evening.

I drop off the last of my dishes in the kitchen before running to change back into my street clothes—black capri cigarette pants, white lace top, and black suede heels. Perfect for a party. Who knows? Maybe I will meet someone tonight. That could maybe even sorta-kinda make up for missing prom. After I freshen up my makeup, I still have about fifteen minutes until I need to meet Clarissa. I'm about to text Dad to see how the auction went when I see that his corner office is lit up. When I walk in, he's sitting at his big antique desk, checking his e-mail. A cardboard box is in front of him, piquing my curiosity.

"Hey, Dad. How'd it go today?" I plop down on the fancy swivel chair opposite his desk.

"Amazing!" He smiles broadly, the first time in weeks. "Wait until you see what I bought. Absolutely incredible." He reaches into the box and pulls out three acrylic cases, certificates of authenticity, and a brochure listing all the auction items. "There was a little casino in Dallas that went belly up. The owner needed cash fast, so I made out like the devil."

I raise an eyebrow at his word choice. "Considering what kinds of things you collect, I'd say that's not too far off. What did you buy?" I lean closer, trying to get a glimpse.

He holds up a small container. "Behold, the bullets taken from the corpses of Bonnie Parker and Clyde Barrow. The silver ones are from Bonnie, the gold ones, Clyde."

"Really?" My jaw drops open as I stare in awe at the five metal chunks mounted on a black velvet pad. "You've wanted to buy a Bonnie and Clyde item for a long time."

"I know. Wait until you see what else I bought." He lifts a clear square container. Mounted inside of it is a nondescript tan beret. "This gorgeous relic cost me seven hundred bucks. Mom would have died if she saw this."

I wince at his accidental slip of the tongue. Despair licks at my heart for a split-second, but I will it away. I did enough crying two years ago to last me a lifetime. "Was this Bonnie's hat?"

"No, don't you recognize it? Faye Dunaway wore it in the Bonnie and Clyde movie. Check it out." His voice catches as he slides a color movie photo toward me. It's a shot of Faye Dunaway leaning against a car wearing the tan beret, looking achingly beautiful.

"Ohmigod, Dad! This is, it's . . ." I can't finish my sentence, but I don't need to. Dad nods and squeezes my hand, both of us choked up. *Bonnie and Clyde* was Mom's all-time favorite movie. We watched it with her every year on her birthday, a tradition I looked forward to. Now it just makes me sad. Haven't watched it since her fifty-first birthday, shortly before she died.

I clear my throat. Dad coughs. "I bought something for you too, Monroe."

"Dad, why?" After all the crap I've put him through lately, I figured the only thing he'd be buying for me is a bus ticket out of town. I hope this means he's starting to forgive me.

"Think of it as an early graduation present." He holds up another clear plastic display case, this one the size of a magazine. He holds it gingerly, like he's presenting a newborn to me. It contains a piece of paper that looks yellow and fragile from age. "I know you like history as much as I do and thought you might like a keepsake for yourself. It's worth a couple grand, so you can either take it home or display it here in the restaurant. It's up to you." He hands it to me with a sweet, genuine smile. "It's a poem Bonnie Parker wrote called 'The Trail's End.'"

"Seriously? Thank you, Dad!" I pop out of my seat to hug him—our first time since the arrest. "This is so cool! I definitely want to bring it home with me, at least for a little while. This is the poem Faye Dunaway reads to Warren Beatty in the movie, right?"

"Yep. Bonnie Parker wrote it while she was in prison for bank robbery, when she was only a little older than you are." He pauses, looking at me.

I avoid his gaze, running a fingertip across his nameplate that reads, "Don't Mess with Gordie Baker or You're Dead," complete with fake bullet holes. I know he's sending me a mental message: If I don't get my act together, I'll be heading to prison too.

He rubs his eye. "She won a few writing awards in high school. Who knows what she could have done with her life if she hadn't dropped out of school at age fifteen to get married."

Something doesn't jibe with the movie. "She married Clyde at fifteen?"

"Not Clyde—a man named Roy Thornton. He just up and left one morning and never came back. Supposedly Bonnie met Clyde at a party not too long afterwards, and they were inseparable until death did them part two years later."

So Bonnie got hitched at fifteen, ditched at sixteen, robbed banks at seventeen, and everyone thinks *I'm* a mess? "A match made in Hell, huh?"

He smiles. "That's what some people say. Do me a favor and read the first two stanzas aloud. I barely got a chance to look at it during the auction." He leans back and relaxes.

"Sure." I glance at the clock and see I still have five minutes until I need to meet Clarissa. I pick up the plastic container and am stupidly amazed to discover that it's written in Bonnie's own handwriting. Duh. No electronics back then. The idea that her fingers touched this piece of paper and it's now millimeters away from my fingers makes my heart race, making me feel both exhilarated and dangerous. All the years separating us evaporate in an instant.

I clear my throat and begin reading. *"You've read the story of Jesse James/ of how he lived and died./ If you're still in need;/ of something to read,/ here's the story of Bonnie and Clyde./ Now Bonnie and Clyde are the Barrow gang/ I'm sure you all have read./ How they rob and steal;/ and those who squeal,/ are usually found dying or dead."*

I picture a girl about my age blowing on the end of her gun, prodding a lifeless body with her shoe. *"Ya shouldn't have snitched,"* she says without emotion. A creepy chill works its way up my spine and I shiver. "Pretty brutal—if it's true."

"Of course it's true. Bonnie and Clyde killed at least twelve people. Most of 'em cops."

Good, I think, but instantly regret it. Cops are great until they bust you—then they suck. Somehow that jolts my memory about the wallet. I dig it out of my purse and toss it on the desk. "One of my customers left this behind tonight. Guy was a scumbag, so it serves him right."

"Why? What did he do?" Dad growls.

I wave in the air dismissively. "Nothing horrible. Just asked me out."

"Jerk." Dad shakes his head in disgust. He picks up the wallet and casually glances inside, like he's looking for identification, but I see him check the dollar bill part. My heart sinks. He obviously thinks of me as criminal first, daughter second. He stands. "I'll be right back. Going to see if Percy can track this guy down. Maybe I'll have a word with him when he shows up."

"Dad, don't," I call out, but he heads down the hall toward his general manager's office.

I can't help smiling. Typical Dad. Always wanting to protect me from the world. I turn the display case over, noticing that the back of the poem is filled with doodles of clouds and flowers, just like I do to my spirals. I imagine a girl my age in a jail cell lying on a cot, writing this poem.

"Hello, Bonnie," I whisper. "Did you have a lot of stuck-up chicks at your school, too? Is that why you dropped out?" I laugh, feeling silly talking to a dead girl. I pull the slug box toward me, thinking how cool it would be to touch one. Like touching death head-on. When I don't hear footsteps, I think, why not? You only live once. Look at my poor mother and how much she missed out on. I dive for the box, pulling at the clear plastic seal. It's stuck tight. I slide a fingernail under the edge of the sticker and slowly pry it up, careful not to rip the seal itself.

A rush of bubbling nervous energy makes my fingers tremble as I lift the cover. A puff of stale air with the scent of rancid meat assaults my nose. I breathe through my mouth as I pull out one of the silver gnarled bits. Is this *the* bullet—the one that actually killed Bonnie Parker? I spy a tiny spot of dark brown nestled between two twisted nibs of steel. Is that her dried blood? Could it be locked inside here after all this time? I lick my finger and touch the spot.

It smudges, turns brownish red. Holy shit—it is her blood! I rub it a bit harder when something sharp pierces my fingertip. A bright red dot from a tiny jagged cut sprouts on the pad of my index finger. I ram my wound into my mouth and glare at the slug. That's when I realize that Bonnie Parker's blood was on my finger and is now on my tongue.

Gross! In a flash, I yank my finger from my mouth and vigorously scrape my tongue on the inside edge of my shirt, hoping to remove all of Bonnie's rehydrated blood cells. A tingling sensation that I'd gotten away with something big rushes through me. I quickly wrestle a Clyde slug out of its slot, close the lid, and smile at my palm. Bonnie and Clyde. Together again. Seconds later, my vision blurs—as if someone smeared Vaseline across my eyes. The slugs in my hand become a swirling mess of flesh and metal. I close my eyes, trying to clear the mess, when a vivid scene floods my mind—one so clear it's like I'm witnessing it live.

I'm riding in the passenger seat of a car, an old-fashioned one too, judging by the three large dials in front of the steering wheel and the long skinny gearshift knob rising up out of the floor. A sleek gray fishtail skirt hugs my legs perfectly, matched with a gorgeous, cream-colored peasant top. The driver looks to be my age, or maybe a couple years older at the most. He's got slicked-back dark brown hair, revealing ears that tip slightly away from his head in a cute, elfish way. He's wearing mocha brown dress pants, a pale blue shirt with the sleeves rolled up, and a striped tie loose around his neck. Like a businessman on a lunch break. Very sexy.

"How ya doing, doll?" He grins at me, his golden brown eyes lighting up his face. He reaches over, a tattoo of a woman's face on his forearm, and pats my knee. "Sure was fine sleeping in a bed for a change last night, huh?"

"Yep. Except now it's already hotter than heck and it's barely nine o'clock," I say in a strange Southern accent. I reach for the crank handle and lower the window partway. A gust of wind blows strands of strawberry blonde hair into my face.

My elf-eared date takes his hand off my leg and thumps the oversized black steering wheel. "Aw, for crying out loud. Will you look at that? Some dumb hack lost his load."

I look ahead of us and see a pickup truck stopped right in the middle of the road, crates of melons scattered everywhere. "Poor sap prolly forgot to latch the gate," I say.

"I ain't stopping either, or we'll be here all day." He grips the wheel harder.

"Don't lose your temper now, Clyde. It might be faster if you help."

As we approach the pickup truck, the intense rat-a-tat-tat of hundreds of bullets whizzing through our car has me ducking for cover. Tiny missiles whistle past my head, leaving penny-sized holes all around me. Clyde's limbs flail uncontrollably as sprays of red blood hit the windshield, my white silk blouse, the cracked leather seat. Shards of glass pelt my neck as I cross my arms in front of my face, screaming. The car careens off the road toward the bushes, bobbing and jerking like an old wooden roller coaster as all four tires get shot out. It makes a final heave of exhaled air and comes to rest ten yards further. I collapse against Clyde's shoulder, my skirt at a jaunty angle halfway up my thigh, but I don't make a move to fix it. I'm left peering through a crumpled mass of tangled hair and torn flesh, staring at Clyde's blood-soaked forehead.

The sound of snapping fingers startles me out of my daydream. The image of Dad's face blends with Clyde's as his office comes into focus. "Earth to Monroe," Dad says, loading his treasures back into the cardboard box—including the velvet-lined bullet case.

I sit up in a flash, inhaling sharply, the slugs still nestled in my palm. How could I have fallen asleep so quickly? It seemed so real, like I was in one of those movie theaters with enhanced sound, scent, and motion. I swallow hard, trying to think of something logical to say as to why I took the slugs out of the box when it was clearly sealed shut, but my mind goes blank.

Dad interlocks the flaps of the box so the top stays closed. "I'm going to lock these babies up now. Don't want dust or moisture to get inside. Ruins their value."

A cannonball of guilt lodges in my chest, knowing I messed up yet again. I can't bring myself to tell him what I've done. After he walks away, I slip the slugs into my pants pocket. I'll guard them with my life tonight and find a way to return them in the morning.

I call out, "By the way, Clarissa invited me to a party tonight." I twirl a lock of my hair, hoping he's not mad. "She's leaving for L.A. soon and we wanted to hang out before she leaves."

He stops walking and turns to me, his forehead heavily creased. "You sure that's a good idea, Monroe? The judge said you needed to stay clean for a whole year or you could—"

"I know," I interrupt, unable to bear hearing another reminder of my fate. "But I learned my lesson, I promise." I look him in the eye, wanting him to trust me again.

He frowns. "You need to make this decision for yourself. But I want you to know that I'm not bailing you out if you get arrested again, nor will I foot the bill for college. Are we clear?"

I glance down at my hands, feeling the heat of his stare. "Yeah. We're clear."

"Okay, then." He sighs, manages to smile. "Have fun and wake me when you get home."

"I will. Bye, Dad." I kiss his cheek and race down the hall to where Clarissa stands waiting for me. Seconds later, I hear a high-pitched squeal of laughter.

I glance over my shoulder, but no one's there.

Clarissa pushes open the door to the parking lot. "Ready for the party of a lifetime?"

"You know it," I say, secretly hoping the party's not *too* crazy. If it looks like it's getting out of control, I'll just take a cab home. I'd rather die than get arrested again.

Be careful what you wish for, girlie.

How odd, I think, as I dash out into the night. My conscience had a Southern accent.

CHAPTER 2

Friday, May 20th // 9:24 P.M.

Clyde

A sudden jolt runs through my bones, swift as lightning and strong as a Texas twister in May. I blink twice, three times, but I can't see nothing. I must be in the bottom of a mineshaft on a moonless night because it's dark and I'm cold. Real cold. I concentrate hard as I can to move my body, one finger even, and finally, after what seems like forever, I give up.

I search my brain trying to figure how I got trapped down here. Last thing I remember was me and Bonnie heading down Potter Lane to go pick up Henry at his pa's house in the middle of nowhere. We'd all visited our kin for two days but we needed to get back on the lam. I slowed down to drive around a fool truck driver who lost his load, when—Christ. It's all coming back.

As I veered past the crates, rounds of gunfire blasted through my head, my neck, my arms and legs—jolting me right outta my seat. Bonnie's spine-chillin' scream was the last thing I heard before blackness came. It's obvious to me looking back now that the sheriff's posse brought along enough ammo to shoot a herd of buffalo. Cold-hearted bastards never even offered us a chance to surrender.

Not that I would, but they dint know that. At least I coulda taken down a few of the laws before me and Bonnie got smoked.

I realize then that I ain't in any mineshaft—I'm in my final resting place. I have a foggy memory of being told I'd need to stay here until my time was up, but I didn't know where "here" was. Then I blacked out. I should prolly be screaming in horror as a man is wont to do when he finds out he's dead, but cryin's for sissies. Don't solve nothing neither. I'd rather plan my revenge, because it's as clear to me as Mama's crystal earrings that my execution wasn't no accident.

My anger festers like an infected wound until I reach a place of pure hatred for the son of a bitch who set me up. Someone tole the feds where I'd be and what time, which narrows it down to about ten people or so, most of 'em family. Soon as I learn how to escape this hellhole I'm in, I'm going to figure out which rat squealed and I'm going to kill the bastard. Make 'em suffer too.

An eye for an eye, my daddy always tole me, and I've always been a dutiful son.

Even if it turns out that it's him that did it to me.

CHAPTER 3

Friday, May 20th // 10:04 P.M.

Monroe

As Clarissa and I walk up the sidewalk to the party, a girl runs out of the front door and leans over the porch railing, puking into the bushes. It's barely 10:00 and there's already a drunk chick? Not good. Clarissa breezes past her, but having been in this same position many times, I stop to pat the girl on the back. "You need anything, hon?"

"Nooo," she moans.

I repeat my mantra: no drinking, no stupid decisions. I'm here to flirt with some football players for a few hours and then go home—alcohol- and hickey-free.

Once inside, the floorboards vibrate from the bass beneath our feet as a party song blasts below us. We head down a flight of wooden stairs to the basement. By the second step, the earthy scent of weed hits my nose. The fourth step adds the obnoxious laughter of drunk kids into the mix. At the bottom, my worries skyrocket. At least fifty people mingle throughout the finished basement, a pack of them huddling around the two kegs. Normally I'd be psyched to be here, but this party has "nosy neighbor police call" written all over it. I'm already queasy and I haven't had any alcohol. I take a deep breath. I am *not* drinking tonight. Not a drop.

Why not? I bet they got good hooch here.

I look left and then right, looking to see who said that. Before I can process what's going on, Clarissa grabs my hand and pulls me through the teenage wasteland. "Isn't this awesome?" she shouts over her shoulder. Every few seconds she announces, "Hey everyone, this is Monroe!" A couple of people raise their beers in acknowledgment, but most are too involved in their own conversations and beer pong games to care to meet someone new. Suits me just fine. Blending into the background is a welcome change.

Clarissa lets go of my hand and squeals, "Hankster!" She races across the room toward a scruffy, bearded, olive-skinned guy with a sleeve of tattoos. He's wearing jeans and a simple gray t-shirt. He holds his muscular arms out wide, grinning widely.

Wait. *That's* her boyfriend? Not at all what I imagined her type to be.

He lifts her off her feet and pulls her into a bear hug, his face beaming with such glee it's as if he hasn't seen her in months. I can't tear my eyes away as he cups her head gently between his hands and gives her one sultry kiss on the mouth. That's so sexy. *He's* so sexy. After he sets her down, she gives me a little finger wave goodbye before getting swallowed up by the crowd.

So much for hanging out with Clarissa tonight.

Of course, if I had a hot boyfriend who gazed at me the way Hank gazed at Clarissa, I wouldn't want to hang out with me either. Before I can decide what to do next, two guys appear in front of me. *Right* in front of me. One guy is blond, has bad acne, and is wearing a t-shirt that says *I'm Higher Than You.* Given that he's so tall he has to duck to avoid hitting the ceiling vents, he's correct no matter how he's defining "high."

The other guy is slim, average height, super cute . . . but *ultra* preppy. He's got dark brown hair with bangs in his eyes, a big silver watch, and of course, signature rich boy attire—a blue Polo with a white t-shirt underneath, designer jeans, and Sperry Top-Siders. By appearances only, neither guy strikes me as my type, but we'll see. Chemistry works in mysterious ways.

"How's it going?" the tall one asks. "I'm Kyle and this is my friend Jack." He hits his friend in the chest with the back of his hand. I recognize Kyle's name—he's hosting the party we're at. He leans in close to my ear and says, "Jack's kind of shy, so I'm helping him out a bit. He thinks you're cute."

21

I'm dying to ask if we're back in middle school, but my friend Anjali's declaration that my sarcasm scares guys away finds me smiling instead. "Hi, I'm Monroe. Nice party, Kyle. Are your parents home?" Prior party experience shows kids stay more chill if parents are around.

Kyle's eyes widen. "Are you kidding? They'd never allow this! They're at a wedding in Texas. Left my brother Turf in charge. That's him in the green shirt." He nods to my right.

I look to see a stocky college-aged guy in a green shirt standing on the coffee table. He's surrounded by a group of people and has a full shot glass in each hand. After a loud whoop, Turf tilts his head back and pours both shots into his mouth at once. He opens his arms wide and points to himself. "Oh yeah! Double-decker!" His friends cheer him on.

"He seems very responsible," I say matter-of-factly.

Kyle laughs, but Jack flicks his hair out of his eyes in what has got to be a rehearsed maneuver. "I never heard the name Monroe before," he says, squinting at me. "Except, you know, Marilyn Monroe."

My chest swells with pride. My name never fails to be a conversation starter. "You're on the right track. My parents love old movies. I have two older sisters—one is named Ginger, after Ginger Rogers, and the other Audrey, after Audrey Hepburn. And obviously me after Marilyn Monroe." I point to the tiny diamond in my upper lip. "Note the Monroe piercing."

"Did it hurt?" Jack asks, wincing.

"No, not really," I answer, thinking that the only other person who ever asked me that was a little girl at Walgreens.

"Shouldn't your name be Marilyn then?" Kyle takes a sip of his beer, smirking.

"Touché," I reply, thinking the smartass might be my type.

"I'm named after someone famous too," Jack says. "Jack Daniel, at your service." He bows at the waist as if meeting royalty.

I raise an eyebrow. "Guess it's a good thing your parents weren't into Wild Turkey."

Kyle cocks a thumb in Jack's direction. "Wild Chicken would fit him better. Dude's scared of everything."

Jack smacks Kyle's hand away. "Shut up. I'm not scared of *everything*—only your dad's creepy company." Jack looks at me. "His dad runs a ghost bus tour that takes you around Chicago to locations where lots of people died. I saw his dad's schedule on the fridge upstairs. There's a group called 'The Half-Dead Society' going on a private tour tomorrow. If that's not scary, I don't know what is."

"The Half-Dead Society?" I ask, amused. "Is that where a group of zombies sit in a circle eating decaying body parts while the therapist asks questions?"

Kyle laughs out loud. "You never know. Lots of groups go on his tours—mystery book clubs, historical museum societies, stuff like that. His company's tagline is 'Where the Dead Come Alive.'" He wiggles his fingers in my face and opens his eyes wide, trying to look scary.

"Sounds fun," I say, intrigued by the idea. Maybe a little by Kyle, too.

Jack wrinkles his nose. "Fun if you like hearing about how people offed themselves."

"Hey guys. What's up?" A pretty Asian girl slips under Kyle's arm.

"Ah, speaking about getting off, here's my little geisha girl now." Kyle leans in to kiss her and she playfully slaps his face. So much for that. He looks over his shoulder at Jack as they walk away. "Good luck tonight, bro!"

If that last comment means that Jack's hoping to hook up with me tonight, he should move along. "Well, it was nice—"

"Wait!" Jack does one of his bang-flipping moves. "You want a beer?"

"Um . . ." I hesitate, twirling a lock of hair around my finger. This is harder than I thought.

23

Before I can answer he adds, "Because it's five bucks a man if you do."

My face flushes with embarrassment. So that whole conversation was a ruse to get beer money? "Not interested," I blurt out quickly before I change my mind.

"No problem," he says with a head nod. "I stopped after two beers because I have a killer practice in the morning. My team is in the state golf tournament this week. I could get kicked off for even *being* at a party like this." He stares, as if waiting for my reaction to that newsflash.

"Wow." As soon as the words leave my lips, I can tell by his expression that he was expecting me to say something nice about his achievement, but forget that. Not only am I not sure if I'm being played, but golf is so boring that the TV commentators have to whisper because they know everyone at home has fallen asleep. I search for Clarissa. Where is that girl?

A glassy-eyed chick stumbles, grabbing onto Jack to keep from falling. "Whoopsy! Sorry, Jack. See you later maybe?" She gives him a drunken wink before weaving toward the keg.

Trollop.

There's that voice again! I look at Jack to see if he said it, but he's blankly staring at the bimbo, a smile on his face. Is it possible for a brain to cough out words and phrases on its own? Unless somehow when I cut myself . . . no. That's stupid. Bonnie Parker is *not* in my head.

Jack leans closer. "That was a slutty girl from school. The guys all call her 7-Eleven because you can get in and get out so quickly. Get it?"

"Um, yeeeaah." I scrunch up my nose, wondering why he'd share that with me. "Don't let me stop you." I look past Jack at a guy running past us with his head tilted up, his arms out to the sides, balancing a screwdriver on his nose.

"Nah. 7-Eleven's not my type." He smiles at me so long that I get the unsettling feeling that he's trying to say that I am. This completely throws me because, up until now, we haven't exactly clicked on any topic in the remotest way.

I take a deep breath, needing to move on before he gets any ideas. "Well, it was nice meeting you, Jack. I'm going to hunt down some water. Good luck on your tournament."

I take two steps toward the stairs when Jack grabs my arm. "Hey, hold up. I know where the Johnsons stash their water bottles. I'll get you one." His face beams with hope.

I wave off his offer, smiling. "Nah, that's okay. Just tell me and I can get it."

"Nope. I'll be right back." Before I can argue, he's gone.

My sister Ginger once told me that when guys at bars send free drinks to you, they feel you owe them a conversation. But if it comes down to a choice between listening to a boring guy drone on about his life and paying for alcohol, I'd rather buy my own drink.

I lean against a pole and scan all the males at this party, trying to find one who looks intelligent or interesting, spying only one guy who doesn't look like a jock. Jeans, plaid button-down shirt, stylish glasses. Having an intense conversation with a guy in a Hawks t-shirt. I glance at my phone and sigh. Right about now, all my friends are dancing their brains out to Manic Devil, the cover band at prom. I wonder if Anjali and her date, Luke, are hitting it off. A giant rush of sadness hits my chest. God, I could use a beer. I bite my fingernail, wondering if I have five bucks on me. Just one will make my pity party less pitiful.

Kyle's brother gets back onto the coffee table and downs two more shots. "Now *that's* what I call a mixed drink, people!" He pounds his chest and howls like Tarzan.

He hops off the table and struts past me, stopping mid-stride. "Titty, titty, bang, bang!" he purrs, checking me out. "You wanna do a shot with me, sexy mama?" He raises his eyebrows twice, suggestively licking his lips.

"Not unless it involves bullets." I turn and walk away. Creep.

"Your tits ain't that great anyway!" he shouts from behind me.

That twit is lower than a snake's belly.

I plug my ears, hoping to silence the woman in my head.

The other fella don't have no fire, but he ain't so bad.

Blood rushes out of my head, making me dizzy. I lean against the wall, dazed. This can't be happening. There's no way Bonnie Parker is speaking to me. She's been dead for like eighty years. This is some sort of stupid brain trick, a cranial hiccup. I run a hand through my hair, needing to come up with a rational excuse. Think, think!

Anjali and Josie are always on my case for writing guys off too quickly, so maybe my conscience is picking up on that. I mean, compared to jerks like Turf, Jack's a gem—he's cute, has goals, is basically a nice guy. There have to be other things Jack likes besides golf, right? When he comes back, I'll ask him questions, talk about his family. This is all a huge misunderstanding.

After willing my brain to shut the hell up, I spy two girls get up off the loveseat and zigzag my way through the crowd, hoping no one sits down before I can get there. Success! I plunk my butt down and set my vintage mesh purse on the seat next to me to save it for Jack. While I wait, I grab my phone and check out what's happening on Facebook. When there's no sign of Jack after several minutes, I wonder if 7-Eleven girl is a convenience he wanted after all. I cross my legs, trying to decide whether to ask Clarissa to take me home or if I should call a cab, when something jabs me in the thigh. The slugs, I quickly realize.

I lean back and slide my fingers into my pocket, repositioning them slightly. The moment my fingers touch the cold steel, the party scene blurs into a murky white fog. I struggle to keep my eyes open. So . . . so . . . sleepy. I dream I'm in some sort of a medical facility. Strong odors of antiseptic, formaldehyde, and death blend into one nauseating aroma, making me gag. An old man in a lab coat checks out what looks like a dead guy on a stainless steel table. Sick! But this dream is even more messed up than that because everything is sideways.

The exam room's light green walls fade in and out, echoing the cadence of the flickering light overhead. The camera zooms in, getting a close-up of the entire left side of the corpse's face and neck coated with dried blood, the hairless chest remarkably clean. Tiny black holes appear all over his body like a morbid connect-the-dots coloring page. The sporadic gasping of fluorescent energy reminds me of strobe lights in a haunted house.

The coroner washes his hands in the white utility sink while peering at a ledger on the desk next to him. There's an old-fashioned black telephone there too, the kind where the earpiece dangles from a wire. After drying his hands on a cloth, he plucks a pair of thick rubber gloves from a box and forces his gnarled arthritic fingers into them. Grabbing a tray of steel instruments from underneath the table, he flips on the gooseneck light. Shining it directly over the victim's face, his examination begins. He lowers the large magnifying glass that's strapped to his forehead and sifts through the corpse's hair, strand by strand, until stopping to peer closely at another spot.

Using one finger to hold his place, he picks up the forceps and inserts them into the corpse's skull, skillfully removing a tidbit. He poises the artifact above a steel tray labeled *Barrow, Clyde / Case #6749*. The coroner drops the slug onto the tray as a metallic *clink!* resonates throughout the antiseptic morgue. My dream self pans the room, noticing diagrams of human body systems tacked onto the wall alongside pin-up girl posters. I continue checking out my surroundings when I look down at myself. I'm lying on a steel examination table, a sheet loosely draped over my naked, blood-caked body. I turn my head slowly and read the label on the steel tray beside my head.

Parker, Bonnie / Case #6750.

I jolt awake and blink a few times, wiping a bit of saliva off the side of my mouth. Kyle's party swims back into focus as the harrowing images of the morgue fade. What the hell? My heart beats wildly in my chest. Everything seemed so real, down to the dried blood on the corpses, the coroner's tools, the name labels on the trays. I sit up and adjust my shirt, which has somehow bunched up under my bra.

Bonnie, are you really in my head? I ask silently, biting my lip.

I listen, one hand covering my mouth. I wait . . . but nothing. I shift in my seat, trying to get comfortable. I have *got* to get to bed soon. Things always look better in the morning. I'll set my alarm to get up early and sneak these slugs back into the safe before Dad gets to work. The sooner these creepy things are out of my possession, the better. I need to find Clarissa.

A blonde girl sitting opposite me looks away when I glance in her direction. I shrug it off. People have thought a lot worse about me than I drank too much and fell asleep. I scan the room, finally spying Clarissa and Hank off by themselves on a recliner. Doesn't look like she's ready to leave any time soon. I sigh, wishing I could meet a guy who fascinates me even half as much as Clarissa seems captivated by Hank. My face blushes when I think of Noah, the actor who plays John Dillinger at our dinner theater. I *meant* someone I could actually date. Noah's got two of my invariables and then some. He's intelligent and interesting for sure, but he's also witty, strong, and debonair in a Rhett Butler sort of way. Sadly for me, he's also very much into his wife. Josie says my having a crush on a married man ten years older than me proves I purposely close myself off to the possibility of having a real boyfriend.

I say it proves I was born in the wrong decade.

Cheers erupt from behind the bar. A guy with funky sideburns raises his glass in celebration. "Take it to the bank! Sox win!"

Jack arrives moments later, smiling as he sits down next to me. His leg brushes mine briefly as he sits, eliciting no response whatsoever from my libido. No worries, I quickly ruminate. I'm not giving up *that* easily.

"Sorry it took so long," he says, handing me a red plastic cup. "They were out of water, so here's a beer on the house."

That was sweet. I hold the beer, staring at it as if it's a poison concoction, trying to decide if I should drink it or not. I deliberate for about four point two seconds. Screw it. I'm supposed to be at prom and instead I'm at a party surrounded by strangers. I hold up my cup. "Thanks, Jack. Cheers." I take a giant sip, letting the liquid roll down my throat. Lukewarm beer never tasted so good.

I lean toward his ear and shout over the music. "Have you seen any good movies lately?"

He shakes his head. "Nah. Haven't been to a movie in like six months."

Strike two. "Really? I go all the time. In fact, I love movies so much I'm even going to major in theater or cinema studies at NYU."

"Theater? You mean plays?" He furrows his brow.

I nod. "Maybe, but I'm leaning more toward film directing." I hold up an imaginary camera and roll the crank, like charades, in case he's having trouble hearing me.

"Movies are okay. Plays suck." He scratches his arm, picking off a fleck of dry skin.

Is he completely oblivious to what I just said was my life's dream? I don't care so much that he hates the arts, but not even trying to fake it for the sake of conversation slams the door on any romantic interest on my part. I gulp down most of my beer to cool my temper before I speak.

"Plays don't suck. My dad owns a dinner theater and right now we're doing a play called *Gangsters of Love*. It's sold out every night." Stick that into your negative attitude and suck it. I down the rest of my beer before dragging my purse strap up onto my shoulder. "Thanks for the beer, Jack. Sorry, but I have to go home now." As I stand, he catches me off-guard and pulls my arm, forcing me to sit back down.

"Hey, come on," he says gently. "Don't be like that, okay? Stay a little longer." He gazes at me with pleading eyes. "Did I say I didn't like plays? I meant I *love* plays."

I tilt my chin down and give him a knowing look.

He grins. "Seriously! A gangster play sounds cool. Is it like the Crips versus the Bloods?" He fakes an intense stare, waiting and watching.

I know he doesn't *really* care, but at least he's trying. I finally cave, setting my purse on my lap. "Actually, it's more of a musical about the 1930s gangsters," I shout at his ear. "We have gangster memorabilia on display, too."

"Like what?"

"Al Capone's cigar cutter and a Tommy gun," I say, picking out two of our dullest items.

He nods, smiling at me. "That's so cool." He leans closer, resting his hand on my knee as he talks. "So uh, you maybe want to hang out tomorrow and you can show it to me?"

Oh God. My stomach drops. Is he serious? I'm trying to like him, but it's just not working. He might be intelligent, *maybe* insanely handsome by some girl's standards, but he's definitely not interesting and worst of all, I think he's faking being into me.

"Um . . ." I say, trying to think of a way out of this. And then it hits me. I can show him the slugs, thereby fulfilling his wish, and then make a quick exit. "I can show you something now and save you the trouble. I happen to have the slugs that killed Bonnie and Clyde with me."

Don't you dare!

I breathe in sharply. Bonnie, is that really you?

"Wow. That'd be cool." He holds out his palm as he watches a scantily clad girl in pink shorts walk by, keeping his eyes on the sizable amount of her butt cheek hanging out the bottom.

I roll my eyes, wondering why I'm even bothering. "Okay, take a quick look and then I have to go."

NO! Leave them in your pocket!

I hesitate, my heart thumping loudly in my ears, waiting for more instructions.

"Come on. Let me see them." He looks at me and smiles.

I shrug. What can it hurt? The sooner I show him, the sooner I can get home and get this mixed-up night over with. As I retrieve them from my pocket, my vision blurs, and Jack's image is swallowed up by footage of two policemen getting shot in the chest and then falling to the ground, writhing in pain. The scene ends the moment I drop the slugs into Jack's hand.

I suck in my breath. I was definitely awake this time. No mistaking the mind movie for a dream. My head pounds with the realization that something isn't right about those slugs.

Jack starts to cough. "Is something burning? My throat stings." I hear him breathe in noisily, making me wonder if he's been wheezing all night, or just since I handed him the bullets.

This makes me shift in my seat. Clearly he's having some kind of reaction. I need them back before they do any damage. "I think the smoke is from all the weed."

"I . . . *cough* . . . don't think . . . *wheeze* . . . that's it." Jack sits up straight, coughing even harder, the slugs gripped tightly in his palm as he pounds his chest with a fist.

Get those slugs back now!

I'm hit with a wave of dizziness. "Can I"—I blink, trying to focus—"have them back now?" What's happening? Did Jack drug the beer he gave me? Why is he coughing so hard?

Get them NOW, you dumb Dora! Before you mess things up!

The piercing wail in my ear increases and the swaying of the room becomes more intense. I can no longer deny that the voice of Bonnie Parker is somehow calling to me from her grave. "I need those—"

Black spots dance in front of my eyes. My head feels too heavy for me to manage.

I hold out my open palm, hoping Jack will get the hint to return the slugs, when a sharp pain hits me in the neck. Clawing at my throat, I reach up to remove whatever's stabbing me, looking to Jack for help. That's when I notice that his eyes are practically bugging out of his face, his cheeks turning redder by the second. I try to pry the slugs from his closed fist, but he won't let go. With his free hand, he clutches at his chest, grabbing his shirt.

Pushing through the fiery agony in my throat, I frantically pull at his fingers, fighting Jack's resistance until finally, the slugs drop from his hand into mine. The scorching pain in my neck instantly ceases, but a new scene dances into focus behind my closed eyes.

I'm sitting in the passenger seat of a car I've never been in before outside of a brick building with a sign that says *Robert H. Brock Hardware*. A woman in a calf-length green dress and black hat breezes past me, pushing a wicker stroller with metal rim wheels. She coos quietly to her baby, who smiles in response. I tap my fingers nervously on my knee.

An alarm sounds and two men with machine guns race out of the store. I watch but don't scream. Before I know what's happening, they hop into my car—one guy into the driver's seat next to me, and the other one in back. "Go, go, go!" the man in back shouts. The car pulls away from the curb jerkily. I squeal, "Hurry, baby!" My stomach twists when I see it's the same well-dressed guy with the outturned ears from my first vision—Clyde Barrow. I turn my head in rapid succession, looking first at the storefront and then at Clyde. He finally pops the gear into place just in time as the shop owner runs outside shooting at us. I scream, ducking down, hearing bullets ricochet off the car's exterior. Clyde floors the gas pedal, tires squealing.

A hard bump against my shoulder makes the scene pop like a pricked soap bubble. I open my eyes, realizing the slugs got knocked out of my hand. I scoop them up and jam them in my pocket. The hailstorm of images flowing through my thoughts are overshadowed by seeing Jack pound on his chest like he's trying to get his lungs working again. He coughs and shouts, "Hallelujah!" followed by a loud gasp for air. Finding out that Jack is a Bible thumper is just one more stop on the crazy train tonight. He blinks several times, his mouth open.

"Whoa! I felt like I was going to die for a second there." He stares at the indentations of the slugs embedded on his palm, as if unsure how they got there.

"Are you okay now?" I ask, biting my lip.

He nods, takes a deep breath. "Yeah. But you got sick at the same time I was." He eyes me warily. "You sure those slugs aren't possessed?"

"I'm starting to wonder myself," I say, hoping he doesn't press further. Were the evil spirits of Bonnie and Clyde locked up tight in that box, and when I unsealed it, did I unwittingly unleash them into the world like the bubonic plague?

Too late to turn back now.

I don't have a second to respond when a loud commotion brings Jack to his feet. I follow suit, watching as a guy flies down the stairs yelling something unintelligible. A girl darts in front of us, grabbing her purse that's on the table next to me.

"What's going on?" I ask her. "Is someone hurt?"

"The cops are here!" she yells, her face white with panic. "Ditch your drugs!"

Damn it! I knew this would happen! I take a quick check for Clarissa, but don't see her anywhere. I turn to look at Jack, but he's standing on the loveseat, pushing open the window. Seconds later, he steps up on the back of the couch and shinnies himself up and out. If there's one thing I've learned, it's that the only way out of getting busted is to run.

"Jack, wait!" He glances right at me, but keeps going. I do exactly like he did, standing first on the back of the couch, and then jumping up to get my stomach to the window ledge. It takes a few tries, but after some major stomach bruising, I manage to get outside. Jack's already halfway down the block. Nice guy, my ass. My dad says if you want to see someone's true colors, wait for an emergency.

Looks like Jack's true color is every-man-for-himself cowardly yellow.

I step on an old branch, which makes a loud *crack*. A cop on the front porch turns and flashes a light in my direction. I duck, but I'm too slow.

"You—get out from behind that bush!" he shouts as he hurries down the steps.

I get one look at his police badge and take off running.

CHAPTER 4

Friday, May 20th // 11:11 P.M.

Clyde

I lie there for a long time, wondering how to get out of this damn coffin, when I see a light—a tiny hole no bigger than a thumbtack—way off in the corner. Light means life so that's got to be the key to my escape. I don't know how come I've been hibernating deep in the earth instead of chumming with the devil, but obviously, the good Lord has His reasons. Maybe He felt bad I'd been taken too soon, or maybe He needs me to get rid of some evildoers on Earth for Him. It'd suit me right fine to be God's personal hit man.

Snuffing out maggot prison guards would do everyone a favor.

For starters though, I have to get out of this solitary confinement if I am going to be of use to anyone. I concentrate on moving my muscles. First a finger, then a toe—hell, even my eyelids, but they is all as dead and useless as an old man's willy. That last part's just a guess though, as I never had no trouble in *that* department. Bonnie would attest to my skillful lovemaking, wild as a tiger with the stamina of an ox. I picture my wisp of a gal—pretty face, tiny hands, small bubs the size of muffins—and it makes my chest hurt.

It enters my head then that I have no idea how many years I'd been gone. Maybe it's been so long that my flesh has started to rot away. I picture my once-virile body looking like a heap of brittle bones, with little worms eating at the last of my innards, and a rotten filthy stench filling the air. Bah! Can't think about that. Gonna focus on getting myself to the guiding light instead. I think about Bonnie, wishing she could get another chance too. Maybe if I do what He asks, the Lord will grant me that wish.

That's when I get the notion that maybe I'm going about this all wrong. Wishing for things never made them happen. The reason I

35

was so good at robbing banks was because I'm a clever son of a bitch. Though I kilt many a man with a Browning Automatic Rifle, my best weapon has always been my brain. Mama always says that the Lord gives each of us a special talent and that it was a sin not to put that talent to good use.

So instead of trying to move my muscles, I stare at the pinhole of light and concentrate on squeezing myself into a tight ball, small enough to go through that hole. I hunker down and let all my thoughts go, all except for one—making my soul obey my command. Bit by bit, I feel a tugging sensation, so I ponder even harder. All at once, a gigantic pull at the center of my core, as powerful as a maelstrom in the ocean, beseeches me to come forward. As I get sucked into my new life, I scream, Hallelujah! with a joy as intense as a man's first time lying with a woman.

I let myself get caught up in the whirlypool, ready to do the Lord's bidding—whatever that may turn out to be.

Amen.

CHAPTER 5

Friday, May 20th // 11:13 P.M.

Monroe

I bolt down the block, adrenaline coursing through me like white-water rapids.

Run, girl, run!

No time to think. I race down the street in the same direction as Jack, staying on the grass and away from the glow of the streetlights. I sail past brick bungalows interspersed with two-flats, not looking back. I leap over flowerbeds and weave around cars in driveways without a thought to my safety, as if a serial killer is on my tail instead of a policeman. It might as well be a serial killer because if I get caught, my future, as I planned it, is dead.

Near the end of the block, I see Jack dart into the gangway between two houses. I follow his path, plowing into him when I turn the corner.

"Hey!" he shouts, sounding more surprised than angry.

"Are they coming?" I ask breathlessly.

He moves aside and peers around the edge of the house, panting. "No, we're good."

"Thank God." I let out a sigh.

"You came out the window too?" Jack steps back into the shadows alongside me, breathing even harder than I am. His face looks pale and sweaty, like he's nervous. Probably about ditching me.

"Like you didn't know." I lean my head back against the wall. "Thanks for helping, by the way. I almost didn't make it. Bruised the shit out of my stomach." I touch the area and wince.

"Seriously. I didn't know." He stares at me with fake confusion. Little scratchy noises escape his mouth with each inhalation.

I glare back at him, not bothering to hide my anger. "Me yelling, 'Jack, wait!' didn't clue you in? You looked right at me and then you ran."

"No, I didn't." He digs something out of his pocket. "Hang on." He lifts the purple plastic inhaler to his mouth and sucks deeply on it.

"You have asthma?" I ask suspiciously, as if he had kept some big secret from me.

He nods and holds his breath, I guess to make the medicine spread through his lungs. When he finally lets it out, he asks, "Why did you think I was grabbing my chest and gasping for air before?"

The thought that the slugs had infected Jack with some sort of dead Clyde Barrow virus disappears in an instant. I smile from relief. "Why didn't you say that earlier?"

He shrugs. "There wasn't exactly a chance. Things went south really fast." He takes another check around the corner of the garage. "No one's coming." He resumes his place and looks at me. "So why are you happy I have asthma?"

I'm disgusted by my insensitivity. "No, it's not that at all. I'm sorry you have asthma." I take a deep breath, wondering how to put this. "It's just that something freaky happened to me at the same time you had your attack. I felt a stabbing pain in my neck, and . . ." I pause, scrambling for any sane reason, "I thought maybe the beer had been poisoned, or maybe you accidentally like, jabbed something in my throat."

I cringe, knowing that sounded dumb, but at least it's better than admitting I thought I had infected our bodies with Bonnie and Clyde's spirits. Especially since everything seems perfectly normal now that we're outside under the stars. Well, if you don't factor in that we're hiding in someone's gangway while all the kids at the party are being arrested.

He shakes his head, his eyebrows pinched together in anger. "So the first conclusion you came to was that I poisoned you and then stabbed you in the throat?"

I bite my lip to keep from smiling. "Okay, when you put it that way, it does sound horrible. But look at it from my perspective. A minute after drinking the beer you gave me, I nearly passed out and there was a searing pain in my throat." I take a deep breath. "But I have this problem about blurting things out without thinking. In head, out mouth."

He shrugs. "I guess I'll never have to worry about where I stand with you."

"Nope." In a few minutes he'll know exactly where he stands with me when I head home without giving him my number. His taking off when he knew I needed help killed the last dying ember of possibility.

He's a fibbing coward anyway. Forget him.

I suck in a breath. Bonnie, if by some cosmic connection that's actually you, can you please just chill out until I get away from the cops?

I look back toward Kyle's house and start twisting my hair, my stomach in knots. "I feel bad leaving without Clarissa."

"Better than staying and getting busted *with* her." Jack swats at a moth that flutters in front of his face. "Since I didn't poison you, what do you really think happened to your neck?"

"Good question." I expose my throat. "Do you see any kind of red mark over here somewhere? Like maybe a spider bite or something?"

"It's too dark to tell. Move into the light a bit."

I step forward into the porch light's rays, pulling my hair to the side. He rests his hand on my shoulder to get a closer look, making me jump. He says, "I was going to tell you I saw two fang holes just to freak you out, but there really is something. The crazy thing is, it's heart-shaped." He sounds surprised.

"Oh yeah, *that*. It's one of those port-wine birthmarks. Anything else?"

"No, but that's so cool. And really pretty," he adds, making me squirm.

I let go of my hair and step back, not wanting him to get any ideas. "Thanks, but I can't take any credit for it. My mom used to say it was God's doodle." I think of her then, guilt flooding in, making my chest hurt. *I'm so sorry about all this, Mom. Please don't hate me.*

A floodlight scoping out the house across the street catches my eye. The nose of a police cruiser pulls forward and the light shifts in our direction. "Hide!" I grab Jack's arm and pull him down into the evergreens. A split-second later, the floodlight beams across the lawn and up the path, pausing on the bushes we're hiding behind. I suck in my bottom lip and slowly slide the tips of my black suede shoes off the sidewalk. A sharp branch jabs into my upper arm, but I don't move. Seconds later, the light moves across the front lawn and onto the next house. When the cruiser drives down the street, I let myself breathe again.

Jack is the first to speak. He whispers, "That was scary. Glad you saw that."

"Me too." I realize my hand is still clamped onto his arm. Letting go, I wipe my sweaty palms on my pants as the cop car turns the corner. "Let's get out of here. If they catch us hiding, we're screwed." I scramble to my feet and brush mulch off of my butt. Blood's coming out of the scratch on my arm, so I pluck a leaf off a nearby hosta plant and dab at it.

Jack licks his thumb and wipes a smudge of wet mud off his gym shoe. "They can't prove we were at the party, so it's not like they could walk up and breathalyze us."

"Hopefully you're right, but I don't want to take any chances." I unzip my purse. "I need to get home. I'm going to try Clarissa." I pull out my phone and see that Clarissa already called and texted me. Six times. The last one was five minutes ago.

Where R U?!!! I got to go bail Hank out. Do you
wanna come with or get a ride home with someone
else?

I text her back that I escaped out the window, that I'll find my
own ride, and wish her luck. "Clarissa left to bail Hank out. I'm
calling a cab."

Jack says, "I'd give you a ride, but my Mustang's in front of Kyle's
house. Don't think I want to risk getting it just yet."

"The gorgeous blue one?" I hate to admit it, but Jack instantly
became more interesting.

He nods. "My parents bought it for me last year. I had golf
practice every day after school and couldn't take the bus."

"Oh." I'm back to not being impressed. A guy who has things
handed to him isn't nearly as alluring as one who worked his tail
off to earn it. "Your car's nice. I ran past it after I escaped from the
basement." I'm dying to add *by myself,* but I don't. No sense in pulling
the scab off that wound. "Thanks for the offer anyway."

"Next time," he says.

I don't let him see me wince as I scroll through my contact list
and call Yellow Cab. "I need a cab for Baker, account 3705." While
the operator's looking up our account, I glance at Jack. "Oh, shoot. I
need an address for the pick-up."

Jack shrugs. "How about the McDonald's at Foster and Kedzie?"
He points to the yellow arches just barely visible over the roofs of the
houses across the street. Nodding, I relay the information, listening
to make sure she repeats it back correctly.

I toss my phone back into my purse. "It's a forty minute wait, so
uh, I guess this is goodbye." I shrug, not sure whether to hug him or
shake his hand. What's the appropriate gesture to give someone I was
just hiding in the bushes with a minute ago?

"Nah, I'll come with you," he says cheerfully. "Where else am I
going to go?"

"Okay, cool," I say, suddenly glad for Jack's company. Ironically, scrambling through a window and running from the cops together gives us something in common. The phrase "partners in crime" comes to mind as we hurry onto the sidewalk, although he wasn't exactly what I'd call a willing participant in our getaway duet.

As we start our walk toward McDonald's, we both crane our necks toward Kyle's house, which is now bustling with activity. Three squad cars are in front and two cops stand guard on the porch. A man about my dad's age strides past us, an angry look on his face. The police are probably having the parents pick their kids up here instead of transporting them all to the station. Jack and I look at each other and wordlessly pick up our pace.

My heels click and clatter against the sidewalk. "I bet the cop that was out scoping the neighborhood was the same one who saw me climb out the window. I can't believe he'd search for me when they have a buttload of teenagers to bust inside."

"Unless he thinks you've got something big to hide." Jack elbows me gently. "You're not an escaped convict with a rap sheet a mile long, are you, Monroe?"

He's not too far off, but I'm not about to tell him that. "I'm wanted for bank robbery in ten states, but other than that, no."

I think for me and Clyde it was only six.

I clench my fists, willing Bonnie to go away. What the hell have I done?

Jack lets out a quiet laugh. "It's so weird you should say that. When I was having my asthma attack, I pictured myself robbing a store. I had a gun and everything."

My heart skips a beat. He did *not* just say that. I strain to sound normal. "Really?"

"Yeah. There was another guy with me and we were both wearing suits and ties. I stuck this huge—" he says, stopping mid-sentence. There's a short break in conversation as we pass a young couple out walking their two dogs. "This huge gun in this scrawny guy's face behind the counter and told him to give me all his money. He opened the cash register and—huh, this is odd." Jack stops talking a second.

"What is?" I ask, not sure I want to know.

He rubs his neck as we turn onto Foster Avenue. Cars of every size and color zoom by, all in a hurry to go somewhere. "It was one of those old-time cash registers. I remember seeing the words 'no sale' pop up in the window on a little white card. Me and the other guy—I called him Ralph—rammed wads of bills into our coat pockets and ran out. Craziest daydream ever."

Panic races through my veins, but I fight to stay calm. Ralph is definitely an old-fashioned name, but that doesn't prove anything. "It's probably because you held those slugs in your hand. Whose mind wouldn't wander if they were holding a piece of history, right?"

He eyes me sideways, grinning. "There was one more thing that happened, but you have to promise not to laugh."

I bite my lip, not sure I want to know. "Okay, I promise."

He pulls open the handle to the McDonald's. "The guy who was with me called me Clyde. Isn't that weird?" He snickers long and hard, like it's the most hilarious thing he ever said.

I, on the other hand, have no trouble keeping my promise.

CHAPTER 6

Clyde

I now reside inside the body of a man I do not know in an era that's as queer to me as women's undergarments. I can see out of his eyes just fine, but I can't hear, can't speak, can't move this new body I'm in no how. Hell, can't even wet the weeds if I felt the need. But at least I saw I got a pecker to wet the weeds with, and for that, I'm mighty grateful.

The good Lord granted me the favor of being thrown into the body of a wild buck with fire in his loins. I was always ready and eager to please the ladies, and did a fine job of it too, every chance I could. Before meeting Bonnie, that is. From then on, it was only me and her. But she didn't need no wedding ring from me before letting herself enjoy the finer things in life. In public, she was as polite as a preacher's wife, but in the back seat, or an occasional hotel room after we pulled a bank job, she was ready and willing. I miss that gal something fierce, along with all the earthly pleasures that came with being with her. Best of all, she was as loyal as they come, and that ain't nothing to snort at.

I see the boy's got himself a pretty gal, too—one with a diamond twinkling on the side of her lip. She's got short black hair that all the high-styling girls are sporting these days, beautiful green eyes the color of freshly cut grass, along with breasts the size of September pumpkins—round and firm, but not too big to handle. Makes me dizzy just looking at 'em. Now if she had some smarts to go along with that fine body of hers, she'd make one slick moll.

She don't seem to like the boy much though, if the lack of kissing means anything. Why if I had a girl that sweet by my side, I'd show her such a good time, she couldn't help but cozy up to me. I'd work hard to get Twinkle to laugh and to let her know all the ways she's a shining star, until finally she broke down and begged me to kiss her. I can imagine her soft lips on mine, or me kissing her neck, getting us both all fired up betwixt and between. Feeling guilty, I make myself stop these thoughts. I'm not the kind of gent that gets his willies from smelling all the daisies in the bunch. Just find one and stick with it. Bonnie's always been my gal, tried and true. My chest hurts thinking about her, wishing she was here.

Course, if the Lord didn't see fit to give Bonnie a second chance, it don't seem right that I should have to do without. A man has needs that require fixing the same way a broken door needs a hinge. I definitely hanker for a taste of Twinkle's nectar—soon as I can work all the necessary parts, that is. I got a feeling I ain't gonna have to wait much longer neither, if what happened at the party is any indication. Lucky for me, I'm rarely wrong. While it's true that I once been dead, I ain't never been stupid.

What happened was this—I watched the boy drink some hooch and then set his sights on courting Twinkle, but the poor girl looked about as bored as a lad in school. That is, until all the partygoers started rushing around. They all looked scairt, making me think there was a raid. Flashing lights rushed in through the boy's eyes into mine, and for a few seconds, I thought I was headed for my face-to-face meeting with my Maker. I even heard music. Even though Mama tole me that the angels play the harp all day long in heaven, this music wasn't nothing sweet. It was a loud, awful squallering, like a sow being slaughtered by a blind butcher.

The quality of music ain't what's important though, it's that I heard it at all. Because them was the first sounds I heard since I had my Second Coming. So imagine my surprise when, instead of standing at the pearly gates, I felt a smooth wooden windowsill beneath my fingertips. It was *my* hand, *my* fingers grabbed that window ledge. If this was a raid, I had to get out of there right quick. I wasn't about to spend a second of my new life in the cooler. Me and Bonnie did enough of that in our first ones and there ain't nothing in this world I hate more.

Before I had a chance to help Twinkle climb out, the flashing lights stopped and I was thrust back into the deathly quiet, only able to see out through the boy's eyes. I could kick myself for being asleep at the switch! Then he did the low-down, dirtiest trick in the book—he left his moll behind. Just took off running and left her with the rap.

What kind of good-for-nothing crumb does that?

I don't know how or why I was able to take the boy over in the first place, but I know one thing I'll do different the next time them flashing lights stream in. I'll push all my energy into becoming the boy and jump into his skin with both feet. And then I'm hanging on tight. Because the next time he stumbles, he's going to fall.

And I'll be right there to catch him when he does.

CHAPTER 7

Monroe

As Jack and I walk toward the counter to order our food, I'm still reeling from his confession that the other bank robber called him Clyde. Jack doesn't seem concerned in the least, ordering a Big Mac Extra Value Meal. With my stomach in knots, I purchase only a small fry and drink to be polite. As we fill our cups at the drink station, I decide to come clean with Jack about his dream, the voices in my head, and the weird power that the slugs hold. I need to gently explain that we might have awakened Bonnie and Clyde's spirits—and then ask for his help brainstorming how we can put them back.

We navigate past group after group of loud teenagers, no empty tables in sight. Jack says, "Looks like everyone has the late night munchies."

We walk aimlessly past occupied tables, the normally mouthwatering aroma of burgers and fries now only adding to my intestinal discomfort. I finally spot a guy in a brown UPS uniform in the farthest corner, loading his trash onto a tray. "There's one." I point to the booth, then zigzag between tables and sidestep people's legs in the aisles to get there. As we approach our table, I notice a guy with shoulder-length brown hair wearing a red knit hat in the booth across from us. I wonder why he's wearing a hat in May, but when I see his torn jeans, his Element logo t-shirt, and his skateboard with a grinning skull alongside him, it's clear.

We slide into our seats, setting our trays onto the table. Jack stuffs three fries in his mouth while unwrapping his burger. "I'm starving. Kyle had nothing but potato chips at his party."

"Typical guy." I pull out my phone and type, "Clyde Barrow gang member, Ralph" in the search window. I wait for the information to load, folding and pinching my bottom lip. I don't even need to click on the blue links to see what I was looking for, because the mini-descriptions are sufficient.

"Clyde Barrow's first gang member, Ralph Fults, joined the gang when he—"

"Ralph Fults met Clyde Barrow when he was only nineteen. Sources say—"

"Hey, Jack. Take a look at this." I turn my phone and hold it closer to his face so he can read the headlines.

He takes a huge bite of his burger, filling his cheeks. "What is it?"

"It's about your dream. Clyde Barrow actually had a fellow gang member named Ralph."

"Oh yeah?" He dabs a stack of fries into his ketchup and bites the ends off. "Aren't you going to eat?"

"In a sec. This is important." I glance over at the skateboarder to make sure he's not listening. He's holding a paperback, his eyes focused on his novel. I lean forward, pushing my tray to the side. "What I'm trying to say is that I think your dream wasn't a dream at all, but an actual replay of a robbery that Clyde Barrow and Ralph Fults pulled off back in the 1930s."

Two guys walk past us laughing loudly, temporarily sidetracking Jack's attention. He wipes his mouth with the back of his hand. "Cool. What are the chances of that?"

I resist the urge to reach over and shake him. "Don't you get it?" I snap, impatient for him to comprehend the magnitude of my revelation. "Your dream wasn't a coincidence. I think that when we touched the slugs, we"—I lean forward so only he can hear me —"unleashed the spirits of Bonnie and Clyde into our bodies. Your dream proves it." I watch, waiting for the light to go on.

Jack has his burger halfway to his mouth, when he stops and looks at me. My irritation must show on my face because he says, "Wait. You're serious?"

"Yes, I'm serious." I take a deep breath. Jack is obviously not the perceptive sort. "And I'm freaking out because other weird stuff has happened ever since I took those slugs from my dad's collection and it has me worried. Really worried."

"Like what?" He pulls a pickle off his burger and drops it to the side.

"Like lots of things." I recount the mind movies in which I play the starring role of Bonnie Parker, the southern voice of a woman in my head taunting me, and finally, how an icy pain ran up my arm and settled in my throat when I touched the slugs at the party.

He sips his Coke. "That was the same time I had my asthma attack, right?"

"Right. Except that maybe it wasn't an asthma attack. Maybe . . ." I glance at Skater, who's still engrossed his book. "Maybe Clyde Barrow inhabited your body right then and was trying to choke you from the inside."

Jack stares at me, his eyebrows raised high, but I can't tell if his expression is shock, suspicion, or worse, mockery.

"So . . . what do you think?" I start tugging at my bottom lip again.

He smiles, looking amused. "Exactly how much did you have to drink tonight?"

Frustrated by his refusal to take me seriously, my face heats up. "Just that one beer. Come on, Jack. I'm not joking around!"

He takes a sip of his drink. "Okay, okay. Chill out, will you? First of all, I really did have an asthma attack. I couldn't fake that. But the other stuff you mentioned could be coincidental. I'll admit my bank-robbing dream seemed authentic, but maybe I saw it on TV or something. Same with you and your Bonnie Parker mind movies."

I pick up a fry and dip it in the ketchup repeatedly, thinking about his conclusion. I want him to be right more than anything, but the queasiness in my stomach tells me otherwise. "I do watch History Channel a lot."

"You see? So stop looking so sad. Unless you wanted us to be possessed by Bonnie and Clyde?" He grabs a handful of fries.

"No! God, no. You're right. I've seen the Bonnie and Clyde movie a ton of times. I'm sure I'm just imagining things." I smile. "It's probably all the pressure I'm under lately, that's all."

"Me too—studying for finals, the golf tournament, work, my parents, you name it."

I nod, mentally adding "missing my mom" and "court case" to my list, as a screeching girl in a pink hoodie races past us. She's holding a baseball cap high in the air while a boy chases after her, laughing. "Give it back, Melanie!"

Jack watches them as he does one of his bang flips. "Plus, I don't believe in all that paranormal stuff—ghosts and spirits and all that other crap."

I shrug. "I don't know. So many people believe in it that part of me thinks it has to be true. Take those ghost bus tours, for example. People must believe or they wouldn't pay to go on it."

"Some people might believe, but that doesn't make it true. Kyle's dad points out places where people actually died, but you have to decide for yourself if you sense ghosts around." He balls up the wrapper from his burger. "Kyle and I went on it once for fun when we were like in fifth grade. We secretively kept touching some of the tour guests with a pigeon feather we found. One lady got totally spooked thinking the ghost of her dead brother was touching her. Kyle and I laughed our heads off behind her back."

"Real nice," I say, smiling. If nothing else, Jack seems to have a good sense of humor.

He goes to dip his fries into the ketchup cup, but knocks over his Coke by accident. "Dang it!" He grabs for it, but not before the lid falls off and Coke starts running across the table in seven directions.

"I'll get napkins." Dashing to the nearest condiment station, I grab a stack about four inches thick and race back, tossing them on top of the brown river tributaries. Jack and I blot up the liquid, throwing the drenched napkins onto my tray, which now has a Coke pond with French fries floating around like dead koi fish.

"Well, that was—" I hear a metallic clink. "Uh-oh." I touch my pocket and feel the outline of only one slug. My heart falls out of my chest. "Shit!" I scoot to the edge of the bench and look down over the side.

"What's wrong?" Jack asks.

"One of the slugs fell out of my pocket!" A gold blur catches my eyes as the slug snakes lazily across the aisle. Skater leans over, stopping it with his foot.

I leap out of my seat as Skater grabs the slug, holding it out to me.

"Sorry about that. Thank you." I open my palm, smiling.

As he places the slug into my palm with one hand, he latches onto my wrist with his other. I'm about to protest when the most intense, pleasurable calmness washes over me. It's the once-in-a-great-while feeling of total happiness, like when you wake up and hear the ocean, or the boy you like smiles at you from across the room.

In a flash, a low buzz surrounds us, blocking out all other sounds and images. When I look into his eyes, I gasp. His irises have turned completely white, with only the pupils visible. They glow dimly from within, as if made of candlelight, making me wonder if he's even human. But if he's not human, what is he—an angel? A demon?

"Do not be afraid," he says in a soft, comforting voice as if reading my thoughts. "I have been sent to bring you a message. Powerful forces have taken up residence within you and your ally—forces that have proven deadly in the past. You two must toil together to appease these spirits with haste, thus ridding them from your body, or they will dwell within you for the rest of your days."

I try to yank my arm out of his grasp, but he gently squeezes my wrist. Another wave of warmth and reassurance courses up my arm, as the intoxicating scent of lilacs fills my nostrils.

His pupils dilate and then contract as he gazes at me, hypnotically pulling me in. "An opportunity exists at the moment of death to purge these spirits from existence. Do not squander this gift like the ones who came before you. While many have been warned, few have taken heed." He presses the slug in my hand and curls my fingers around it before releasing my wrist.

The scream of death accompanied by live footage of a machine gun fills my vision. Gold casings flip out from the side of the machine gun in an explosion of blasts. I stuff the slug into my pocket and the image stops. I don't take my eyes off Skater, half-expecting angels to swoop down and bring him back to heaven. When nothing happens, my mouth falls open in disbelief. "Did you—"

The tranquility of a moment ago is gone and I'm left standing in a noisy McDonald's, staring at a skateboarder. I whisper, "Wait. Was that for real?" I have to ask him straight out because I could swear he just told me that if Jack and I don't get rid of the spirits inside of us quickly, we'd share our bodies with them forever.

A cock and bull story. Don't believe it.

I'm not sure if I should scream, "Shut up!" or check myself in to the mental ward when Jack walks up, swirling the ice in his newly refilled cup. "What are you guys doing?" His voice is as jarring as the machine gun blasts of a moment ago.

Skater blinks and whips around, as if someone is about to attack him from behind. His dark brown eyes dart from mine to Jack's as he nervously licks his lips.

He looks freaked out, but I need clarification about all those crazy things he just said to me. "Why did you say that stuff? What did it all mean?" I reach out to touch his forearm, wanting another sweet hit of that warmth and reassurance I felt a moment ago.

Skater backs away, his hands out in front of him, as if he's afraid of me. "That . . . that wasn't me." He grabs his skateboard and dashes out the emergency door. McDonald's's ear-piercing alarm goes off throughout the restaurant, shocking my body into action.

"Hey, wait!" I run after him. A person can't say the kinds of things he said to me, and then bolt without explanation.

"Where you going, Monroe?" Jack calls out.

Without looking back, I push open the door and race outside. Skater's already halfway across the parking lot, cruising fast on his skateboard toward the back alleyway. I chase after him, waving my arms, screaming, "Come back! I just want to talk!"

He throws a quick glance over his shoulder but doesn't stop. I keep running and nearly get hit by a gray Dodge exiting the drive-through. Darting around the car, I resume my chase, but Skater turns the corner and is gone.

"Noooo!" I stop my pursuit, knowing I'll never catch him on foot. Interlocking my fingers on top of my head I wait a few seconds, but he doesn't reappear. I turn and trudge slowly toward the restaurant. Assuming Jack didn't put him up to this, could mean trouble.

Life and death trouble.

"Damn it!" I only needed two minutes to talk to him. Two minutes and I would have been able to tell if he was really some sort of legit messenger, or if he's a sicko who gets off on saying weird shit to people at McDonald's and then running away. I kick an empty can, sending it skittering across the pavement. What am I going to do now?

When I'm nearly back to the restaurant, I look up. A burly man with a full mustache stands at the door with a group of teenagers behind him—all of them staring at me. Judging by the yellow arches embroidered on the front pocket of his dress shirt, he's the manager. He's shut off the alarm, but apparently not his anger.

He props the door open with his foot, leaning his head out. "This door is for emergencies only," he barks. "I can call the police on smartass kids, you know. If you don't leave right now, I'll do it too."

He doesn't move to let me through, so I yank the door open, pulling it out of his grasp. "I didn't set off your alarm, that skateboarder did." I indicate the direction Skater went, but of course, he's long gone. The manager doesn't even bother to look where I'm pointing. I step past him, but he continues to glower at me, keys jangling in his fingers.

Jack appears beside the manager. "It's true. That dude left so fast, he even forgot his book." He holds it up as proof. It's a copy of George Orwell's *1984*.

A possible clue to his identity. "Can I see that a second?" I snatch it from his hand before he can answer. The onlookers have lost interest in the false alarm scandal and now file back to their seats. I flip open the inside cover, smiling when I see the words, Property of Lane Technical High School, stamped across the top. Underneath that, there's a list of about seven students' names, each one crossed off in succession. The bottom name reads Milo Ricci, 6th period.

You can run but you can't hide, Milo, I think as I stuff the book into my purse sideways.

"Time to leave," the manager says, crossing his arms in front of his chest.

"Fine. Let's go, Monroe." Jack swirls the ice in his drink and heads toward the front door.

Part of me, the rebel half, wants to turn and race back out the emergency door just to be a bitch, but I decide against it. That was the old me, the fun impulsive crazy girl. Probation Girl needs to be more mature, not so rebellious.

I follow Jack outside, anxious to share what Skater said. Before I can speak, Jack says, "Weird how that skateboarder flew out of there like that, huh?"

"What was even weirder was what he said. Either he's on drugs or he's possessed."

Jack squints at me. "Why would you say that?"

I pause, trying to find the words to best describe what happened. "I wish you could have heard him. First, his voice got all soft and whispery and he told me that we have evil spirits within us."

"We?" Jack interrupts. "As in both of us?"

"Yes, both of us. He even called us allies," I confirm, waving a finger between us. "He said that we needed to get rid of the evil spirits right away or we'd share our bodies with them forever. Then his eyes glowed like headlights and the only thing I could see were his pupils." Rubbing my forehead, I keep trying to digest what I witnessed. Surely Jack will believe me now.

"He whispered weird things and his eyes glowed like headlights?" Jack smirks, his eyes sparkling with amusement. "All in the time it took to refill my drink?" A car full of girls cruises past us toward the drive-through. Jack's head turns in perfect sync, watching them.

I throw my hands in the air, as much to make my point as to regain his full attention. "I know it sounds crazy, but it's true! Didn't you see *anything*?"

"Nope," Jack says, craning his neck to watch the girls. Apparently Jack's interest in me disappeared when possible complications showed up. Just like how he fled the basement when the police arrived.

"Jack, this is serious. Milo—if the name in the book is right— went into this trance and he said all these things that sounded like warnings. What should we do?"

"Do?" Jack shrugs, a look of irritation on his face. "I'm not *doing* anything, except going home and trying to get some sleep. I have to be at the golf course at six."

"But he was talking about Bonnie and Clyde! The mind dreams, the asthma attack, his message. It all adds up. We can't blow this off, don't you get it?"

A yellow taxi drives slowly through the lot and pulls into a slot a few spaces away. I want to run away, to forget this whole night, but I can't leave until Jack and I decide what to do.

He chuckles. "Whoa. Now you're the scary one, Monroe." He holds his fingers up in the shape of a cross, as if to ward off evil spirits. "Like I said, I'm not into that paranormal stuff, but you can believe what you want. Anyway, one of those girls was at the party and I want to find out what happened." He walks backward. "You take care now. And stay away from those ghosts!" He takes off running, but not before I hear him laugh.

"It's not a joke, Jack!" I shout, desperate now. "You'd better be careful!"

Jack doesn't even bother turning around.

As I step down off the curb toward my waiting taxi, I hear a girl— Bonnie Parker if my suspicions are correct—laughing hysterically inside my head.

CHAPTER 8

Saturday, May 21st // 12:18 A.M.

Clyde

I'm so mad I could rip my eyes out. Several tiny flashes of bright light hit me while the boy was at a diner, but none of them lasted long enough for me to jump into. They were only itty-bitty pops, like the spark that flashes after I pull the trigger on my granddaddy's flintlock rifle. Here's the thing: I saw the boy serve himself Coca-Cola, not moonshine this time, which means there's got to be something else that triggers my chance to take over instead of drunkenness. I need to think about this systematically, cuz that's what I do best.

The flashing lights was the strongest inside his head, *our* head, when we was escaping out the window. I know that much for sure. And I know he'd been drinking but I ain't for sure if he was drunk. But what I didn't think about then but I'm considering now, was that he was also prolly scared to death of getting collared by the laws. Even though I ain't a betting man, I'd wager that fear is what made him lose hisself for those precious few seconds. I need to remember if he was scared of anything at the diner too, that way I'll know for sure what makes us trade up.

I remember at one point a stranger started chatting with Twinkle, going as far as to hold her hand. If I was in charge, I woulda told that dumb cluck to get his hands off my flame. But that didn't seem to bother the boy—he just went and fetched himself another sody-pop—so jealousy ain't the trigger neither.

The stranger musta flimflammed Twinkle because when he hightails it out of there, she runs after him. Hoo boy! Gotta admire a gal like that. Ain't afraid of nothing, just like me. But instead of running to defend her, the dumb biff sat there sipping his sody-pop—just like one of them old ladies at the church social who sets in the shade waiting for her date with Jesus. That's when it hits me. Maybe he and them old biddies got more in common than I thought. The boy's afraid of fighting, I 'spect. I laugh, despite my own bleak situation. It's only fitting that his fear will be my salvation because I ain't never been afraid of nobody and no thing. While I didn't like dying, I certainly didn't fear it. My favorite Bible verse says it all— *Yea, though I walk through the valley of the shadow of death, I will fear no evil: for Thou art with me.*

Now if only I could find a way to get the boy into a situation where he is looking down the barrel of a gun or in front of a hungry coyote, that oughta do it. The next time those flashing lights appear for longer than an instant, I'm taking over. I don't know how long it'll be before the boy gets afraid again, but I hope it's soon. I wish I could scare him from the inside, but it don't seem like the boy even knows I exist.

But when I get my chance, the whole world will know I'm back. And I'm here to stay.

CHAPTER 9

Saturday, May 21st // 10:55 A.M.

Monroe

When I wake the next morning, the first thing I see makes all the madness of yesterday return like an avalanche. Propped up against my stained glass lamp is Bonnie Parker's poem, a sticky note tacked onto the plastic case. "Your first collector's item!" I ball up the note and throw it on top of the piles of books and study guides scattered alongside my bed.

Snippets from last night return full blast—me and Jack running from the police, Jack's asthma attack, Milo and I stuck in a hazy cocoon as serenity rushed out through him and into me, his words scaring the crap out of me: *Powerful forces have taken up residence within you and your ally—forces that have proven deadly in the past.*

Anger seeps into my face and neck when I picture Jack laughing at me, forming his fingers into crosses like he was defending himself against the devil. I whip the blankets off of me and stand. What a douche. I walk over and crack the window for some air. But when I look at things from his perspective, would I have believed Jack if he told me that some random guy at McDonald's said we were possessed by evil spirits? Not likely.

I consider calling Josie, my go-to girl for advice, but a glance at the time lets me know that Senior Picnic is already under way. Another once-in-a-lifetime moment ripped from me. Yeah, what I did was stupid, but I paid for it by getting arrested. The school didn't have to punish me double. I wonder if all the things stressing me out— school obligations, Dad's disappointment, my heavy work schedule, and my upcoming court case—have finally pushed me over the edge.

Could all that pressure have forced me to inflate the events of last night? I know for certain that I didn't imagine Milo's words,

59

but I'm not positive about his intentions, or his sanity for that matter. Maybe he's just a troubled guy who forgot to take his meds and what I witnessed was some sort of bipolar episode. As far as his glowing eyes, I've seen all sorts of novelty contact lenses at the online Halloween shop.

I'm going to try and forget all about last night and instead, concentrate on my future. As long as I walk through the doors at NYU in August, any lunatic can say anything they want to me and I won't care. I close my eyes and send a plea to my mother: *If you see me about to ruin my life, please send a warning. Make it one I can't miss—like a giant bird landing on my head or an asteroid falling at my feet—because I'm not the best decision maker. Love you, Mom!*

Talk about an understatement. Some of the decisions I've made lately are not even on the same continent as "not the best." A sudden breeze makes the sheet of yellow paper pinned to my corkboard flutter wildly. I groan when I remember what it is—questions that Dr. Hanson wants me to journal about before our session today. *Fine, Mom,* I tell her with a wry smile. *But next time, save the sign for something really important.*

As I slide my feet into my slippers, I make a plan. I'll write up a few answers, shower, drop off the slugs, and then walk to Dr. Hanson's office. If last night's craziness was due to some sort of anxiety overload, hopefully everything will return to normal once the slugs are back where they belong. Luckily, Dad doesn't leave for work until 4:00 on Saturdays, so I have plenty of time to get in and out before he even leaves the house.

As I unpin the paper, I realize then that I need to be extremely careful not to mention anything to Dr. Hanson about last night. If he even gets a hint that I thought I heard voices of dead people, he'll put me on heavy drugs and commit me to a psych ward for further testing. No thanks. Saint Joseph's Center for Mental Health does not award Bachelor of Arts degrees in film studies or drama production.

I grab my journal from my nightstand drawer and head toward the window bench. I pick up the purple fuzzy pillow, the one Mom bought for me before she got sick. I hug it to my chest and stare down onto Lake Shore Drive from my bedroom on the 51st floor of the John Hancock Center building. The sun is nearly overhead, so there are no shadows over Oak Street Beach. Looking down at the pretty scene below should lift my spirits, but instead I feel trapped, like I'm under an overturned cup. I take a deep breath and read Dr. Hanson's assignment.

> **Monroe: Make a list of everything you stand to lose if convicted of felony vandalism. Rank them in order of importance. Bring your list to our next meeting. See you then ~ Dr. Hanson**

My heart sinks. Great. Just what I *don't* want to do—be reminded of the terrible things that will happen to me if I get in any more trouble this year. I crack my knuckles, heave a big sigh, and let all the negativity flow onto the paper.

Things That Would Suck If Convicted
1. I'd have to go to the dumpy local college instead of NYU. Ugh—kill me now!!
2. I'd get a huge fine, continue on probation, maybe go to jail?
3. I'd have a criminal record, so employment would be limited to strip clubs and pimps.
4. No guys except creeps and lowlifes would date, much less marry, a girl who is an ex-con. Bye-bye hot husband, kids, and a French bulldog named Pierre.

As I reread my list, each option feels like I'm being stabbed in the heart. I'm not sure if the jail part is true or if the judge was just trying to scare me, but either way, it worked. I realize for the millionth time just how stupid and impulsive it was to retaliate against Talia. Of course, if I hadn't done anything, I'd have zero shreds of self-respect left, so I don't completely regret what I did. Like my lawyer did for the judge, I review the facts of the case.

Fact # 1: I agreed to go to Starbucks after school with Pierce Donovan, a hot guy with freckles and a ton of charm, who tried to slide his grubby paw between my legs twenty minutes later, so I called him a dick and left.

Fact # 2: His apparently *not*-ex-girlfriend Talia found out that we hung out. So for the next four days she yelled "Slut!" really loud every time we passed in the hall and wrote a ton of lies about me online.

Fact # 3: I told her to shut the hell up and then wrote mean shit about her online too.

Fact # 4: No, I didn't consider going to the principal or the social worker.

Fact # 5: One of my guy friends told Pierce to "settle his bitch down," but she didn't settle. On the fourth day after my date with her scumbag boyfriend, she rammed into me in the hall, making my entire Starbucks coffee spill down the front of my shirt.

Fact # 6: When I walked past her car, I thought of the perfect way to show her that she picked the wrong person to mess with. I keyed BITCH in twelve-inch letters across her trunk.

Fact # 7: I enjoyed all eight seconds of it.

Fact # 8: No, I didn't wipe her red car paint off of my key. Big mistake.

Fact # 9: Both of us spent hours in the office with school administration, were warned not to even look in each other's direction, and had privileges taken away—mine worse than hers.

Fact # 10: The douche and the bitch got back together and lived crappily ever after.

I fold up my list, deciding I'd better grab the slugs now too and stick both things into my purse before I forget. When I pick my pants up off the floor so I can grab the slugs, I hesitate. After I return these bullets to the safe, Dad will put them into one of his display cases and that'll be the end of the mind movies. As horrifying as some of the events were, I have to admit they were also pretty cool—especially from a director's standpoint. Shouldn't I experience just one more, observing from a purely cinematic standpoint?

I pause, as if waiting for someone to disagree with me.

When no one does, I take a deep breath. There's no time like the present to witness the past. Bracing myself for some horrific scene to follow, I slip my hand into the pocket, making contact with the slugs. My bedroom swirls into a blurry cocktail of whites and grays, followed by a graphic scene that bursts into full color before my eyes.

This time I'm sitting with Clyde on an old wooden porch swing. I have on a flouncy yellow skirt with a white cotton top complete with frilly ruffles and pearl buttons. Clyde has his shirtsleeves rolled up and his top buttons undone. We clink mason jars filled with a cloudy brown liquid and take a sip. I swallow the putrid concoction—kerosene trying to pass as homemade whiskey would be my guess—which burns as it slides down my throat. I shield my eyes from the sun blasting over the large maple in front of the house. The paint-peeled planks scald the soles of my bare feet, so I swipe off bits of dirt from my feet and curl them under me.

Clyde drapes his arm casually over the back of the swing, his hand resting behind my neck. He pushes off the ground with his toe and the swing starts to sway. "You're as pretty as a postcard in that fancy new outfit," he says with a smile, his thumb making lazy circles on the nape of my neck. A pleasurable zing electrifies my entire body, neck to toes and back up again.

Clyde grins devilishly, a dimple appearing on his right cheek. "This dress is almost as nice as the birthday dress you got underneath it. Sure would like to see that one." He winks and seductively lifts the hem of my skirt. "It's a sin to cover up gams as gorgeous as these." He puts his hand on my knee, and ever so slowly, slides one finger up my inner thigh. At the same time, he leans in and kisses my neck. He expertly locates all the right places with his tongue. I close my eyes, writhing with pleasure until I can't take it anymore.

I tilt his chin up and plant a passionate kiss on his lips. He responds eagerly, gently sucking on my bottom lip before softly whispering, "Let's go inside, baby." He rises to his feet and holds my hand, gently tugging me off the porch swing. "I want to give you a glimpse of what heaven feels like right here on Earth." Clyde leads me through the squeaky screen door and into a dimly lit bedroom. Slits of sunlight filter into the room from around the edges of the shades. "I've been dreaming about this." He kisses me, lifting me off my feet, and tenderly places me on the bed.

The daydream fades to black, ending the show. Based on the slick film of sweat in all of my restricted zones, I realize my brain was a lot more turned on by Clyde than I knew. I sigh, a tiny smile of satisfaction on my face. Now that's what I call a dream with benefits.

That's why I ended it. You started breathing way too heavy for my liking.

I bolt to a sitting position and clutch the neckline of the NYU t-shirt I wore to bed. "You again! Stop popping in and out and talk to me already!" My eyes dart around my room, watching for her image to appear inside a cocoon of white light or floating in a sea of black mist.

No response. "This is stupid! If you want my attention, show yourself!" I demand, slightly louder this time. Still nothing. No voice, no halo of light, no ink cloud of gloom.

"Damn you!" I slap my hand down onto the bed. "If you're really Bonnie Parker, then prove it! Stop screwing around and let's have it out right here, right now!"

Fine! You want proof, you got it. My full name is Bonnie Elizabeth Parker and I was born on October 1st, 1910, in Rowena, Texas. My daddy's name was Charles and he died when I was four. My mama's name was Emma. I loved Clyde Chestnut Barrow more than anything in the whole wide world until we got gunned down in 1934. Satisfied, darlin'?

My heart skips a beat. No. Please no. Let it be that my overworked brain made all that stuff up to confuse me. I lunge for my laptop and quickly type "Bonnie Parker" in a Google window, clicking on the first website. I only have to read the intro to see Bonnie's full name, birthdate, and hometown. I shove the laptop away in a daze. It's true. Every word of it. I am sharing my body with a woman who died over eighty years ago. "How? How can this be?"

You know how. You meddled where you wasn't supposed to.

"So being infected by a dead gangster is my punishment for being nosy?"

I don't make the rules 'round here. Once you're dead, your opinion don't matter no more.

I get up and start pacing from window to dresser. My red-painted toes embed themselves in the thick gray carpet. Like drops of blood on decaying flesh, I think before I can stop myself. I nervously twirl my hair around a finger trying to think of what to ask next when I rush to my mirror. Black bob messy from sleeping, green eyes with eyeliner smudges around them. Same as always.

My heart races so fast that I can hear my loud exhalations. I take a deep breath, trying to calm down. "So let me get this straight. I made one little mistake and then *bam!* you wake from the grave and start talking to me?"

Oh honey, I ain't just talking to you. I'm IN you.

My stomach twists with disgust and I stumble, unsteady on my feet. I plop down onto the bed, my head reeling. "No. No way."

Think what you want. Like I said, I don't make the rules. I just follow them.

I replay her words, trying to take this all in. "Okay, so let's say I believe you. I meddled where I wasn't supposed to and now you're my punishment. How do I get rid of you?"

Silence.

"Well? You going to tell me what to do so we can both get back to our lives?"

Who says I want to go back?

My head feels light, disoriented. I lie back on my bed, my ears shrieking with panic. I hug my pillow tightly, wondering if I could possibly be imagining all of this.

Nope, you're not woolgathering. I've been given a second chance.

Her response hits me like a bucket of water to the face. A realization comes over me that rocks my core. Did you just read my mind? I ask silently.

Yes, of course. You can read mine too. What do you think those things you call "mind movies" are? They're my memories, you dumb Dora.

"Fuck you," I say aloud, refusing to mind-talk with her. It's just too creepy.

It ain't polite to swear. Drink all ya want, but talk like a lady.

"I'll talk how I want—fuck, fuck, fuck."

Real grown up of you.

"Shut! Up!" I squeeze the sides of my head until it hurts, willing her to go away. I stop and stare at my hands. Can she control my body too? I clench my hands into fists and wiggle my toes. I let out a quick sigh of relief. At least not that.

I can hear and see just fine, but I haven't had any luck moving your body parts yet.

Yet? Alarms go off in my brain and my stomach lurches at the thought of Bonnie being able to control my body. I sit on the bed, holding my gut, waiting for the cramp to ease. "Are you saying you'll . . ." I stop, not wanting to say the rest aloud, but unable to prevent myself from thinking it. Will she eventually take me over completely?

I don't rightly know. It ain't like there's a rulebook, if that's what you're asking. But dying does give you an instant education on how the afterlife works. The lucky ones go someplace nice, while the rest of us have to wait around and see what's going to happen in a place called Limbo.

My mind reels, her words conflicting with everything I've believed my whole life. "Limbo? I thought that was a place for babies. Not only that, but you and Clyde killed people—lots of them! You belong in hell!"

From what I know, there's only two places to go: heaven, and waiting to get in heaven.

Furiously twisting my hair, I replay what she said. Can that be true? There isn't a hell? Or is she lying to make me think the way she wants? "If that's true, then how come you're here? Inside of me? Why aren't you still in the waiting place?"

Because you done something to bring me here, like I said. One look through your mind and I can see you ain't no stranger to scandal. In my day, people would've lined up to scorn you for all the things you done— drinking, swearing, fornicating, stealing. Ever hear the preacher say, "Let the one who is without sin cast the first stone?"

I'm about to argue that at least I've never robbed a bank, never stolen a car, never killed anyone—but can't deny she's right. I've done plenty of things I'm not proud of—things I wish I could take back. I'm in no position to be the accuser, to act upon her sentence. I drop my mental handful of stones to the floor.

My, oh my. You're weaker than I thought. When I was able to take over your hearing without no trouble, I knew you wasn't a very good listener. I guess I'll figure out your other weaknesses as we go along and then I'll take those over too. She laughs—a high-pitched, obnoxious chortle. *Soon I'll be in control and you'll be the one chatting inside my head.*

My insides become liquid, threatening to bubble over. I whisper-shout so as not to wake my dad, "No, you won't! Get the hell out of me right now!"

Does your mama know you talk like that? Bonnie tsks loudly. *Oh wait. You ain't got a mama no more. She's probably turning in her resting spot right now. Time to grow up and accept the fate you've been handed— or should I say the one you created because you're a thief?*

"I'm not a thief, and leave my mother out of this!" Eyeing Bonnie's poem on the nightstand, I drop it to the ground, stomping on it again and again. The plastic breaks into pieces with a series of satisfying cracks. "How do you like that, huh?"

You are such a child. I don't think I want to stick around with the likes of you after all. I'll tell you what: If you can find Clyde, I'll leave.

"Find Clyde?" I throw my hands in the air. "That's impossible, you moron! He's dead."

He died, but he's somewhere, same as me. When you opened the box, I felt his presence for a few seconds. I called out to him, but I was too late. Go find him.

I lean against my dresser, my thoughts drifting back to last night. If I can't see Bonnie, then maybe Clyde is hidden too. Milo jabbered on like he was possessed, and then Jack told me that he imagined himself robbing a bank. Could Clyde be inside one of them?

Take me to them now. Until you find Clyde, I'm staying in your head and sharing your life, all the way until the end of your time. Could be another eighty years or so if you live right.

"Shut up! No, you aren't!" Storming into the bathroom, I slam the door behind me before realizing my mistake. I wince, waiting for Dad to yell for me to keep it down. When he doesn't, I sit on the closed toilet seat, my stomach in knots the size of fists. Bonnie Parker is going to live inside my body for the rest of my life, all because I touched some old artifact that didn't belong to me? That's so not fair.

Seems fair to me after what you done. Better than prison.

Ha! I'd choose prison over you any day.

You are such a child. You have no idea.

The enormity of it all hits me then and I sob as quietly as I can into my hands for a long while. When I'm finally spent, I blow my nose and wipe my tears away. Time to toughen up.

Should I wake Dad and ask his advice? He's the closest thing to an expert on gangsters that I know. I could come clean, begging his forgiveness, explaining how I wasn't thinking straight when I took the slugs. But then I remember how he said he'd refuse to pay for college if I got into trouble again. Would this count as trouble? And forget about asking my sisters. Ginger would tell me to grow up, and Audrey would probably laugh. Even if Anjali and Josie weren't having the times of their lives doing all the Senior Weekend activities, what could they do to help me anyway? Say, "Wow, that sucks," and "Hope Bonnie leaves soon?"

This is one problem I'm going to have to fix all on my own.

Maybe a shower will help me think. While I wait for the water to heat up, I make a few decisions. First off, I need to talk to Jack or Milo and find out if anything creepy has happened to them. If either one says yes, together we'll figure out a plan to get rid of Bonnie and Clyde. I quickly strip down, leaving my clothes in a heap. As soon as I'm done with my shower, I'll try and private message them on Facebook.

Just bring them to me. I'll know straightaway if my Chestnut is inside.

At the sound of her voice, I instinctively cover my chest. "Geez! Could you give me some privacy please?" I step into the hot spray, pissed that I can't even be naked by myself, can't even have a thought that goes unheard. I take a deep breath and try not to think about her listening to me. Let's assume Clyde is in Jack or Milo, how would I reunite Bonnie with Clyde anyway? When I think about the traditional way couples unite, my stomach drops. Oh God. Please not *that*. There's got to be some other way. I squirt shampoo onto my hand and vigorously scrub, when I suddenly get an idea. Putting the slugs back where they belong might do it. Lying side by side with Clyde in that little plastic box ought to make Bonnie happy.

We were locked up together in that box all those years, so 'fraid not.

Shoot! She's right. Besides, maybe if Milo holds on to the slugs again, he can give me more details about how to fix this mess.

Don't believe anything he said. He's the messenger of Satan.

Satan? I thought you said there was no hell.

I never said there was no Satan. He's in the waiting place too.

And never getting out, just like you.

Maybe you neither.

I don't have time to waste worrying about where I'll end up, because I need to plan for the here and now. If Milo isn't a guardian angel that was sent to try and warn me, I'm completely on my own. My chest feels thick, congested with fear. What now? I'm out of the shower and nearly done drying my hair when it hits me. How stupid am I? Why would Bonnie help me figure out how to get rid of her? She's probably lying—about everything! I bet that's why she doesn't want me to listen to Milo—because he can help me.

"Ain't that right, Bonnie Dearest?" I ask, mimicking her accent. When I don't hear a response, I smile. I might not be a good listener, but I'm not stupid. If there is a way out of this, some sort of loophole, I'm going to find it. Then I'm sending Bonnie Parker back in her grave. Just like Talia, Bonnie picked the wrong girl to fuck with.

But this time, I'm not the one who's going down.

CHAPTER 10

Clyde

The boy lies around in his bedroom doing absolutely nothing. All he does is sit on his bed and watch cartoon people play golf all day long. Nothing scary about that. My pappy would have tanned my hide for being so lazy. But there ain't nothing I can do until I'm in control.

No matter how hard I try to concentrate on moving his bones, it ain't happening. So he must be strong as well as pig-headed, because I can't read his thoughts neither. But I'm sick to death of watching him waste time, especially now that I know how precious time is. When I take over, I'm going to get to work right quick. When the papers find out that Clyde Champion Barrow is back in town, it'll be the headline on every newspaper from California to New York. And I'm gonna make sure they say Champion, not Chestnut like my God-given name. I love you, Mama, but a man has to put his foot down sometimes when it comes to his repute.

The boy picks up a small metal contraption with glass on the front for the hundredth time. He touches squares of letters, and words come up on the glass. Good thing I learned to read and write. I know something about typing letters too, because Mama owned a typewriter. When I squint, I can read the word "Dad" at the top. The words under his name say, "I'm in the ICU. Aunt Ruth had a stroke. It doesn't look good."

I don't know what the ICU is, but I know that after the boy reads the news, something unexpected happens—something very, very good.

Speckles of lights flash in the corner of the boy's fool head.

Hoo-wee! Is the boy afraid of someone dying? Then he ain't never lived through hard times, that's for sure. I seen many a hungry man in the west Dallas slums come to blows over a loaf of bread or a pair of shoes without holes in the bottom. Saw a lad so desperate for food once that he killed a rabbit with his bare hands and then asked me if I knew how to cook it.

The boy types, "Can I see her?" And the lights flash a bit more, so I start concentrating real hard, hoping this time the switchover will take hold. A few seconds later, the response comes. "I think you might be too late. I got to go now. Sorry."

Giant streaks of light as bold as lightning bolts fire off, so right then, I focus on taking over and push my soul with all my might. I feel the boy's spirit fighting mine but I'm stronger than him. After several seconds, the cyclone feeling comes over me, and then *whoosh!* The next thing I know, I'm sitting on his bed with the metal contraption in my hand.

Me! Clyde Barrow, in the flesh.

"Hot dang!" I shout, my voice sounding strange to my ears. "I'm alive again! Yes sir!" I leap to my feet, happy as can be, but my legs wobble and I flop back down. Maybe it's best I sit here a while and figure out a plan while I learn to use my new body.

I'm still smiling from ear to ear, nearly apoplectic from joy, when the contraption in my hand starts blasting wretched music—horrible screeches and loud whistles. I push all the buttons and hit the damn thing a few times, but it won't shut up. Slamming it to the floor finally makes the music stop, praise Jesus. I clear my throat and look around. Maybe I ought to give standing another shot. I push up with both arms, bend my knees, and soon I'm on my feet.

I'm a bit unsteady but it's only a second before the blood runs through my legs. I pat my pockets until I find the boy's wallet and pull it out, along with a comb and some gum wrappers. When I open up his billfold, I find that the stupid buzzard ain't got no cash. No matter. I'll change that soon as I get my hands on a car and a gun.

I slide out the identification card to see my new name: Jack Daniel Hale. I laugh out loud. Jack *Daniel*? His pappy musta liked whiskey as much as mine did. Doesn't have as fine a ring to it as Clyde Champion Barrow, but it ain't bad. I glance at the year he was born and the smile drops off my face. Shiest, I been gone a long time. Somewhere around eighty years, if my calculating's any good. I let that sink in a moment.

If the sheriff's posse didn't gun me down, I'd be over a hundred. Of course, no one lives to a hundred, so I woulda been dead anyway. I think of Mama and Pappy, knowing they's been laid to rest. My four brothers and sisters too. Hell, everyone I know is prolly dead and gone. I sit down, the squeezing feeling in my chest almost too much to bear. I whisper my final goodbye, tell them I love them, and then set my mind to other things. No sense crying over people who ain't nothing but worm food.

Too bad they ain't here because maybe now I could afford to buy them some nice things. I spy a mirror over the dresser and lumber over to it to have me a closer look. I can barely see my face with all the hair in front of my eyes. I push the fool's bangs off my forehead and hold it there a few seconds, shocked at what I see. I'm young—younger than I was when I got bumped! I surely got a long life ahead of me now. Course I ain't as good-looking as before, but I ain't half-bad neither. Lean and muscular, brown hair and brown eyes with yellow speckles in them, all the same as before. 'Cept now I got freckles, lots of 'em, but I don't mind. They remind me of my brother Buck.

A hot pain stabs me in my heart, like the burn of whiskey that's been setting in the sun. Buck was the best friend I had, and I let him down. I push out the memory of his last day on Earth, not wanting my eyes to turn to water. I swallow back a mountain of guilt and look at myself square in the mirror. "I'm gonna make you proud of me, Buckie Boy. I'll get back at the cops for taking you from me." I feel better, knowing I got me a real purpose here on Earth.

I let go of my hair and it falls back in front of my eyes. Jesus H. Whittakers! What the devil's wrong with Jack Daniel, keeping his hair in his eyes like a sanitarium patient? I spy a pair of scissors setting in a cup along with a bunch of pencils. Dumb cluck. I'll give him a haircut for free. I hold out his bangs, *our* bangs, and snip 'em straight across. I drop the hair onto the ground and look for some pomade to slick it back, but there ain't none. No matter. I can pick me up some at the drug store—after I rob the place, that is. In the meantime, I can use this tube of cream he's got here. I squirt some onto my palm, rub my hands together, and smooth it into my hair, nice and thick. After I part my hair on the left side and comb it back, I look a lot more like my old self. Feel like my old self too.

I spy a green bottle with a fancy wooden knob at the top. Looks like a bottle of men's toilet water. I smile, remembering Bonnie's first job with me. How she sidetracked the owner in the back of the store while I robbed the cash register up front. I was so cocksure that I even slapped on some fancy cologne from Paris, France, before I took off. After we got away, we had us a good laugh over it. Bonnie cozied up to me and said I looked and smelled as handsome as a movie star. Started to kiss me right while I was driving. I'm no fool. I pulled down a dirt path about ten miles out, and me and Bonnie had fun right there in the back seat.

Looking down at my manhood, I smile. Looks like all of Jack's equipment belongs to me now. I'm getting a rise just thinking about being with a woman. Poor bastard is probably looking through my eyes right now wondering what the hell happened to him.

I smile at the mirror, knowing Jack Daniel can see me. "Too bad, pally. I'm here to stay. You might be stubborn, but I'm stronger and smarter than you, you little sissy."

I unscrew the wooden knob of the cologne and look up at the ceiling. "Bonnie, honey? This here's for you, girl." I take off the lid and give the bottle a whiff to see if I fancy it. The second that piney smell hits my nose, a tiny light flashes through the corner of my vision. Damn it to hell! I slam the lid on and stumble backward a few steps, landing on the bed. I pick up the side of the quilt and blow my nose real hard, case any of that toilet water got into my nostrils.

As I rub the gunk off my fingers onto his bedcovering, I realize that the flashing lights was the boy trying to come back and reclaim his body. Shiest! I gotta be more careful.

I stare into the mirror, so's Jack can see me, maybe read my lips. "Do you want your body back, boy? Well, too bad! I ain't never wearing cologne again, so you can stay right where you're at." I stick my thumb on the end of my nose and waggle my fingers, getting a good belly laugh over it.

I picture myself getting cozy with Twinkle, knowing Jack will be watching from inside my head. That oughta really rile him up. He can't do nothing about it, neither. The funny thing is, she won't even know the difference. What am I saying? Of course she'll know—cuz I'll show her how a real man romances a woman—putting her needs first above all else. I'll woo her with flowers, tell her how pretty she looks, and then we'll talk about everything under the sun until she begs me to kiss her. Yeah, that'll be real nice. I reckon Jack will garner a few pointers from watching me in action, too.

Even though the communicating device gives me the heebie-jeebies, I grab it off the floor and shove it in my pocket. Don't know what my future holds, but I have to be ready for anything. I take three steps toward the door and stop. I walk back to the bed, then over to the dresser two times. I can't believe it! I ain't got no limp no more! Ever since I axed off two of my toes to get early release from Eastham Prison, I've had to hobble round like an old man. I chuckle and strut down the hall looking at my feet, happy as a preacher on Sunday. Guess what happened in the past don't matter none now, do it? I got all my toes back. Thank you, Jack Daniel.

When I wander into the kitchen, I see a guy about my age with curly blond hair sitting at the table reading the paper. His clothes are smooth and fresh, like this chump is loaded. I consider hightailing it out of there, but I'm too late. Curly looks at me. "What were you yelling about in your room?"

I need to play it cool until I find out who he is and what he wants. This guy could be a lawman for all I know. "Nothing, just mutterin' to myself." I lean on the counter, casual-like, sizing him up. "But I got to get my hands on some cash. Can you spare a sawbuck?"

"Why you talking so weird? What the hell's a sawbuck?" the twit asks, frowning.

If'n I want to fit in, looks like I got to "tone down the Texan" like Daddy used to say. I try to remember how to make myself sound a high brow Yankee. "Just being funny is all. About the money, if ten is too much, I'll take a fin, uh, five dollars. Whatever you got."

"What the hell did you do to your hair?" the pip asks as he pulls out his wallet.

"You like it, eh?" I slick it back with my hands.

"Like it? You look like a dork." He hands me a ten-spot, no questions asked. My kind of fella. "Pay me back when you get your next paycheck, loser."

I size him up, tempted to make him give me all his cash after calling me a loser. But since I ain't got my bearings just yet, I settle for the ten. Not sure how much things cost nowadays, but this ought to be enough to buy me a gun. "I'll give you that and double," I tell him, knowing I ain't never gonna see him ever again. "You know where I can get me a car?"

Curly slides his wallet back into his pocket and laughs. "Your keys are right behind you on the table, dumbass."

"What did you call me?" I ball up my fists, ready to pound on his face.

He yawns, waving a hand at me. "Chill out. What's wrong with you? Are you high or something?"

Taking a deep breath, I decide to let the curse slide for now. If I knew for sure that I'd see this bum again, I'd let him know that no one calls me names and gets away with it. He's lucky I didn't ram his teeth down his throat. I turn around and snatch up the keys, but they don't look like none I ever seen. I can't help smiling when I see Ford on the key fob. Hope like heck that it's an 8-cylinder. "Thanks, kid."

He looks confused. "Who are you calling 'kid'? And why are you still talking with that accent? You in a play at school or something?"

"Yeah, I'm James Cagney." I open the door, wanting to get out quick.

"Don't be gone long," Curly yells. "Dad said he's bringing a pizza home."

Looks like Curly is my new brother. He ain't nothing like Buck though. Buck was smart and a true gentleman in every way, while Curly is just surly. Ha! Ain't that a hoot. Surly Curly.

"Yup," I tell him. "Shouldn't take but half-hour to get my business done."

As I head out the door, I remember the first time I heard about pizza, from my wop friend, Gino. Said it had tomato sauce and cheese on a crispy bakery crust and was all the rage in New York. Now, while getting dinner in my empty belly sounds mighty tempting, I got me a job to do. I need cash so I can drive to West Dallas, my hometown in Texas. I want to see if one of my relatives still owns our filling station, maybe a niece or nephew. I need a place to hole up while I track down who set me up and got me kilt. Because if by some miracle he's alive, he ain't gonna be for long.

When I step outside, saliva near falls out my mouth. There are big, fancy houses all in a row and cars in every color under the sun. Everyone has green grass and flowers are blooming everywhere, which means people around here have money to blow. Things have really changed since I been gone—changed for the better. I stroll over to the shiny blue car in the carport out front and run my hand along its side. I whistle in admiration. This is one gorgeous vehicle. By the sight of all the money all these folks got, the Ain't-So-Great Depression is long gone.

My hand is jiggly from excitement as I yank open the door and hop inside. Sweet Jesus! Looks like Jack Daniel is rolling in dough!

Leather seats, gadgets and gears, fancy radio with lots of buttons. I feel the smooth leather on my palms and my heart starts racing. I can't wait to see how much power this beauty has. Even my pecker is excited about driving this sweet ride. I spent the last two years of my life in cars so I love and respect Mr. Ford's invention. Because of that, they love and respect me right back. After I search high and low for the ignition, I finally find it on the steering column. I slip the key into the slot and the engine roars into life.

"I'm going to have me some fun tonight!" I don't know how to work all these levers, but I'm sure I can figure it out. I peer over and under, studying the different parts and how they work, amazed at all the jazzy gizmos they got now. When I see there's no clutch, I realize—it don't need one! This car shifts by itself! And different speeds on the windscreen wipers? Talk about swanky. I take a deep breath and set the gear to "D" for "Drive."

Slick as rain, I maneuver this baby onto the street like I've been doing it my whole life. I drive slow at first, testing things out. It's like a dream how easy it is to steer this thing. I cruise down the road, awed that there ain't no wheel or carriage ruts to slow me down. As I get the hang of it, I press the accelerator and let this automobile zoom into high speed. "Yee-ha!" I shout, loud as I can. Even though the power of this auto ain't nothing like the 12-cylinder Packards, it's still mighty fine.

A cad pushing a baby buggy shakes his fist at me from the sidewalk, but I don't pay him no mind. He's prolly jealous of my driving skills, like everyone else. Ain't nothing new. I turn onto a big street choked with cars and people and trucks. I nearly ram the vehicle in front of me when it comes to a stop right in the middle of the road. I notice all the other cars stop too and traffic goes the other way. I'm confused, 'til I remember those new stop-and-go lights that started popping up in all the big towns right before I got smoked. Soon as I think about how I got tricked, I feel my face getting hot. When I find out which son of a bitch set me up, someone in his family will die as horrible a death as their kin bestowed on me.

First things first. I need cash and I need it now. I drive up the road a mile or two looking for a store with lots of loot and nary a customer. I finally spy a filling station, which ought to be just perfect for my needs. I pull in and park right in front of the door so I can make a fast getaway. I turn around and check the back seat for Jack Daniel's weapons, but don't see a Tommy gun or a Browning Automatic Rifle in sight. What a total jelly bean, a good for nothing do-gooder.

For a second, I get an inkling that maybe I should start over and try my hand at making a clean living. I can turn around and go back to Curly and his family. Hook up with that dame, Twinkle. Could be kinda nice not to have to be on the lam all the time. No one here in this town knows me for nothing. As far as they know, Clyde Champion Barrow is long gone. Sure would be nice not to have to worry about going to the Big House again. I rub my chin, thinking it over, wishing Bonnie was here. She'd jabber with me about this. Was always good for that.

I sit up straighter and look around. What am I thinking? How can I go back and live with a family I don't know? And make a decent wage doing what exactly? Farming's too much work and I'm too set in my ways to learn a new skill. Damned if I want to work for no boss, neither. I ain't gone farther in school than the sixth grade, so what else am I good at besides robbing?

Nothing, that's what.

That's when I glimpse a tire iron laying on the floor in the back. I know straightaway that this is a sign from God that I'm doing the right thing. I'll head inside to case the joint first and then come back outside for my convincer. The tire iron's no gun, but it sure oughta convince whoever's behind the counter to give me all his money.

A bell jingles over the door when I walk in, just like our place back home in Texas. As much as it pains me to not mind my manners, I don't say "Howdy" to the dollface coming out. But she don't even notice—walking past like I'm made of air. Her ignorance suits me fine. One less citizen to identify me later on. I keep my head down and walk clear through to the back end of the store. I want to have a gander around the joint before I rob it. I pretend to shop, but all the while, I'm checking the layout of the place. I take in the back door exit and then count eight customers that could get in my way. I'll have to make sure the palookas leave before I do anything else. If more than five of 'em jump me, I could be in for a spot of bad luck.

I'm amazed that they got a whole aisle filled with nothing but pretzels and potato chips. Hundreds of kinds and flavors, some I ain't never even heard of before. I finally grab a bag of pretzels with a fancy blue wrapper and make my way to the front counter. When I get close to the register, I see a small movie screen up on the wall. It's like the kind you see at a theater, 'cepting it's a lot smaller. I watch for a moment, fascinated that you can see a movie picture for free, but I don't recognize any of the actors. James Cagney's not even in it, and he's in just about everything. Of course, now that I ponder that idea, he's got to be dead, too.

I rub my hand across my hair to slick it back, when the man in the movie does the same. I try a few more actions—waving, grabbing a white box off the shelf, bobbing my head back and forth. Sure enough, I'm the leading man. I toss the pretzels on the newspaper rack and dart out of there fast. No way to weasel out of that robbery, not with solid proof staring me in the face. There's got to be other stores to rob around these parts—ones without fancy movie cameras.

I get in my car and start the engine, mad that everything is so queer in this new world. Lots of things have changed—some of them not in my favor. I tap the steering wheel, pondering my next move, when a plump buttercup walks up to a tall metal box that's fifteen feet from the door. I'm curious what that contraption is, so I watch. She shoves a card in a slot, pushes some buttons, and right before my eyes, dough comes spitting out of the machine! While I'm still staring, wondering if I'm seeing things, another stoolie comes up and does the same thing!

Hell, I don't need a gun to pull this job off. I grab hold of the tire iron and pull up so there's only five feet between my car and the cash-making machine. All I gotta do is wait for the next halfwit to come by and stick his card in the slot, and I'll have me an easy stack of greenbacks. To pass the time, I whistle Bonnie's favorite tune, "We're in the Money." I only get through the song once when a slim dame wearing close to nothing sallies up and puts her card in.

I linger inside my car until the money is shooting out the machine before I make my move. I dash out, leaving the car door open, and cozy up right behind her. I push the tire iron into her back. "Don't scream or I'll kill you. Give me all your money." She starts to turn around when I tighten the grip on her arm. "Don't look at me. Just hand me the loot. NOW!"

"Here!" She holds the cash over her shoulder. "Take it!"

I stuff the wad into my back pocket and push the tire iron in her back as a reminder. "Now keep quiet until I get to my car or I'll shoot."

I dash off, thinking this job was easier than falling off a log.

I barely take three steps when she screams, "Help! Help me someone!"

"Shut up!" I snarl, gritting my teeth, running at her.

She's frantic, pointing, backing away. "Heeeelp! Thieeeef!"

"I said close your head!" I hoist the tire iron and wallop her on the side of her skull with one swift blow. Not hard enough to kill her—but enough to make the trollop shut her trap. She crumples to the ground in an instant. I run like a jackrabbit and hop in the car, hightailing it out of that gas station before anyone can figure out who or what she was snapping a cap about. I drive away with a handful of loot and no cop on my tail. Just like old times.

Turns out there are some things even a person with a sixth-grade education never forgets.

I drive a few blocks and turn down onto a side road to count my cash and reckon what to do next. I pull in front of a house under a shady tree and put the car into park. Next door, a man pushes a lawn mower around his yard, the putt-putt sound of the motor the same like when I was a kid. I count my money. "Yes, sir. Eighty bucks! That lady was loaded."

I lean my head back, thinking about where to go next. If Bonnie was here, we'd drive about fifty miles and then go out for a nice meal. We'd scoot from town to town, living in fancy hotels for weeks on this bounty. The smell of freshly cut grass reaches my nose and I take a deep whiff, longing for the country. I sorely wish my moll were here to celebrate with me.

Flashing lights go off inside my head, like the kind I remember from Prohibition raids.

Before I know what's happening, *Whoosh!* I'm back inside Jack's head. Alone. In the dark, soundless. If I had that tire iron in my hand right now, I'd hit myself over the head with it for letting my guard down. Must not be the smell of cologne that lets Jack get back in after all.

I can't believe my Second Coming is done as quickly as it arrived.

CHAPTER 11

Saturday, May 21st // 12:33 P.M.

Monroe

After my shower, I dress in one of my favorite outfits, hoping to lift my spirits—a red floral vintage-style halter top with wide lapels, coupled with black, high-waisted shorts with two rows of buttons down the front panels. I finish it off with a red feather clip in my hair.

You look swell—for a chippy. Once I take over your body, I'll lose five pounds and those clothes will look right as rain.

Shut up. They look fine now.

Men like their women as lean as flagpoles.

Not anymore they don't. It's unhealthy.

As cool as I thought the legend of Bonnie Parker was, she's way better as a footnote than a companion. All that's left to do now is to lock up these slugs and pray she leaves.

That's a waste of time. Go find Clyde instead.

It could be my infantile aversion to authority figures, but the way she's protesting my putting the slugs back makes me suspicious. It doesn't matter what she says anyway, because I don't trust her one bit. She's not about to give me advice that will make her situation worse.

On the other hand, if she's right and she *is* still around after I've put the slugs back, I need to know what I'm up against. If she can hear through my ears because I'm a bad listener, it makes sense that I need to find out her weaknesses. Hopefully it'll give me an advantage. So far, I know she's a love slave to Clyde, enjoys rotgut whiskey, and sits in the car like a dumbass waiting for Clyde to rob banks. I want to know more, but first I need to locate Jack and Milo to see if anything is up with either of them.

I flip open my laptop, log on to my social network, and do a search for Jack Hale—Chicago. There are only about ten listings, so it doesn't take me long to find the one I want. I request his friendship and send a generic message along with it, hoping he'll shed some light on my dream.

> Weird scene yesterday. I'm checking to see if everything's okay with you today. Just curious
> ~Monroe

Then I do the same for Milo Ricci. Turns out he's the only one with his name in all of Chicago. I send him a message similar to Jack's and start racing around, getting ready to leave. The sooner I get these slugs locked away, the sooner I'll know if I can get rid of Bonnie before she gains any more power.

I slip on a pair of black sandals and am halfway to the door when I come across the smashed document frame with Bonnie's poem inside on the floor next to my dresser. Plastic shards are everywhere, and parts of the exposed poem stick up between the sharp edges. Another impulsive act—why can't I control myself? If Dad sees this when he wakes up, he'll be furious at me. I kneel down and start picking up the pieces of the container, made even more tedious because I have to be careful not to tear the poem. After several painstaking minutes, I finally free the poem without any damage. "Thank God!" Bonnie and I say at the same time, surprising me. I fold it up and slide it into my back pocket so I can buy a replacement frame at the craft store.

Hey, I wrote that!

"Yeah, I know, genius," I whisper, imitating her.

She begins narrating the poem as I tiptoe past Dad's closed door, desperate not to wake him. I hate lying to him, so I'd rather not have to make up a story about where I was going, which is what I'd have to do if he saw me now. Luckily I manage to stay quiet enough to sneak out. I take the elevator downstairs, pick up a coffee in the lobby, and catch a Yellow Cab. On the way I come up with an alibi if anyone sees me at the restaurant—that I left a textbook in my dad's office and need it to study for finals.

When the cabbie pulls up at The Clip Joint, I charge my ride to my dad's account before racing to the employee entrance. The door slams behind me, helped by a gust of wind. I make a covert sprint for my dad's office when from behind me I hear, "Monroe!"

My heart stops. It's Dad.

I spin around, and see him walking toward me. "What are you doing here?" he asks.

I smile, my excuse temporarily forgotten in the panic of seeing my father here, so I settle for a detour instead. "I should ask you the same thing. I thought you were still at home sleeping."

"Guess some of us can actually be quiet enough not to wake the others in the household." He clears his throat and gives me a wry smile.

"I am quiet," I reply. He tilts his chin down and stares at me. "Sometimes," I add.

"I want you to come check something out." He tugs on my elbow, leading me toward the front lobby. "Billy and Denny are here too." As I follow him, I'm hoping upon hope that he's got something inconsequential to show me—sturdier hangers in the coat room, revised menu items, maybe a fancy new doorknob on the front door. But when we turn the corner, I see Billy kneeling on the floor next to the toolbox. Denny's standing a few feet away, wiping his forehead with a red bandana.

And there's a brand spanking new display case mounted on the wall between them.

Several spotlights are aimed at a three-foot square glass rectangle that has two glass shelves. The tan beret that Faye Dunaway wore in the 1967 *Bonnie and Clyde* movie is on one shelf, alongside a letter of authenticity and press kit photos of her and Warren Beatty.

The velvet-lined plastic box containing three slugs is on the other.

"Wow," I manage, the coffee I drank in the cab percolating in my stomach. My face heats up, like I'm leaning over a hot toaster. "The display looks stuper, I mean super, guys," I stammer, anxiety building in my chest.

Dad gives me a sideways glance. "Thanks. We've been working on it all morning. I asked Denny and Billy to help me today in exchange for an extra day off."

"Gonna go fishing," Denny says. "Maybe I can convince your dad to come, too."

"That's nice. For all of you." I force a smile when all I really want to do is turn around and race outside before Dad asks me about the missing slugs. Because I know he will. Nothing gets past him. My phone vibrates and dings loudly inside my purse. I dig out my phone and see that Jack Hale has accepted my friend request. Underneath my message is his reply:

Everything is not okay! We need to talk! I'll stay online waiting for you. PLEASE HURRY!! JACK

The urgency in his reply must mean Clyde started talking inside Jack's head, too. I need to return these slugs now more than ever. But how am I going to do that with the clear plastic box locked up inside the display case? Serves me right for sleeping past ten! I send Jack a quick reply that I'll be online in two minutes and toss my phone back in my purse.

When I look up, Denny's next to me, cleaning his glasses with the bottom of his t-shirt. Billy watches us, twisting a bit out of the drill.

"Did you ask Monroe about the slugs yet?" Denny asks, staring at Dad as if challenging him to make good on some promise. His face is stone cold—no smile, no warmth in his eyes.

"No, but I will now." Dad turns his attention to me. The pride in his face from a moment ago is completely gone, replaced with confusion or anger, I can't tell which. "I paid for five slugs, but there were only three in the box this morning. Did you take two of them out of the box yesterday by any chance?" He watches me, his eyebrows pinched together, his lips a straight line. "Like maybe to show off at the party?"

I change my mind. His expression is definitely anger.

I open my mouth to admit that yes I did take them and that I'm really really sorry, praying he'll forgive me, when he adds, "Even though I told you it would decrease their value by removing them from their original case? You wouldn't have ruined my investment just to have a good time, right?"

Three sets of eyes glare at me. If I tell the truth, I'll be a thieving scumbag in all of their eyes. If I lie, I'll only be a loser in my own.

Denny nods. "Yeah, once the dried blood rubs off, they're not nearly as valuable. Worth thousands one second, scrap metal the next."

Scrap metal? Is he serious? I want to explain that I took them before I realized it would ruin their value, but hearing Denny say they'd be worthless puts me in a quandary. Should I admit I took them in front of Dad's friends who will then know they're junk, or tell Dad privately so maybe he can concoct some story about how the auction house shipped the last two slugs separately? Anxiety races up my chest and into my face in a flash fire of heat.

What to do? I decide on the second choice. He can always tell them the truth later if he wants, but once I admit I took them, I can't take it back. I twist my hair around my finger, hoping to look casual. "Are you sure there were five? I only remember three in the box when you showed me."

Who's the liar now, huh?

Shut up. I'm eventually going to tell him the truth.

"Really?" Dad scratches his head. "I'm positive I bought five. I remember looking at them on the auction floor before I wrote the check, but I didn't actually look after they packed them up for me to take home."

Billy looks me right in the eye. "Guess you can't trust anyone these days."

Was he referring to the auction house or to me?

Denny shakes his head. "I can't believe they'd risk their reputation like that. No one will want to do business with them after this. After all that money you spent, Gordo."

I glance at Denny and he diverts his eyes. Good thing they can't see inside my chest or they'd see a swirling black tornado of guilt, along with the Wicked Witch riding on her bike, pointing her bony green finger at me, screeching, *I'll get you, my little pretty!*

Dad shakes his head, his mouth tight with apprehension. "I guess the Brownstone Brothers duped me then."

For a second, I almost think he looks relieved. Like he was hoping it wasn't me. How can I tell him the truth now? A temporary solution pops into my head. "Maybe two of the slugs fell out when we were looking at them yesterday. I can go check your office right now." The thought of being the hero crosses my mind as I picture myself finding the "lost" slugs under his desk. I take two steps when Dad stops me.

"Thanks for offering, Monroe, but the slugs couldn't have fallen out. The auction seal was firmly intact on the box when I bought them. Archival packaging is meant to be permanent. Someone would have had to deliberately remove them—like slicing the seal with a razor blade."

"Oh, I see," I say, wanting to tell him that it wasn't nearly that difficult. "Well, I hope you get them back." I stare at an imaginary hangnail on my finger, while trying to figure out what to do next. If I head for his office, I can text him to come meet me back there so I can talk to him privately. "Did you see my Trig notebook in your office, Dad? I need it for a test on Monday."

"No, but you can go check while we finish up." Dad wipes his forehead with his sleeve. "I'll be there in a minute. I've got to call the auction house right away."

"The display looks awesome, guys," I call out, desperately hoping to sound like a girl who isn't hiding a horrible secret. I dash off, glad the Morality Inquisition is over. I don't care what anyone says—you can run from your problems. Or at least dodge them until you have a chance to confess in private. My phone buzzes loudly. It's a message from Jack.

Where are you? Message me or call me right away: 555-348-9757. PLEASE!!!

I hurry into Dad's office, now wondering if I should call Jack first or wait for my father. Either option sucks because one guy is already pissed off at me and the other one soon will be. I punch in Jack's number. He answers on the first ring.

"Monroe! My God! What did you do to me?" Before I speak, he launches into a long explanation about how, after I left, he kept seeing flashing lights in his head. "I thought I was having a migraine, or maybe a seizure. But then this morning, I was texting my dad about my aunt dying in the hospital, all of a sudden, he took over my body." He pauses, breathing hard. "Oh no! The lights just flickered again!"

"He—you mean Clyde?" I hold my breath.

"Yes, I mean Clyde! He robbed a woman at an ATM! He bashed her over the head with a tire iron and then stole eighty bucks—in my body! It's probably on video and everything!"

"Whaat? How?" I ask, although I heard him perfectly.

He repeats his explanation, adding, "Except, I swear to God, it wasn't me! What if he killed her, Monroe? It's all going to be on me." His voice cracks, almost like he's about to cry.

"Oh my God, no," I whisper. The realization that Clyde can take over Jack's body makes me cringe. What if he started robbing banks again, killing people like he did back in the twenties?

He clears his throat, his voice octaves higher than normal. "You've got to help me, Monroe. Whatever you did, you've got to undo it. I don't want to go to jail! Please!" I hear what sounds like a fist slamming into the bed. "Oh no! There the lights go again!"

"Calm down, Jack! Maybe the lights are flashing because you're going to faint. Every time you yell, you see those flashing lights, so stop yelling. It's not helping anyway."

I hear him take in a deep breath and blow it out in one big whoosh of air. "Okay, okay. You're right. But it's hard. I'm so nervous. I've never been more nervous in my life."

"I get that. But we're in this together. Bonnie's inside of me, too. Now tell me exactly what happened when Clyde took over. Has he given any hints about what his plans are?"

Clyde's much too clever for that, honey. He's got a plan all right, but he ain't telling.

"Hints about his plans? What are you talking about? He hasn't spoken to me at all. I was just sitting on my bed and then *POW!* the next thing I know, I'm inside my own body watching out of my eyes—helpless. I couldn't hear a thing!"

Now I'm really confused. I look at the door, listening for Dad. "I can't exactly talk now, but I'm desperately hoping that all of this ends when I put the slugs back in the box."

That ain't gonna work! I already tole you that!

"Then hurry up and put them back!" Jack screeches. "I don't want—"

Just then, the door opens. I quickly end the call and leap to my feet, looking to the side of the couch. On the coffee table, I spy the copy of Bonnie's poem that Dad made for himself.

"Did you find your book, Monroe?" Dad pulls his desk chair out and sits down.

"No, but I found this." I hold up the paper. "And I want to tell you that I've been thinking about it and decided you can put my poem in the display case. I don't need it at home anymore."

"Oh, okay. Thanks. That'd be nice. It'd still officially belong to you, of course, and I'll make note of that on the explanation card." He sets a can of Diet Coke onto his desk. "Have you read the whole poem through yet? It's quite good." He pops open his drink and takes a sip.

"Yep, twice in fact." I decide not to mention that, the second time, it was narrated by the author herself. I can't seem to bring myself to launch into my confession, so I postpone the inevitable. "I had a couple of questions though. This stanza kind of stood out to me: *They call them cold-blooded killers/ they say they are heartless and mean./ But I say this with pride/ that I once knew Clyde,/ when he was honest and upright and clean.*" I make a face. "What—did she know him when he was five?"

Dad smiles. "He wasn't always corrupt, but his family lived in one of the worst slum areas of the Depression. Good people do bad things when they're in desperate situations."

I nod, thinking that I'm in a pretty desperate situation myself. I skim the next few lines: *The road was so dimly lighted/ there were no highway signs to guide./ But they made up their minds;/ if all roads were blind,/ they wouldn't give up till they died.*

I flash back to the death scene. I message Bonnie: I bet you'd change your mind now that you know how it feels to get executed roadside, wouldn't you?

Nope. I'd rather be six feet under than locked up in a filthy cage like an animal.

Dad looks at his watch. "What time are you seeing Dr. Hanson today?"

"At 2:00. What about this: *If a policeman is killed in Dallas/ and they have no clue or guide./ If they can't find a fiend,/ they just wipe their slate clean/ and hang it on Bonnie and Clyde.*" I look at him. "Do you think the cops actually charged them with all unsolved crimes, or is Bonnie, I mean, *was* Bonnie being melodramatic?"

Dad clicks on his spacebar to wake up his computer. "I'm sure they had more than their fair share of false accusations, but they did kill a lot of people. I think it was ten or twelve, mostly cops." He stares at the screen, scrolling and tapping the keys, then sits back and waits.

I never killed anyone.

"Bonnie, too?" I ask, doubting her words.

Dad rubs his chin. "That's up for discussion. Some historians say she did, others say that she mostly stayed in the getaway car and waited for Clyde and his gang to come out."

Only cuz my leg got all crippled after the accident. Clyde made me stay in the car.

To protect his personal hooker, I think as I grab the poem, still not finding the guts to tell him that I have the slugs. "This part's the creepiest: *Some day they'll go down together/ they'll bury them side by side./ To few it'll be grief,/ to the law a relief/ but it's death for Bonnie and Clyde.* It was like she knew her and Clyde would get gunned down together before it actually happened."

Didn't know for sure, but I suspected.

Dad takes a sip of his soda. "They lived in the 1930s, Monroe. The police routinely shot and killed known criminals back then." He pulls a copy of *Restaurant Owner* magazine off the stack next to him and sets his drippy can on top of it. "Enough talk. I have to call the auction house now." He sighs, picking up his cell phone. "I'm not looking forward to this." He wakes his computer and scans the screen, squinting. "Contact info, contact info . . ." he says aloud.

I take a deep breath. It's now or never. "Um . . . about that."

Hush now! You need those slugs to reunite me and Clyde!

"Ah. Here's the number." He enters the number, looking from phone to computer screen.

I shift my weight from one foot to the other. "Dad, I actually—"

"Not now, honey." Dad presses the last button and then holds the phone to his ear.

This time I need to make myself clear. "Hmmph . . ." When I go to speak, I can't part my lips—as if they've been bound by super glue. "Immt," I try again, but it's no use. My lips are literally sealed.

Dad says, "Yes, I'd like to speak to a manager, please. It's regarding a purchase I made yesterday." He turns his chair away from me, as if wanting privacy.

I dive for my purse. Bonnie forcing my mouth shut can only mean one thing—that she knows she'll disappear completely if I put the slugs back where they came from. I knew it! Bonnie thinks she's so smart, but I'll just toss the slugs on Dad's desk, and he'll put them back for me. Sure, he'll be angry that I took them, but he'll be relieved that he doesn't have to file a report. I reach for the slugs when I realize I can't breathe. I put a hand on my throat and concentrate on sucking air in through my nose. Nothing. Both nostrils are blocked solid.

Stop it, Bonnie! You'll kill us both!

Child, I'm already dead. Now skedaddle before you faint dead away too. She laughs.

Black spots dance in the corners of my eyes as I unzip the inside pocket of my purse. I'm going to give these nasty things to Dad no matter what. The moment my fingers grab the bullets, the room swirls into bright colors, lights, patterns—a mind movie on mushrooms.

Dad clears his throat. "Yes, I have a question about my auction purchase."

Damn you, Bonnie! I need to breathe!

Then leave NOW!

My ears ring from lack of oxygen and my head feels disconnected from my body. In a stroke of genius, I grab my phone and toss my purse onto the couch. If I can't take the slugs out of my purse, I'll leave my purse here. I only make one step when my knees buckle.

Foolish girl.

I fall to the ground, my world dissolving into blackness.

CHAPTER 12

Saturday, May 21st // 1:40 P.M.

Clyde

Ever since I robbed that woman and Jack Daniel took over our body in his Ford, he's been busier than a honeybee in spring. That fool took one look at the blood on the tire iron and threw all the money out the window. Then he went driving off like a dog with its tail between his legs and tossed the only weapon I got into a big metal garbage bin.

One thing is certain—if I ever wake up with money in my lap that someone else stole, I'm keeping it. Money is money and the cops don't know where it came from. Jack Daniel's a sniveling little piker who deserves to hide inside me while I take care of business. If he's too much of a sissy to be a man, then step aside.

After his hands stopped shaking, the dewdropper headed for home. I have to say that Jack Daniel is the sorriest excuse for a getaway man I ever seen. He jerks and stomps on the gas pedal, and people honk at him left and right. We might share the same body, but we sure don't share the same driving skills. I can beat him in a race flat out drunk and with one hand tied behind my back. Heck, I'd bet on my grandmother if she was in a race against him, and Gammy was blind in one eye and had the tremors.

After he got home, he ran up to his bedroom and kept looking out the window. Reminded me of how I made my brother Buck check for laws when we was hiding out. Jack Daniel finally gave up his fretting to sit in front of a machine with a window screen with typewriter letters. Good thing I learned how to read and write because all kinds of words come jumping out at me.

Milo Ricci: How did you get my name?

I have no idea who Milo is or what he wants, but I watch the boy type back:

Jack Hale: Monroe told me. It was in your book that you left on the table.

Milo Ricci: Monroe? Is that the chick who was with you?

Jack Hale: Yeah.

Milo Ricci: She your girlfriend?

Jack Hale: Nah. Just met her last night at a party. She starting saying all this weird stuff about Bonnie and Clyde infecting us, but I didn't believe her. Later on she told me that you gave her some sort of message and I wondered what it was. Maybe it can help me out of this mess.

Hey! They's talking about me. I watch closely, excited that people still know me after all this time. Why, once I take over Jack's body, I'll make headlines all over again.

Milo Ricci: Out of what mess exactly?

Jack Hale: I think Clyde somehow invaded my body. Like he's trying to take over.

There's such a long wait before Milo Ricci answers that I think maybe he fell asleep.

Milo Ricci: I don't know much, but since last night, it's all I can think about. All that insane stuff I said to her. I swear it wasn't me talking—it was an angel or a devil or something. So freaking crazy.

Jack Hale: For sure. FWIW, Monroe told me she's returning the slugs today. She hopes that'll be the end of it, but we have to wait and see. Did you have any more visions?

Milo Ricci: No visions, but other weird stuff. Really weird stuff. Almost too embarrassing to tell you, but here goes. After I got home I noticed I had a G burned into one palm and a bunch of numbers and the word DEADLINE on the other. Looks like someone tattooed me with a branding iron, except the crazy thing is, it doesn't hurt at all.

So the boy uses letters for code words in case the police are nosing around. I wonder if FWIW is a kind of weapon, like my favorite, the BAR. I'd bet anything that G is for G-men.

Jack Hale: Whoa! That's crazy, man! What do you think the G stands for?

Milo Ricci: I don't know. I was thinking maybe . . . Get the hell out of town?

Jack Hale: Really?

Milo Ricci: No, dude, not really. But I overheard you guys talking about Bonnie and Clyde so I

Googled them when I got home. Obviously, G could stand for gangster, but I found out about something called qwvv9900

Googled? Another code word? Maybe Milo's a cop. He's acting awfully sneaky, like laws do. Them weird letters and numbers at the end don't make a lick of sense to me, neither.

> Milo Ricci: Sorry. My cat ran across my laptop. I found out about something called the Grapevine killings. Happened in Grapevine, Texas. Bonnie and Clyde knocked off two cops who had stopped to help them fix a flat.

> Jack Hale: That's pretty low.

> Milo Ricci: Except Clyde claims it was this kid who joined their gang, Henry Methvin, who did it. Who knows? Hang on. My work's calling me.

I'd swear on a Bible that's what happened. The fool Henry didn't understand what I meant and shot the deputy right in the neck, point-blank. I had no choice but to kill the other one. Always felt bad about that. The papers made me and Bonnie out to be monsters, all because it happened on Easter Sunday. That's when we stopped being America's Sweethearts and got on the Ten Most Wanted list. I shoulda never let Henry join us. But after I helped him and my friend Ray Hamilton break out of jail, Henry followed me around like a puppy, lapping up everything I said. Guess my head swole a bit.

I can forgive Henry for shooting the law and I can even forgive Frank "The Hammer" Hamer's posse for killing me. But I will never forgive the rat-fink-lying-sack-of-cow-dung who told The

Hammer where and when I'd be heading out of town the day I got kilt. I know I ain't led a good life, but whoever ratted me out should tend to their own business and leave Judgment Day for the Lord.

If the squealer is dead, which he prolly is, given the time I been gone, I'll do the next best thing—wipe out all of his or her remaining kin. When Daddy went on a drinking binge, he'd warn me that I'd be in trouble one day because "The Lord punishes the child for the sins of the father." So it's clear the Lord wants me to punish the sons of my betrayer. It'd be a sin for me not to follow the plan.

Jack Hale: No problem. I'll wait.

This time, Jack gets his lazy buttocks off the divan and gets himself a Coca-Cola from the icebox. It looks so wet and cold that I ache to taste it. He tilts his head back and guzzles that sweet soda, but I don't taste nothing in my mouth 'cept the bitter taste of being made a patsy.

Blue flashing lights like the fancy kind coppers use start swirling round the bedroom. As Jack makes a run for the window, I see flashing lights inside my head—but they're white, not blue. Holy hell—I know what's going on! I push with all my might and the next thing I know, I'm watching a police car race past the house lickety-split with my very own eyes. Jack got scared again—and the coppers wasn't even after him! Hot dang if he ain't the biggest chicken this side of the Mississippi.

I stroll on back to the desk and guzzle the rest of his Coca-Cola in one swallow. It's cold, bubbly, and sweet—just like I remember. Lord, if this ain't heaven on earth, I don't know what is. I set in his chair and put my feet up on the desk, waiting for Milo to tell me all he knows.

Milo Ricci: I'm back, but only for like five minutes. My boss wants me to come in early. I remember telling Monroe during my trance or whatever that an opportunity existed at the moment of death. So maybe the G stands for garden, a place Bonnie and Clyde buried money. Or a grave with more dead bodies that was never discovered. Who knows? If you check the old photos, the ones they took with all the stuff they stole, maybe you can find their stash.

I wish I had buried some loot that I could go dig up right now, but there ain't none. I spent it as soon as I got it. I remember the day I took that pitchur of Bonnie that made the front page. It was right after the Oklahoma job, before anyone knew about us. Bonnie put her foot up on the fender of that sweet Ford V-8. At the last second, she grabbed a pistol and shoved my cigar in her mouth. After that, the papers started calling her a tramp. They said it wasn't ladylike to smoke a cigar, but I told her I didn't give a dead rat what anyone thought. She sent a letter to the papers sayin' she didn't smoke cigars and was only funning around.

Milo Ricci: Hello—you still there? What do you think the letter G stands for?

Shiest, he's talking to me. How does this thing work? I pull the contraption closer and look at the letters. I know what I want to say. I try pushing a letter when an amazing thing happens—the letter pops up in the window. My spelling ain't perfect, but it ain't bad neither.

Jack Hale: maybe g is for grate. wat else you know

Milo Ricci: Grate? I don't follow. Anyway, I'm not sure what's important but I read that Clyde once got reckless and crashed a car during one of their getaways. Bonnie's leg got burned real bad with battery acid. Maybe G for is for gimp, lol.

Stinking liar! I was the best driver around—and it's a sin to say otherwise. I spit onto the floor to curse his mother and set Milo straight about that day.

Jack Hale: Aint my fault the axel broke. Made me druve off the road and then the engin cawt fire. I drug Bonnie out and wrapt my shirt round her leg best I could

Milo Ricci: Wow, good impression. At least I hope that's all this is, ha ha. I read that Bonnie limped so bad that Clyde had to carry her all the time.

I get a twisting in my heart. Too bad she didn't get another chance because I'd like to make it up to her. But being lovesick ain't helping me none now. What I need now is the answer to the one niggling question that won't let me rest.

Jack Hale: do you know witch spineless bastard ratted me out

Milo Ricci: Ratted YOU out??? You're scaring me now, dude. Anyway, you remember that kid Henry I mentioned before? His dad set them up so his kid would get an easier sentence.

Son of a bitch! I knew I shoulda never trusted Ivy Methvin! I slam my fist into the desk. After everything I done for his son, too! Made him into something when he was a whole lot of nothing! I whip the empty Coca-Cola can to the ground, stomping it under my foot.

> Jack Hale: Clyde should kill all his kin and burn down there houses. Someone is gonna pay
>
> Milo Ricci: WTF??? Are you being serious right now? You're totally making me nervous, man.

I got to simmer down or I'm gonna blow my cover. I need to act more like a scairt jackrabbit, quivering in my little den. I smile. Like a scairt Jack Daniel rabbit, that is.

> Jack Hale: just pulling your leg is all.
>
> Milo Ricci: Well stop it. It's too creepy. Last thing and I gotta go. Under the word DEADLINE on my palm, it says 5-2-3-9-10.
>
> Jack Hale: whats it meen
>
> Milo Ricci: I gotta go to work now, that's why I'm telling you. You'll have to figure this one out yourself. Later

I stare at the numbers. For the life of me, I don't know what they's from. It ain't my birthday and I don't think it's Bonnie's neither. Maybe it's some sort of safe combination? A telephone number? I give up for now but I memorize them anyway, because everyone knows deadlines ain't meant to be broken.

My first line of business is to find Henry Methvin's kin and pay them a visit. No confusion about what the letter G and the deadline means. At least not to me.

Get even and bury the bastards soon. Before time runs out.

CHAPTER 13

Saturday, May 21st // 2:08 P.M.

Monroe

I came to with Dad in front of me, shaking me gently and calling my name. Apparently Bonnie decided to let me breathe again—but not without first issuing a warning.

You try another stunt like that, and the next time, you won't wake up.

This time, I got the message. I made up an excuse, telling Dad I hadn't eaten and had gotten up too quickly, and that I was fine. But he made me wait while he ran to the kitchen and whipped me up some scrambled eggs. Meanwhile, I called Dr. Hanson and said I'd be a few minutes late. When Dad was positive that I was okay, he let me leave.

Now I'm sitting in the same leather chair that I sit in every time I come to Dr. Hanson's office. But this time I'm emotionally exhausted and petrified about my future. Dad is going to call the Brownstone Brothers, maybe even the police, and there isn't a thing I can do about it.

Thanks for ruining my life, Bonnie.

As soon as you get me and Clyde together, you're free to ruin it all on your own.

The fifty-something and slim Dr. Hanson sits down across from me, notepad in hand. "So tell me about your week."

I grip my thighs hard to remind myself to proceed with caution. I start with small talk about work, my family, and about being sad that I missed prom and all the Senior Weekend events. He asks me to take out my homework and we chat about that for a while, too. We end the discussion by agreeing that my future now hangs by a very thin and delicate thread, and that I'm the one holding the scissors.

"I wish I could just throw the scissors away," I say, trying to lighten the mood. "I don't want to be tempted to cut the thread just to see how things turn out."

Dr. Hanson jots something down on his notepad. Whenever he does that, I always get a weird feeling in my stomach. He obviously thinks I said something so crazy or abnormal that he wants to remember it later on. He probably wrote, "patient has death wish," or "Monroe should not be given scissors." After his note taking is over, he clears his throat. "With that thought in mind, I'd like to talk to you about hypnosis. I spoke to your father on the phone yesterday at length and suggested that hypnosis might work really well for you. It could help you to quell your impulsive tendencies."

I tinker with my ring. There's no way I'm going under hypnosis, not after last night. I have a lot to keep hidden. "I don't think I'm any more impulsive than anyone else my age. I just get caught more often." I shrug apologetically.

Hypnosis? I heard about that. Let's do it!

No! Be quiet and mind your own business.

Dr. Hanson squints, a perplexed look on his face. "I think you might be confused about the purpose of therapeutic suggestion. While you're under hypnosis, I will replace your misguided pleasurable associations to violent or thrill-seeking behaviors with subconscious negative ones. Thus, when you consider doing something illegal or inappropriate, you'll have an immediate aversion for the activity." He smiles warmly then, like he's offering me a slice of French silk pie instead of a brain scramble.

I smile back. "Yes, well, thanks for the offer, but no thanks." I click on my phone. 2:24. I've only been here twelve minutes? I shift in my seat and feel something jab me in the back. I reach around behind me and grab the offending object. It's Bonnie's poem. I quickly try to slide it back into my pocket, but my fingers clamp down on it and I can't let go. I concentrate on prying my fingers apart, but I can't do it.

Stop it, Bonnie. Let go!

No!

"Is there a problem?" Dr. Hanson asks, his forehead wrinkled in confusion.

"No, sir. No problem at all," I say, with a thick hillbilly drawl that sounds exactly how Bonnie sounds in my head. I can feel my cheeks rise as I break into a wide grin.

My face flushes hot and my heart pounds hard. Is she taking over my body, like Clyde has done to Jack? Hot bile mixed with scrambled eggs come partially up my throat, burning as they recede.

Bonnie, no! Don't you dare do this to me.

You be quiet. I'm in charge now.

Dr. Hanson taps his pencil. "I see you're uncomfortable with hypnosis, but are you aware that it can also help calm those anxiety attacks you mentioned? You'll learn to recognize when your stress level increases and can begin those self-calming techniques we discussed."

"Some people think hypnosis is whole lot of booshwash," Bonnie drawls, "but Hubert brought home an advertisement about hypnosis a few months back. Thought it sounded keen. So you know what, doc? I'm gonna change my mind. Let's do it!"

Heat roars up my neck, my face. With every molecule of my brain, I concentrate on moving my lips even one millimeter. They won't budge. Damn you, Bonnie!

Dr. Hanson clears his throat. "A southern accent. Interesting." He scribbles something down on his notepad, the pen making scratchy sounds across the paper. He rises to his feet. "Terrific. We'll get started right away. I'll notify my assistant to start up the recording equipment."

Recording equipment? My eyes must pop out of my head, because Dr. Hanson holds up a hand. "Now don't let that worry you. Recording hypnotic sessions is standard procedure—for your protection and for mine. It all takes place behind that two-way mirror so you don't have to see it." He glances up at the large mirror mounted on the wall behind him. "In fact, if you can even forget it's there, that'd make things go a lot smoother. Like everything else we discuss, anything you say under hypnosis will remain confidential."

I take another stab at telling Dr. Hanson that I don't want to go through with this, but my lips won't cooperate. "Mmmph."

"Excuse me?" he asks, concerned.

I shake my head, shrugging.

"My mistake." Dr. Hanson points to the couch and smiles. "How about you go lie down over there and make yourself comfortable?"

So as not to draw more attention to myself, I stumble to my feet in a daze. I try not to let panic register on my face, even though inside of me, there's a freaking five-alarm fire.

Stop this right now, Bonnie. What the hell do you think you're doing?

What does it look like I'm doing? I'm gonna get hypnotized. You can do what you want.

My eyes dart around the room. The couch is three feet to my left, the door five feet to my right. I take two steps toward the door, ready to bolt, when Dr. Hanson turns around.

"Do you need to use the restroom?" he asks politely, but his tone shows he's concerned.

"No, sir! I tripped is all. I'm clumsier than a drunk mule." Bonnie lets out one of her horsey laughs.

Stop saying weird shit. You'll make him even more suspicious!

Stop your bellyaching and relax. This will be fun.

Sweat breaks out under my arms, across my forehead. If I run, he'll conclude I'm even more messed up than he already thinks I am. Probably call my dad and suggest residential treatment. I force myself to lie down on the couch, hypnosis being the lesser of two horrible outcomes. My fingers still clutch the poem so tightly that my muscles are beginning to ache.

Wait a second. Is the poem the thing that's giving her control right now?

I do a quick check on Dr. Hanson's whereabouts, finding him by the door speaking with his assistant. Perfect. Trying to flick the poem out of my hands, I shake my wrist forcefully several times, but it's no use. I can't get my fingers to release her poem.

So that's it, huh? When I touch something that belonged to you, you have more power?

You think I'm tellin' you my secrets? I ain't no squealer. She laughs.

I squeeze her poem tightly, wishing it were her neck.

I don't know why you're doing this, Bonnie, but listen carefully. Whatever you do, don't mention Clyde, jail, or robbing banks, or he'll commit us to the psych ward.

Of course. I ain't stupid.

A brick lands in the floor of my belly. I just referred to myself as "us."

"Alrighty then." Dr. Hanson sits in the straight back chair next to the couch and crosses his legs. "I'm going to put you in a very relaxed state and then I'll ask you some questions. After about ten minutes, I'll wake you up, and we'll go from there. Okay so far?"

"Yes, sir. Everything's dandy," Bonnie chirps.

"I'm going to ask you to tense and then relax each muscle group from your feet all the way to your shoulders. Let's start with your toes."

I wiggle my toes, then ankles, then knees, trying to get this over with as quickly as possible.

"No, not like that," Dr. Hanson corrects. "You have to clench the muscle, hold for five seconds, and then relax it before moving on to the next one. Let's try this again."

With an impatient sigh, I clench and hold as he asks, before moving on to do the same with my calves, my knees, and on up, all the way to my shoulders. His voice softens. "That's it. Now concentrate on your inhalations and exhalations as you let go of all conscious thought."

Behind my eyelids there's an ocean of blackness with two white squares superimposed in the center—which I figure must be the negative images of the sun coming in through Dr. Hanson's office windows. Despite all the relaxation exercises, my breath booms loudly in my ears—in, out, in, out. I can't wait for this to start so it can be over.

"Are you fully relaxed and ready to begin?" he asks.

Bonnie replies with a guttural, "Uh-huh." Trancelike, but still alert.

Not me, I think. I'm so hyped up, it's like I drank a swimming pool's worth of iced coffee.

Dr. Hanson begins then, speaking quietly. "Let your mind wander. Think about the first time you got in trouble with the law. Let the images rush in and don't edit what you're seeing or feeling. Just give me a running commentary of everything you see and hear."

Images of places I've never been flood into my mind—barns, silos, prairie grasslands with a few skinny cows grazing off in the distance. I'm in some sort of antique car with a ton of headroom above me. An emblem with the words *Ford Motor Company—1927* is mounted on the glove compartment. I'm waving a white handkerchief in front of my face, as if to cool down. I look to the driver's seat and see Clyde there, with his greased-back haircut and ears that stick out, younger now than he was in the autopsy. He smiles at me. *"Hey beautiful. You all set to lose your virginity?"* He laughs, elbowing me. *"Your virginal criminal record, that is."*

My hand slides down Clyde's slim arm. "I'm in Tellico, Texas," I tell Dr. Hanson, "sitting in a car with the love of my life. Lord, he looks good!"

Keep things vague, Bonnie. Don't mention any names.

The scene in my brain pans to my left, and then zooms in for a close-up, getting an interior shot of the car. There are unfamiliar foot pedals, a gearshift knob on the end of a long skinny bar, and an outdated dashboard with big dials. *"Ready to go, doll?"* Clyde squeezes my knee, smiling. I look over at the small white building with wooden siding, complete with peeling paint and raggedy, faded blue awnings. I can make out the words *Colleyville Drugs* in white paint across the picture window.

"It's the day of the first job we pulled together," I say, my voice all twangy and breathless. "After I helped him break out of prison, that is. That's a whole other story, though."

I hear Dr. Hanson's pencil furiously scribbling notes.

Prison! I screech. Are you crazy? Take that back now! Say "just kidding, Doctor!"

Bonnie doesn't respond. I need to end this session now before Bonnie says any more incriminating details about her life. I'll tell Dr. Hanson that hypnosis is not working for me and that I feel uncomfortable. But when I attempt to slide my legs to the side so I can sit up, I can't. They have become two beached whales that have melded with the couch.

My ears ring with panic. Could her side of the brain be so entranced that she's under hypnosis even though I'm not? Temporarily down for the count? Inaccessible? If she is, I guess that means I am, too. I quickly rattle off a prayer to my mom, to God, to anyone who will listen: *Please don't let Bonnie say anything that will make Dr. Hanson decide to commit me for residential treatment. Please, please, please!*

"We're sitting in the car, talking about our plan and Chestnut—that's his real middle name, you know, not Champion like he tole everyone—looks so handsome and sweet, it's breaking my heart."

"What happens next?" Dr. Hanson says, sounding intrigued.

I watch through Bonnie's eyes as Clyde reaches under his seat and hands me a gun. I twist the two knobs on the black purse on my lap and toss the pistol inside. *"You're gonna do swell, doll. I just know it,"* he tells me. *"You were born to this life, same as me."*

"I can't wait to show Clyde I can pull this job off," Bonnie tells Dr. Hanson, "but I'm a tad scared about using a gun. I shot plenty of cans out behind Turtle Creek, but that's not the same as shooting a live person. Made me feel kinda sick in my belly, you know?" She—or maybe it's me since I don't know at this point—sighs loudly. "Clyde said it made no matter because I shouldn't fire at anyone unless they's aiming a gun at me first. Made that very clear. He ain't no monster like everyone thinks. Only shot people when he had no choice."

"Tell me about the job you pulled," Dr. Hanson directs.

"Clyde decided Colleyville Drugs would be an easy target because the owner was older than God himself. I told Clyde it was blasphemy to say that and he told me that I'd see for myself that he wasn't lying. That was Clyde for you, always kidding around." I giggle and snort loudly, unable to stop myself. My heart rate increases with her every word. I need to stop her.

Wake up, Bonnie! I beg. Open your eyes. Session's over.

Dr. Hanson clears his throat. "Uh-huh. Keep going."

I try again, this time louder, more urgent. The cops are here! Raid! Run for your life!

"Sure," Bonnie says, deaf to my pleas. "So then Clyde told me that my job was to go in and distract Mr. Rogers by bringing him to the back of the store, while he robbed the register up front. Clyde said the man behind the counter was one lucky bastard because he got to see my great gams." When I giggle-snort again, a bit of drool runs out the side of my mouth. I go to wipe it when I realize Bonnie's hypnotic trance prevents me from moving.

My dream self daintily dabs the sweat off my forehead with a handkerchief before taking a deep breath and exiting the car. After smoothing my dress, I stroll over and pull open the squeaky screen door of the drugstore, hearing it thump as it swings shut behind me. I'm in an old-fashioned country store with built-in shelves all the way to the ceiling. An old man in a butcher's apron stands on a tall sliding ladder, like the kind you see in ancient college libraries. He sets a box on a shelf. *"Howdy, ma'am! Let me know if you need anything."*

"Thank ya kindly," Bonnie replies.

"So I go in and walk around," Bonnie tells Dr. Hanson, "and pretend I'm looking for something. I'm real nervous, this being my first job and all, but I know Chestnut's counting on me to do it right." With my eyes still closed, I can feel Bonnie smiling.

"Uh-huh. Then what?" Dr. Hanson presses.

"Then I pick up a few boxes and put them back down, like I can't find what I want. Mama always says I should've gone into acting because I'm so good at it. Anyhow, I saunter up to the old man at the counter and make my voice sound sweet, smilin' just the way men like. Then I ask him if he can help me find rose water, because that's what Clyde told me to ask for. Said they kept it way back in the far corner of the store when he came here to case the joint."

I try to yawn, bite my tongue—anything to regain control of my mouth, but it's no use. Bonnie keeps on blathering away—telling Dr. Hanson every last freaking detail of her first robbery. And it sounds like she's enjoying herself. Bragging about it even. "Of course, the old guy is pleased as punch to help me. Tells me to follow him. As I do, I make my heels clunk loudly on the wooden floor. That was my own idea, the clunking. I figured the noise was good cover for Clyde."

"What did you and Clyde do next?" he asks, making me wonder when he's going to do his part with the alternative suggestions so Bonnie will shut the hell up.

"I touch the geezer's arm so he thinks I'm flirting with him. When I hear a *toot-toot* out front a minute later, I tell the old man I can't make up my mind and need to come back later. Turned out to be the easiest job we ever pulled. Got away with fifty-two dollars and Clyde didn't even have to shoot no one. Funniest thing was, he came out smelling handsome too. He had dabbed some fancy cologne on at the register, right after he swiped the cash. Ain't he a hoot?"

I can hear Dr. Hanson scribbling like mad. "Yes, I see. Very good." He clears his throat. "I think that's enough for now. On the count of three, I want you to start waking up slowly, coming back to being in my office. 1 . . . 2 . . . 3. When you're ready, open your eyes."

The light in my eyes flickers and my head feels lighter, as if I'm coming to the surface from being underwater. I bolt to a sitting position, hoping to catch Bonnie off-guard. I'm rewarded for my efforts by being able to whip the poem into my open purse. I take a deep breath, ready to tell Dr. Hanson that the things I spoke about weren't from my memories, but from Bonnie Parker's. That I never robbed a drug store at gunpoint in my life and that this is all a huge mistake. My heart races, as I sputter, "Oh my God, that was not me talking just then, Dr. Hanson. I know this sounds crazy, but last night, I think I might have awakened the spirit of—"

You say my name and we both end up in the sanitarium. Ain't that what you said?

A mental sledgehammer pounds my skull. I clear my throat. "Never mind."

Dr. Hanson narrows his eyes. "Awakened the spirit of who? It's all right. You can tell me." Judging by the slick line of sweat on his forehead, he's on high alert for a juicy revelation.

I'm plagued with indecision. Let Dr. Hanson think I have schizophrenia or say I've been inhabited by Bonnie Fucking Parker. I realize it probably doesn't matter what I say.

Either way, I can kiss my future goodbye.

CHAPTER 14

Saturday, May 21st // 5:18 P.M.

Clyde

After deciding to drive to Texas to find Methvin's kin, I realize I ain't got me no map. When Bonnie was around, I didn't have to worry. That girl was an expert at stealing maps whenever we stopped to fuel up. *Lookie what I got here*, she'd say, teasing me as she waved it in my face. I swear that gal had flypaper for fingers. Swift and sure, never getting caught.

White light flickers for a second. Is Jack about to take me over? Shiest! I concentrate on staying put when I realize it musta been the sun shining off a car window as it drove past the house. I get up and look in the mirror. "Ha! You ain't getting back that easy." I plug my fingers into my ears and waggle my tongue, like I used to do to my brother Buck when we was kids.

The door slams somewhere nearby and a man yells, "Jack? Sean? Pizza's here!"

I rub my belly. Sure would be good to eat. I smell garlic, cheese, and tomato sauce, which make my stomach growl loudly. I laugh, remembering the time Bonnie bamboozled a slice from a pizza man in Chicago by giving him a kiss.

Before I knew what hit me, thunderous bolts of lightning flash through my head and I'm plunged into darkness. I'm so angry at myself for letting my guard down that I wish I could beat the daylights out of Jack Daniel. Take him outside and cuff him again and again until blood was squirtin' out his nose like a faucet.

I look out through Jack's eyes and see him pick up a pen and paper off his desk. He writes, "FUCK YOU, CLYDE! LEAVE ME ALONE!" in giant letters. Is that all he's got—a few curse words? Looking at his pretty boy face and straight nose, I'd bet Jack never got a licking in his life. Defending yourself is something all men should know how to do. Ranks right up there with another event all men should know about, something I doubt Jack knows anything about either. My first time was with Sweet Norma Rae. She was worth all two dollars my daddy paid for her as my sixteenth birthday gift.

After wetting his hair and messing up all the stylin' I done for him, Jackrabbit runs out of his room and heads to the kitchen. He grabs a plate and sticks four wedges of that mouthwatering pizza pie onto it. Them wops know what they're doing. The white cheese is all melted and gooey, and little pepperonis sit on top just begging to be eaten. But eating four whole slices on his own? My God, they don't got a care in the world about food these days. I seen men fighting over a rich family's table scraps, just hoping to have enough to survive.

Jack stuffs it into his mouth, chewin' and swallowin' again and again, but I can't taste a thing. For the second time since I been sharing Jack Daniel's body, I'm green with envy. First time was watching him make a turrible attempt at wooing Twinkle, knowing I coulda sweet-talked her into giving me a kiss, and now this. He don't deserve none of it the way he lays around all day like one of those poor army fellers who ain't got no legs.

He sits at the table, jawing with Curly and his daddy. I try to read their lips to learn something. They keep looking at a square box on the counter with moving pictures on it. But this one don't look like the one at the gas station. They's watching a baseball game, but we ain't even at a ball park. This new world is strange all right, but with all the dough they have, I could get used to it right quick.

As Jack heads back to his bedroom after dinner, I start going over every detail of how and when the lights inside my head started flashing. Because if I don't figure this out soon, I'm going to be left behind like a sissy. Since that boy can't do nothing without holding his mama's hand, it means I did something that opened the door for scairt little Jackrabbit to come in.

I was at the desk sitting and thinking about how to get to Texas when I first seen the lights. Could it be that I was homesick for Texas, and that made me lose myself for a few seconds? Nah, that's not it. I was hungry and I started remembering how Bonnie sweet-talked the pizza man into giving her a free slice. I let that sink in a few seconds. Could thinking about Bonnie make me lose my head?

If so, that's an easy fix. I done all the caterwaulering I need about Bonnie. If I want to stay a real man, I have to forget about her altogether, at least when I'm out working my new body. I call out to her, hoping somehow she can hear my thoughts, wherever she may be. *Sorry, doll, but I need to move on. Maybe I'll see you in heaven after my time is done here on Earth. Amen.*

I think a bit longer, not settling on the first idea that comes to me, because that's how men fail. Being so hogsure of themselves that they don't look at all the options. Right before the switchover, I remember smelling the garlic and onions of the pizza. And the first time it happened, I smelled fresh cut grass, then it was the men's toilet water. So until I'm one hundred percent positive what's causing the change, I'll stay away from thinking about Bonnie and from smelling things. Hell, I'll stuff corks in my nose if I need to.

Jack Daniel sits at his desk and opens that writing contraption I was using earlier when I talked to Milo. A bit of despair hits me square in the chest. Looks like I ain't gonna change back anytime soon because sitting in his room writing words isn't going to scare him. Jack Daniel types and types, lickety split like he's a dang secretary, and then stares at the screen. When I read what's written at the top, I tune in real good. It's a newspaper with the headline "Ivy Methvin Dead" in big letters across the top. Luckily, the boy ain't a fast reader, so I can follow along.

Turns out Henry's father, Ivan Methvin, the dirty filthy squealer who set me up, got kilt by a hit-and-run driver in 1948. The article says the perpetrator never got caught. I chuckle when I read that most people think it was my kin or my sympathizers who did it.

Thank you, secret avenger. I hope good luck shone down upon you all the rest of your days.

The boy clicks onto the pictures and they get real big on the screen. Henry Methvin looks exactly the way I remember him, strong as a bulldog with piercing blue eyes. Eyes I now want to poke out with a sharp stick and roast over a fire for what he done to me. But when I read a bit further, I'm giddy with happiness. Turns out Henry met as gruesome a death as me and Bonnie. Got run over by a train that took off right when he was scampering beneath it. Ha! Looks like God took care of my vengeance for me just fine. *Thank you, Lord!*

My only perturbance is that I didn't get to do it myself.

My eyes get wide as pancakes when I see pictures of me and Bonnie—the ones we sent to the papers. There was the time I scooped her up in my arms like we was newlyweds. Pictures of me and Henry in our trench coats, our arms draped over each other's shoulders like we was best friends. God, I was stupider than a stump of wood. After some reminiscing, my eyes freeze on a large ad at the bottom. When I read what it says, I nearly wet myself from shock.

BONNIE AND CLYDE AMBUSH MUSEUM

See it all as it really happened!

Visit the spot where the outlaws were gunned down!

Photos galore!

Check us out in Gibsland, Louisiana!

They got a whole museum about us? Pride springs forth from my innards as bright as the first day of spring. Right as I'm gloating about how lucky I am, horrible pictures loom big onto the screen— snapshots of my getaway car blown to pieces, my body lying sideways in the car, mouth open, blood everywhere. I wish I could look away, but I can't.

Jackrabbit scrawls something on a paper and holds it up alongside the writing contraption. There's an arrow pointing at my corpse. "You're dead. Stay that way."

Have your fun now, Jack Daniel, because soon, you're all mine.

Looking at them pictures does make me realize how life can turn on a dime. One minute we was riding high, ready to blow through Texas and on to Missouri, and then next we was dead. Only a hair past twenty years old, the two of us. I get a pain in my chest thinking about it. But then I make myself cheer right back up. The Lord gave me a Second Coming, just like He'll have one day, so there ain't nothing to wail about.

At the bottom is a picture of me and Bonnie sitting together with our arms around each other. It says "Together Forever ~ May 23, 1934 ~ 9:10 A.M."

Something about that date irks me. But I don't have time to think because the fool shuts the lid and reaches for his communicating device. He holds it up to his ear, so it must be some sort of newfangled telephone. Course, I can't hear nothing anyhow. A minute later, he pushes a button and sets the contraption down. Lo and behold, the cockroach finally bathes.

As he washes up, I think about that date again, trying to figure out why it's getting under my skin. Did I get slaughtered on Mama's birthday? No, that was March 23rd, not May. Is May 23rd a holiday? I run through every holiday I know, and it ain't that neither. I try to block out everything and remember the numbers I memorized that Milo tole me.

5-2-3-9-10.

That's when I figure it out. The answer's as clear as if an angel brought me Jack Daniel's head on a silver platter. I'd fall to my knees and thank the Lord for providing me with the answer if I had my body back right now.

May 23, 1934 at 9:10 A.M.

The deadline is our dead time.

Hot damn! Now I know the truth! I'd bet anything that the thick-headed dimwit didn't pick up on that. God sent *me* that message, not him. God's trying to tell me that whoever has control of this body on the anniversary of my death wins the grand prize—L-I-F-E. Maybe we ain't got to share bodies no more. Out with the Jackrabbit, in with the Clydesdale.

It's now plain to see that G stands for Gibsland, which is where I aim to be when our deadline hits—in the same spot I died—and I'll need to be there for my un-dying, too. Hallelujah! Then I'll set forth on my task to end the lives of all the Methvin kin.

A niggling thought winds its way into my mind. Killing someone's grandkids ain't the same as sticking it to the one who brought you down. None of them was even alive at the time, so that don't seem right. Looks like I need to think a mite longer about what I want to do. I know one thing for certain—I ain't gonna live like dirt the way my folks did—always scrambling for money, never having enough to eat, having to move when we couldn't pay the rent. And while I didn't much like running from the laws my whole life, I did fancy being famous. Not even pitching woo with Bonnie in the back seat compares with the rush of pride I got whenever my name was bantered about by strangers. I almost think about Bonnie then, but catch myself. Better train myself now to deflect them thoughts whenever they hit me—like cheap bullets off of steel.

Since I been sent on a mission from God, I need to do something good for the world. Maybe I should spend my time eliminating the worthless bastards that hide behind their badges committing worse crimes than the henchmen they should be collaring. All I have to do is get friendly with some hammer and saws so they can tell me which ones among them went rotten.

Once I hunt down all the club-swinging coppers and dirthole lovin' prison guards, and wipe them from the face of the Earth, the world will thank me. Why, they'll erect a real museum about me—just me this time. Not just one about how I died, but showing all the things I did during my Second Coming. Folks will visit the Clyde Barrow Museum every year to talk about what a fine man I am. I can see it now. But the only way I can do the Lord's bidding is if Jack Daniel gets scairt again so I can push myself back into his body.

My body.

The boy ain't out the shower five minutes before he's checking out the window again. If he thinks the cops are coming cuz of me clubbing that woman, he best be on his way. Because if I do take over his body, I'll fight to our death before I go to the Big House again. Not going to sit around and get humiliated by some fat-as-lard prison guard, that's for sure.

Jack Daniel runs around, shoving things into his pockets before he heads out to his sweet ride. He gets in and drives not even two blocks when he pulls over next to some bushes on a dead-end street. I'm kinda perplexed when he walks round to the back of the car. He pulls a fat marking pen out of his jacket pocket and kneels down 'til he's nose to nose with his license tag. He changes a P to a B and a 3 to an 8 before hopping back into the driver's seat. Well, I'll be danged! He ain't as dumb as I thought.

He drives for a while, following in a line, not changing lanes at all. He finally parks and heads into a shop with a coffee cup on the window. He orders something, a cup of joe I guess, but it's in a paper cup and has a lid on it, so I don't know for sure. He takes a seat at a little brown table with two chairs. He keeps looking around, checking his watch. A couple minutes later I want to cry out for joy when who should come in, but Twinkle herself!

When I see her, my heart beats a little faster. Damn, that girl looks fine with her tight clothes hugging them curves—nothing like the girls in my day. She's got on a red top that lets me get an eyeful of her luscious breasts along with black shorts that shows off those long sexy legs. Makes me want to tell her all the things I like about her if, no when, I get the chance.

She goes up to the counter to order herself a drink while the weasely little boy stays put in his chair. Why, he's not a gentleman at all! Made her buy her own coffee—which costs nothing but a few cents. She must think he's a total flat tire. She finally gets her drink and sets down across from Jack Daniel—across from me—the diamond in her lip sparkling in the sun each time she moves her pretty little head.

If I was in charge of this date, I'd have already told Twinkle how swell she is and pulled her close so everyone knew she was my gal. I'd kiss her and whisper sweet things in her ear, just so I could see her smile. Wish she was smiling now, cuz she sure don't look very chipper. Course, meeting up with a Johnny-Come-Lately with sawdust for brains wouldn't make any dame light up, much less a swell one like Twinkle.

Jack Daniel must be flapping his gums a mile a minute cuz all Twinkle does is nod, and then nod some more, her face all twisted up like she missed her train and there ain't another coming anytime soon. I reckon Jack Daniel's going on about me and how I took him over. I wait and wait, hoping to see some flashing lights, but nothing. Maybe he's getting tougher, trying not to be scairt so easy. That's gonna make my job a tad harder, but I ain't worried. A chicken's still a chicken, even if it learns to bark. Why, he's so afraid of getting turned down by Twinkle, he don't even try to touch her. Stupid fool.

After what seems like forever, Twinkle slides her chair over closer and opens up a silver contraption—a lot like the one the boy had in his room. I want to hold her hand, to ask her all about her family, what she likes and doesn't like, but I have to settle for the heavenly view of her gorgeous bubs. Hard to avoid doing so since Jack Daniel keeps eyeing them every chance he gets. Twinkle types "getting rid of spirits living inside you" inside a little box and then starts talking and pointing to the screen, like she's explaining something. So she's a planner, just like me. She takes out a communicating device, something like Chickenshit has, but hers is red. Her thumbs start doing a jitterbug dance on top of the glass. Finally, Jack Daniel takes his eyes off her chest and looks at the writing contraption.

In big black letters across the top it says, "Half-Dead Society" with a picture of a ghastly creature jumping up and down, spreading his arms and legs. A jumping jack is what I think the maggot called it when they took us out in the yard for daily calisthenics. I stare at the creature, wondering what on Earth it is. The left half is a handsome fella in a suit and tie, a dapper dresser like myself, while the right half has a decaying face of an old man, wearing dirty, ripped clothes. Shiest, that thing is ugly. The whole thing don't make a lick of sense 'til I put two and two together. Can't believe I didn't catch on sooner. Jack and me is what they's calling a half-dead, and apparently, we're not the only ones.

Maybe I can get a few reliable ones that I can trust to keep their mouths shut to form a new gang with me. Why, we'll wipe out all the crooked guards and cops in no time. The Clyde Barrow Museum might be up sooner than I had hoped. Blinking words catch my eye.

~ REMINDER ~ REMINDER ~ REMINDER ~

Join us tomorrow

SUNDAY, MAY 22nd

THE CHICAGOLAND GHOST BUS TOUR

is the perfect opportunity to meet

other half-deads from

around the globe.

THIS IS THE FINAL EVENT OF OUR

3rd ANNUAL HALF-DEAD REUNION.

Don't miss out!

MEET AT The Hard Rock Café

63 W. Ontario @ 2 p.m. SHARP!

Before I can read any farther, Jack Daniel pushes the screen away—prolly so I can't read it. The fool has some sense after all. Not as much as me though. If I play my cards right, then in two days' time when the deadline hits, I'll be in charge of our brand spankin' new life, ready to rid the world of crooked laws or anything else I please—like bringing Twinkle flowers and telling her that I'm sweet on her.

Then she'll be all mine.

CHAPTER 15

Saturday, May 21st // 8:37 P.M.

Monroe

A heavy throb starts up on my right eyebrow above the bridge of my nose. I lie back on my pillow, pushing hard into the pain with two fingertips. After apologizing to an angry Dr. Hanson for "pretending" to be hypnotized, I left his office more freaked out about having Bonnie in my body than when I went in. If that's even possible. Not only did Dr. Hanson tell me that he didn't appreciate me wasting his time like that, he's going to tell my dad, I just know it.

Yeah. You almost balled that up back there.

Me? If it weren't for you blabbing about your first robbery, I wouldn't be in this trouble.

I already tole you I don't remember none of it, so stop your woolgathering and move on.

Whatever. Any lecture Dad gives me can't compare to knowing what would have happened if I told Dr. Hanson the truth—a minimum three-day stay under twenty-four-hour surveillance at a residential treatment center. I check my phone and find texts from both Anjali and Josie with a ton of pics from the prom and the Senior Picnic. Anjali wrote "Miss u, Roe!!" and Josie texted, "Isn't the same without u here, Moo-Moo!"

I text them back, telling them I miss them too. Wish they could help me figure out what to do, but as far as I know, neither of them has been inhabited by a dead outlaw either. If I don't figure this out soon though, they'll be best friends with one. For what seems like the ten-thousandth time, I rehash all that's happened, hoping to stumble upon some answers.

The number one thing that bothers me most is Milo's statement when he was in the trance. He had said an opportunity existed for

Jack and I at the moment of death, but he didn't say *whose* death or *what* opportunity. I'd like to assume he didn't mean our deaths, but I'm not naive enough to believe that's not an option. When we go on the ghost bus tour tomorrow with the Half-Dead Society, I'm going to ask around about that. And finally, I want to figure out what Clyde's weakness is so that Jack can switch right back if Clyde ever takes him over again.

Give up, you bug-eyed Betty. Clyde ain't afraid of no one and no thing.

I squeeze my pillow as hard as I can. Is there a way to turn her off? Unless . . .

Who said he's afraid of something? I taunt. Maybe there's something he just can't resist.

Sure there is—me!

Bonnie lets out a hideous laugh, giving me a second to tuck that information away. Bonnie's weakness is definitely Clyde, no doubt about that, but is Clyde's weakness Bonnie? Or did she mean sex was his weakness? I roll my eyes. Isn't sex every guy's weakness?

It sure is. I still can't believe that my Chestnut is inside your fellow.

He's not my fellow. He's just a random guy who is as unlucky as I am.

I groan then, recalling her squeals of excitement after she found out Clyde was inside Jack back at the coffee shop.

Clyde is here? she had said, letting out her hyena laugh. *Thank you, Lord! Now hurry up and find a way to reunite us so we can leave you two pills to fend for yourselves.*

Then five minutes later . . . *Touch him! Maybe I can link with Clyde and get out of here!*

And two minutes after that . . . *What are you waiting for?*

And on and on and on until I finally told her that her constant interruptions were hurting, not helping, our mutual goal. That as soon as we could positively reunite them without harming ourselves, we'd do it. She let out a loud *harumph!* but stayed quiet. She obviously has figured out that using the choking strategy won't work anymore, because if I die, she dies. She's like a soul-sucking tapeworm who needs her human host to live. The thought sickens me.

When I mentioned to Jack that Bonnie thought that if I touched him, she could link to Clyde, he got all nervous and backed his chair away from mine—as if I was going to try it right then. He obviously thinks so highly of me. I said that, even though it was scary, maybe we should test it somehow. Maybe she actually could connect with Clyde and then they'd leave our bodies—isn't that what we wanted? To my surprise, Jack got totally pissed, bitching at me for five minutes straight about how much worse it was for him than for me. That I didn't realize how horrible it was to be inside your own head and not be able to control your own body and that he didn't want me touching him again until we knew for sure what would happen. Before I could say, *Hey, calm down, we're on the same team*, he crumpled up his cup and headed for the john.

When he finally came back, I told him he needed to start trusting me. And that if we worked together "everything would turn out all right in the end," just like the saying goes. He didn't necessarily buy it, but at least he wasn't still mad at me. We decided to go home and spend the rest of the night researching Bonnie and Clyde, hoping to uncover some clues. Tomorrow we'd meet at 1:45 P.M. at the Walgreens across the street from the Hard Rock. It felt good that we were doing something concrete instead of only talking about things.

I decide to private-message Milo on Facebook to see if anything new came up. When he doesn't answer, I spend the next three hours scanning a million websites about Bonnie and Clyde. I know where they lived (West Dallas, Texas), how many brothers and sisters they each had (Bonnie; one brother, one sister. Clyde; three brothers, three sisters), first arrests (Bonnie; age 22—burglary. Clyde; age 16—failing to return a rental car on time), and hobbies (Bonnie; fashion. Clyde; guns and cars).

When I hear the front door slam, announcing Dad's arrival home from work, I shut off my light and hop under the covers. There's no way I want to have a confrontation right now about the missing slugs or my awkward visit with Dr. Hanson. I lie still, faking sleep in case he pops his head in my room. I hear his footsteps stop outside my door, but after a few seconds, he heads down the hall to the bathroom. Ten minutes later, I tiptoe across the room to plug in my phone to recharge, not daring to turn on the lights.

The next morning, I still have two hours until I have to meet Jack. After a shower, I decide on a red flared skirt and a white lace top, along with my silver cross necklace for good luck. Trying to be super quiet so as not to wake my dad, I eat a granola bar that's been on my dresser for weeks instead of messing around in the kitchen. After I print out all of Bonnie's poems, I glance at the time and freak out when I see it's already 1:25. How could I have been so careless? I rush around, shoving everything I need into my purse when there's a knock on my bedroom door.

Not now! "Yeah?" I ask, holding my breath.

"Can we talk?" It's Dad.

Does he know the truth? Did he talk to the Brownstone Brothers? I do a quick scan of my room to make sure there's nothing incriminating lying around. "I'm kind of in a hurry. I'm meeting some friends at Hard Rock for lunch in fifteen minutes. Can we talk later?" I bite my lip, hoping he goes for it. He doesn't.

"This will only take a second."

I open the door to him standing there in his blue terrycloth bathrobe, a steaming cup of coffee in his hand. He leans against the doorjamb. "I received a rather disturbing e-mail from Dr. Hanson yesterday. Says you acted deranged during hypnosis and then laughed about it."

"He said I acted deranged? Wow. Real nice, Dr. Hanson." I roll my eyes. "And I didn't laugh about it. At least not the way you think. More out of awkwardness than ha-ha." I head over to my bed and straighten the covers to have something to do other than look him in the eye.

"What happened exactly?" Dad steps into my room and rests his arm on top of my dresser. I pray that he doesn't look down into the garbage can. The plastic document frame that I stomped into pieces is inside.

"The hypnosis wasn't working, so I started saying stuff that I thought he wanted to hear, that's all." I scurry around my room, gathering everything I need. Phone, notes, slugs, poem, printed voucher for the bus tour. I need to leave now or I'll be late.

"You thought he'd want to hear that you robbed a pharmacy in Texas?" he asks, his tone laden with sarcasm.

"Oh, *that*." Warmth races up my face like a Ferrari. If I was ever going to come clean, now would be the time. Of course I don't actually have time to spare, not now. Should I, shouldn't I?

He raises his voice. "What do you mean, 'oh that?' I'm paying good money for you to see him, hoping he could help you to sort things out before college, and that's all you have to say? He thinks medication might help, and suggests continued psychiatric treatment in New York."

Okay, so definitely *not* sharing now. I whip around and face him. "Dad, no! I'm sorry I wasn't taking hypnosis seriously, but that doesn't mean I need medication! And definitely *not* continued therapy treatments at NYU. Dr. Hanson is exaggerating to make me look bad." I sling my vintage black fringe purse over my head and arm so it lies diagonally across my body. I grab handfuls of tissue from my nightstand.

Dad narrows his eyes, keeping his lips tight. "Why would he do that?"

I fake-blow my nose and casually deposit the unused tissues into my garbage can, partially covering the plastic shards inside. That'll have to do. "Doctors like to make situations sound worse than they are so you have to keep going to them. If I earned two hundred bucks an hour, I'd make up shit about people too."

"One-fifty an hour and watch your language."

"Sorry, but seriously, I'm fine." I give him my most reassuring smile. "Now please, can I go? I don't want to be late."

"What time will you be home?"

I scoot past him. "Um, not sure," I say, hoping to sound casual. "We're having lunch but afterward, we might head to Michigan Avenue or catch a Cubs game. I'll text you later, okay?"

"Don't forget." He sips his coffee. "Stay out of trouble today. *Please?*"

Hearing the pleading tone in his voice makes a boulder form in my throat. "I will!" I race down the hall before he remembers to ask about the missing slugs. If only he knew how much trouble I was already in, he'd be choking on that coffee. *I'm so sorry, Dad,* I say in my head. *I'd explain more, but I don't want you to worry any more than you already are.*

After catching Every. Single. Light, the cabbie finally drops me off in front of the Walgreens across the street from the Hard Rock. Jack's already there, standing just outside the entrance, wearing jeans and a black golf shirt. He looks at his watch and scans the street, his jaw tight like he's angry. I glance at the time on the digital marquee. 1:58! I start running. Stupid cab driver drove like it was his first day in Chicago. Probably was, knowing the typical cabbie.

The second Jack sees me, he starts jogging away from me and toward the tour bus. He waves his arm and shouts, neck tendons raised and taut, "Come on! Let's go!"

I run faster, catching up with him. "Sorry I'm late," I blurt out, slightly out of breath.

"It's almost 2:00," he snaps, glancing at me. "We'd better not miss it."

"We won't. It's right there." I point to a small school bus painted black with the words "Chicagoland Ghost Bus" painted in white along the sides. It waits at the curb kitty-corner from us. "I'm really sorry, but my dad sidetracked me at the last second. I had no choice."

"Whatever. Just hurry!" he says, both of us out of breath from running.

"I am. It'll be fine." I hope my confidence helps Jack stay calm. The last thing I need is to be face-to-face with Clyde Barrow himself. As soon as the green arrow lets the cars make their turn onto Ontario, we sprint across the street. Only one more street to cross and we'll be all set.

Jack jogs next to me. "And don't forget that Mr. Johnson knows my family. Don't slip and say anything weird. If anyone asks, we came on this tour because it's your sister and her husband that are inhabited by Bonnie and Clyde, not us."

"I know. Ginger and Greg." I want to remind him that I'm the one who came up with the alibi, but decide not to bring it up. He's mad enough at me already. A taxi turning right on red blares his horn at a messenger in a neon green vest riding fast through the intersection, making us wait. As soon as the road clears, we race across, only twenty yards to go. But before we can get there, the bus revs its engine and starts pulling away from the curb.

"Hey, wait!" Jack takes off running, waving his arms. "Stop! Stop the bus!" he screams.

An avalanche of dread blankets my body as I continue full-speed ahead, my lungs on fire. If we miss this bus, I'll have ruined everything. Jack pounds on the side as he runs alongside it, shouting. *Please, please stop*, I beg.

A moment later, the bus screeches to a halt with a loud *hiss* of air. The doors open and surprisingly, Jack waits for me on the bottom step to let me go ahead. As soon as I get on board, I hold my chest, gasping for air. I smile at the bus driver. "Thanks for waiting!"

The chubby black bus driver tips his gray, flat-topped hat. "No problem, miss."

The bus has eight or ten rows of seats, all upholstered in the same blue-gray fabric. A middle-aged guy in the first row, dressed in a black t-shirt with the Ghost Bus logo on the breast pocket, leaps to his feet.

"Looks like we have two more passengers. Welcome aboard!" He does a double-take. "Hey there, Jack! I wondered if you were still coming. Thought maybe you changed your mind." He holds out his hand and Jack shakes it. Mr. Johnson turns to the group and says, "This is my son's best friend, Jack, who I've been trying to get to come on this thing with me for years. Everything changes when there's a pretty girl around, I guess."

A guy in a Bob Marley shirt whistles, making the others laugh. I smile awkwardly, uncomfortable having to pretend that Jack and I are on a date. I glance at the twenty or so faces and, despite the wildly varying ages, genders, and ethnicities, I'm both surprised and relieved that they all look normal. Not sure what I expected a group of half-deads to look like, but certainly not like regular people, I guess.

Mr. Johnson pats Jack on the back. "You missed all the introductions, so why don't you tell everyone who you and your friend are real quick and we'll get on our way."

Jack nods. "Hey y'all! I'm Jack Daniel and this here's Twinkle!" he shouts way louder than necessary, his words dripping with a thick Southern drawl. He holds both hands up in fists.

I stare at him, wondering what the hell he's doing. After we just decided to lay low.

Oh my Lord, that sounds like Clyde!

No, it's not. Jack's just being stupid.

I swallow hard. A horrible sense of dread creeps into my gut. God, I hope that's what he's doing, but part of me wonders if—no. No way. Not that quickly.

An old guy sitting in the fourth row calls out, "Is either of you half-dead, yah?" His accent is thick and guttural, like Alfons Shoenhofer's, the old German guy who has manned our stuffy little coat room at the restaurant for as long as I can remember.

Jack grins. "No, sir. I never do nothing halfway. It's all or none for me and this pretty little woman." He puts his hand on my shoulder.

Before I know what's happening, Bonnie's words spew from my lips, "Yep, I'm his gal."

Everyone laughs, but my stomach churns like whitewater. Bonnie can suddenly control my mouth even when I'm not touching an object that belonged to her? Is she getting stronger? I start heading toward the back of the bus, too stunned to look anywhere but the floor.

How did you do that? I demand.

I can do whatever I want, whenever I want.

I don't believe her. Something's changed. Bonnie's way too chatty to have stayed quiet all this time if she could have been talking. Is it because Jack touched me? When she doesn't challenge that thought, I know I'm right. Anxiety creeps into my neck and runs up my face. What if she takes me over completely? Since I haven't told anyone about this, can I ever be rescued?

Mr. Johnson chuckles. "Looks like Jack and his date are up for some role-playing today. Hit it, Lionel."

The bus cruises slowly forward as Jack and I stumble down the aisle, making our way toward the only available seats, the last row. I slide into the seat next to the window, and Jack sits next to me. "Why'd you talk like that?" I half-whisper, half-hiss. "I thought you didn't want to make Mr. Johnson suspicious."

Jack shrugs, looks away.

Mr. Johnson says, "Well, let's try this again. Welcome one and all to the Chicagoland Ghost Bus Tour. I'm going to take you to places where the dead come alive." He pushes a button on the wallboard and the theme from *The Twilight Zone* plays. "But based on the fact that you're all a part of the Half-Dead Society, I guess the dead come alive every day at your place." There are a few chuckles, but not many.

"I guess that's what they call 'dead' silence." He lets out a loud snort, but again, only a couple tour-goers laugh.

I lean toward Jack. "Whoa. Tough crowd."

"Not as tough as you, little woman," Jack says, grinning.

My heart drops. "What's wrong with you? Why are you still using that fake accent?"

"Nothing fake about me. I'm one hundred percent man, not like Jack Daniel, who is five percent man and ninety-five percent Grade-A chicken." He elbows me and winks.

Bonnie screams in my head, *Sweet Jesus! It IS Clyde!*

No, it's not. It's Jack, thinking he's being funny.

But Jack's words, along with Bonnie's thoughts, make my stomach contents churn. I picture us sprinting, screaming for the bus to stop. Jack did tell me that Clyde took him over when something scared him. But could running to catch the bus have triggered that much fear? I turn slowly and stare at the guy next to me.

"What's the matter with you? You look like you seen a ghost." Jack tilts his head back and lets out a belly laugh. "Ha! That's a good one, ain't it?"

"Ohmigod. Are you . . . ?" I can't bring myself to speak his name out loud.

Jack winks at me. "You know who I am, but like all good molls, you know we go by aliases when we're out in public. So you can call me baby or sweetheart, or heck, Paul Bunyan if you like." He shrugs.

Paul Bunyan? How lame. Now I know it's Jack. "You're not funny. Stop kidding around *right now*. I mean it."

"I ain't the kidding type, Twinkle. I say what I mean, and I mean what I say." Jack leans in close, his tone soft. "I been watching you all the while I been inside Jack Daniel and I like what I seen. You are one hotsy-totsy dame—curvaceous and pretty as all get out. Smart as a whip too, the way you was writing down a plan. I couldn't wait to get rid of Jackrabbit so I could have you all to myself. He don't deserve a firecracker like you, but I'd sure like a chance to court you myself, to give you all the good things you deserve. What do you say, doll? Want to see what it's like to be with a real man?"

My mouth dries up and I feel sick. My heart beats so fast, I'm sure that any second now, it's going to burst from my chest. Every cell in my body tells me that the guy talking to me isn't Jack Hale anymore. Mr. Johnson begins speaking about the scary legend surrounding our first stop, but I'm way more freaked out by the guy sitting next to me than some old ghost stories.

He puts his hand on top of mine, his forehead wrinkled in concern. "What's wrong? Why you so quiet all of a sudden? You're not afraid of me, are you, kitten?"

I'm about to push his hand off of me when Bonnie blurts out, "Afraid of you? Of course not, sugar. I can't wait to cozy up to you."

Jack, or should I say Clyde, grins. "That's more like it. We'll take things slow and easy. I want to know everything about you." He reaches up and tucks a hair behind my ear.

I try desperately to clamp my lips together, but just like in Dr. Hanson's office, I'm suddenly not in control of my mouth. "Kiss me, baby," Bonnie says breathily.

What the hell are you doing, Bonnie?

I miss him so much!!

But I don't want to kiss him!

You won't be, I will. Relax.

"My, my. You are more of a bearcat than I knew." Clyde smiles so broadly, it lights up Jack's entire face.

I stare, frozen inside my own skin. I don't know whether to shake my head, spit on him, or let him kiss me. Based on historical information alone, Clyde Barrow does not seem like the kind of guy you should piss off.

"No wonder Jack's been holding back. You're way too much for him to handle. But not too much for me." He winks. "I been staring at this here heart for days and it's been driving me wild. I know it ain't proper for a man to kiss a woman till he gets to know her better, but maybe just a little one won't hurt nobody none. Especially since you asked."

I sit statuesque, my eyes shut tight, waiting for him to force his mouth on mine. But instead, he gently traces my birthmark with his fingertip. "You're so pretty. Did Jack ever tell you that?" The next thing I know, I feel his warm breath on my neck as his lips flit softly across my skin, sending a pleasurable zing racing through me. I swallow. He'd better not do that again.

"Sweet as the summer rain," he whispers, kissing me again, releasing another jolt of electricity. I had no idea that spot was so sensitive. I'm about to push him away when his lips skim the part of my neck that meets my shoulder. Bonnie moans in response. At least I hope it was her and not me. I might be dying to have a guy say sweet things to me, but not *this* guy. Certainly not an infamous criminal. A dead one at that. The bus hits a bump and we're both jostled, allowing me a small window of opportunity to push him away.

"That's enough," I say.

Clyde squints at me, looking hurt. "What's the matter, doll? Did I do something wrong? You want me to kiss you on the lips instead? Because I can if you want. Just didn't want to rush things is all. I didn't want to be improper." He strokes my hand softly, waiting for my answer.

That's when I notice that Jack's petroleum brown eyes have been replaced by lighter, hazelnut-colored ones with tiny golden flecks. How could I have been so blind? Everything about Clyde is different from Jack—his carefree smile, the way he sits with his legs apart and his shoulders relaxed, even his smooth pick-up lines. He's . . . he's slick and confident, whereas Jack is anything but.

Told you he was something. Now you see why I want him back.

That's when I know for sure that physical contact with Clyde is what allows Bonnie to control my voice. Clyde once belonged to her, the same way the poem did. How could I be so stupid? I'm about to pull my hand out from under his, when Bonnie says, "I want to kiss you, but this trollop won't let me. As soon as you find a way to ditch her—"

What the hell? Ditch me? I yank my hand out of his grasp and pretend to scratch my forehead. "Hello, hello?" I whisper, testing out my theory. I'm relieved when my own words leave my lips.

Touch him again! I was about to tell him that we can be together!

Right. You called me a tramp and told him to ditch me.

I warned you not to mess with me and Clyde.

My airway closes and I can't take another breath. Hot bile rises up my esophagus as I fight to get air. This time though, I'm not giving in.

Clyde looks at me, his forehead wrinkled in confusion. "What was you just saying? Something about a trollop?" He eyes me suspiciously.

I hold up one finger as if asking him to wait, sending Bonnie a message: If you kill me, you die, too. Then you can kiss Clyde goodbye. Oh wait. I meant, *I'll* kiss him goodbye, I add rebelliously.

Don't even think of kissing him!

Then let me breathe.

After two more seconds of cement-filled lungs, she finally relents.

Fine! But this ain't the end. I'll find a way to tell him I'm here. Just you wait and see.

"Our first stop is the *Eastland* disaster," Mr. Johnson says as we pull up along the Chicago River. "The event took place on July 24th, 1915."

I breathe in huge lungfuls of air. "I said that trollop over there gave me a dirty look, that's all." I point toward a woman in her thirties two seats ahead of us.

The old man from the seat in front of us clucks his tongue and turns partway around. "Can you two quiet down? I can't hear a thing!"

Clyde leans forward, his hand on my thigh. "What did you say, you old weasel?"

A mixture of anger and surprise crosses the old guy's face. Before I can stop her, Bonnie mouths off, too. "They say curiosity killed the cat, but they're wrong. Tell them, honey. It was you that kilt that cat, isn't that right?" I yank my leg out from under his hand before Bonnie can say anything else.

"You got that right," Clyde says, rubbing his chin. "And I ain't afraid to kill more, too."

A disheveled guy in a Bob Marley t-shirt across the aisle from us makes a face. "I'm sorry but do you think you or your other half could talk a little quieter by any chance?" He blinks and shivers, causing his whole demeanor to change. He puffs out his chest and curls his lip, a gravelly voice erupting from his mouth. "Yeah. Pipe down, you stinking maggots." He blinks and shivers again, and we're back to the stoner, who stares at the ceiling and says, "Cut that out, Tony, or you'll get us in another fight!" He looks back at us and mumbles, "Sorry about that. My other half is a bitter old man. Total asshole."

He turns away, continuing to argue with his other half.

Disgust rolls through me. I *cannot* live like this for the rest of my life. How many half-dead people are there in the world? I never even heard of them until yesterday, but now here's an entire bus filled with them. I wish I knew if any of them would be willing to help us, or if that's even possible.

Mr. Johnson continues, "The *Eastland* tipped from an unstable ballast, toppling hundreds into the water and trapping even more inside. Eight hundred and forty-four people died that day before the voyage began."

"I have an idea," Clyde says quietly. "How about you and I take a voyage all our own? One without talking." He holds a finger to his lips as he inches toward me, his eyes closed.

I don't want to make him angry, but I don't want to lead him on either. "Maybe later. People nowadays don't like PDA."

He opens his eyes. "PDA? That some kind of code word for the police?" He slouches lower in his seat before peeking out the back window of the bus.

That's when I remember that Jack thought that either strong smells or fear sent Clyde packing. Looking at him sweat it out after hearing the word "police," I take a stab at it. "Yeah. PDA is short for Police Department Agents. They come on tour buses these days searching for criminals. Look! I think that guy is one!" I point to the front of the bus, praying that fear of getting caught will jumpstart Jack back into place.

"Where?" Clyde ducks down, only his eyes peeking above the seat.

"Up there. In the blue shirt. I saw a gun on his belt." I wait, holding my breath.

Clyde squints. "That ain't no gun. It's one of them communicatin' devices like you have." He sits up straighter, grinning. "False alarm."

"Oh." Strike one. Fear must not be it. I paw through my purse, finding my perfume. I casually tilt my head to the side and squirt a hefty amount of Chanel No. 5. onto my neck. "Mmm. Doesn't that smell nice?"

Clyde pinches his fingers over his nostrils. "Don't much care for it."

Hope starts to build in my chest. He's definitely avoiding my perfume.

Mr. Johnson clears his throat. "A few notes before you head off the bus. Ghost experts agree that the spirits of the dead roam the place they were killed until justice is served. The city of Chicago probably hoped they'd be forgiven by erecting this bronze plaque in the deceased's honor, but folks who live near the river still report frequent wailings in the night."

I squirt a puff of perfume into the air when Clyde snatches it from my hand and whips it to the floor. The silver tip breaks off and flies under someone's seat. "I said I don't like it, woman!"

I cross my hands in front of my face as protection, my heart pounding through my shirt.

Clyde's tone immediately softens. "Come on now. Put your hands down, Twinkle. I ain't never hit a woman in all my life and I ain't gonna start now. I just got me a quick temper is all."

Nearly everyone on the bus turns to look at us. "Is there a problem?" Mr. Johnson asks.

"No, everything's fine," Clyde calls out. "I dropped something and it broke."

Mr. Johnson nods. "Okay then. So as I was saying, screams and panicked pleas—kind of like what you just heard in the last row back there—are often heard when the moon is full. But check out the area and judge for yourselves if the ghosts of the *Eastland* disaster are still around."

Glancing at Clyde, I see him staring at me like he's got bullets in his eyes with my name on them. It can't be good to make a killer mad. I tap my foot, ready to spring out of this seat and away from Clyde the moment our row vacates. I've got to find a way to ask some other half-deads for advice without Clyde overhearing me. As the seconds tick by, my mind reels about what to do next. Should I tell Clyde that Bonnie's inside of me and wants to hook up with him in the afterlife? Yell for Jack to come back to the surface and see if that works? Run away, go to the police, call my dad?

The last one makes me wonder what I'd tell my father if I did call him. That Jack and I are possessed by Bonnie and Clyde—come get me? What good would he do? He's no exorcist. No matter how protective he is, running home to Daddy isn't going to solve this problem. As the passengers shuffle their way toward the door, a debilitating thought hits me. One that feels like a kickboxing sidekick to the gut. If Clyde realizes I'm not into him, will he decide to run off and commit another crime in Jack's body instead of trying to kiss me?

Oh God. There's only one way I know to make sure Clyde sticks around.

I've got to make him believe I'm falling for him.

CHAPTER 16

Sunday, May 22nd // 2:40 P.M.

Clyde

I look at Twinkle, standing there in the aisle waiting for me, but something don't seem right. At first, she seemed to like it when I turned on my charm, getting all cozy with me and surprising me to no end when she asked me to kiss her. But just as quick as it started, she turned all cold. And if my reckoning is on track, it almost seemed like she wanted me to get a whiff of her perfume, the way she sprayed it all around. Could Jack Daniel have figured out my suspicions and then tole Twinkle about it when they was at the coffee shop? I need to test her, to see what she knows.

"Forget the tour, Twinkle. Let's stay here and talk." I reach over and grab her by the waist, hoping to pull her back down into the seat.

"Clyde!" she yelps and hops up the aisle, fast, like she stepped on a hot coal.

"Come on, now. Don't you want to get to know me better?" I try again when she elbows me hard. Makes me hit my arm against a sharp edge of the seat in front of me. I check out the underside of my forearm and see a bloody scratch. "Dagummit! Look what you done to me."

"Oh my gosh! I'm sorry!" She sucks in her bottom lip, fretting over how she hurt me.

I smile, thinking it's mighty sweet that she's got such slick moves. Bonnie always waited for me to do the dirty work, to put up a fight. It's kinda nice to see a strong woman that can defend herself.

She says, "It's just that I have this um, this phobia about being touched."

That don't sound good. "Phobia? That some kind of disease?"

She shakes her head back and forth fast, like a wet dog drying off. "No! It means you have an intense fear about something. Like some people have with spiders, or being in the dark?"

I nod, grinning. "I got one of them myself—'bout being in prison."

"See? You know how it is then. You hate something so much that you can't stand to think about it." She smiles. "So as long as you don't touch me anymore, we'll be fine."

There's no way I'm agreeing to that. "How can I kiss you if I can't touch you, Twinkle?"

Her eyes widen, like she's giving it some thought. A second later, she tilts her head toward the exit. "How about we go outside?" she asks, avoiding my question. "I want to see where the *Eastland* disaster happened. Come on!"

I let it go—for now. Looks like this little lady wants me to work to win her affection, but I love a challenge. I get up off the seat and follow her. "How'd you get that phobia, Twinkle? Did some fella hurt you? Because you tell me who it is, and I'll make sure he don't hurt you ever again."

She shakes her head. "No, it's nothing like that. It's just . . . a quirk. I'm sure I'll get over it one day." She shrugs, tossing me a forlorn smile over her shoulder as she walks down the bus steps.

Poor thing. Prolly just needs the right man to help her overcome this. I know just the man. When I get outside, she's waiting for me. I like that. "You know, I can help you conquer your fear of being touched, Twinkle."

"My name's Monroe," she says, smiling.

I bring my finger to my lips as we step onto the boardwalk. "Code names, remember? Besides, Twinkle fits you better. That diamond in your lip twinkles in the light every time you turn that pretty head of yours." Sure enough, she looks at me to answer and a tiny spark of sunshine reflects off her little jewel. "See! Just like that!"

She smiles shyly, like she's not used to getting compliments. "Okay . . . Sly."

"That's a good one." I'm about to reach out and hold her hand—but I stop. I don't want to risk getting her ire up. Could ruin all my plans. "Hell hath no fury like a woman scorned," my daddy used to say. I seen it for myself a hundred times, with Bonnie mostly. I catch myself and quickly get her out of my mind. Not thinking about my old moll might be harder than I thought.

We belly up alongside the guardrail with all the other folks milling about. I look down into the murky green waters of the river and can barely believe my good fortune. I ain't in Jack's body one hour and Twinkle's already taken a liking to me—even if she ain't ready to show it just yet. I close my eyes and let the sun warm my face. *Thank you, Lord Jesus, for my second chance.*

A nagging thought about my mission flies into my head before I can stop it. What if ridding the world of crooked laws has me ending my second chance the same way as my first? While I ain't afraid of dying, I can't say I liked it much neither. I'd ax off another toe before admitting that out loud. Never let your enemies know your weakness. Such an important rule is prolly in the Good Book. If it ain't, it should be.

Luckily, there's plenty of time for me to decide what I want to do—unless the coppers figure out it was me who clubbed that hussy. Course, if she didn't scream none of this would have happened, so she's got no one to blame 'cept herself. Still, if they come after me, I'm taking off—with Twinkle or without.

As I stroll along the concourse, cars of every color zip past us and men in suits march by, their heads down to push against the strong breeze. I look across the way and see flags atop the bridge tower rippling like mad. Giant buildings line the river, making my head spin when I look up at them. The wind blows, sending a strong scent of dead fish up my nose. I pinch my nostrils tight, hoping I didn't get enough in me to let Jack back in. I wait a few seconds, but luckily, no flashing lights shine in my head. I take a deep breath with my mouth, holding my nose closed as I look around.

How the heck am I going to rid the world of all the evil cops if I have to hold my nose shut whenever there's a strong smell nearby? I ponder that a second. My mama liked to say that if you wanted flowers, you needed to accept the rain along with the sunshine. If not smelling things is God's idea of giving me rain, I ain't gonna complain.

"I'm going to read that bronze plaque real quick, okay?" Twinkle says, looking at me funny, like I came from outer space. "You feel all right?"

I like how she checked with me first. "I'm just holding back a sneeze," I tell her. "But yeah, you can go on without me."

"You want some Kleenex?" She digs in her handbag and hands me a tissue. Right as I'm about to grab them, she pulls them away. "Wait. Don't touch me when you take them, okay?" She watches me, biting her lip, nervous as a fly caught in a web.

I do as she asks—without letting on that I'm skeptical, but I aim to test it soon as I can. Just not now, when she's out here in the open. My gut tells me we need to stick together. Since my instincts saved my sorry butt many a time, I ain't gonna question it now. I rip the tissue in half, ball up each piece, and shove one wad up each nostril. There. Problem solved.

As she strolls over to the sign, I realize Twinkle looks as good going as she does coming.

A young woman, about as curvy as a telephone pole, passes Twinkle and heads my way. Her skirt's so short it'd make a two-bit whore blush. Right then, a breeze blows it up, showing off her keister. She pushes it down and looks my way, like she was worried I saw.

I saw all right. "Nice drawers," I tell her with a smile.

"Screw you," she says, hustling past me.

"Name your time."

She holds up her middle finger and hurries off toward the stop-and-go light.

I'm half-tempted to follow after her and let her know that she'd better be careful who she points that vulgar gesture at. No one cusses out Clyde Champion Barrow and gets away with it. Especially not a streetwalker.

The tour man sets down a little wooden box right in front of me, stepping up on it to make himself taller. "Okay, people. Listen up if you want to hear about ghosts and how to make them happy. Of course, given your circumstances, I expect most of you are even more knowledgeable about ghosts than I am." He chuckles. "I'll tell you what I know, and you can straighten me out on the parts I get wrong."

A bunch of folks move in closer. I need all the information I can get, so I aim to listen.

"Hauntings in and around large bodies of water are quite common. That's because proper burials and last wishes of the deceased aren't carried out when victims drown, so their souls can't rest in peace. A discordant soul wanders the earth waiting for his wishes to be resolved, or until the good Lord decides his time is up."

I pray the good Lord don't think bad of me, but I'd sure like for his watch to break when he's eyeing my time on Earth.

The tour man pauses a second, raising his finger in the air. "So, if you don't want your deceased loved one drifting around aimlessly, I advise you to find out their last wishes and carry them out, or they may end up wandering around on Earth for a *looong* time."

An older woman in the back calls out, "Does anyone know how it works for us? I have no idea how to find out what my other half wants and she won't tell me." She stops talking and looks up in the air. "No, *you* be quiet," she says aloud, looking at no one. She waits, listens. "Yeah, well I'm sick of you too. So tell me what you want, so I can do it and you can leave."

The way the lady looks like she's talking to someone who ain't there makes me wonder if Jack can hear things I'm thinking. Just in case, I send him a message: *The only thing I want is to live forever.*

Since I can't have that, I'd be much obliged if you just stayed locked up in my head until the Lord decides He wants me back.

I chuckle out loud at the thought of living to a ripe old age. A codger with a great big belly turns and stares at me, like he's got a bone to pick.

"You got a problem?" I ask him.

"Nope." He scurries toward a seagull preening itself in the sun on the handrail. I look for Twinkle and see her chatting with a bald feller. I'm about to holler and tell her to get back over by me but something stops me. I watch to see if she's a dame I can trust. I position myself behind some people taking pictures of the water where the boat sank, so that Twinkle can't see me observing her.

I slide my thumbnail between two of my bottom teeth, waiting and seeing. The bald feller reaches into his back pocket and hands her a folded-up glossy pamphlet—like the kind they give out at the picture show with the names of all the actors. I wonder if he's asking her out to the movies, but just as quick, I know I'm worrying about nothing.

Twinkle wouldn't go for a dud like him, not when she's got a better-looking, whole lot tougher man around. Why, he's twice her age and has as much hair on top of his head as a hog's behind. I squint at the design on the front of his shirt, trying to figure out what it is. That's when I realize it's that ugly creature doing jumping jacks that Twinkle and Jackrabbit was looking at in the coffee shop. I'm about to make my way over there to find out what they's up to when she up and leaves him, heading my way. She breaks into a big smile when she sees me. Makes me feel like I won first place at the county fair.

"Five minutes, people," the tour man announces. "Then we need to load up."

I smile at Twinkle as she comes toward me, when someone bumps me from behind. I whip around. "Hey, watch where—" But before I can give him a what-for, it turns out it's a crippled gent about my age, his arms and legs herking and jerking with every step. Seems like the poor guy don't got a single limb that's straight.

"Sor-r-ry," he says, unable to keep his arms at his sides.

"Yup, me too," I tell him, sending him off with a wink. Seeing him hobble away like that makes me think about Bonnie and how her leg got all burnt and twisted up after that car accident. My heart gets a searing pain in the center, wishing I could have them five minutes back when the car went out of control. Before I can turn to talk to Twinkle and ask to see the propaganda sheet the man gave her, powerful lights flash through my brain like God himself was paying me a visit.

I fight to stick around, but Jack Daniel beats me at my own game. Next thing I know, I'm a bystander inside his sad little head! I knew I had to keep Bonnie outta my brain and I didn't do it. I got what I deserved for acting like a schoolboy instead of a man. And at the worst time too. I'd bet my left arm Twinkle would be getting over her phobia if I had just a little more time.

Why, Jack couldn't coax a dog to take a bone, much less convince a firecracker like Twinkle to go on a date with him. I felt her squirm when I kissed the heart tattoo on her neck, which got my own heart all fired up. Other parts of me, too. Her face pinches up like a raisin in the sun, so I have a hunch that Jack Daniel's babbling about how it was me wooing her, not him. As if she couldn't tell. All I can do now is sit back and wait for the boy to be scared again.

It shouldn't take long. Everyone can see Jack Daniel is a big ole fraidy cat.

CHAPTER 17

Sunday, May 22nd // 3:36 P.M.

Monroe

When I walk back to Clyde, he starts right in—pacing, arms flailing. "What's wrong with you? Are you kidding me right now? Are you trying to get me to leave or what?"

For a second, I'm confused. A minute ago, he was trying to kiss me, and now this?

Without even needing to check his eyes, I realize what's happened. It's clear by his tight jaw, his hands closed into fists, every inch of his body racked with *fury*, that Jack is back. I stare at him, my stomach in knots. "Calm down, Jack. What are you talking about?"

"Back on the bus, please!" Mr. Johnson stands by the door of the bus waving us toward him, his wooden stepstool in his free hand. "Time to go to our next location."

Jack pulls the Kleenex balls out of his nostrils and flicks them on the pavement. He sticks his face right up to mine, and starts bitching at me between clenched teeth. "You didn't even care that he took over, did you? I swear, it looked like you wanted him to kiss you! Like you were on a fricking date! What's going on, Monroe?"

My face flashes hot and my palms break out in a sweat. Jack's back ten seconds and he's already accusing me of being sketchy? Without even bothering to ask what I was doing?

"Maybe I did want him to kiss me. A date with him would be way better than one with you," I snap. "He's way nicer and doesn't yell at me, either." I turn and stomp up the bus stairs, hearing Jack right behind me.

"I hope you're fucking kidding," he says, loud enough for the Asian guy in the first row to look at his wife and shake his head.

Five steps later, I feel a pain in my throat.

You'd better not be trying to steal my man!

I don't like him! I was just mad at Jack.

Bonnie lets go a few seconds later. I resolve to watch what I say. Bonnie's got almost as short a temper as Clyde. No wonder they killed so many people.

Mr. Johnson lifts the microphone to his lips. "In a few minutes, we'll be driving past the famed spot of the Saint Valentine's Day Massacre, where seven men from Bugs Moran's gang were executed after Al Capone gave the order." I can't help but think how much Dad would love this tour. I need to come back with him sometime.

Ha! When I take over, I ain't sticking around with your Pa.

I breathe in sharply, the idea of being separated from my dad almost too much to bear. For both of us. First he loses my mom, then me? It would completely destroy him. That's when I realize what she's doing.

Stop threatening me, Bonnie. You already admitted you don't know if you can take me over completely, so stop pretending you do. I'm doing my best to reunite you guys, so lay off.

I might not know how to trade places yet, but I bet Clyde will figure it out and tell me.

He's not as smart as you think.

As I head down the aisle toward the back of the bus, a flickering image of Clyde's eyes whisks into my brain. He sure seemed like he had total confidence in his ability to stay alive, as if he knew something he wasn't telling. If he does know how to do a permanent switch, maybe I can charm it out of him.

He'll never fall for it. Or you, for that matter. Not once he finds out I'm around.

My heart skips a beat. If her relationship is as strong as they say—and why wouldn't it be?—of course he'll choose her. Even more reason I need to make sure Clyde doesn't find out she's inside of me. We pass the old guy that Clyde and I harassed earlier, but now he's moved to the second row. When he glances up, I grab onto the back of his seat so I don't fall from the motion of the bus. "Sorry about before. I don't know what got into me."

"Or who," he says, pursing his lips. "Half-deads got a mind of their own, so no offense taken."

I jump in to clarify. "Oh, no. I don't have a half-dead in me. We're just here—"

"—for some friends. I know. Started out saying the same thing myself." He nods, unsmiling, giving me such a knowing look, it's like he can read my mind.

As I walk down the narrow bus aisle to my seat, I realize that, for all I know, he can read my mind. We end up behind the two heavyset women, a gray-haired mother and thirty-something daughter, who I had overheard talking when I was outside. The daughter complained that the stress and awkwardness of going to gay bars to satisfy her other half, Lamar, was making her sick. The mother said they needed to talk to Bob because he might have some suggestions. My nosiness paid off. As soon as they were done talking to him, I ran over there. Hopefully the Half-Dead Society brochure he gave me will help.

I stand to the side to let Jack slide into the seat first. He doesn't even look at me as he passes by. Suits me fine. I perch on the very outside edge of the seat so as not to have accidental contact with him. At least Jack won't question my "phobia" the way Clyde did.

Clyde don't want to touch you anyway.

Good. I don't want to him to touch me, either.

Despite saying this, thoughts of his mouth on my neck, along with his sexy banter, send an unexpected reminder that ricochets from my brain down to my thighs. Stop it. He's an ex-con with a PhD in Player. I'd bet anything he has used the same lines on all the girls he charmed.

There wasn't no other girls, and there never will be, neither!

Damn her and her ability to hear my every thought. The bus takes a right turn and I fight to keep my weight from shifting into Jack. I look at him then, his arms crossed, not looking my way. What are we doing? How completely immature of us to ignore each other when we've got huge problems to fix and a ton of questions to answer. I take a deep breath. "Look, Jack. I'm sorry I said I wanted him to kiss me before, but you started accusing me before you even asked me what happened or why I did it."

He doesn't respond, but he nods imperceptibly.

I shift my butt so I can face him. Jack responds by inching up as close to the window as he can. He must remember how I said Bonnie thought she could make Clyde resurface if I touched him. I don't know if she can bring him out, but when Clyde was around, she sure was ready to resume their romance.

I fiddle with my ring. "I only acted nice to him because I didn't want Clyde—I mean, you—to bolt. I thought if I pretended to be interested in him, he'd—I mean, you'd—stick around." I let out a huge sigh. Trying not to offend Jack is making speaking and thinking to him very difficult.

"I guess." Jack shrugs one shoulder, which I take to mean he accepts my apology.

Even though I deserve one back, I keep quiet. "Okay, good." I smile, needing Jack to be in a better mood. "We will figure this out, you know. It's probably like one of those wooden labyrinth games. All the knobs and levels have to be exactly right to maneuver past the holes and get to the end. Soon as we figure the sequence out, we're free."

"At least I've got Clyde figured out now. But I can't tell you what I know because his girlfriend is listening." He looks at me.

For a brief horrifying moment, I think he's referring to me. I'm about to deny having any feelings whatsoever for Clyde when I realize with relief he means Bonnie.

Tell him he can trust me. She lets out a loud chortle.

I bite my lip. "I don't know, Jack. Don't you think it's important that I know the details in case he comes back? I need to be able to help you return."

149

"Don't worry. He's not coming back. I promise."

His words are not reassuring. Meanwhile, I'm saving Bonnie's presence inside of me as my ace in the hole. If Clyde ever does come back and it seems like he's about to skip out on me, I'll let him know his little gangster whore is inside of me. That ought to make him stick around.

Whores are girls who pretend to like someone, which is what you're doing, not me.

A few seconds later the bus squeals to a stop in front of a gated parking lot on Clark Street. Mr. Johnson says, "We can't exit because there's nowhere to park our bus, but if you look between those two buildings in front of us, you'll see a parking lot, which is where the garage once stood and where the murders took place." He pauses to let the tour goers peek through the windows. "Four of Capone's goons, some dressed as police, paid a visit to George 'Bugs' Moran and his gang. A few seconds later, seven men lay dead, and many say the ghosts of the slain gangsters still walk the streets. If you should ever find yourself in this part of Chicago late at night, be sure to hang on to your wallets."

All this talk about Al Capone makes me think of our display case at the restaurant. A huge rush of guilt floods in, hitting my chest like I slammed into a glass wall. Why did I touch those stupid slugs in the first place? If only I'd kept my hands to myself, I'd be home watching TV or shopping at Water Tower. Anywhere but here. No more reckless decisions, Monroe!

Jack's voice jerks me out of my reflection. "Is that the paper that bald guy gave you?" He points at the Half-Dead Society packet.

"Yeah." I release my death grip on it and flip it open. "His name is Bob."

Jack nods. "I saw you talking to him. What'd he say?" The bus hits a big pothole, making all the passengers shift forward and then back in unison.

"He told me that I should have my sister Ginger and her husband Greg contact him." The left side of the three-fold pamphlet shows the Half-Dead Society's two founding members and their bios. "Hey, this is him. The guy I was talking to." I point to the picture of the balding man.

> Bob O'Reilly, 53, father of two sons, divorced. *Fortune* 500 Chief Financial Officer. Was on vacation skiing in Aspen in Dec. 2007 when he suffered a severe head injury. While in a coma, he became inhabited by the ghost of Silke Hildebrent, a Swedish housewife who died on that slope in 1969. (AMICABLE)

> Deondra Johnson, 38, single, never married. Tarot card reader and fortune teller. Small business owner of *Psychic Enlightenment*. Infected in spring of 2008 during an epileptic seizure while conjuring the spirit of Lizzie Borden. If seen carrying an ax, DO NOT APPROACH.

"Is that a joke?" Jack points to the last sentence of Deondra's bio.

"I don't think so." I grimace at the thought of being approached by someone with an ax, and quickly change the subject. "Speaking about crimes, have you heard anything else about what Clyde did at the gas station?"

"No, thank God." He points to the right side of the pamphlet. "What's this section about?"

When I read the title, my adrenaline starts to flow. "Yes! This is exactly what we need!" I put the sheet between us so we can both read, and then dive in, ready to devour the words as quickly as possible, when Jack stops me.

"Better read it out loud to me," he says, sighing. "I don't want Asshole to know any more than he has to."

"Right." I whisper the entire page to Jack, not stopping until I'm finished.

CO-HABITATION THEORY

(Will remain in place until proven otherwise)

According to our medieval pastoral forefathers, when humans die, a guardian comes to escort them to one of two resting places: **heaven or limbo**. Souls going to heaven immediately begin eternal rest, but those in limbo, known heretofore as LIMBOTIC SOULS, do not.

1. Limbotic Souls remain asleep until their fate is resolved, or until the end of time, whichever occurs first. IF, however, a Limbotic Soul is awakened (through conjuring, séance, witchcraft, or exhumation), they return to Earth and may attempt to rush in and occupy the nearest living human, or SAPIEN. Sapiens can easily prevent Limbotic Souls from entry UNLESS they are compromised in some way, e.g., in a coma, unconscious, anesthetized, or in rare cases, through blood-to-blood contact.

2. If the Limbotic Soul does not successfully locate a Sapien in a compromised state, he or she will wander the Earth until their fate is decided. Limbotic Souls who are awake but without a bodily residence are commonly referred to as GHOSTS. In the rare occasion that they successfully overtake a compromised Sapien, both souls share a body, rendering them each HALF-DEAD.

3. Half-deads remain that way until the end of the Sapien's natural life. If the Sapien regains consciousness, each of the cohabitating souls will exert varying amounts of control on the physical body, depending on the strengths and weaknesses of the two individuals involved. Thus, half-dead embodiment differs widely from person to person.

POSSIBLE LOOPHOLE (three unconfirmed cases)—The Sapien must perform a ritual that fulfills the wishes of his or her Limbotic Soul on the anniversary of his or her original death, within the first year of cohabitation.

"At least there's a possible loophole—better than anything else we've got," Jack says. "I'd better check when they died." He pulls out his phone, shaking his head. "Can't believe Asshole got in because of my asthma attack."

I nod, secretly feeling better knowing that the blame doesn't rest solely on my shoulders. "You check on that and I'll check on Milo. Maybe our guardian angel has more info." I grab my phone from my purse, careful not to touch Bonnie's poem nestled alongside it, and zip that section closed.

When I navigate to my app, there's a response from Milo. "Listen to this, Jack. Milo wrote, 'I had a horrible nightmare about running through a graveyard last night. I'm wondering if that means G is for graves.'" I look at Jack and wince. "Hopefully theirs, not ours."

"Don't say stuff like that," Jack barks, his dark eyes filling with anger. "First it sucks to think about, and second, it's not helping to keep me calm."

He's right. "Sorry, bad habit. I'm a blurter."

"I noticed." He taps the surface of his cracked cell phone screen, courtesy of Clyde. "Says here that Bonnie and Clyde died on May 23, 1934; 9:10 A.M., to be precise."

I look at Jack, my eyes wide with panic. "Wait a second. That's tomorrow!" The familiar buzz of anxiety builds in my rib cage. "It says we need to do some sort of ritual to get rid of them, but what exactly—kill a sheep, dance in a circle, throw salt?"

Jack runs his hands through his hair, staring straight ahead.

I want to shake him. "Well?"

"I'm thinking."

Tapping my foot against the vibrating floor, I do some thinking of my own. Something else about that date sounds familiar. "Hold up. What were the numbers Milo gave you—the ones that were burned onto his palm under the word 'deadline'?"

"I'll check." Jack reads through his messages on his phone. "Here it is. 5-2-3-9-10." He looks at me. "Why?"

Bells of recognition sound off in my head. "Don't you see? Now we know for sure. 5-2-3-9-10 is May 23rd at 9:10 A.M. Tomorrow *is* the deadline!" I look around, sizing up the people around us. "I think we need to come clean to someone and get their advice so we get this ritual right. The question is who can we trust?"

Jack shakes his head violently. "No, forget it. We're not telling anyone. If it gets back to Mr. Johnson, he'll tell my father. You have to realize that my dad is a retired marine sergeant. He'll go ballistic if he hears about this. Besides, you're jumping to conclusions. Let's say the deadline is tomorrow. Maybe that signals the time Bonnie and Clyde have to go back to their graves." He shrugs. "Like they have twenty-four hours on earth and *ziiip!* they're gone. You're assuming the worst."

I wish with all my heart what he said is true, but it doesn't add up. "Do you seriously think that if Clyde knew he only had one day to live, he'd spend it on a tour bus with me?"

"Quiet!" The daughter from the mother-daughter team sitting in front of us glances over her shoulder, making a sourpuss face. I itch to tell her that if talking about dead people offends her, maybe she shouldn't be on a ghost tour. She suddenly licks her lips and stares at Jack, rolling her shoulder seductively. She lowers her voice. "Forget what Chunky Monkey says, sugar. You can come by my place and talk all you want. Ditch the chick first."

Jack looks at her, frowning. "Uh, no thanks."

When she turns back around, Jack sticks out his tongue in disgust before beckoning me closer. I strain to listen. "Remember how Mr. Johnson said the dead roam around until their unresolved final requests are granted? Ask Bonnie what she wants."

I frown. "I did. All she'd say is she wanted to be with Clyde forever. She told me if I hooked them up, she'd be happy and leave. Either she was lying, or they need something extra to allow them to stay together. When you were Clyde and you touched me, she spoke out of my mouth. That means that technically they were 'together' for several seconds, but nothing happened."

"Did they both know the other one was around?"

"Bonnie knew, but Clyde didn't," I admit. "I'm afraid to let him find out. I mean, what if he grabs on and doesn't let go, and then Bonnie is able to take over my body completely?"

Jack rolls his eyes. "Will you stop coming up with all this horrible stuff? We could play the What-If game forever. See if Bonnie knows anything about Clyde's last request, and then, at the next stop, we can casually ask some people about what others have done for the ritual."

I take a deep breath. He's right again. I need to think more rationally. "Good idea."

Clyde's last request was the same as mine—to be with me forever.

Yeah, yeah. That's your answer for everything.

Bonnie's absolutely no help. Not that I trust her anyway. I skim a Wikipedia website on half-deads, looking for some new information to jump out at me, when Mr. Johnson starts back up with his narration. "Soon we'll be at the Biograph Theater, the famous location where John Dillinger was gunned down following his attendance of the movie *Manhattan Melodrama*." He pauses, rubbing his chin dramatically. "Or was he? An interesting controversy still exists over whether the FBI killed the right man that evening."

The tour group starts to buzz about Dillinger when Jack says, "Hey, listen to this. Bonnie and Clyde were both buried in Dallas, but in *different* cemeteries."

"Are you sure?" I tinker with my ring, thinking. "Something about being buried together rings a bell." I try to remember what I'd heard, but nothing clicks. "Let me check my notes." I pull out my phone.

The bus pulls to the side as a wailing fire truck and three police cars approach. Jack scrunches down in his seat, as he peeks ever so slightly over the top of the glass. They sail past us and he sits back up.

Mr. Johnson's commentary resumes, "The fingerprints on the deceased did not match the ones on file with the police, so some historians believe that Dillinger had a friend on the police force who gave him a heads-up. Dillinger cleverly arranged to have a look-alike patsy accompany the lady in red to the theater that night. Roam around and see if you can speak to the ghost of whichever man was killed that evening and find out the truth once and for all. I've scheduled fifteen minutes for this stop."

The same way that Jack will be Clyde's patsy. Just you wait and see.

For once, Bonnie's annoying comments helped trigger a memory. Passengers stand and shuffle their way to the front, but Jack and I stay seated. Going on a hunch, I type in, "The Trail's End" in a search window. Seconds later, I have the info I need. "Listen to this, Jack. This is the last stanza of a famous poem Bonnie wrote." I clear my throat and read over the noise of the exiting Half-Dead Society members. "*Some day they'll go down together/ they'll bury them side by side./ To few it'll be grief,/ to the law a relief/ but it's death for Bonnie and Clyde.*"

Jack's eyebrows pinch together as if confused. "What's your point?"

"My point is that Bonnie hoped they'd be buried *side by side,* but their families buried them in separate cemeteries."

"Whoa. That could be significant." He rubs a finger along the ridge of his chin, gazing at me.

"Exactly. And here's the thing: Bonnie keeps telling me that the only thing they wanted, both in life and in death, was to be together. And their families screwed that up."

Watch what you say about my family. I'm sure my mama had her reasons.

Sounds like I touched a nerve. "I think that would qualify as a last request, don't you?"

Jack frowns, shaking his head. "Yeah, but if it does, we're screwed. We can't unbury them."

I shrug. "Unless there's some spiritual way out of this. Let's have a little chat with Bob and see what we can dig up." I glance at Jack. "Sorry. No pun intended."

We hurry down the bus steps, rushing to find Bob. On the way we pass Lionel, who smokes a cigarette in the shade, waving his bus driver hat in front of his face as if to cool himself. We stand waiting for Bob to conclude his conversation with the German guy before jumping in to talk to him ourselves.

After introductions, Bob rubs his chin. "I've been thinking about your sister and her husband. They must be pretty scared having known criminals as cohabitators, huh?"

"Definitely. I'm scared for them too," I agree, not having any trouble looking authentically sick to my stomach.

Jack nods. "To try and help them out, we wanted to ask you a question about last requests. What if someone hadn't been buried where they wanted? How could you make *that* ghost happy?" Several cars screech, narrowly missing a drunk guy jaywalking unsteadily across the street.

Bob clears his throat. "The thing with burial sites is that the final resting place usually has more to do with where the *souls* of the dead rest, not their bodies. So if you bury a special memento of the deceased at the spot they wished to have been buried, that usually appeases them. If you're talking about Bonnie and Clyde, you could probably purchase an object that belonged to them online somewhere. People sell stuff like that all the time."

Hope swells in my chest. At least we already have Bonnie's poem. "Okay, cool. I'll let my sister know about that." A troubling thought hits me then. "By the way, wouldn't everyone's last request be that they wouldn't die?"

Bob swats a swarm of gnats away from his face. "Yes, but having only one life to live is a basic and unyielding rule—similar to the idea that a person who gets three wishes cannot wish for unlimited wishes." He smiles at a couple from the tour. "How's it going, Mark? Tammy?"

Jack waits until they pass before jumping in to the conversation. "Except that doesn't make sense, because aren't all of these half-deads getting a second life?"

Bob nods. "Good point. But as you may have read in the brochure I gave you, there are specific, very unusual circumstances that allow limbotic spirits to inhabit a sapien's body. Those spirits who successfully transition into a second body are few and far between. More luck than intent. Wishing for a second life is an exercise in futility." He checks his watch.

Jack clears his throat. "What about the loophole that's mentioned? How does that work?"

Bob shrugs, looks uncomfortable. "There is one woman, Jeanette Finnegan, who has been a member for quite some time. She claims that she was inhabited by a French woman named Suzette. Some doubt Jeanette was ever half-dead—but she seems like the honest type to me. Anyway, Jeanette says she got rid of Suzette by satisfying her last wishes on the anniversary of the date, time, and location of Suzette's original death."

"Date, time, and location?" Jack asks, sounding alarmed. "It didn't say anything like that in the pamphlet. Just 'the anniversary of his or her death within the first year.'" Jack looks at me, as if to confirm.

Bob rubs his hairless head and squints at Jack. "Really? We'll have to fix that. Because I know for certain that Jeanette flew out to Paris when she did her ritual."

Panic builds in my chest, along with a sour taste of dread on my tongue. My mind starts racing, wondering where the hell Bonnie and Clyde died and how we can possibly get there by tomorrow morning at nine o'clock. "What kind of ritual did she do?"

Bob frowns, pausing as if he's unsure if he should continue. "Now, don't get your hopes up. There have only been a few half-deads who claimed that it worked. Two of them live in other countries and I've never met them in person, but I did have a chance to talk to Jeanette last year."

Bob smiles at the guy in the Bob Marley t-shirt. "Staying out of trouble, Mike?"

"Trying to," the stoner replies, shaking his head.

Turning back to us, Bob resumes his story. "Anyway, Jeanette told me she buried a locket that had been given to her limbotic spirit by her lover. Along with that, she also tossed in a copy of her lover's death certificate that she had ordered online, and then buried both items at the actual spot where he had committed suicide." The space between his eyebrows creases. "Along the River Seine, I believe. She told me she lit a candle and recited the Last Rites and supposedly, by the time she was done reciting the words, her half-dead spirit was gone."

"Wow! That's awesome," I say, as hope floods in, rinsing away some of the anxiety.

You hear that, Bonnie? You're going down!

He don't know nothing. The man's a fool.

Bob shrugs. "Might sound awesome, but in practice, not so much."

His words puncture my heart. I can almost feel the hope oozing out. "Why not?"

"Because dozens of us have tried it since and we were all unsuccessful." Bob holds up a finger to wait and then looks off to his left as if listening. "Uh-huh, okay. I'll tell them." He looks at us. "My other half, Silke, insists it's possible, but not likely. Most limbotic souls prefer living as a half-dead as opposed to lying asleep in limbo, so they're not about to share what to do to send them back." Bob points to his head. "She's one of them. She's content to live upstairs from me, as I like to call it, watching and listening as I lead my life. I've come to enjoy her company. My wife left me because of her, but maybe it was for the best."

"I'm sorry," I say, feeling awkward. But how could he possibly like someone else living in his head like a parasite, devouring his thoughts and analyzing his actions?

"Don't be," Bob says with a grin. "I'm never lonely."

Ask him if the dead can change places with the living.

Bonnie's question unsettles me but I need to know if it's even possible. "Can the limbotic spirit ever like, completely take over the human?"

Bob leans in close. "Every now and then some lunatic comes onto the website claiming they've taken over the bodies of their humans. There's one guy who swears he's Buddy Holly, and a gal who says she's been taking over new bodies ever since the Civil War."

Hearing Bob admit that the dead overtaking the living is even a remote possibility makes my insides twist in fear. Jack suddenly looks sweaty and pale, like he might throw up.

Ha! I tole you it was possible! Clyde will figure out how. Might even know already.

If Clyde's so smart, how come he didn't figure out your death ambush ahead of time, huh?

Bob must sense our discomfort because he dismisses the idea with a wave of his hand. "But there's absolutely no proof, so we—Silke and I—think it's all a sham. Let's face it. There are all kinds of crazies out there, along with a ton of skeptics, who think being half-dead is a joke. Truthfully, don't even bother mentioning that switcheroo part to your sister. Tell her and her husband to join our society and visit our members' only forum." He checks his watch again. "We only have about five more minutes left, so I need to start giving people a heads-up."

"Oh, of course," I gush, embarrassed we'd taken up all his time. "Thanks for everything!"

After Bob walks away, Jack says, "That was some crazy stuff. What did you think?"

What I think is that we're in even bigger trouble than we knew, but I don't want to scare Jack. "Based on that conversation, I think we have to head to the place where they were gunned down and do the ritual tomorrow morning." I swallow hard, unable to believe what I'm saying. "I don't want to risk Bonnie switching places with me." I get out my phone and start tapping like crazy. "I'm sending a quick text to my dad, telling him I'm going to stay at Anjali's tonight."

"Why would you do that?" Jack stares at me like I've sprouted a mustache. "He just said that the people who claimed they switched places were lunatics! And that it was all a sham."

"But he wasn't positive," I retort. "Either way, I don't want someone living in my body even one more day, much less for the rest of our lives, do you?" I know I should be trying to keep him calm, but he needs to wake the hell up.

Jack slides his hands into his pockets, glaring at me with a sarcastic look on his face. "So you think we need to head to their death spot, bury some crap, say prayers, and hope they go away? Isn't that a little nuts?"

"You have any better ideas?" I do a search, clicking on the first link. I need to keep my hands busy so I don't choke some urgency into him.

Jack lets out a loud sigh. "I just don't know. The whole idea seems ridiculous."

"No, *you're* ridiculous," I snap, rolling my eyes. "Sorry, Jack, but there's no other way out. So stop angsting over this and accept what we have to do already." I hold up my phone, hoping my stern tone has convinced him. "I'm looking up the place where they died."

"Okay, okay." He rubs his neck, red blotches dotting the surface. "I guess."

My mouth drops open when I read the results. "You're never going to believe this, Jack. If this isn't proof, I don't know what is. Listen to this—they died in *Gibsland*, Louisiana."

"The letter G." Jack stares at me, his jaw slack.

"Exactly." I reach for a lock of hair, twisting it around my finger. "How far is that from here?"

He shrugs. "I don't know. A few hours by plane probably. But are we seriously doing this?"

I grit my teeth, wanting to shake him. "Yes, for God sakes! Now stop dragging your feet. You need to be eighteen to order plane tickets, but my birthday's not until July. How about you?"

"August." He runs a hand through his hair. "I guess we'll have to drive. Let me map it." Jack slides his phone out of his pocket. "This is weird. Nine missed calls." He stares at the screen. "Uh-oh. My dad left me six texts."

"Is that bad?" I ask, not following.

"He never texts me." His face contorts as if in pain as he rapidly reads through the messages. "Oh no. Oh my God." He clicks through the messages faster, his eyes skimming, his lips moving as he reads.

"What, Jack? Tell me." I bite my lip, afraid to hear his answer.

He tilts his head back and looks up. "I'm fucking screwed!"

"Calm down! What's wrong?" My heart's racing and I don't even know what the problem is yet.

He hands me his phone. "Read the texts. All of them. Then you'll know."

I take his phone, my hands trembling with nervous anticipation.

The police have been sitting in front of the house for five minutes now. Are you in some sort of trouble?

They are saying you robbed a woman at an ATM?? Call me right now!

Answer your phone, damn it!!!

The victim has a head trauma and the police are searching your room. They showed me pictures of you and your car.

How could you do this, Jack?! I'm calling our lawyer. If they arrest you, don't say a word.

They just found your car downtown and towed it to the police pound for evidence. Why, Jack, why? What were you thinking?

When I look into Jack's eyes, I know what he's thinking. He picked the wrong girl to talk to at the party.

CHAPTER 18

Sunday, May 22nd // 4:32 P.M.

Clyde

The longer I'm inside Chickenshit's head, the madder I get. He's getting better at controlling his fear, I'll give him that much. He gets scairt as much as a boy on his first hunt, who draws his gun at every little sound. I saw a ton of them itty-bitty pops of light—fright lights I call 'em—but none of them lasted long enough for me to slide into.

Jack Daniel's the type to let his troubles build up inside him instead of forgetting about them. Prolly won't take nothing more than a person shouting, "Boo!" to push him over the cliff. It's like getting drunk. At first you don't feel nothing, you're just drinking and having fun. You have two, three, four drinks and you're happy as a lark, telling stories and bragging 'bout the things you done with a bit more mustard than the real McCoy.

You take a few shots of whiskey and have another drink to toast in the start of a new day. That's about when you notice your tongue has gotten fat in your mouth like a swollen toad and the words ain't as smooth as before. You think maybe you'll hit the road soon before you fall off the barstool or swear at another drunk bastard defending the boxer you think will win the title, when all of a sudden, an old chum strolls into the tavern and offers to buy you a drink.

You know you had enough, but you ain't saying no. Not after years of having to sneak around, drinking bootleg booze out of buckets. Not when you ain't got two nickels to your name.

So you clink your mug in thanks and guzzle down that seventh drink.

When you stand up to go take a piss, you can't barely walk. Your legs don't work, you're dizzy as a dame on bubbly, and you're considering taking that piss right where you stand. That seventh drink is like jumping off a cliff—too late to climb back up after you've gone over the edge.

The way I see it, Jack Daniel's already guzzled six drinks filled to the brim with trouble. He's been standing on the edge with his toes curled up tight, trying not to fall. But seeing all those itty bitty fright lights means something big is brewing. Any time now, Jack is gonna tip the shot glass and topple right off that cliff, and I'll be there to take over when he does.

Bottom's up, JD.

CHAPTER 19

Sunday, May 22nd // 4:38 P.M.

Monroe

Since I'm not very good at keeping cool when I'm stressed, I can easily recognize when someone's about to flip a shit, and clearly, Jack's about to do just that. But if he doesn't calm down now, Clyde's going to come back. The last thing I need right now is a criminal psychopath to deal with—one who wouldn't blink when trying to kill me.

I pause. Or would he?

Truthfully I'm not sure if he'd kiss me or kill me if he got me alone again, but I don't plan to find out.

I'd kill you myself if I could.

I ignore Bonnie and concentrate on Jack. "Deep breaths, Jack! I know your situation sucks, but don't dwell on it now. Think about puppies, or playing golf—whatever makes you happy." I fold and unfold my lip between my fingers, waiting, hoping he can pull it together.

Jack nods, doing as I ask. After his third inhalation, he says, "Okay. I'm better now. That was close. Asshole was trying to get in. The lights in my head were flashing like crazy."

A guy and his girlfriend sharing a waxy bag filled with Garrett cheese popcorn stroll toward us. Orange fluffy kernels roll down their chests and fall to the ground with each bite.

I allow myself to breathe while we wait for the couple to pass. "I know having Clyde lurking inside of you sucks, but at least you know when he's trying to take over and how to avoid it. We'll figure out how to clear your name later on, but right now we've got to get to Gibsland. Since the cops impounded your car, we'll have to rent one." A small group of pigeons swoops down off the top of the marquee and begins feasting on the gourmet popcorn treat on the ground.

Jack shakes his head. "Can't. You got to be twenty-five to rent a car. Maybe twenty-one, but either way, it won't work." He starts pacing, running his hands through his choppy Clyde haircut. Pigeons dart out of his way. "There's no way we can borrow my dad's car. Even if the cops were gone, he'd make me go to the police station and turn myself in. And my buddy Liam's car is at the shop right now. How about your friends?"

"Let me think. Not sure who . . ." I fiddle with the cross on my necklace, mentally rattling through a list of my friends who drive. Everyone either uses their parents' cars, or the ones who have their own cars aren't good enough friends that they'd lend me theirs. My brain leaps to my sisters Ginger and Audrey, but that won't work. They both live hours away.

I shake my head, frustrated. "No. There's no one I can ask. How long does it take to drive there anyway?" I type in the two locations in my GPS and wait for them to load. "It says Biograph Theater to Gibsland by car is fourteen hours and thirty-two minutes." I look at him and frown. "*Without* traffic."

Jack raises his arm and stares at his watch. "Let's see, it's roughly five o'clock now and we have to be there by nine A.M., so that gives us . . ." He winces. "Sixteen hours. And that's not counting traffic jams or stopping to pee. Check Amtrak."

Cars race down Lincoln Avenue, spewing exhaust. As I wait for the train schedule to load, I say, "Too bad we can't hijack a car. We could be on our way right this second."

"Yeah, I guess." Jack sighs, shaking his head. "What's the deal with the train?"

I peer at my screen, turning my phone sideways to make the schedule easier to read. "The next train from Chicago to Louisiana is . . . 7:08 tonight. Gets into New Orleans tomorrow afternoon at four. Damn it!" I kick a crushed soda can to the curb, sending pigeons waddling away fast. "What else? Come on, think!" I snap, wanting to whip my phone down in frustration. "There's got to be another way!"

Nope. Might as well give up. She lets out a chilling cackle.

Jack rubs his face, groaning. "There's not, unless you can afford to rent a private jet. Face it, Monroe. Driving's the only answer, but who? How?"

That's when it hits me. "Hey—we could take a taxi!" I could slap myself for being so dumb. "My dad has an account. Let me call them." As I wait for the operator to come on, I start pacing back and forth. We're wasting time here.

"That'll cost a ton," Jack warns.

"I know, but this is an emergency. Money won't matter if we're dead." When no one picks up, I check my phone to see if the call failed. There's an error message written in red font. I shield the phone from the daylight so I can see it better, squinting at the words. "'Your account has temporarily been suspended.'" I wriggle up my face, confused. "Liar. No, it hasn't." I try again and get the same message. "What the hell?"

Jack rubs his chin, staring at me. "Your name and address were on a notepad in my room. Do you think the cops could have called your dad and now they're trying to prevent us from leaving?"

"That's probably it!" This news makes me wonder if the lady at the ATM got hurt worse than Jack thought. I glance over at Mr. Johnson, who's chatting with the Asian guy from the front row. "Hey—Mr. Johnson could drive us! Out of all the people in the world, the half-deads would understand if their tour was cancelled, right?"

"Understand?" Jack's forehead contorts into an angry, wrinkled mess. "These people came from all over the world to be here. And besides, this is Mr. Johnson's business. He's not going to drop everything and drive us to Louisiana! Wake up, Monroe!" He throws his hands in the air.

"Don't yell at me! We've got to do something!" Fear wraps around my gut and squeezes.

"Well, not *that*. That was stupid." Jack shoves his hands in his pockets.

"Let's not call each other names, all right?" Twisting my hair until I feel a painful tug, I wonder if Jack's right. Am I blowing this all out of proportion?

I send a desperate plea to my mother: *I need your advice, Mom. Should I forget this whole thing and hope it works out, like Jack wants me to do?* I pace a few more steps, waiting for a definitive sign—a gust of wind, a rattling of chains, something. When nothing happens, I try again with a different question. *Do you think we should head to Louisiana to do the ceremony?*

The entire flock of pigeons suddenly rises up and flies off a few feet over my head in a giant flurry of wings and feathers, making me cry out in surprise. I realize without a doubt that my mother orchestrated that sendoff. *Thank you, Mom! I love you!* Her undeniable presence gives me the courage I need for my next task.

I lean close to Jack. "Mr. Johnson can't say no if we don't ask permission."

Jack looks confused for a few seconds, before the light bulb turns on. Speaking between clenched teeth, he growls, "Steal it? What's wrong with you?" He glares at me. "No. No effing way, Monroe!"

"Listen for one second, will you? We only need the bus to get out of the city. Then we can stop at a used car lot somewhere and buy a cheap car with my debit card. I have like six hundred bucks saved. It's our only chance!"

He rubs his chin silently, which I take to mean he's considering my plan. I need to do my strongest convincing yet or we're never going to do this. "Ten miles out of town you can text Kyle and tell him where they can pick up the bus." I stare into Jack's eyes, pleading with all my might. "If we don't do it, Bonnie and Clyde will stay in our bodies forever, or worse, maybe even trade places with us! Which would you rather do—steal a bus or die?"

"This sucks. This totally sucks." He breathes in through his nose, scowling at me for what seems like forever. After a deep breath, he says, "Shit! I don't see any other way, either. Let's do it now before I lose my nerve." And with that, Jack races the few yards to the bus.

I follow him, climbing the bus stairs two at a time, ecstatic that he agreed to my idea, yet terrified at the same time. I've done a couple of illegal things in my life, but nothing as over the top as this. But strangely, for the first time ever, doing this wrong thing feels right.

Jack hops in the driver's seat, which is good since I can't remember the last time I drove a car, much less a huge fricking school bus. His eyes scan the dials and levers. "It's like a car, only everything's in a different place and bigger."

"Start it up and let's go!" I crouch down in the front passenger seat, sneaking a peek at Lionel. He's leaning against a pole about thirty feet away, smoking another cigarette. He turns slightly, blowing smoke from his mouth, glancing casually at the bus. He does a double-take, squinting our way. He takes a final drag on his cigarette and stamps it out, strolling toward the bus as if to investigate.

"Don't freak out, Jack, but the bus driver's heading this way."

"No problem. I can do this," Jack replies in a Zen-like tone. He bumps a lever, causing the windshield wipers to start up, which scrape noisily across the dry window. "Crap!" He shuts them off and turns the key in the ignition. The engine sputters into life.

This causes Lionel to start running, his huge belly jiggling with each step.

I leap to my feet and pull the red handle, making the door unfold into the locking position.

Lionel arrives seconds later and pounds on the doors. "Hey, get out of there! What the hell are you kids doing?"

"Drive!" I scream at Jack, not able to rein in my terror. So much for being the voice of serenity.

"Let me in *now!*" Saliva globules land on the glass with each word. Lionel presses his face up against the window, flattening his nose and leaving small steam circles from his exhalations.

One of Lionel's thick fingers inches into the crevice between the doors. I squeal and try pushing his fingers back through, but he's strong. "Hurry, Jack!"

"I'm trying, but it won't go." Jack's voice is steady but rising. "I'm pressing the gas."

"Check the parking brake!" I screech.

Lionel now has the doors about two inches apart in the center. A few seconds more and he'll have the doors pried far enough apart that they'll open automatically. Not knowing what else to do, I snatch the industrial metal Thermos from the cup holder and pound his fingers. He finally lets go, accompanied by a yelp and a "son of a bitch!"

"I'm so sorry!" I shriek. He winces, trying to shake off the pain. Panic and disgust build inside of me in equal measure. Are we really doing this—stealing a bus? The acid in my stomach rises up my throat, but I swallow it back down. I cannot get sick now.

Lionel cups his hands around his mouth. "Boss! Come quick!"

In the huge side view mirror, I see Mr. Johnson running full-speed alongside the bus, pounding it as he moves toward the door. "What's going on? Stop, stop!"

Jack releases a side lever and pounces on the gas. The bus jolts forward. "That was it!" He pulls into traffic amid a blaring of car horns and screeching tires. Mr. Johnson and Lionel run after us, waving their arms.

I drop the Thermos and watch it clunk down the steps, landing against the door. "Step on it, Jack!"

"Stop yelling at me," Jack says calmly, pressing the gas gently.

I swallow hard, nodding. "Sorry. You're right." The bus cruises slowly down Fullerton, heading toward Lake Shore Drive. Please God, let us get away. Please, please, please.

God can't help you now, but Clyde can.

Shut up and go away!

Looking out the back window, I see Mr. Johnson on his phone. I pray he's trying to call Jack to find out what's going on and not the police, but I know I'm fooling myself. Jack plods through the intersection, cars blaring their horns as they whiz past us.

"Maybe I should pull over so you can drive," he offers.

"There's no time. You're doing fine." I hope saying it will make it true, even though I'm dying to take over. As little practice as I get driving, I'm way better than Jack. Does he not get that we're in a hurry?

Clyde was the best driver anyone ever saw. He could drive this bus like a pro. He'd be fast, too.

I don't care, Bonnie. Go away!

When Jack veers over the center line, a truck blasts his air horn, making me jump. I bite my lip, praying he doesn't get us into an accident. That would make this the quickest end of a getaway in the history of robberies. He turns, tires squealing, onto Lake Shore Drive, rumbling toward Michigan Avenue. Soon we'll be in the middle of the worst traffic in downtown Chicago, but we've got no choice. This is the most direct route to where we need to go. I perch on the edge of the first row seat, kitty-corner from him. "According to my GPS, the highway's less than three miles. Can't you go *any* faster?" I'm trying not to sound bitchy, but what the hell? We stole a bus and are making a run for it, not going for a scenic Sunday afternoon drive.

"No, I can't go faster." He brakes hard, the car in front of him a football field away. "Don't you see how heavy traffic is?"

What I see is cars flying past us on both sides. "Just keep up and we'll be fine."

"What does it matter?" Jack says, sounding miserable. "They're going to catch us as soon as we get stuck in that traffic."

"Not if we don't pull over."

"What's wrong with you?" He glances over his shoulder at me briefly, his face screwed up in anger. "We're not in the movies, Monroe. We can't outrun the cops in a school bus!"

What happened to Jack-Ass, the guy so desperate to get away from the cops at the party that he tried to ditch me? But I can't press this any further and cause Clyde to reappear. "Okay, okay." I spy a red metal box under the dashboard in the center. "Hey, we could trade up for a car instead. Go down a side street and you can hotwire something smaller." I kneel down and tug on the heavy toolbox, which is nearly impossible to drag over the rubberized flooring. "What tools you need for that?"

Jack glances down at me, a trickle of sweat rolling down the side of his face. "You're kidding, right? Clyde might be inside of me, but I've never stolen a vehicle in my life."

I don't point out that he just stole one. "I didn't say you did, but you know *how* to do it, right?" I figure hotwiring a car is a guy thing, same as cutting the lawn and grilling burgers.

Clyde knows how. Stole a million cars. Does it in ten seconds flat, too.

"No, Monroe, I don't know how to hotwire a car. What kind of people do you hang out with anyway?" Jack shoots me a dirty look.

"Fine, forget I asked. Let's just carjack someone instead. Pull in front of someone's car and force the driver to get out."

"With what? My fists?" His eyes meet mine in the mirror above his head as he cruises through a yellow, but drives so slowly that the light turns red not even halfway across. A guy in a black SUV guns it as soon as his light turns green, nearly hitting us. Horn blasts follow.

I lift a hefty wrench out of the toolbox. "Would this work as a weapon?"

"I don't know, does it work for you? Because *I'm* not doing it." His eyebrows pinch together in the center. "I'm in enough trouble already."

My hands grip the wrench tighter. Like I'm not? "Okay, fine! I'll do it then." The ominous wail of multiple sirens makes me whip around and look out the back window. At first I don't see anything, but when a truck changes lanes, blue flashing lights are only several blocks behind us.

"Are they close?" Jack asks, his voice wavering.

"We have time," I lie, my tongue feeling as if it's coated with chalk dust. The two cop cars, lights flashing, try to maneuver around the lethargic traffic. My heart pounds, my ears ring. We need to do something fast. "Let's ditch the bus and hide until they pass!"

"Now? On Lake Shore Drive?"

"No, but as soon as we turn onto Michigan. Do it now!" Grabbing the cross on my necklace, I murmur, *Help me, God!* as I watch the cops close the gap between us.

"Oh God. I can't get over. No one will let me in." Jack grips the steering wheel with both hands, his knuckles white. "I'm sorry, Monroe, but I'm not cut out for this." His voice cracks, like he might cry. "Let's give ourselves up and hope for the best."

My brain screams for air. "There is no hope if we get arrested! We'll be sitting in jail when the deadline passes, and then Bonnie and Clyde will share our bodies forever! Make them move."

He manages to slowly change lanes and maneuver onto Michigan Avenue, where we're met with even more traffic. "Cross this street and then pull over by that red car," I direct, pointing to where I want him to go.

Jack shakes his head, his forehead slick with sweat. "No, Monroe. Listen to me. We do have a choice. We should turn ourselves in right now, before we rack up any more crimes. Then we can explain—"

"Explain?" I yell, throwing my hands in the air. "Explain what? That we're possessed by Bonnie and Clyde, who've been dead for almost a century? And then ask the cops if they can pretty please drive us to Louisiana right away so we don't die? Come on, Jack! It won't work!"

"You don't know that. Besides, we don't know for sure what will happen at the deadline. It's not worth risking my future over. If you want to keep going, you'll have to do it alone."

Clyde could get you out of this mess in a blink of an eye.

A high-pitched squeal pierces my eardrum and my chest feels tight. When I try to take a deep breath, the air has become thick, like corn syrup. I claw at my neck, trying to swallow.

Let me breathe, Bonnie.

This time, honey, it's not me.

Part of me wants to let Jack go ahead and pull over. Sit on the curb until the cops come, then hold my hands up and surrender.

But the other part of me knows that if we both don't arrive in Gibsland by 9:10 tomorrow morning, something terrible will happen. For the first time in years, I realize how much I like being Monroe Baker, police record and all. That I might be impulsive, sarcastic, and do lots of stupid things that I later regret, but I want the chance to do better, to try again to make my dad proud of me. *And you too, Mom.* I suck in my lips hard, trying to keep from crying.

The sirens blare loudly, closer now. Black splotches flit at the corners of my vision just as a welcome sight comes into view—the underground parking garage below Millennium Park. "Drive down that ramp! We can hide down there while we figure out another plan!"

Yes! Do it now!

Instead of flooring it down the ramp, Jack stomps on the brakes, tires squealing loudly in protest. My chest slams into the cross bar in the front of me. "No! I won't do it. I'm turning myself in. You run if you want, Monroe, but count me out."

"No! We *both* need to go to Gibsland. Remember the poem—one day they'll go down *together*? I can't do this alone. I need you, Jack."

He shakes his head slowly, steering the bus toward the curb. At that moment, I know I need to pull out all the stops or we'll both be half-dead permanently, or worse, tomorrow morning. Win big or go home. I hate what I'm about to do, but I'm out of options.

With a heavy heart, I ratchet up the meanest, evilest, most psychotic face I can muster and grit my teeth. I wrap my fingers around the Goliath-sized wrench from the toolbox and hold it up over my shoulder. In a loud, commanding voice, I yell, "Listen, you pussy! Drive down the fucking ramp *now* or I'll smash your head in!"

His eyes widen and his lips peel backward. "What are—" is all he can get out. He gives me one last traitorous glare before his eyes roll and his shoulders twitch.

"Drive!" I scream in his face.

Jack hits the gas and aims the bus down into the garage, his body still contorting with small jagged motions. I pray I made the right move—if we can survive driving down this ramp without ramming head-on into a parked car at the bottom.

Letting the wrench fall to the floor, I watch in horror as Jack's elbow, then his neck, jerk as if being electrocuted. "I'm so sorry, Jack," I wail, a hand covering my mouth. "But you left me no choice."

Atta girl! First bright thing you done all day.

He skims the side of the cement wall, sparks flying as metal meets concrete, making the bus swerve wildly. Jack plunges into the darkness, his driving erratic. Maybe I didn't scare him enough for Clyde to take over. As my eyes adjust to the sudden darkness, the shadowy outlines of a mom and two kids appear fifty feet in front of us. I shout, "Watch out!"

The mother yanks her children out the way, one by the collar of his shirt. Jack sails past the group, missing them by inches. Oh my God, what have I done? I look back and see the youngest child crying, as the mother kneels to attend to him. Jack finally brakes, getting the bus under control.

I spy an empty spot over to the right, against the wall, my heart pounding out of my chest. "Park it and turn off the engine. Quick!"

The sirens are softer, farther. Please let us escape, I beg to whoever upstairs is listening. Please, please. I'll be good the rest of my life. I promise.

He pulls into the parking space and shuts off the engine, not a word spoken. I grab my purse and pull the door handle, hoping that whichever guy is behind that handsome face will follow me off the bus. Running down the steps, I yell, "Hurry! Let's go!" I leap onto the cement floor, turning around when I don't hear footsteps behind me.

"Aren't you coming?" I ask nervously, hoping that the guy I've been avoiding all morning will be the one to answer me back.

CHAPTER 20

Sunday, May 22nd // 5:02 P.M.

Clyde

So there I was, watching Jack Daniel drive the bus like a pantywaist, when all of a sudden, flashing lights appeared in front of my eyes as bright as tractor headlights at night. For a moment, I thought they really was headlights, so I kept watching. Then I realized Chickenshit was scared again . . . this time of Twinkle! I seized the opportunity, pushing my soul right back into his body.

Hot damn! I knew Twinkle had some spit and fire in her, but I never thought in a million years that she'd be the one to help bring me forth. She must have figured out that I'm the guy who will protect her and who can outmaneuver any police car, not that half-wit Jack Daniel. If my pappy were here, he'd have said that a girl with that much gumption was rarer than hen's teeth and twice as valuable.

"Aren't you coming?" Twinkle stands outside the bus, her face all rumpled, like she's frightened. Even in this underground tunnel, I can see the diamond in her lip sparkle and her breasts aglow in the dim light. Sweet Jesus, she's pretty. And she has legs for days.

I go to rise up, but a leather strap tethers me to the chair. I push and pull at the silver buckle until the dang thing finally lets go. I stand, wobbly at first, but I find my balance right quick. "I'll go anywhere with you, Twinkle."

"Oh, thank goodness it's you!" She holds a hand over her heart.

I can't help smiling. Twinkle is sweet on me, just like I suspected. Seems hard to believe I got so lucky right out of the gate, but the Lord is a kind and merciful man.

"Come on!" She waves for me to follow.

And just like that, she takes off in a mad dash, like there's something bad about to happen. I'm no fool. I ain't waiting around to take the heat. By the time I get down the steps, she's near thirty yards ahead of me, light on her feet like she's got wings instead of legs. I'm awed at the sight. Bonnie ain't never ran that fast. Not even before battery acid twisted up that leg of hers.

"Wait for me, woman!" I shout, rushing after her. I'll be damned if my lame foot is going to land me back in prison. Five steps later, I remember Jack Daniel has all his toes. My chest swells, tickled by the idea of being whole again. But Twinkle ain't waiting for me the way Bonnie would. She races ahead, like we got to catch the last train out of town. I aim to stick with her, at least until the deadline hits. And then, if we're both still around, I'll do my best to convince her to be my moll and take her with me.

Twinkle screeches, "The cops are coming. Hurry!"

Sure enough, I hear sirens not too far off in the distance, like a swarm of angry hornets. "Why dint you say so in the first place?" I get a burst of energy twice that of the sun, zigging and zagging around cars. "Why are you—"

"Shh! Come here." She stops and hunches down behind a big silver car.

I kneel next to her, not even a foot away. Face to face with Twinkle like this, I can barely breathe. Her green eyes are the color of a Christmas pine, her hair as black as the winter wheat fields after the burn. "Why are the cops after us?"

She scrunches up her cute nose. "Does clubbing a woman over the head ring a bell?"

I think about yesterday and it don't make sense. "They's chasing after us just for that? Why, I barely hit her. Not enough to hurt her, just knock her down." I ponder that a second. "Course, I got away with a tidy sum of money, too." I pat my wallet and grin.

"Not to mention we just stole a bus." She looks around, catching her breath.

"Whose fool idea was that anyway? It's akin to stealing an elephant—big, slow, and old."

She tilts her chin down like she's annoyed with me, but I see a hint of a smirk on her lips. "Real funny." The sound of sirens overhead makes Twinkle's face collapse. "We've got to get out of here and fast. Do you know how to hotwire a car?" She looks at me with eyes as wide as saucers, like she's afraid I'm gonna say no.

Makes me want to pull her close and tell her not to worry—that I'll take care of everything. That gives me an idea. I lift my chin and scratch my neck. "I reckon I can remember how. All's I need is one little kiss from you to start my engine first." I grin, leaning closer, hoping she'll meet me halfway.

Instead, she backs away from me, fast. "I can't. My phobia, remember?"

This phobia of hers is making my patience fade quicker than daylight in December. Right then I decide I'm making it my mission to cure her, one kiss at a time. "I'm staying put until I get one kiss." I fold my arms over my chest, like I aim to set here awhile. Next thing I know she catches me off-guard, planting one soft, sweet kiss on my lips.

"Okay, let's go!" she says, her voice filled with worry. "Please, Clyde!"

If we had more time, I would've wrapped my arms around her and showed her there was nothing to be afraid of, 'cept right then, the volume of sirens gets louder.

I leap to my feet and pull the handle of the silver car we've been leaning against, but the door don't budge. I look for the rubber lining so I can slide my finger under and pop the button, but there ain't one. "Hmm . . . I ain't familiar with this here sort of car." I peer inside, cupping my hands to my face to block out the light. "No wonder. This one ain't got the wires poking out the bottom like it's supposed to."

"Oh, I get it. An old car. The kind like when you were alive."

That lights a fire under my pride. "I am alive, damn it!"

"Okay, okay. Sorry." She holds her hands up like she's surrendering. "I didn't know you were sensitive about that."

What am I doing? Yelling at her ain't no way to woo a woman. I take a deep breath. "I guess I ain't learned how to deal with my past just yet. Now let's hunt us down a car with the wires sticking out so I can get us out of here."

We race down the aisle, hunched over, looking left and right. All of a sudden, red and blue lights ricochet off the ceiling, not fifty yards away. We both dive behind the closest car, holding our breaths as the cop car drives slowly past us. I turn my head, looking around for a weapon in case I need one. Instead, I find something else I need—a rusty blue Ford pickup with fat tires and shiny fenders—just like ones I used to steal, only smaller, sleeker. Not in the best shape, but it don't look half bad neither. I hear the cop's tires roll over a stick about five cars up the aisle.

"They're going to find the bus any second." Twinkle's voice gets high and whiny, like she might cry. That'll never work. Blanche nearly got us killed with her constant fretting.

"Hold it together, woman. I think I got us a ride." I point to the truck across the aisle and two spots over.

And just like that, she goes from sad to glad. "Oh, thank God! Let's go!"

Now don't that beat all? Twinkle's beautiful, tough, and a God-fearing woman to boot. After I check to make sure the coast is clear, we scurry across the aisle, staying low. The oval sign on the truck door says *Rojas Landscaping*. Peeking under the tarp covering the load, there are shovels, cutting shears, motors, and all sorts of farming tools. Don't matter to me what kind of getaway car I drive. I pull on the driver's handle and this time, the door opens right up. Twinkle shimmies in first and I follow. First thing I do is lean under the steering wheel and yank the ignition cap.

"Hurry!" she whispers. "They're going to find the bus any second!"

"Hold your horses, I got this." I press the two red wires together and like magic, the truck roars into life. "I tole you I could do it."

"Yes! Good job." Her eyes dart every which way while she wrings her hands. "There are about five exits out of here, so I think you'd better—"

"Lookie here," I explain, cutting her off mid-sentence. I pull the truck into reverse but I don't back up. Let her sweat it out a bit. I lay my arm atop the steering wheel and turn toward her. "As cute as you is, I been on the lam since looong before you were born, which makes me the boss, got it?"

"Yep, you're the boss." She turns her head and I swear I hear her say, "for now," but I let it go. She might think she wants to be in charge, but if things get rough, she'll be begging me to take the lead, just wait and see.

I grab the blue baseball cap that's lying on the seat between us and pop it on my head. "Time for you to disappear, Twinkle."

She grabs a shoulder belt and snaps it in place. "No. I'm not going anywhere. I'll be quiet as a mouse from now on." She clamps her lips shut, zips them shut, and throws away the key.

I hide a smile. I know I should be mad at the way she's sassing me, but I never met a woman so cocksure before. "I meant that the cops is looking for a man *and* a woman, so uh . . ." I look at the floor by her feet.

"Oh, whoops. Sorry." She unsnaps her buckle and slides her curvy bottom onto the floor, scrunching down in a ball like a snake. "Ready."

I back up, grinning like a fool, aiming the truck the opposite way of the cop lights flickering on the ceiling. Heading for the patch of daylight one room over, I drive slow as molasses so I don't call no attention to me. I turn onto the ramp and drive straight up toward the sunlight as the cop car passes behind us. When he don't follow, I grin. Already outsmarted one cop. Looks like I ain't lost my touch.

When we get on the street, I whistle as I whiz past all the tall buildings. "Chicago sure got a whole lot bigger since last time I was here." I pat the seat next to me. "The coast is clear. Come on up here. I want everyone to see what a gorgeous gal I got by my side."

She ignores my compliment, but climbs up all the same. "That was so scary." She slips onto the seat and fastens her seat belt. "I can't believe we did it!"

"We?"

"Okay, you," she says with a smile. "Thank you." She gasps, pointing to a sign on the right. "Hey! Take 41 South, coming up in a quarter mile. That's what we want."

I pinch my cheeks to keep from smiling. Twinkle said "we." Means she's starting to think of us as a couple. My plan is afoot. I switch lanes, trusting that her navigating skills are better than Bonnie's. That girl could steal maps, but she couldn't read one any better than she could read Chinese. Flashes of light spark in my head and I realize my blunder.

I concentrate on naming the cars around me to get my mind on something else. There's a red Buick, a tiny gray car no bigger than a tin can, big brown truck that says UPS—and that's as far as I need to go. The flashing lights in my head fade, and then disappear. I take a deep breath. Forgetting about my old gal is going to be harder than I thought. After the deadline tomorrow, I'm hoping it won't make no difference who I think about. In the meantime, I got me a good-looking dame to set my sights on.

"Where you heading, Twinkle?" As long as it's in the direction of Texas, I'll be fine.

"Anywhere but here. How about south?" She digs in her purse and pulls out her red communicating device. "I can get directions on my GPS."

I don't like secret codes unless I'm in on them. "Come again?"

"Global Positioning System. You type in where you want to go and then a satellite—it's this robot thing that circles the earth—sends back information about how to get there."

I eye her sideways. "You expect me to believe that, Twinkle?"

She laughs. "It's true! A lot of stuff has happened since you"—she pauses, her face gets all scrambled like she's trying to suck the words back in—"I mean, in the last eighty years."

"How's about you stop talking about how long I been asleep, and concentrate on our future? How's about we head to Texas and see if any of my kin can lend us some money? Unless you got some?"

"Sorry. I spend my cash as soon as I get it."

I chuckle. "Same as me." As I guide the truck onto the highway, I can barely believe my eyes. The road is four lanes wide and smooth as a lake on a breezeless afternoon. "Sweet Jesus!" I press the accelerator, feeling the power under my foot. "Yeeee-haaa!"

Twinkle looks behind us, her face a mess of worry. "Don't go crazy, Clyde. If the cops pull us over, we're screwed. They'll run our plates and—"

I cut her off. "Relax, kitten. I know what I'm doing. I'm the best driver there ever was. Got away every time."

"Not *every* time," she mutters, facing forward.

I wish she hadn't brought that up. "You're right. Every time *except* the last time. But that had nothing to do with my driving. It's because a stoolie named Henry Methvin opened his trap and got me kilt. Goddam squealer." I picture his face and feel the steam rising up my innards, threatening to choke me. I open the window to get more air in this truck.

"Yeah, I'm sure it was horrible. But try and forget about all of that for now and concentrate on driving. Just so you know, today's cops have radar—electronic equipment that measures speed," she says, sounding like a schoolmarm. "Better not drive faster than eight miles per hour over the limit until we get out of the city."

I like a woman who's strong, but not one who's bossy. "You know what? I got this under control. When I need your advice, I'll ask you for it. Until then, just sit there and look pretty."

"Ohmigod, you are so . . . what's the word?" She twists her hair round her finger, looking up.

"Exciting?" I ask.

She shakes her head.

"Handsome?"

A tiny smirk appears and then fades. "No, um . . ."

"Sexy?"

She laughs. "No! I was thinking stubborn or chauvinistic."

I don't know the second word, but I ain't got time for book learning. "Stubborn's about right. But only for your own good. Now what about my idea about heading to Texas?"

She takes a deep breath, fussing with her ring. "Actually, I need to head to Shreveport."

"In Louisiana?" I rub my chin, wondering what she's up to. I know there's a deadline, but the way she was fretting over my speeding means maybe she ain't as worried about it as I'd think she'd be. "Why? You got kin there?"

She picks up her communicating device. "Um, yeah. And my mom's buried there. I was thinking I'd stay with my grandma for a while until this whole thing blows over. So, if you don't mind, we'll need to take 55 South all the way to Memphis. Then 40 to Little Rock."

I ain't sure how much to believe. I got a million questions, and some stuff she's telling me don't add up, but I'll play along until she slips. Because she will. I know firsthand how fibbing gets you into a bigger heap of trouble than the truth. So I'll pretend I'm a country rube and when she stumbles, I'll make her do things my way.

"Route 55 South to Route 40 West. The little robot thing called my brain has got it." I take a deep breath, relishing the warmth on my face and the fresh air in my lungs. Feels good to be doing, not watching. We settle in for a stretch, watching traffic and commenting on the buildings. Finally I say, "So why'd you run in the first place? From what I seen through Jack Daniel's eyes, you was the one wanting to steal the bus and get out of town, not him. You running from the law, Twinkle?" I smile, having fun teasing her.

"What? No." She makes a face like she smells something bad. She adjusts her shirt when it don't need adjusting.

I can't believe my eyes. "Ha! You're lying! I can tell by the way you're acting."

"No, I'm not. You're crazy." She stares straight ahead, taking her ring off and setting it on a different finger, and then back again.

I seen her do that same thing on the bus when they was trying to get away. "Look at you, all nervous. Come now, Twinkle, fess up. Nothing I hate worse than liars."

She sighs, rubs her eyes. "Okay, yes, sort of. I'm on probation right now." She aims her finger at me. "Don't get all weird about it. It's not what you think."

I grin. "A fellow con! Will you look at you? What you on the lam for?"

"Vandalism—but I haven't been convicted, so I'm not a con," she snaps. "Not yet anyway. They'll drop the charges as long as I stay out of trouble for a year." She leans back on the headrest. "Of course, I just screwed that up, didn't I?" Her voice cracks, like she might cry.

My heart pinches up in my chest. I remember my first arrest, the one I got for not bringing back a rental car on time. "Not for sure you didn't. There's lots of ways to get out of it. Coppers arrest the wrong person, or they don't got no evidence." I smile—not to cheer her up, but because knowing this about her puts me into an even finer spot. I can make her do anything, go anywhere I want, under the threat of avoiding arrest. Sticking with me is her best bet. I know she's got to arrive at that idea on her own, but there ain't no crime in helping her see the light. "Besides, if you keep on the run, they might never catch you."

"I don't want to keep on the run." She examines her fingernails, picking dirt out from under one. "I've never been to jail, but it can't be as bad as hiding out for the rest of my life."

Anger claws at my ribs, trying to get out. But I can't lose my temper again so quick, or she'll harden her heart to me and become bored—the way she looked when she was with Jack Daniel at the party. I take a deep breath and work at keeping my voice even. "If you ain't ever been, you really don't know which is worse now, do you?" The big buildings on the side of the road are gone and small shabby houses have taken their place. I bring the truck up to eighty, feeling the power increase.

"Fair enough. But I want to go to college and if I ran, that would be the end of that. This whole conversation is pointless." She opens her window. "Can we talk about something else?"

"College? My, you really are a smart one!" I can't stop grinning, wondering how I got me such a fine woman at my side with both brains and beauty. I watch the sun hitting bits of glass on the side of the road, and the patches of wildflowers mixed along with garbage, thinking about all the million questions I have for Twinkle. I finally settle on the one that's most pressing—what will happen at the deadline. I need to be sneaky about it though because I ain't even positive she knows there is one. "How's about once we get to Memphis, you and me get a room at Harbin's and go see hear some Memphis blues in the city?" A sign announces distances to cities I never heard of. "We could hear some music, drink some wine, maybe get cozy . . ." I raise an eyebrow, wondering what she'll say to that last idea.

Twinkle sits up right quick. "What? No, we have to drive straight through. We can take turns driving, but I need to get there by tomorrow morning."

That means she must know about the deadline too, or she wouldn't be in such a rush. I'm going to stir the hornet's nest a bit and see what flies out. "Why is that? No disrespect to your mama, but she ain't going nowheres. It'd sure be sweet for us to have some time to get to know each other. You and me got a lot in common. If you give me a chance, you might even like me back." I switch lanes, going around a slowpoke that keeps patting the brakes for no good reason.

"Who knows, but unfortunately, I won't have time. I have to go to a funeral. Starts at nine." She starts fussing with the folds of her skirt, twisting the fabric between her fingers.

"Is that right?" Her lies are getting thicker and more troubling. "Who died?"

She glances my way, enough for me to know that her eyes read scared, not sad. "My Uncle Tim. Crazy dude. Drank too much." She fusses with her ring again. "It was very sudden."

"Oh good. Because I thought maybe you was worried about some sort of deadline."

"Deadline?" Her eyes flicker, but she tries to shrug it off. "What are you talking about?"

I've pulled her chain long enough. "Come now, Twinkle. I already tole you I don't like liars. I figured out the deadline way before Dimwit did. You tell me what you know, and I'll get you there safe and sound—and on time." As long as I'm alive at the end of that rainbow, that is.

She plays with the doodad on her necklace. "There's nothing to tell. All I know is that tomorrow morning we'll find out if we'll continue sharing our bodies—I mean, if you and Jack will keep sharing your body—or if you'll go back to where you came from."

I knew she'd slip. I heard that sour note and I ain't gonna let it pass. "What was that? Why'd you say sharing 'our' bodies like you is sharing a body too?"

"Nothing. No reason. Wasn't thinking, that's all."

Twinkle's hand lies on the seat between us. I wonder if that phobia of hers could come in handy now. I reach over and place my hand on top of hers, holding it tight. "Tell me the truth and I'll let go of you."

She shakes like a rattler before squealing, "It's me, baby! I am trapped inside of her, the same way you are. She's lying to you, Clydehopper!" Twinkle's voice sounds different, like she's from Texas too.

Hearing her use Bonnie's nickname for me makes me let go of Twinkle's hand like it's on fire. Alarms go off in my head. "So it's true! Bonnie's inside of you!" I check the road and then look back at Twinkle. A tiny flash of light races past my eyes. *Go away!* I roar. The lights fade.

"No, but I do a pretty good imitation of her, don't I?" She folds her hands up by her neck, eyes fluttering. "Oh, Clydehopper," she drawls. "I'll do anything you want because I've got no personality of my own." She shrugs. "See? I'm a good actor, aren't I?"

I stare at her, a grenade ticking in my chest. I'm not fooled. "Eyes don't lie. You been keeping this from me. Bonnie's inside of you. I heard it with my own ears."

She looks out her window. "No, Clyde, she's not. You're just mad because I used her baby nickname for you."

"It's not a baby nickname. She called me that when—" I remember how she used that name whenever she was trying to lighten the mood, make me laugh. Lights flash across my mind.

"When what? When wittle Clydehopper got a boo-boo?" She giggles.

The lights flash again, brighter, faster. "Stop it, I said!" I point my finger in her face. "You say it again and I'll push you out the truck." That ought to make her heed my word from now on.

She narrows her eyes. "Push me out of the truck? Wow, Clyde. I was only teasing."

And still she backtalks me? I stare at her, wondering if I lost my touch, or if women today say whatever they want. "You do know I killed twelve men, right?"

Talk about passive-aggressive. Yes, Clyde, I do know. So are you saying you'll kill me if I tease you again?" She stares at me, waiting for an answer instead of backing down.

I never seen a woman so forthright and headstrong. Looks like I need to come up with a threat that'll make Twinkle mind her mouth, to make her fear me properly, since reminding her I'm a killer didn't do it. Then I come up with the perfect solution—a lie so powerful that it'll make her skinny knees knock together and keep that brazen tongue at bay. "Something just occurred to me, Twinkle. Something so important that you oughta pay heed."

Out of the corner of my eye, I see her turn my way. "Oh yeah, what?"

I give her my meanest son-of-a-bitch stare, no smile on my face, silence. I wait until she's squirming in her seat, eagerly fretting to hear what I got to say. "No matter what you say, I know Bonnie's inside of you, waiting for the deadline same as me. And you might think that will keep you safe, but you're wrong. Because though I once loved Bonnie, I'm sure I can get another gal to keep my bed warm. So you ought to know that if you keep on sassing me, I would just as soon kill you as keep you. I'm good with a tire iron and I ain't afraid to use it. Even if you are the prettiest thing I ever seen."

I turn my head toward the window so she can't see the grin on my face.

For once, Twinkle ain't got nothing to say. Glad to see she's finally minding her manners.

CHAPTER 21

Sunday, May 22nd // 8:58 P.M.

Monroe

After Clyde threatened to kill me if I sassed him again, I shrink down in my seat and stare out the window at the setting sun flickering at me between rows of trees, staying silent. What an ass! Is this how he always was? If he doesn't like someone, he threatens to kill them?

Oh, please. He was only saying that to make you stop talking.

Didn't seem like it to me.

He hates quibbling more than anything. He's actually quite a peace-loving fella.

Right.

I take a deep breath, leaning back on the headrest, trying to make sense of everything Clyde said. He thinks he's the master of the game, but I'm no idiot. My mom used to say that when people are angry, there's an ounce of truth along with a pound of snake venom in their argument. But what part of Clyde's tirade was truth and what part was snake venom? I think of my mom then. *Stay with me, Mom. I need you today more than ever.* A strong breeze makes the truck shake from side-to-side as Clyde grabs the wheel with two hands. *Thanks for the signal, Mom. I knew you wouldn't leave me.*

I get back to thinking about what Clyde said. If Clyde actually did love Bonnie, how could he talk about replacing her so easily? Is there a chance that he just kept her around because she followed him like a lovesick puppy and had sex with him whenever he wanted? I mean, how many girls would go for a life running from the cops? Makes me wonder about Bonnie's final request. Together forever? It sure doesn't sound like that was Clyde's last wish.

How dare you! Clyde's not going to tell you nothing. He's too smart for that. He loved me as much as I loved him. True, not many gals would go on the lam with their men, but it proves I loved him most of all.

I grip the armrest. Having Bonnie know every thought of mine sucks! She's probably right though. Why would Clyde tell me anything? He's manipulating me the same way I'm manipulating him. Everyone knows Bonnie and Clyde's romance is right up there with Romeo and Juliet's. You can see it in all the newspaper clippings—Clyde holding Bonnie in his arms, Bonnie playfully posing with a shotgun at Clyde's chest, all her romantic poems about him. Unless . . .

I stop reminiscing and start replaying exactly what he said.

Every time I said "Clydehopper," he got more and more angry. Could thinking of Bonnie cause him to relax so much that it allows Jack to take over? Bonnie did say Clyde's weakness was sex. Maybe when Clyde thinks about Bonnie, Jack can take over. I bet that's why he wanted me to shut up—because the lights were flashing and Jack was trying to take back his own body!

You're woolgathering, girl. Talking nonsense.

I grin. Sounds like my theory has Bonnie worried. I can't test it now, but as soon as Clyde cools down again, I will. Or should I say as soon as Clydehopper cools down? I search my hair for split ends, thinking about what else Clyde said. He told me he could just as easily kill me as keep me. Was he serious, or was he trying to bulldoze his way into making me do what he wants by threatening me? Anger runs up my spine and lodges in my throat, simmering, building up, until finally I can't take it anymore.

"Just so you know, Clyde, if you did kill me with a tire iron, they'd sentence you to die by the electric chair. We have high-voltage chairs that'll fry your brains in an instant these days."

Instead of being scared, he roars with laughter. "You are one funny gal, Twinkle." He chuckles, shaking his head. "I ain't gonna kill you—I mean, not unless you try and kill me first." He pauses. "You

192

ain't planning to rid the world of me and your sissified girlfriend, Jackie Daniel, in one fell swoop now are you?" He smiles, teasing me.

I bite my lip, trying not to laugh at Clyde's assessment of Jack. "No, Clyde, I'm not going to kill either of you. I might like to strangle you, though."

"Good. Sounds like a game we could play together." He winks, like that's the end of the story. I want to believe that he won't hurt me, but I'm not gullible. He's killed twelve men to my zero, so to be safe, I'm not saying anything else to piss him off. It's crazy but it almost feels like I can trust Clyde when he's probably the least trustworthy guy around, while the opposite is true of Jack. Thinking of bringing Jack back makes my stomach do a flip. What will I do if he comes back and wants to turn himself in again? Threatening him won't work twice.

"Just so you know," Clyde says, imitating me, "we had them same frying pans back in the thirties. Nasty things. Nothing worse than the smell of burning flesh in the morning—stunk up the whole prison for a week. Made it hard to eat."

Grimacing at the thought, I cross my arms over my chest. "Gross. But I'm glad you're afraid of it. You don't want to end up as the breakfast special of the day now, do you, Cowardly Clyde?"

His light-hearted expression darkens. "You're crossing the line again with that name, too. I ain't a good person, that's true. I'm a cheater, a gambler, a killer, and a thief, but there's two things I ain't—a liar or a coward. And no one who knew me would say different."

What am I supposed to say to that—good job, Clyde, you're well-rounded?

You ain't never been in our shoes, sister. Living in filth and starving to death made everyone thieves. Clyde tried to make an honest living, but there wasn't none to be had. He's not lying about being brave, neither. Clyde was the first one in and the last one out on all our bank jobs. Once he took a bullet in the leg trying to stall the coppers because I was hobbling so slow. And he always drove the getaway car. Mostly because he was so good at it, but also so the rest of us could lie down low.

Clyde glances at me. "Well? What you got to say about that?"

Bonnie's testimonial makes me queasy. It just doesn't jibe. Everyone knows that Clyde was a monster who killed a bunch of cops and innocent people, not an overprotective guy who worried about everyone. "I'm not sure what to say. I get it that the Depression sucked and you and Bonnie wanted a better life, but why'd you kill people? How could you look someone in the eye and shoot them? I mean, I feel sad when one of my goldfish dies. That's nothing compared to a human." I shiver, rubbing my arms to get the creepy feeling off of me.

He throws his hands up, shifting higher in his seat. He looks over his shoulder and floors it past three cars. "I didn't want to kill no one neither! I only did it when they was reaching for their gun. When it was going to be me or them." He purses his lips, shakes his head as if he's thinking of things in his head. "Always hated it too. Got to be such a mess. But after a couple of bad turns, I realized there wasn't no way out of it without me and Bonnie ending up dead."

Oh, Clyde! I miss you, baby!

A sense of déjà vu rolls through me. "I get it that one bad thing leads to another. That's exactly how I got myself in trouble. But wasn't there a time, like after your first time in prison, that you thought about going straight and not doing more crimes? I mean, that's where I am right now. Well, where I was." I think about losing my NYU scholarship and my chest gets heavy. I close my eyes and pinch my thighs, willing that horrible ache to go away so I don't cry.

"So you see what I mean then? Sometimes things don't work out the way you want!" He grips the wheel until his knuckles turn white. "You really don't know a damn thing 'bout prison, do you? They are filthy, lawless places that make decent men turn into rabid dogs. I knew if I got caught again, I'd have to kill more cops to avoid going back. More killing—that was what I was running from. If hating prison makes me a coward, then so be it."

I shrug. "You killed people so you wouldn't have to kill? You're not making any sense."

He stares at me, his golden brown eyes searching out mine. He sighs, shaking his head. "I killed 'em, but I didn't want to, don't you see? Because I couldn't go back in. Ever. While I was there, things happened to me that no man should *ever*—" He stops talking, clenching his mouth shut, as if physically forcing himself to stop. "And I was only sixteen!"

He doesn't need to tell me the rest. I can fill in the blanks myself, if all the horrible prison stories I've heard about are true. "I'm sorry, Clyde. You want to talk about it?"

He breathes in and out loudly through his nose, his mouth tight. "No, woman, I don't! There are some things I never want to speak about again." He accelerates and changes lanes, darting around cars, left and right.

I check to make sure my seat belt is tight. "You can chill out, Clyde. There are plenty of things I don't want to talk about either. Just ask me next time. You don't have to yell."

Hush, girl! Don't press no further. Clyde's sister told me that he came out of prison a changed man. Harder, never smiling. He never told me much about those days and I didn't ask.

That surprises me. Maybe they weren't as close as everyone thinks. I mean, if my boyfriend had a terrible secret that made him so sad and angry, I don't think we could keep dating until he shared it with me, let me help him get through it. Scratching a mosquito bite behind my knee, I try to think of something that'll lighten the mood. "So . . . did you date a lot of girls when you were younger?"

"It ain't polite to talk about other girls when you're with one." He smiles, glancing my way. "I'd much rather talk about you, Twinkle. The things you've told me so far makes me think we've been cut from the same cloth. We're more alike than not—you feel it, too?"

Our similarities had crossed my mind, but the fact that Clyde Barrow noticed them too worries me. I force myself to laugh, deciding to take advantage of his mood swing. "Maybe a little. But hey, I was wondering if I can ask you a favor." I shift my legs to get comfortable, making sure my limbs aren't anywhere close to his.

"A favor?" He lifts one eyebrow, a smirk on the edges of his lips. "You need me to find a quiet spot off on the side of the road so we can neck awhile?" He grins at me. "I remember how nice it was kissing you on the bus, before you realized what you was doing. You sure rev my engine. Go on. Admit that you liked it too. I heard you moan."

Wait. Who is he talking to?

A pleasurable reminder jolts through my system at the memory of his soft kisses on my neck. Of course, I can never admit that out loud or I think he really would pull over. "It was more like a grumble. I don't like being touched, remember?"

He lets out another belly laugh. "You ain't still thinking I believe you have a phobia, are you? When are you gonna realize you can't hide things from me, Twinkle?"

His words are like a fist to my gut. How can he know? "What are you talking about?"

"I know when I touch you, Bonnie can talk. There ain't no phobia. You can deny it all you want, but I could see it in your eyes, and hear it in the way you lost your breath, that you liked when I kissed you. If you let your guard down awhile and stop pretending you hate me, I promise that, after an hour with me, you'd be begging for more." He grins widely. "How 'bout it?"

I roll my eyes, laughing at his bravado. "Please. Make me beg for more?"

"Please make you beg for more? Like right now?" he asks, his voice deep and sexy. He gives me a sideways grin. "My pleasure. A girl as fine as you don't have to ask me twice. Let's pull off here and

I'll take care of all your needs right quick." He swerves into the right lane. "I can make up for lost time with my driving."

He's only ribbing you. Don't you believe a word of it.

My heart rate leaps into high gear. "That's not the favor I was going to ask for and you know it."

He snaps his fingers, faking disappointment. "Too bad. But hopefully when all is said and done, we will have us some free time on our hands. But until then, what favor was you wanting?"

"Since we've got a long ride ahead of us and things are scary enough as is, can we both just agree to be ourselves? I'll quit lying to you and you can quit threatening me." I quickly add, "And maybe you can quit talking about us being a couple too. Deal?"

He wasn't talking about you and him! He meant me, you dumb Dora!

He rubs his chin, as if thinking. "I can agree to stop threatening you." He smiles.

I ignore his purposeful avoidance of my last request, deciding to change the topic altogether. "Great. So in the spirit of honesty and having a fresh start, can you tell me about . . ." I pause, desperate to find a topic that won't lead to more romance talk. "Oh, I don't know, the first time you robbed a bank? How did you do it?" I can't believe I just asked Clyde Barrow that. As if he's going to tell me. Think before you speak, Monroe.

He eyes me sideways. "Sure—as soon as you tell me why you threatened Jack Daniel with the wrench. You two get in a rift about something, or did you miss me?"

He turns the radio lower and I realize he's fishing for clues. If I spill some information, maybe he'll trust me and share something he knows in return. "Actually, a little of both," I joke, but realize it's partially true. Jack's constant whining made me even more anxious than I already was. "But mostly because Jack was about to turn us in to the police and I didn't want him to." I leave off the part about Jack's belief that deadline meant the end of Bonnie and Clyde. If

Clyde thought he'd be a goner in the morning, I bet his agenda for today would be radically different.

"Without even trying to escape? What a sissy." He tilts the rearview mirror and looks at himself. "Ugly too. Would probably get me five years just for that."

I smile. "Ha! Jack's good-looking and you know it. And he doesn't have monkey ears like someone else I know."

"How'd you know that?" He looks confused. "You seen pictures of me?"

I don't dare mention the mind movies. "I've seen lots of pictures of you and Bonnie. Movies, too. The *Bonnie and Clyde* movie was my mom's favorite."

I love the picture show! My mama would be so proud!

Proud you were an outlaw who killed and robbed people? I don't think so.

Clyde's eyes get wide. "A movie? Now don't that beat all?" He lets out such a loud, boisterous laugh, that I can't help but laugh too. "Sounds like your ma was pretty taken with me, huh, Twinkle? Maybe you're taking after her, trying to find out my life story and all." He chuckles long and hard. "I sure would like to see that movie sometime. If it's you and me after the deadline, maybe I can accompany you to the picture show. How about it, Miss Twinkle? May I take you for a night on the town? I'm hoping that you have such a nice time, you'll consider giving me a kiss goodnight." He smiles at me then, genuine and sweet.

He's only saying that because he knows it'll be me using your body.

She's probably right. He's definitely a charmer, a guy who knows that flattery wins a girl's heart every time. And stupidly, I keep falling into his trap. As long as I remember this is all a game, I'll be fine. "I'd go with you, but I doubt you'd like the movie. They made you . . . never mind." I wince, wishing I could learn to keep my thoughts to myself for once.

"Made me *what?*"

"Nothing." I smile dismissively. "Forget it."

"I thought you said we was gonna be honest with each other. I want to know."

I close my eyes, rubbing them. "Oh, God. Now don't get mad at me—I'm only the messenger."

"Say it already, girl!"

"Okay, okay. They made it seem like you were . . ." I take a deep breath, wanting to break it to him gently. "Impotent."

"What's that mean—weak? Dumb? Mean? Tell me."

Could this be more awkward? "No. It means you can't get it up in bed."

"Whaaat!?" His face contorts, like he's panic-stricken, before he busts out laughing. "They finally tell my life story, and they lie about the one thing I'm best at? I can't think of nothing lower to do to a man than lying about his manhood. That's Hollywood for you, I guess." He sighs, shaking his head. "Say, does that movie show anything about, you know, me killing some deputies on Easter Sunday in Grapevine, Texas?"

The name of the town makes the words "Grapevine Killings" jump out at me. I remember Jack saying it was a turning point, but I can't remember why. "I've seen the movie a bunch of times, but not since my mom died. What happened again?"

He checks the mirrors, switches lanes. "Was a big mistake, that's all. One that haunts me to this day."

My brain screams *LIAR*, but I keep it to myself. "A *mistake*? Ordering the wrong flavor of ice cream is a mistake. Killing a cop is intentional." I might be gullible, but I'm not stupid.

"It hurts me to hear you say that, but honest to God, it was a misunderstanding. When I yelled, 'take him,' on that hot spring day, I meant that Henry should grab the officer closest to him so we could kidnap him. I did that a lot—kidnap, not kill. But that dumb cluck Henry thought I meant to kill the cop nearest him, so's he did." He shifts in his seat uneasily. "Left me no choice but to shoot mine, too."

He looks over at me, his eyes filled with pain. "Wish you could see it for yourself."

Do it! Touch them slugs and I'll show you!

No! I don't want to see cops being killed.

Yes, you do. I can read your mind, remember? You're dying to find out if he's lying, so go on, touch them. I'll remember that day and you watch it. Then you can judge for yourself.

I take a deep breath. There's no denying she's right about my being curious, but it'd be wrong to watch something so terrible. Still . . . I peek into my purse and unzip the side pocket. For a panicked couple of seconds, I don't see anything in the blackness of my purse.

I'm just checking that the slugs are there, Bonnie. I'm not trying to see what happened.

Oh, okay. You do that. Meanwhile I'll think about the time I ordered a vanilla ice cream cone instead of chocolate. I mean, since you don't want to know and all.

Damn you, Bonnie. Okay fine, yes. I want to see what happened that day.

"I'm going to close my eyes a second," I tell Clyde. "I've got a bit of a headache."

My, my. For all the times you accuse Clyde and me of being liars, turns out you're a pretty good one, too.

Just do it already.

I close my eyes, discreetly reaching into the side pocket. The moment my flesh touches the metal, an image of an old-fashioned car with enormous fenders and a flat right front passenger tire fills my vision. I'm sitting on the grassy shoulder next to the car, wearing a red, calf-length dress. A big white bunny is on the ground next to me, munching on a blade of grass. I reach out and pet him. "Eat all you can, Sonny Boy. Next stop is who knows when." I shield my eyes from the sun, looking at a man with his back to me who squats alongside the car, a tire iron on the ground by his feet.

The rumbling of motorcycles makes me look down the road. Seconds later, two uniformed policemen appear, their gas tanks painted with the words "Texas Highway Patrol." I can't hear what they say over the rumbling of the motors, but one of the patrolmen points at the tire. The owner of the car finally stands and wipes his brow with his forearm. I instantly recognize the greased-back hair and suspenders as those belonging to Clyde. He animatedly goes through the motions of driving and pulling over, apparently telling how the tire blew. He smiles warmly, looking like an average guy who got stuck having to fix a flat.

Clyde shakes his head no, refusing the patrolmen's offer of assistance but they insist, parking their motorbikes ten feet ahead of the car. As they're both removing their helmets, Clyde grabs something off the front seat and turns to speak to someone in the back seat, who I hadn't noticed before. I pull Sonny Boy onto my lap and squint into the car. A badass but completely gorgeous teenage guy nods in response to whatever Clyde told him, before leaning down and grabbing something by his feet. I glimpse the end of a rifle for a split-second before it disappears below the window level.

My stomach lurches. I don't want to watch, but I don't want to miss it, either. I need to know if what Clyde was saying was true, or if history had it all wrong.

As the police officers approach, Clyde raises a hand in greeting. "While it's awful nice of you to stop, I'm sure you have more important business that needs tending to. I can change this flat in no time."

The shorter officer replies, "Horsefeathers! We're happy to lend a hand." He wipes his forehead with a handkerchief, while the other policeman—the taller, older of the two—strolls toward the car, definitely trying to sneak a peek at the inside. I'm halfway to my feet, Sonny Boy clutched in my arms, yelling, "Excuse me, Officer!" but he doesn't look my way. Instead, he continues to creep forward until he's only a foot away from popping his head into the back seat. I'm untangling my skirt from my legs, trying to hustle over and distract the cop, when Clyde yells, "Take him, Henry!" Gunshots from an automatic rifle ring out and I scream. The tall policeman falls to his knees not five feet from me, struck in the throat. The younger one ducks, reaching for his gun. He's too late. "That ain't what I meant!" Clyde yells, pulling out a small handgun he had concealed in his pocket and opening fire. The cop clutches his chest, landing in the first officer's pool of blood. Clyde yells, "Clear out—now!" I step around the two cops—the live one sucking air, groaning in pain. Clyde pulls the car up five feet and I jump into the front seat. The moment I slam the car door, my grip on the slugs relaxes and the image stops.

Oh. My. God.

But you see now what Clyde was telling you? Stupid lug Henry pumped the nosy cop full of lead, so Clyde had no choice but to off the other bleeding heart copper.

What a heartless thing to say, Bonnie, I tell her as I open my eyes. I hold a hand over my own heart, trying to catch my breath. What a horrible, horrible day that was.

"Feeling better already, Twinkle?" He looks down at the dashboard. "We're almost on empty so we'll need to fill up pretty soon. Grab us some supper too, while we're at it. That ought to make you right as rain."

Although my stomach growls in hunger, I'm a bit queasy after what I witnessed. "Sure, but we need to be quick."

"You're preaching to the choir, sister." He points to a blue highway sign advertising restaurants and gas stations that are coming up at the next exit. He licks his lips. "I sure got me a mighty hankering for fried chicken."

"Okay by me," I reply, not that he's asked my opinion. About anything, since we started. I hate how I've become so accustomed to Clyde's rules that I've fallen into an almost comfortable rhythm with this dead bandit. At least he's not racing off to rob another bank or trying to kill me. As long as I'm cooperative, I'm hoping I can come out of this alive.

Of course, if Jack were in control of his own body right now, he'd probably start yelling at me for threatening him with that wrench. He probably wouldn't even give me a chance to explain that I only did it to save our lives. As the prairie landscape whisks past me, part of me begins to worry why Jack hasn't switched back in over four hours. Is it because Clyde is stronger-minded than Jack? The thought saddens me. I need to test the Clydehopper theory soon to see if it brings Jack back. A shiver of fear runs up my back. Before it's too late to bring him back at all.

"I miss my brother Buck," Clyde says, seemingly out of nowhere. He doesn't bother with a turn signal as he speeds toward the off-ramp. "Fried chicken got him killed."

"Seriously?" I half-expect him to laugh and say I'm as dumb as a cow if I believed that. But when I look at him, I notice his lips are pressed together tightly and his shoulders sag.

Clyde nods. "Every time we'd get a bit of cash and hole up somewhere, I'd want fried chicken." His lips curve up in a sad smile. "Buck joked that I had cravings worse than a pregnant woman." He glances at me and I smile back awkwardly, knowing the story is going to eventually take a bad turn. "Anyway, Buck or his wife Blanche would sneak out and order us six fried chicken dinners to go. Bonnie and I stayed back because our pictures were in the papers an awful lot. Turns out the cops was onto how much I fancied chicken."

"Why? What happened?" Anxiety builds in my chest, afraid to hear the rest.

He shrugs, his voice quieter now. "We was staying at the Red Crown Hotel that night, in Missouri. We ordered our meals from the tavern the hotel owned. I'd gotten us a bottle of some fine bourbon too, so we could all relax and have a good time. Twenty minutes later, right when we was all in the middle of supper, bullets came straight through the walls from a hundred different directions. The chicken leg I was eating got shot right out my hand."

"That was close." I wipe my sweaty palms on my skirt.

"Yeah, I got lucky that day, but can't say the same for Buck. When we got up to make a run for it, he got a bullet in the side of his head. Right here." His voice catches as he points to the spot above his ear and he quickly clears his throat.

I clutch my neck, imagining the scene. "How horrible!"

Clyde nods, his knuckles white as he grips the steering wheel. "Yeah, but that ain't the worst of it. The bullet didn't kill him. Somehow we managed to escape, even with Buck's head bleeding like a faucet and Blanche blinded from glass splinters. I drove out of that two-horse town like a madman, speeding so fast and taking crazy turns up on two wheels, making the cops suck my exhaust."

And Jack couldn't even hotwire a car.

Your fella is kind of prissy, ain't he?

He isn't my fella, but yeah.

I shake Bonnie from my mind. "Then what did you do? Did you get away?"

"Yeah. I got a bunch of medical supplies from a pharmacy, then Bonnie spent three days tending to them while I drove. Blanche kept wailing about not being able to see, but Buck? He never complained. We ended up camping out in the car, sleeping in the woods. I'd pour rubbing alcohol into Buck's bullet hole and change his bandages three times a day, but it was no use. The wound started smelling bad. Oozing lots of yellow gunk too. Watching him die nearly killed me at the same time." As we stop for a traffic light, he opens his window and spits. "You know what? I lost my taste for chicken. Let's get something else."

"I lost my taste for eating, period." I hold my arm over my stomach.

The horrendous scene Clyde has described leaves me shaken. Even though I know he and his gang did terrible things to other people and they deserved major payback, I can't bring myself to feel any enjoyment in the idea that he witnessed his brother's grisly death. "I'm sorry about your brother. Sounds like you two were real close—like how I was with my mom. Seeing someone you love die . . ."

I can't finish my sentence. Images of my mom lying in the hospital bed, weak with cancer, whir through my mind—her skin a ghastly white, an oxygen tube up her nose, fluids attached to a post dripping into an IV. A crushing pain hits my chest as I fight not to relive that emotionally crushing last day. Stop it! I tell myself. Stop right now! You've put this behind you now. Don't open this wound—you don't know how deep it goes.

But I can't stop. I remember her asking how I was feeling when I should've been the one asking her! How lame was that? She was the one dying, not me! The pain rushes back like a runaway freight train. A small whimper escapes my lips. *I love you, Mom. I'm so sorry I wasn't a better listener in the end. I miss you every single day.*

"Thinking about your ma?" Clyde asks quietly, as if he, too, can read my mind.

I glance over, his eyes filled with concern. Which is exactly what I *didn't* need. I put both feet up on the dashboard, barefoot now from the four-hour drive. "Yeah, she was sick for a long time," I tell him, shrugging, trying to swallow the guilt in my throat. "Breast cancer. I was fifteen." I think about my dad then, knowing how much pain he went through, too. How he tried to help me and my sisters, but all of us were so lost without Mom, we had to grieve in our own ways.

He clucks his tongue, shakes his head. "Sad you lost your mama so young. That's the worst pain a child can have. I loved my mother with all my heart. I can't imagine—"

"Stop," I manage to squeak out, despite the huge lump in my throat.

He continues as if he doesn't hear me, "—how awful that must have been for a young girl to lose her mama at the age she needs her most. I'm really sorry, Twinkle."

And that's it. His kindness punctures a hole into some forbidden fragile boundary I never knew existed, the place I've kept my emotions stockpiled so as not to have to visit them again. "Thanks." A whimper escapes my lips, so I do my best to turn it into a cough.

"Aw, girl. Let it out. Tell me what happened," he says gently, causing more stress fractures in my Wall of Denial.

Leaks threaten to sprout everywhere. I bite my lip to keep from crying. Because once this wall comes down, I don't know what will happen. The car slows, pulls to a stop. I look up and see that we're on a residential street, out of the glaring beams of the streetlight. The oxygen in the car escapes a moment later, making me fight for each breath. "What are—*gulp*—you doing?"

"Shh. Nothing." Seconds later, he unbuckles his seat belt and faces me. "Just taking a little break is all."

I shake my head violently. "No—*gulp*—we have no time." My chest tight with pain, I know now I'm facing a full-out anxiety attack—the kind that sent my dad rushing me to the hospital. I need to relax so I can breathe.

"I ain't moving 'til you're better, Twinkle." He reaches out and pushes my hair away from my face in one quick motion, apparently catching Bonnie off-guard because she stays silent.

His one tiny gesture of kindness detonates that wall. Two years of bottled-up sadness erupt from me and tears spring from my eyes. I wipe them on the inside of my shirt—first my right eye, then my left—and then when it seems impossible to keep up, I close my eyes and sob loudly, keeping my shirt up over my eyes so Clyde can't see what an ugly psychotic crybaby I am.

I'm dying to tell him that I'm fine, that I'm always fine. That I am *not* a girl who cries. Which is ridiculous, given that I'm crying my guts out and can't stop.

"My sweet, sweet girl. Look at me," he whispers, tugging gently at my lacy shirt sleeve. When Bonnie doesn't call out to him, it makes me wonder if it's skin-to-skin contact that lets her speak aloud. I look into his eyes and he says, "I'm here, kitten. Tell me all about it."

Stop feeling sorry for yourself, tramp!

I ignore Bonnie, taking several deep breaths, at last relaxing into a hiccupping mess. My lungs open and I can breathe. I begin my story by describing in aching detail how much I loved my mom. How funny, pretty, and smart she was. How she loved me unconditionally and was always there for me. And finally, how the nasty disease withered her up into a shriveled bony nothing, yet she never complained—exactly like his brother Buck.

He listens, nodding, occasionally murmuring some consoling words. I apologize for my breakdown, explaining that I've kept those emotions locked inside of me ever since her death. He relays the story about his own mother then, how she fretted over him, begging him to go straight but always "happier than a sheared sheep in July" to see him whenever he could arrange it. I smile at his crazy expressions, stupidly amazed at how much he loved his mom too. I guess we do have more in common than I thought. That's when it hits me. What the hell am I doing? Spilling my guts and delaying our trip is the last thing I should be doing.

I pull it together. What troubles me most of all is that riding on top of the wave of emotions is something bigger, something scarier than grief—affection. I take a final, deep breath and with it, the horrible pain in my chest leaves, purged from my body. "Thanks, Clyde. I had no idea how much was bottled up inside of me." I smile at him. "I'm better now. We should go."

"We should, but not just yet," he says, sliding closer to me. "Something I have to do first."

I look at his eyes filled with such warmth for me. Every cell in my body wants me to grab on to him and kiss him, but I know that the moment his skin touches mine, Bonnie will blab my plan to complete a ritual to get rid of him at the deadline. That plan is my ace in the hole, the one secret I still have that's safe. "Clyde—don't," I warn, pressing my shoulder up against the window, fumbling for the handle. If he touches me, I'm jumping out of the car.

"Just trust me, okay?" He unbuckles my seat belt, his hand brushing ever so softly against my thigh, sending an electric current zipping through my body. Wanting to kiss him is wrong on so many levels. And yet I do.

"I-I'm sorry. I can't." I finally look down to physically see the handle, which is all the time Clyde needs to move in even closer. He wraps his arms around me and pulls me tight to his chest. My internal alarm goes into panic mode. I squirm to get free, but he's too strong.

Bonnie blurts out, "Clyde! Tell her it's me you want. I need to hear you say it!"

Instead of replying, Clyde gently kisses the top of my head, then my cheek, and finally tilts my face toward his. He wipes the last bit of my tears with his thumbs. "I don't rightly know how to say this, but I've really taken a shine to you." He gazes at me, his golden eyes melting into mine. "Every second I'm with you, I like you even more."

My heart beats out of control. Is he talking to me or to Bonnie? I stop fighting and listen.

A small grin appears on his lips. "I love how you laugh, how you're so smart, even how you're not afraid to speak your mind. Even though I was raised to believe that a woman needs to mind what her man tells her to do, I'm coming around to the idea that it's better when we're true partners. So while I'm hungering for a kiss, it's only worth it if you want to kiss me back."

My heart races full-speed, along with my emotions. Everything about the idea of a partnership between us is wrong. When I open my mouth to tell him that, despite his sweet declaration, I absolutely should not—cannot—kiss him, Bonnie's shrill voice butts in. "Who are you talking to, Chestnut? Me or this two-bit hussy? Because if you think—"

Gazing into Clyde's eyes, I see his pained expression as he ignores Bonnie and waits for my answer. Even though he has all of my invariables, including being insanely handsome, I tell myself that I'm going to kiss him solely to guarantee my future. Knowing that I'm probably sealing my destiny to go to Limbo for a very long time, I nod. Clyde's face relaxes into a warm smile and he covers my lips with his, pulling me into a passionate kiss, and best of all, drowning out Bonnie's whiny pleas.

CHAPTER 22

Clyde

While I sat there listening to Twinkle tell me about her mama, all I could do was watch her pretty green eyes water up, but inside, I was dying to comfort her. I knew if I held her, Bonnie would start begging and pleading for me to reassure her that I loved her best. And while it was true once, I ain't sure I can rightly say that no more. Bonnie buttered my bread for two years, but why settle for bread when I can have that, plus a whole fried chicken and dessert with Twinkle?

So I listened and twiddled my thumbs, keeping my hands off of her when all's I wanted to do was draw her close to me. My heart swole big as a house when she tole me she ain't never shared that story with no one before—not even her gal pals. I can't recall a time I ever wanted to kiss anyone as badly as I wanted to kiss Twinkle right then. My heart ached to show her, not just tell her, how I was feeling. And that's when I decided I had to kiss her—even though I knew that doing that could allow Jack Daniel to rise from his slumber and railroad his way back in. Knowing that I was risking everything to kiss Twinkle, I did it anyway.

Turns out Twinkle wanted to kiss me as much as I did her. Bonnie too, I think, but I cleverly stifled her by making my move on Twinkle. The moment my lips met hers, my heart felt like it could burst out of my chest. I wanted to ravage her, to kiss her until we lost control, but we didn't have time. But it was sweet while it lasted—our mouths gently meeting—not awkward, like first kisses often are. After that one amazing, heart-stopping kiss, Twinkle gently pushed me away.

No matter. Now I know how she feels about me and that's all I need.

"I've been dying to do that all day," I say, stroking her cheek. "Can't I have one more?"

"Clyde Chestnut Barrow," she snarls in response, her top lip pulled back like a rabid coon. "Are you two-timing me, or is romancing this know-nothing tramp part of your plan? I need to hear the truth right this minute or we're through!"

I back away fast, regretfully tearing my hands from Twinkle's curvy hip. As much as I was enjoying Twinkle's kiss, Bonnie's threat reminds me I've gotten myself in a quandary.

Twinkle must think she made a mistake because her face gets redder than a radish. When I keep quiet, Twinkle says softly, "She's got a point. I'd kind of like to know, too."

I take a deep breath and move back into the driver's seat, recalling how much of a jealous streak Bonnie had. I get a cannonball-sized pain in my chest knowing how much that kiss must have hurt Bonnie's feelings. That gal had spunk and she always had my back. My mind goes back and forth between the two gals, making me dizzy. Am I making the right choice here?

Lights flash in my head like a goddam circus and I curse myself for being weak as a puppy. I start the engine up, picturing my old farm dog Jezebel I had growing up so as to get my mind off of my former moll. "Don't worry your pretty little heads about it. I got it all figured out."

Twinkle crosses her arms over her luscious breasts, signaling that she don't like my answer, but for once, she stays quiet. Thank the Lord for small favors, because if pressed, I don't think she'd be too tickled by the news that I got a Plan A and a Plan B. I pull onto the street, racing to the corner. I ain't about to tell either moll that the plan I'll go with will depend on which gal will be the one to help me stick around. Above making headlines, above getting my own museum, and most of all, above romance, is staying alive past morning.

Plan A is to take over Jack completely and have Twinkle by my side. A shiny new gal for my shiny new life. But until I figure out the rules about how this works, I need to keep my weakness a secret. Otherwise, Twinkle could let Bonnie start yammering at me right at the deadline, which could allow Jack back in charge. I suspect Twinkle already knows that my weakness is thinking about Bonnie, but I can't ask her straight out or it'll tip her off. As much as I hate lying to her, I need to plant a little reminder in Twinkle's mind that smelling something strong is what makes me change.

If I can't get Twinkle to spill the beans about what'll happen at the end, I've got no choice but to resort to Plan B—convincing Bonnie that wooing Twinkle was all part of my game. Shouldn't be too hard. Bonnie's the kind of woman who needs a man to tell her what to feel, how to think—and I'm that man. A streak of light no bigger than a wink of an eye whizzes past my brain, then dies.

"You sure had your share of heartaches," I tell Twinkle, hoping to get her back into a sharing mood. "Sad that your mama left us early, but it sure explains why you're tougher than an armadillo."

She raises her eyebrows. "Do I say thank you to that?"

I laugh. "I reckon so. I don't know about you, but losing Buck changed me. I wasn't no angel before, but afterward, I did things I normally wouldn't, trying to rid myself of the guilt and the sadness. Ain't no excuse. Just saying I wasn't in my right mind for a while after, you know?"

She nods slowly, her eyebrows wrinkled up. "I never thought of it that way, but my first arrest was only a few months after my mom died. Stole the brand and color of the lipstick she used to wear. Was holding it, thinking of her, and just walked out with it. That one was an accident. But it gave me such a rush, I thought, let me try that again! So I stole an expensive bottle of perfume, and that's when I got caught." She sighs. "Second time indirectly had to do with my mom, too. Was at the after-homecoming party, thinking about how much I wished she could have seen me in my dress, so I did a few shots to numb the pain. And then a few more until finally, when the cops busted the party, I was passed out on the couch."

"Strange, ain't it? How we both got ourselves in trouble thinking about someone that we was missing?"

"Is that when you, um, started killing people? After Buck died?" Her voice goes up at the end, like she ain't sure she should be asking about stuff like that.

I shift in my seat, figuring it can't hurt for her to know. "Nah. Sorry to say, I'd already killed a few by then." I pause, adding, "But only when I felt I had to. But after Buck was gone, I got ruthless, trying to find a way to get rid of the pain in my chest. I wanted to punish everyone, especially the Texas prison system. Goddam guards beat us, stuffed us in sweatboxes outside on hundred-degree days, hoping we'd die in there. Did even worse stuff—stuff I can't talk about." Before I can stop myself, I picture the first guy I killed, a guard named Crowder, and the things he did to me when I was just a babe in prison, so young I still had peach fuzz on my chin. I ball up my fist and punch the seat next to me. Fucking Crowder—nastiest piece of lowlife scum that ever walked the earth.

"What's wrong?" Twinkle fiddles with her necklace nervously.

"Nothing." I veer in front of a red sports car, narrowly sliding between two cars before hitting the gas. I picture his ugly face, his gray sweat-stained undershirt, his pants around his ankles, pinning my scrawny sixteen-year-old arms down like they was toothpicks. I grip the wheel harder, trying with all my might to block out the rest of those scenes, day after day, while the other guards sat around and played cards, laughing. Cocksuckers. I swerve around cars left and right, doing forty, then fifty, blind with anger.

Twinkle grabs the armrests, craning her neck to look behind us. "What's wrong, Clyde? Are the cops after us?"

A slow-moving car exits the mall parking lot, pulling into my lane.

"Watch out!" she screams, covering her face.

I swerve around Granny with an inch to spare. The tires squeal and the seat belt bites my shoulder. "Have you ever felt what it's like when you ain't in control and no one comes to help?"

Twinkle grips the dashboard, holding on tight. "Yes, right now!" she wails. "If there weren't cops before, there will be now! Please, Clyde, stop this!"

Her words wake me up. She's right. I need to get control of myself. I brake hard and swerve into an empty filling station on my right, so fast that the truck hitches up on two wheels for a short stretch before hitting the ground. I get the truck under control and pull into a spot alongside a pump at the far end, too juiced up to drive another moment longer. I throw the pickup into park and lean my head forward on the steering wheel, panting heavily.

"What was that? Were you trying to get us killed?" she screeches, staring at me.

"Not us, a memory." I shut off the engine and get out, slamming the door. I kick the tire twice and rest my arms over the back hatch, trying to cool off. If Crowder was in front of me now, I'd pound his face in with the shovel, stab his eyes with the weed puller, and cut off his manhood with the shears. I let him off way too easy when I slugged him with that lead pipe, killing him with a single blow.

Makes me realize I lied to Twinkle earlier. I did enjoy killing him.

Twinkle gets out, staring at me with rattlesnake eyes, lids half-closed and waiting to pounce. "I'm buying food and going to the bathroom. When I come back, I'm driving."

"Afraid not," I say, teasing her.

"You still pulling that 'you're the boss' stuff again?" She puts her hands on her hips, all tough-like. "You're not the only one who likes speed and power, you know. Trust me when I say that when I get behind the wheel, I'll drive like the devil."

Hearing her talk like that makes me like her even more. I stare at her, smiling. "The devil, huh? You and me truly was cut from the same cloth, you know that? We're both hot-headed, hot-blooded, forthright, and smart as whips. Really good-looking, too." I step closer to her, grinning. "You still ain't driving, but how's about another kiss to last me until you get back?"

"You make me crazy!" She storms off toward the market, without kissing me, but I see a smirk on her lips.

"Crazy about me, I bet!" I call out, teasing.

"Nope!"

I shake my head, smiling. That girl got more sass than a blister beetle. Good thing I saw in her eyes and in her kiss how she felt about me earlier, or I'd be worried right now.

Taking a deep breath to settle my nerves, I look around for a car that we can trade up for. After checking out the five cars that are here, none of 'em look "old" like Twinkle called it. It's risky keeping the pickup, but there ain't another option, lessing I steal one that's running. Course, we've driven near five hours, all the way to Mt. Vernon, Illinois, in this truck without a hitch, so maybe I'm fretting about nothing. Besides, it'll be hard to see the license tag with no light on it. I kneel down and untwist the two tiny light bulbs that shine on the numbers. There. Hopefully there won't be no moon out tonight neither. When I look at the sky, I see a lightning bolt way off in the distance. And I smile. Coppers don't like to be out driving in the rain.

I stick the hose into the gas spout and squeeze the handle, but nothing comes out. I try again, but the gas line is either dry or broken. A dull brown car pulls up across from me. I watch a scrawny white-haired gent inch his way out of the car, take a plastic card from his wallet, and then slide it through the slot on the pump. So that's what I need. I grab Jack Daniel's wallet, flip it open, and lo and behold, what do I see but a shiny silver card smiling up at me.

I did exactly as the old coot did. I try again and this time, it works. The numbers on the pump fly so fast they make me dizzy. My stomach gets an ache watching the price go up, until I remember that Jack Daniel's footing the bill. While it's filling up, I use the time to take a piss in the bushes. When I'm zipping up, Twinkle hustles toward me with a brown bag in her arm.

And she's not smiling.

My heart sinks. "What's wrong, woman?"

"Please tell me you didn't use Jack's credit card to get gas." She stares at me, her bright green eyes filled with worry.

"A silver plastic card with numbers on it?" I ask, not admitting nothing until she tells me why she wants to know.

"Damn it!" She looks over her shoulder, scanning the street with her eyes. "If they're looking for you, for us, the cops might be tracking its usage." She grabs her forehead like her head hurts. "I just realized. Maybe our phones, too."

"What? How?" I freeze, wanting answers.

"Remember the robot satellite system I told you about? The one for the GPS maps? Well, the cops can use that system to pinpoint where we are. We need to turn the power off right now." She holds up her phone and pushes a button before tossing it back into her purse. "And the credit card transactions go through a computer and they can find us that way too."

I don't understand all she's saying, but I know it ain't good. I dig into my pocket and pull out my communicating device. "Here. Do mine."

She grabs it from my hand, our skin touching briefly. I hear Bonnie yelp, "Hey!"

Twinkle rolls her eyes, slides a button on the side of Jack Daniel's phone, and hands it back to me—this time making sure our skin don't touch. "And no more credit cards, either."

"Agreed. Let's go." We turn toward the truck, but to my surprise, Twinkle races to the driver's side and leaps in behind the wheel.

"What are you doing?" I stand next to the open door. "We ain't got time to mess around."

"I ain't messing round," she says, imitating me, a Texas-sized drawl dripping from her lips.

My stomach drops. "Bonnie?"

She laughs. "Nah, I'm just teasing you. But come on, please? I want to drive a while."

I trot out my proper Northerner talk, making sure to pronounce my endings. "Now is not the time. Please take your cute little bee-hind out of the driver's seat, Miss Twinkle."

Her mouth drops open. "How did you do that? I couldn't hear your accent at all!"

I grin. "I'm mighty talented, Twinkle. I tole you that before. Wait. I *told* you that before." I hold my hand out, as to assist her out of the car. "Now please don't argue with me for once."

"What happened to the true partners thing you said before?" She eyes me squinty-like, waiting for my answer.

"I meant it. It's just that now's not the right time—please?"

She smiles. "Fine. But at some point I really do want to drive, okay?" She sets the bag down on the floor between the two seats and gets out, her breasts brushing my chest as she scoots past me, sending a chill up and down my body.

She bites her lip, grinning. "Oops, sorry."

"I ain't." I can't stand being this close without kissing her. I put my arm up, blocking her off from leaving. "About that kiss." She's so close her breath is warm on my cheek.

"I want to, but I don't know if we should," she says, looking up at me with those green eyes that draw me in like a moth to a flame. "I mean, Bonnie got awfully mad and I'm—"

And just like last time, I lean in and kiss her before I have any more reminders that could cause me trouble. Her tongue is spicy hot as it teases mine, slowly, playfully—so different than any other girl. We kiss for several seconds, the heavenly scent of cinnamon rousing all my senses—which makes me realize once and for all that smelling something strong don't have nothing to do with letting Jack back in.

Still, I'm careful not to let my body press close to hers, lest I get carried away. I'm about to end the kiss so we can get back on the road, when her hands reach up around my back and pull me closer. I know precious time is escaping, but kissing her is so interesting and new, a few seconds more won't hurt. My fingers stroke her neck, across her shoulder blades, and end at her shoulders, where I give a gentle squeeze to signal that we need to make tracks.

Apparently that's not enough for Twinkle—she wants more.

She puts a hand on each of my butt cheeks and forcefully pulls my hips forward into hers. She moans, moving slowly in circles and twisting her head to kiss me first left, then right, her tongue flitting in and out of my mouth fast, the same way that—I stop, pull away, confused. Twinkle told me that Bonnie could only speak through her when I touched her, but that she controlled her own body. But something ain't right with that last kiss because those moves was exactly like Bonnie's—fast and urgent.

"Bonnie?" I ask, stepping back, a lump in my throat the size of a gopher. "Is that you?"

Flashing lights start up behind my eyes, so I fight back with my mind. I'm stronger than Jackie Daniel, I just . . . have to . . . hold on. A taste as vile as death itself comes into my mouth, so I turn my head and spit onto the ground.

"You have to ask?" She reaches for my belt. "How's about we start up where we left off."

I look into Twinkle's eyes and see the pain of not being in control of her own body. I grab on to both her wrists and peel them off me before Jack Daniel takes over, too. Before I let go, Bonnie yammers, "Don't let go, baby. I'm getting stronger each second you're holding on to me. She's been keeping secrets from you!"

"Is that right?" Knowing Bonnie's right here, ready to pitch woo along with anything else I tell her to do, should make me as happy as the day I got freed from Eastham Prison. But instead, I'm feeling out of sorts, maybe even a little sad. I guess I've taken an even more powerful shine to Twinkle than I thought. I know we need to get back on the road and fast, but not before I hear what Bonnie has to say about what's really in Twinkle's heart.

Bonnie, or maybe it's Twinkle, squirms in my grip. "The little tramp figured out that it's our own strengths and weaknesses that let us flow into each other. Running her mouth is her weakness, but you're my strength, Honey Bear. Turns out that the longer you hold me, the stronger I get. So you'd better not let go, y'hear?" If I keep on wasting time, I could miss my opportunity to switch places with Jack Daniel forever. As I start leading her toward the passenger side of the truck, Twinkle tries to dig her feet into the ground, fighting me. Like coaxing a sick child into the doctor's office, I push and tug her.

The white-haired gent walks toward us with a sourpuss face. "Everything okay?"

"Yup! She done twisted her ankle," I call out, with a friendly wave. "She'll be fine."

After he nods his approval, I turn to see Twinkle's mouth opening and closing like a dying fish. She's aching to talk I bet, to tell me she hates what I'm doing to her. My heart aches because it feels like I'm betraying Twinkle. Course, if she's been fibbing, I need to know the truth. "So what else did Twinkle tell you?"

Bonnie prattles on, "She knows your weakness is me, Sugar, so stay strong so Jack don't take over. If we're there at the deadline, we can be the ones staying. The tour man told her so."

Lights flash behind my eyes—bigger, more powerful. Every second hanging on to Bonnie takes every ounce of strength to not relax my mind. Batting away images of Bonnie and me together is near impossible, but I can't let go of her, not yet, not until I know the whole truth of what's to come. "What are you saying? How?"

"She's going to do a ritual, hoping to get rid of us!" Twinkle pulls and twists to get out of my grasp. I close my eyes and think about my dog Jezebel again, trying to fight off Jack Daniel. Beams of light like a reporter's flashbulb flutter through my mind. *Go away!* I roar, hoping to scare Chickenshit off, but the lights don't stop. "What else—quick! I'm fading fast!"

"Some half-dead folks think there's a way we can trade places with them—permanently! Please baby, figure that out so it can be you and me together again—just like the old times." Twinkle really kicks in then, squirming and twisting more than a worm on a fishing hook, but after that shocking news, I need to know more.

"Trade places altogether? How? Did they say?"

"No, not even sure it's true, but this tramp I'm in is worried about it, that much I know. But I ain't saying any more until you swear it's me you love. If you don't stop—"

As Bonnie rambles on, I shake my head in awe. Twinkle is one smart schemer. I sure could use a gal by my side who's not only clever, but can keep secrets—though I'm mad as a hornet that she was keeping 'em from me. Can't exactly blame her though, since I tole her it's every man and woman for himself.

"—you'll be sorry."

Course, as much as she's complaining right now, there ain't no moll more loyal than Bonnie. She'd sit in the car in the blazing heat, honking when she saw me running out of the bank so I'd know where she was. Anytime I asked, she'd rub my sore feet or fetch me a cool drink. How is a guy supposed to choose when one gal satisfies his heart *and* his mind, but the other worships you so much she'd do anything for you?

The decision is a tough one for sure, but the heart knows what it wants and there ain't no use in trying to persuade it otherwise. "Don't worry, darlin'. I'm taking you with me in the end," I lie. Before I know what hit me, Twinkle leans against the truck and aims her two feet squarely in the center of my chest. She pushes me back with such force that I lose my balance, making me lose hold of her wrists. Hot damn, that girl is stronger than a Brahma bull. The sky explodes in a raging storm of light, and I feel like I'm being lifted up into a funnel cloud.

On my way down to the cement, I know for certain which dame I want to be with.

It's a shame I'll never get to tell her.

CHAPTER 23

Sunday, May 22nd // 10:12 P.M.

Monroe

Clyde lies on the ground near my feet, slow to sit up. Judging from the heavy thud I heard when his head hit the ground, I'm hoping he sustained a blow strong enough to keep him at bay while I decide what to do. He groans, gripping the back of his skull, his eyes closed. I scurry sideways to grab a hefty chunk of tree branch off the ground to use as a makeshift weapon, not wanting to turn my back on him. There's a jagged end of the branch where it split from the tree, which I can use as a dagger if he tries to grab on to me again.

I glance around, wondering what to say if a bystander asks if I need help. Turns out I don't have to worry about that. For now, we're the only ones here. Maybe it's better that way. I don't need any witnesses if I end up having to defend myself. The thought of stabbing Clyde turns my already queasy stomach into an even bigger jumble.

You stupid, stupid tramp! Get back over there and help him up!

I'm not touching him again, you idiot!

My brain is still reeling from the revelation that Bonnie's ability to control my limbs kicks in the longer Clyde touches me. I felt her gaining strength with each passing second—first my hands, then my arms, and near the end, my feet. If he held on any longer, would I have been able to stop her from heading into the back seat to heat things up even further?

Would you have wanted to stop? my foggy brain asks.

Shut up, I scream. What's wrong with me? Not only is he a half-dead gangster, but he's a skilled liar who probably doesn't give a flip about me—only about staying alive.

That's right. Now get your dirty thoughts off of my man, you scheming little whore.

222

Geez, Bonnie, chill out! I just said I don't want to be with him, so relax!

I look toward the mini-market, relieved that the cashier has his nose in a book, too busy to notice what's going on out here. What will I do if Clyde drags me into the truck, clamps onto me, and doesn't let go? I won't even be able to make a run for it in the end. And if the rumor is true they actually can trade places with us, where will I be? Lying in Bonnie's grave somewhere? Or up in the waiting place, lingering about until the end of time?

Panic rises up my chest and lodges in my throat. I picture Bonnie and Clyde using our bodies and going back on the run. Black spots appear on the edges of my vision and a high-pitched whine, like the sound of cicadas in the summer, fills my ears. An overwhelming sensation of needing to vomit blindsides me, so I hold on to the truck's mirror and lean forward. Having not eaten in over eight hours, all I manage is a few dry heaves. I stay like this for a few more seconds, waiting until the feeling passes. Slowly, I stand up. My head pounds in unison with the throbbing of my heart, as thunder rumbles overhead.

While confident I won't faint from lack of circulation, I can't guarantee I won't blackout from pure disgust—of myself, of what I've brought on to me and Jack, and of having a dead woman inside me who wants my body for herself.

Too late now, chickadee.

Clyde finally opens his eyes and looks at me, moaning quietly. I feel equal parts victorious and horrified that I put him there. I take a deep breath, deciding to ask about his intentions straight out. "Who were you talking to when you said that you'd take them with you in the end, Clyde? Me or Bonnie?"

My pulse races while I wait for his answer, hoping he's going to say my name. And even if he does, why would I believe him? I'm not one of those gullible girls who believes everything a guy whispers to her. I don't even find badass guys attractive, so what's wrong with me? It's completely ridiculous and illogical. Still, I barely breathe, not wanting to miss his reply.

If he says Bonnie, I'm screwed. I'll need to run for it and hope I'm still alive tomorrow.

If he says my name, I'm not sure what he expects from me, but at least I'll have a chance.

Clyde removes his hand from the back of his head and looks at it, as if checking for blood, his face contorted in pain. Groaning, he pushes himself up, dusting off his palms. He watches me silently as I watch him—unsure if I should run away, cry, or scream for help. Clyde shuffles forward, glaring at me, as the first raindrops begin to fall.

"Don't touch me," I warn, holding up the stick, "or I'll stab you in the throat." My nerves are on such high alert now, I bet I could do it, too. A whimper of anguish escapes my mouth as hot tears lick my cheeks. What am I saying? No matter who's in charge of the body, this is a living, breathing teenage boy in front of me who deserves none of this, and whom I need alive and well with me at the deadline so we can end this nightmare. But I don't throw my weapon away just yet.

I can wound him without killing him if I need to.

"You think I'm scared of you, Monroe?" Clyde asks between gritted teeth.

"Stay back!" I raise the pointy branch, realizing I've made a huge mistake. It's obvious Clyde meant to take Bonnie with him, not me. My options are now extremely limited—fight to the finish or die trying.

Wait a second.

Did he just call me Monroe?

He throws his hands up, his face reddening by the second. "Why'd you do it? What if I wasn't able to come back, huh? What then?" He grabs a shovel out of the back of the pickup truck. "Maybe I should just bash your head in right now, like you threatened to do to me. What do you think of that?"

My knees buckle. I back up, leaning against the truck for support. "Jack? Is that you?" The fluttering of a million moths in my gut brings the queasy feeling right back. Is this really Jack in front of me, or is this Clyde using his Northern accent to trick me? "How did you—"

"Come back? I'm not telling you." He glares at me, clenching and unclenching his fists. "Because you'll just use it to turn me back into Clyde, you fucking traitor."

"No, don't say that! I'm sorry, Jack. I didn't know what else to do!" I lower the branch, but still I don't throw it away. Judging by his anger, I'm not sure who the enemy is anymore. "If you had gone to the police, we'd be sitting in jail right now. Then Bonnie and Clyde would hang around for the rest of our lives while we sat there doing nothing to stop them. Surely you believe that now, don't you?"

He starts pacing. "Only thing I see now is that you're a selfish liar, only concerned about yourself. I told you I didn't want to do it and now I'm in even worse trouble than before."

His words are bullets to my heart. He's obviously so pissed at me that he cannot see my side of things whatsoever. Even so, I'm convinced that we still need to be together in the end to make this work. And even though Clyde can be completely compelling and charismatic, he and Bonnie already had lives to live and they blew it. Jack and I didn't. At least not yet.

"No, that's not true, Jack!" I plead. "I want to save both of us. Please don't be like this."

"Like what—human?" He rakes his hair with his fingers. "Look at it from my point of view, will you? Here I was, driving a stolen bus—which I now realize makes no sense whatsoever—and when I'm trying to convince you that we made a mistake, you threaten me with a wrench." He tosses the spade in the back of the truck, resulting in a loud *clunk!* "What the hell, Monroe? And then, not only that, but you did nothing to help me come back. You knew if he thought about Bonnie, it'd give me a chance to take back my life. But instead, you let him kiss you! How could you do that? He's a fucking dead gangster!"

Was once dead, but not for long.

Jack stares at me, waiting for an answer. He's deeply hurt, understandably so, but we're wasting precious time. I need him to calm down and forgive me so we can make up for lost time. "I only did what I did because I was afraid we'd stay half-dead forever, like Mr. Johnson said. Or worst of all, have them trade places with us altogether. But seriously, Jack, I'm glad you're back. Please just trust me on this, okay?" When I look into Jack's dark brown eyes, I remember sitting with him on the couch at Kyle's party, trying unsuccessfully to pick me up.

"How can I ever trust you again, Monroe? I couldn't hear what you guys said to each other while I was locked up inside my own head, but you looked pretty happy the entire ride. Oh wait, except for when you were crying your eyes out, like you were pouring your guts out to him. What was *that* all about?"

I can't deny that I was getting used to, okay maybe even enjoying, Clyde's constant flirtatious remarks. I'm sure it was fueled in part by the emotional connection of two people running from the police together. But discovering that this infamous outlaw had a soft side would make any girl's resolve to stay away from him falter, at least a little bit.

"It was all an act, Jack." I'm desperate for him to let go of his questions and believe, once and for all, that we need to get to Gibsland together or we fail.

"So you were pretending to make out with him just now? You even grabbed him and pulled him close, like you were ready to get it on in the back seat!" He eyes me suspiciously.

"That was Bonnie taking over my body—I didn't want to kiss him!" I'm glad Jack doesn't know the pounding in my heart, the flood of emotions inside me while I kissed Clyde. The intensity I felt during those two heart-stopping kisses will have to remain my little secret.

You little trollop! Clyde was kissing me, not you!

Go away! I scream at Bonnie. Clyde's gone now, so leave me alone.

I glance at the digital clock mounted above the gas station prices. "But it's all over anyway. We need to get back on the road now, or we'll never make it on time. It's past ten."

Jack shakes his head. "I'm not going with you, Monroe, and I don't think you should go, either. Hear me out and then decide." He looks down at his hands and then back at me. "After Asshole took over my body, I fermented for four solid hours. Gave me time to do some thinking of my own. And you know what? I've come to the conclusion that Bonnie and Clyde are mind-fucking us. They want us to go to Gibsland because that's the only way they can take us over."

I want to believe him, to give up and go home, but I now believe with every fiber of my being that doing so would be the end of me, of us. "No, Jack. That's not true. Remember the warnings from the Half-Dead Society? We thought this through already and there's no other way. It has to be tomorrow or never." The high whiny buzz of panic starts to squeal in my ear as my plan unravels more quickly than I can repair it. "Think about all the clues Milo had—the G, the numbers, the deadline. It all adds up."

"They mind-fucked Milo too! I mean, they're ghosts, right? They can do anything they want." He slides his hands in his pockets and leans against the truck, legs crossed at the ankles. If I needed convincing that this was truly Jack and not Clyde faking it, Jack's no-urgency stance is a dead giveaway. "How about we go to the police and confess while they're still in us? Maybe they can do a blood test or something to prove it."

I throw my arms up in the air. "A blood test? That's ridiculous!"

He stands up straight. "More ridiculous than stealing cars and driving fourteen hours on a whim?" Jack opens the truck door and puts a foot up on the ledge. "Look, I'm not going with you. Your calling me a pussy was a wake-up call to grow a set of balls. It's time I used them." He hops into the truck and slams the door. "Get in, Monroe. Let's get this over with."

The mosquito buzz in my ear has now become a 747 at takeoff. I leap onto the foot ledge, pleading with him face to face. "Please, Jack. I beg you. We'll turn ourselves in tomorrow!"

He starts the truck. "No, *now*! This is what I think will save our lives. Get in or get off."

Tears well up in my eyes, as the first raindrops begin falling. "You're making a mistake."

"No, you are. I'll serve time, but then I'll be free to live the rest of my life. Maybe you should do the same." He leans down under the steering column and hotwires the ignition. "At least I learned one thing from Asshole. Last chance, Monroe."

Get your butt in that truck right this minute! Don't let him go. We need Clyde!

I step down and pat the truck. "Good luck, Jack. I hope at least one of us is right."

"Yeah, me too, Monroe. Sucks it has to end like this." He gives me one last wistful smile before driving off toward the road. Three seconds later, he turns and accelerates away from me.

As sure as I was ten seconds ago, I realize I don't want to do this alone. I race to the street, hoping he was bluffing. Please come back, Jack. *Change your mind, change your mind* I chant until his taillights are two red dots in a tunnel of blackness. Knowing he's gone suddenly makes breathing an Olympic feat. I look up at the sky, knowing that unless I'm somehow magically transported to Gibsland in the next ten hours, Bonnie will forever share my body.

I sink to my knees, my tears blending with the raindrops.

Looks like you win after all, Bonnie.

CHAPTER 24

Sunday, May 22nd // 10:36 P.M.

Clyde

I watch as the weak-kneed bastard gets into the truck and drives away—leaving Twinkle behind. If only I'd made up my mind a minute sooner, I wouldn't be in this mess! I try to holler directly into Jack Daniel's brain that he's a fool—to go back and get her no matter what the cost. But either he doesn't hear me or he doesn't care, because he pays me no mind. Just keeps on driving slow, both hands on the wheel like a muddled old woman, the automatic wipers going lickety-split across the front window even though it ain't barely raining.

All I can think about is Twinkle's face, her eyes filling with tears as she begged Jack to go with her. I should be mad at her since she's the one who kicked me to the ground, but I know she got scairt, thinking she was turning into Bonnie right there and then. Can't say I blame her. Being in someone else's skin is the most infuriating thing that's ever happened to me. It's like being in prison without knowing your release date.

This whole thing has me plum on edge because I can't calculate a clear way out.

He drives a few blocks before I know for sure that Jack ain't changing his mind. What kind of man leaves his moll behind? A lousy piker is what. I start concentrating hard, like a fox with one foot caught in a steel trap, thinking on how to get out of this coward's mind and into his body, but I ain't having no luck.

I need something bad to happen right quick, something that'll scare Jack Daniel right out of his body so I can take over again. *Lord, I'd sure appreciate some help here. I have to get to Gibsland and I want Twinkle by my side. I want to let her know that what I said before was the real deal, not a con job.* A speedy silver car cuts in front of us with no room to spare.

May lightning strike me dead if that ain't a sign that my plea went straight to God's ear.

Jack Daniel turns the wheel hard to the left, attempting to swerve out of the way, but since the ground is slick with rain, the back end fishtails. Instead of trying to even things out by making little adjustments, he turns the wheel back and forth fast, like he's doing a jig. Why, he's worse at driving a car than a three-legged mule! The next few moments are a blur of lights and colors as Crybaby runs off the side of the road, up the curb, and into a big ole light pole. The hood crunches up and Jack closes his eyes, so I can't see nothing.

I stare into blackness, wondering what's going on. Did Jack Daniel get hurt so bad he conked out? Is he dead, but I'm still alive somehow? *Please Lord, don't let me die again on the side of the road.* I pray another ten seconds before realizing I hear a hissing sound of steam escaping the engine. Like a dumb cluck, I finally open my eyes. I hadn't realized that I'd been catapulted back into Jack's body. I knew Jack was a chickenshit, but I didn't think a little run-in with a pole would make him fizzle out faster than a candle in a windstorm. Hallelujah! The Lord is surely looking down on me now. *Thank you, Jesus!*

I move the deflated white balloon to the side so I can lift my middle finger in front of my face. "You see this, you cowardly bastard? Serves you right for cutting out on Twinkle."

Warm liquid drips onto my lips and chin, so I swipe it away with my hand. Turns out it's blood coming out my nose, quicker than I can whisk it away. I flip open the glovebox, hoping to find some napkins, but instead, a fancy silver flask catches my eye. I smile like a fool when I shake the thing and hear booze sloshing around inside. Opening the lid, I take a big swig, loving the burn of the whiskey strolling down my throat. Someone raps on the window and I nearly choke. It's an old fella sporting an umbrella.

"Are you okay in there?" he asks, his face all wrinkled with worry.

I shove the flask in my back pocket before bolting out the truck, grinning like a madman. "Am I okay?" I repeat, smiling. "I'm alive, ain't I?" Another gush of blood runs out my nose and into my mouth. I wipe my nose on my t-shirt, then pinch it shut at the top where the blood flows out, like my mama taught me, not at the bottom like most folks tend to do.

"Take it easy, son." The man herds me toward the sidewalk, holding on to my elbow. "Go sit over there on the bench and wait for the ambulance to come."

"Ambulance? No thanks!" Damn do-gooder ought to mind his own business. I take off running, still pinching my nose. Last thing I need are docs with the laws on their coattails. A few more seconds and the blood will stop flowing anyways.

"Hey!" the man shouts in alarm. "Come back! Where you going?"

I fly toward Twinkle as fast as Jack Daniel's legs can take me. Hang in there, girl. Clyde's coming back for you. If I run fast enough, maybe she'll still be there waiting for me. The way she looked so sad makes me hope she didn't call her daddy and give up. I don't know how all this Second Coming stuff works, but if the rules Bonnie tole me about were true, getting to Gibsland before the deadline is my only priority. If there's even a chance of trading places with Crybaby permanently—putting him in limbo and me on Earth—I need to figure out what to do. I'm counting on Twinkle to know what sort of ritual that'll take.

I stick close to the buildings, making sure to stay in the shadows as much as I can. Which is hard to do, since all the cars' headlights is brighter than the center ring at the county fair. I stop for a second beside a boarded-up shop to catch my breath. I let go of my nose and find that the bleeding's nearly stopped. I'm about to run again when I realize I should cover my tracks in case that old geezer gives the coppers my description.

I toss my blue gardener's hat into the bushes and strip off the black shirt I got on, leaving me only wearing Jack's white undershirt—a peculiar one with no sleeves. I take off running. The rain is coming down hard now and my shirt gets soaked within a minute. An occasional drop of blood from my nose lands on my shirt, making it look like a kid's painting, but I don't care. I got to get to Twinkle before she leaves.

When I see the gas station sign up ahead, my legs find new strength. I jump over a row of bushes and cut through another parking lot, this one a liquor store. As I race past the door, I see a sleek silver car setting there with its engine on—with no one behind the wheel.

I look up at the sky, grinning. "Why, thank you, Lord. I don't mind if I do." I hop inside and see that it's got near a full tank of gas. I put it into drive and zip away, just like that. "Hold on, Twinkle!" I yell, hitting the gas. Four stores down and thirty seconds later, I zoom into the gas station and scan the lot, looking for my moll.

You'd think it was a sunny afternoon instead of half-past eleven the way the overhead lights make the parking lot glow so bright. I thought I'd be able to see her right quick if she was here, with that red skirt and white top she had on. But she's nowhere to be found. Could she have hitched a ride with someone else already? Then I realize how dumb I am. It's raining out, so she prolly went inside. I coast in front of the market, driver's side closest to the entrance.

I'm about to park and run in when a middle-aged lady from inside the store waddles up to the door and throws it open, strutting her wide butt through. I yell, "Twink-kuuul!" as loud as I can, hoping if she's in there, she'll come running. The lady puckers up her lips in contempt, as if she thought I was admiring her overstuffed carriage.

I sneer right back. "Move along, Mrs. Grundy. I wasn't talking to you."

From behind the biddy's shoulder, Twinkle's head pops up. She busts outside and hustles toward me—her eyes all red and watery, like she'd been weeping—then stops when she gets within five feet of the car.

I smile at her and ask all casual-like, "Hey, Beautiful. Need a ride?"

"Is that you, Clyde?" She winces, like she done something wrong. "I mean, Sly."

Right now I'm so happy to see her she could have called me Clyde Chestnut Barrow on a loudspeaker and I wouldn't have minded. "It sure is. Get in, woman. We got ourselves a deadline to make and I want to meet it with you."

Her face goes from looking as scared as a sow in a slaughterhouse to as joyous as a preacher on Christmas Day. She runs round the front of the car to the passenger side. But instead of getting in, she leans in the window. "Where did you get—?"

"I'll explain later. Hop in." I pat the seat.

She pinches her eyebrows close together, as if deciding. "I'm not sure I should."

Looks like I need to make her trust me again. "Don't say that, kitten. I want you with me. I promise to keep my hands to myself."

She stares at me with those big green eyes, shaking her head. "I want to believe you, Clyde, but I'm not gullible like Bonnie. If you grab on to me—"

"—then Jack Daniel will come back and take me over," I finish. "I know you like to inspect things logically, same as me, so have a look at the facts. Chickenshit's gotten a lot stronger and knows how to flip back into hisself way quicker than before. If he takes over, we're both doomed. Same with you-know-who. When she's here, I'm weak, but then again, so are you. So it's got to be me and you, don't you see?"

She twists her hair around her finger in that cute way, thinking over my proposal.

I give her my last plea. "I promise I'm being honest with you. Come with me. I want it to be you, Twinkle. I should have tole you that before. No one else matters."

She looks at me, biting her lip, the worry of the whole world showing up on her face. After a deep breath, she mumbles, "Screw it," before getting in the car alongside me. She slams the door shut. "Hit it," she demands, strapping on her seat belt.

And even though I'm the boss, I do. Soon as I sail out of the gas station I pull a U-turn and make tracks back toward the highway. I let out a belly laugh, giddy with happiness. "Atta, girl! I knew you was smart."

"We'll see. Coming with you was either the smartest, or the dumbest, thing I've done in my entire life." She gives me a stern look. "You'd better not screw me over, Clyde, or I'll never forgive you."

I like the sound of never. Goes along with always, which is where I want to be with her. "I'll be a gentleman. Cross my heart and hope to—" I stop, grit my teeth in mock horror. "Don't want to say that now, do I?"

"I suppose not." Twinkle lets out a quiet chuckle, before turning all this way and that, checking out our ride. "Wow, nice car. Where'd you get it?"

I'm so happy to be back in business, I can't stop smiling as we head onto the interstate. "From God," I tell her with a nod. "He said I could borrow it for a little while."

"Amen to that!" Twinkle says with a flirty laugh.

And amen to hoping Twinkle feels the same way about me that I do about her. A thought that I'm double-crossing my old gal hits me hard in the chest, but I shrug it off. I done all I could for that gal when we was together, but the circumstances have changed, which means I need to change, too.

A lump of coal rattles around in my rib cage. It suddenly occurs to me that Twinkle ain't never said nothing about wanting to be with me. Making decisions without proof is dead man's chatter. I need to ask her straight out if it's him or me she wants in the end. If I get even a hint that it's Spineless Jack she pines for, I'll have no choice but to jump ship and choose Bonnie.

I merge onto the highway and bring the car to eighty-five without a hitch. I run my fingers along the black leather wheel and leather seats that ain't got nary a scratch. This ride is smooth too, smoother than twenty-year-old scotch. Must belong to a man who respects his car's strength, beauty, and power—same as me. "I got a question for you, Twinkle. Were you truly happy to see me, or were you just pretending so I'd bring you with me to Gibsland?"

"I was beyond happy." Her grin lights up the whole car. The spark in her eyes tells me she's not fibbing. "As soon as Jack drove away, I realized I didn't have a Plan B. I started freaking out, worrying about, you know, my future."

She's not the only one. "We've got eight, nine hours until you have to think about that again, so how about we agree to stop talking about it and enjoy the ride?"

"Fine by me." She sighs and puts her feet up on the dashboard.

A trickle of blood leaks out my nose, so I quick pinch it shut. "Damn. It's starting up again."

She grimaces, looks worried. "Let me get some tissues." She reaches for the glove box.

"A big white balloon popped in my face when Jack Daniel crashed into a pole," I say, my voice all nasally. "Fool drives worse than a one-eyed goat."

"No comment." She shuffles things around. "Hopefully there's a . . . whoa!"

"A whoa?" I crane my neck to see what she's gawking over. When I hear the clunking and shifting around of metal against plastic, I smile.

She slams the glove box. "Yeah. As in, whoa, look at what I found—a ton of napkins!" She hands me a stack. "Here you go."

I rip one in half, twist each side into an upside-down tornado, and stuff one up each nostril. Works every time. "You found a gun in there, didn't you?"

"What? No. Just a bunch of junk." She waves me off, but she don't look at me.

I cluck my tongue and shake my head. "Come now, Twinkle, fess up. You know how I feel about liars."

She grabs the side of her head. "God, I suck at lying! Yes, Clyde, there's a gun." She turns to face me. "But I didn't want to tell you because the last thing we need is for you to shoot someone. You agree with me on that, right? I mean, just forget it's there. Seriously. Please."

"Forget what's where?" I lift the bottom of my shirt to dry my face, but it's as wet as I am.

"Oh, hang on. Let me check in back for a towel," she says, reading my mind. She unhooks her seat belt and gets on her knees, facing the back seat. Lets me get a gander at her curvy bottom. Right then, I see flashes of light whiz past my eyes.

"Was that lightning?" I ask, not sure if what I saw was in my head or for real.

"Sorry, wasn't looking," she says, sounding distracted. The sound a zipper makes as it moves down its track makes me wonder what she's up to back there.

If it wasn't a streak of good old-fashioned lightning, was that Jack Daniel fighting to come back—even when I wasn't thinking about Bonnie? A bucket of worry hits my gut. I don't like when the rules change in the middle of the game. I try to anticipate what I'll do if he tries again, but I let it go just as quick as it came. If Chickenshit wants to fight me, I'll fight back. I turn my attention back to driving, the road a line of tiny white dots flying past me, the sky a black tent surrounding us. Few cars are out and about, making traveling at night the best time for cruising over state lines. Some things never change, and for that, I'm grateful.

I look down at the speedometer and check the clock. Nearly midnight already and we still got a whole lot of mileage to cover. I press the car to ninety. Bonnie would have been hollering by now, but Twinkle don't seem to mind one bit. "So Twinkle, why did Jack Daniel run off and try to ditch you this time? You tell him you're sweet on me?"

"Very funny." I hear her shuffling things around back there. "Perfect!" She flips back around to the front seat with a pile of stuff in her hands. "Looks like God works out in his spare time. He had a gym bag back there filled with extra clothes." She hands me a white dress shirt. "I'll take the t-shirt, you can have this."

I check out the goods. "Mighty nice. I always wore the finest suits when I could afford to buy 'em." I nod toward the empty space between us. "Just set it there until I dry off a spell." I look for the crank to lower the window, but there ain't none. "How do you get air in here?"

"There's a button on the armrest, but let me turn on the air conditioning instead." Twinkle touches a few buttons and cool air blows out little flap holes.

"Air conditioning? Now ain't that a hoot?" I hold my hand into the air stream, and sure enough, it's cold. "Well, I'll be damned." My soggy shirt is irritating my skin. "Say, can you mind the wheel a second while I change out of this wet shirt?"

"Wow. You actually *asked* me to do something instead of ordering me." She looks at me, like she's considering my request. "But sorry, not happening."

I make a mental note to try and mind my manners more. "Why not? Afraid you're gonna go crazy when you see how good I look without my shirt?" I smile at her, loving the idea of Twinkle thinking about me without my shirt on.

"No, I'm worried you'll grab on to me and try to ask Bonnie more questions when I reach over to grab the steering wheel."

Now I see what's got her all stirred up. "I'd only do that if that meant I'd get to kiss you again."

"I knew it!" she says in a huff, scooting away from me.

"Come now, settle down. I'm just trying to tell you how much I like you, since I can't show you no more."

She nibbles the end of a fingernail, like she's worried I'm telling a yarn. I need to give it to her as clear as I can. "I'm a man of my word. I won't touch you."

She sighs, relaxing her shoulders. She looks at me all sly-like before leaning over and grabbing hold of the wheel, giving me a great close-up of them gorgeous bubs of hers.

"Not until *after* the deadline anyway," I add with a smirk. Then, lickety-split, I strip off the wet, bloody t-shirt and toss it in the back seat. She don't huff or puff none about what I said, which I take it to mean she's thinking about our kiss, too. Fate keeps bringing us together, so that's how Fate wants us to end up. Nothing I can do to change that, nor do I want to, neither.

"I got it now, thank you." I take back the wheel, rubbing my chest and stomach a few times to get air to it.

When I catch her staring at me, she quickly looks away. I grin as I pass two trucks, getting the car back up to speed. "Okay. Your turn to change out of that wet shirt."

She laughs. "Ha, ha. I'm fine, but thanks for looking out for my best interests."

"Your breast interests, too." I grin at her and she rolls her eyes. "Hey, you never answered me before. Was Jack Daniel heading off to the police station again?"

She looks out the window. "Yeah. He thinks turning ourselves in will be best in the long run. Do time now and then we'd be free."

My blood boils at the thought of wasting away inside a prison cell. "What a fool." I stomp even harder on the gas pedal, wishing I could teach Jack Daniel a lesson, face to face. Course, in the end, I shall hopefully live on in his place. With his dame. Ain't no better lesson than that.

She shrugs. "I don't think he was being foolish. He was doing what he thought was right, same as me. He thinks that you and

Bonnie will go back to where you came from when the deadline hits." Her face droops, her eyes look sad. "What was it like, where you were?"

I think about it, trying to find the right words. "It was dark and silent. Peaceful. Not happy like heaven, but after what I done, I thought I'd be standing in line at the devil's barbecue." I shrug. "When God brought me back for my Second Coming, He didn't give me no directions. All I know is that I want things to be different this time. I don't want to live like I did before."

"That's good to hear," she says. "Maybe you learned your lesson."

"I think so. What can you tell me about the ritual?" I'm real quiet now, hoping she'll slip and give me a clue about how this whole thing works. I hit the gas and bring it up to ninety-five. Now that most law-abiding folks are in bed, traffic's thinned out quite a bit. Hope there's less laws on the road too.

"All I know is that the ritual involves a last request. What was yours?" She sounds all coy and innocent, but I know better. We're both playing a game of cat and mouse, toying with each other, hoping to catch the other off-guard.

Enough of this. I'm tired of this game. "Why are you asking— you gonna try calling Jack Daniel out of me again, like you did with the perfume when we was on the bus?"

After a long bout of silence, Twinkle sighs. "Okay, so it's true. I did try to call Jack out of you on the bus. But I'm the one who did this to him in the first place," she adds hastily, "so it was only right that I tried to bring him back. You can understand that, right?"

I don't look at her. "Yeah. But it don't mean I have to like it."

"But since thinking about you-know-who is the thing that lets Jack back in and not strong scents, you threw away my perfume for nothing." She props her knees up, her feet pushed against the dashboard, giving me a nice eyeful of her shapely legs.

I rub my chin, liking the view, but finding this discussion unsettling. I need to put some doubt in her mind about the state of

Jack Daniel. "Could be we're both wrong about how we all switch places. Could be that God will decide our fate and nothing you or I do will make a difference. It could even turn out that I'm the one that gets to decide which of you gals I want, instead of you deciding which guy deserves to stay. Ever think of that?"

"No. But now that you say it, I don't know the rules either." She toys with her skirt, folding and unfolding the pleats.

We cruise along, falling into a smooth rhythm of talking about everything and nothing, when I realize I'm near the end of the first set of directions she gave me. I look over and see her hands clasped together on her lap. "Twinkle, do you remember the rest of the highway numbers we need to take to get there? We don't have any time to spare getting lost. Wish I'd nabbed a map when we stopped for gas."

"Actually," she reaches into her bra and pulls out a piece of yellow paper, "when I was at the gas station, they had a wall map so I wrote the directions down."

Leave it to Twinkle to be so wily. She unfolds the paper, narrating the directions. I plug them into my elephant mind—cuz I never forget.

"I asked the guy who works there how long it'd take to drive to Gibsland, but he said he never heard of the place."

My head turns to look at her so fast it nearly breaks off at the shoulder blade. "Gibsland? That ain't even a town. That's just a place a horse did his business and they put a sign up pointing it out. Why go there?"

She fidgets with her ring—putting it on one finger, then the next. "That's the last spot where you and you-know-who were together."

I nod, getting the picture. Makes sense we start where we ended.

She lifts the crinkly paper. "But the clerk did say he had a son who lives in Little Rock. Takes him around six hours to get there."

"And Little Rock to Dallas is about five hours. But Gibsland ain't near as far as Dallas. Maybe three hours, I reckon."

"That means we have roughly nine hours to go, give or take." She scratches her arm, staring at the clock. "It's twelve thirty now, so that's . . ." Her voice trails off as she calculates. "Whoa! We've only got eight hours and forty minutes left. And we're going to have to stop for gas!"

"Don't cast no kittens now. Take a nap and leave the worrying to me." I press the accelerator hard. Doing ninety-five should give us time for one roadside piss and get us there with twenty minutes to spare, provided we don't encounter no more time swallowers.

Which means I got eight hours and forty minutes to come up with my own goodbye ritual—one that'll get rid of Jack Daniel permanently—and then I'm home free.

CHAPTER 25

Monday, May 23rd // 4:23 A.M.

Monroe

After finding out we had even less time than I hoped, I freaked out for another twenty minutes before Clyde finally pulled out a silver flask from his back pocket. "Almost forgot I had this," he said gleefully. He held out the flask and basically ordered me to take some or he'd have to hold on to me and make Bonnie drink it.

I knew, well hoped anyway, that he was only kidding about the Bonnie part, but I also knew I was being an angsting pain in the ass, so I took the flask and slugged some down, then a bit more. Even though I asked him not to, Clyde took two sips as well—one for "fortitude" and one for "concentration," as he called it. He stuck it under the front seat, promising he'd have no more.

I must have eventually dozed off, because I wake up some time later drenched in sweat. "What time is it?" I bolt to a sitting position, my body in full alarm.

"Halfway to Tuesday, doll."

Moving my hair from my eyes, I try to blink the world into focus. "I slept through the deadline?"

"Yep. It's you and me from now on."

I look at the clock and then outside. "Wait. It's only 4:00 A.M."

Clyde laughs, slapping his leg. "Had you fooled for a second there, didn't I?"

With a hand on my chest, I catch my breath. "Don't scare me like that. My heart's going crazy."

"Probably cuz you're thinking about you and me together, ain't you?" He smiles at me.

He's talking to me, sweetheart. Hope you enjoyed the show I sent of Clyde and me while you slept. Now that you saw how much we love each other, you can forget about coming between us.

I sift through my dreams—snippets of Clyde and I having sex in the back of cars, in hotel rooms, on a blanket on a mountaintop. He definitely wasn't lying about his bedroom skills. I know I should keep quiet, but I can't help gloating.

You must have forgotten that I was in your body, Bonnie. Thanks for the sweet dreams.

She cuts off my airway for several seconds, but just when I'm about to alert Clyde, she lets go.

That's for being a low-life tramp.

I want to remind her that it was *her* life I was reliving, but don't want to risk her wrath. I run my tongue around the inside of my mouth, which feels drier than dirt. Dabbing the sleep out of my eye, I yawn. "I can't believe I slept for four hours."

"Almost five. And you was snoring," Clyde says, sounding amused, relaxed. He laughs, his arm casually laid across the top of the seat. "Good thing I got a good memory, Twinkle." He lifts the silver flask from between his legs and takes a sip.

My eyes widen. "You're drinking? You said you wouldn't."

"You want some?" He offers the flask to me.

"No! And you shouldn't have had any either. Pull over and let's switch places."

"Come on now. I wouldn't risk our lives, not when I'm about to have a second chance. I'm the best driver in history, with or without liquid fortitude. And don't fret. I ain't had much—a tiny sip now and then to wet my whistle is all—and I ain't tired in the least. But sorry to say, I don't plan to give up the wheel to no one, especially not a female."

"I hope you're kidding because things have changed—a lot. Women are equal to men now, Clyde. We have full-time jobs, we own houses—hell, we even build houses! Anything a man can do, a woman can too. There are even females in the Indy 500."

He laughs. "As what—flag wavers?" Before I can say something snarky in response, he glances at the rearview mirror. "Uh-oh. Don't look now, but we got us some company."

I turn and look out the back window. There are blue flashing lights—approaching fast.

"I just said not to look!"

"Sorry!" My panic jumps from slightly nervous to pure terror. "What're we going to do now?" I cycle through possible excuses, cracking my knuckles. "Should we say this is my sister's car? Or that we just bought it and don't have the paperwork yet?" I'm about to check back again, when I stop myself. "You should pull over, Clyde." I look down at his crotch. "And get rid of the flask!"

"Settle down, woman! They're going to think you're hiding something with all that fidgeting. Sit still and let me handle this." Clyde hits the brakes, and for the first time during our trip, he uses his turn signal to move into the right lane. He doesn't pull over, just drives slow, as if waiting to see what happens.

"Handle it how?" I remember the gun. My heart drops.

Clyde shrugs. "I'll wait for the coppers to get out and walk almost all the way over to our car, then I'll take off like ammo from a Winchester. I'll ditch them in under two miles with this baby." He pats the dashboard lovingly. He must mean it too, because he makes no effort to hide the flask.

Based on the way the trees on the side of the road light up in split-second intervals of blue light, I know they're right behind us. "Okay, fine. You're the boss."

"About time you came around." Clyde grins, pointing toward the glove box. "Now hand me that gun, just in case."

"No, Clyde!" I jam both feet against the glove box. "Don't even think about it."

Fool! You might need it!

"Don't be like that. Now hand it over." With his palm up, he wiggles his fingers, gesturing for me to hand it to him.

"No! I've been doing some thinking, too, and I decided that Jack was right about one thing. As soon as the deadline's over, I'm turning myself in. The fewer illegal things I've done, the better." The sirens are louder, lights right behind us. I close my eyes, my hands gripped together in prayer. *Mom, God, anyone? Help me to get through this. I don't want Bonnie sharing my body. Please!*

"Crybaby's tomfoolery is making you change your mind about being with me?"

"It's just that . . ." I swallow my words, realizing that once again, I've revealed too much.

"Can't believe a girl as smart as you could be so dumb, Twinkle."

He suddenly chuckles, staring straight ahead. "Well, what do you know? God must like you and me both. Looks like they's heading to arrest some other sad sack!"

It can't be. I watch open-mouthed as the police car zooms past us. I lift trembling hands to wipe the tears lining my eyes. "I can't believe it. I always get caught."

"Now that you're with me, maybe your luck is changing." He smiles for a second before snapping his fingers. "Oh, wait. You're choosing jail, not me." He shakes his head. "Too bad about that. Not sure what I'm going to do now. Shame to have to get rid of such a sweet moll."

I can't tell if he's serious or not. But I sense that I need to fix this now or I might not be going anywhere except a roadside ditch. "I only said that so you'd stop asking for the gun! I didn't want you to shoot another police officer. Truthfully, I don't know what I'm going to do after the deadline. I'm taking this one day at a time, okay?" I hold out my hand. "Look how bad I'm shaking."

Clyde glances at my hand and his expression immediately softens. "You're quivering more than a wet cat. If we wasn't in this predicament, I'd pull over right here on the side of the highway and hold you 'til you calmed down. But since I can't, you'd better have some of this." He hands the flask to me. "Have a swig or two. That'll cure the shakes."

"No, thanks. I plan to drive the next time we stop. That'll make me feel better." It'll also give me more control over the situation, but I'm not mentioning that. If Clyde decides to drive past the death memorial instead of stopping to let me do some sort of ritual, I can't do a thing to stop him.

Good Lord, girl! You are testing his patience. Keep quiet or he'll get rid of us!

Clyde clucks his tongue and smiles. "I wouldn't have thought it possible, but I kinda like your feistiness." He shakes his head, chuckling. "I never dreamed a woman could be so headstrong as to stand up to a man. I tell you what I'm gonna do, Twinkle." He nods at a glowing gas station sign atop a towering post that boasts *Open 24 Hours!* "We need to stop for gas now, so maybe I'll *consider* letting you drive after we fill up."

"Perfect, thanks!" I know Clyde's not the type of guy to come out and admit he's taking a woman's suggestion, so I take his consideration as a yes.

He pulls off the highway at the next exit, and a quarter-mile of roadside farmland later, we drive into the gas station. "We ain't got any time to spare. How about you pump gas and fill the tires this time while I relieve myself indoors?"

"Me?" Wish I hadn't been so gung-ho about equal rights. "I guess." I glance over at him and shrug. "It's just that I never worked an air pump before."

He busts out laughing. "I'm just having fun with you, Twinkle. Let's do it like last time. Hurry inside and let out your water and bring some more food if you can."

"Ha ha. Press *Pay Inside*," I say, realizing I can't risk paying at all. "I'll be back in two minutes and then I'll drive so you can nap." I dash out of the car before he can argue with me.

You're making a mistake. Clyde'll get us there faster.

Mind your own business.

Racing through the store, I head toward the restroom sign. My mouth waters as I dash past hot coffee dispensers touting delicious-sounding flavors, rows of juicy hot dogs spiraling in uniform precision on steel rollers, followed by rows of chips and candy bars. My stomach growls, letting me know I need food. Badly. But I can't use credit and I don't have any more cash. I lock myself in the tiny disgusting bathroom, trying to pee as fast as I can.

When I finish and wash my hands, I'm stunned at the sight of the disheveled bag lady staring back at me in the mirror. Self-pity floods into my chest, along with an ocean of guilt and a wave of sadness. Four and a half hours before I know whether I'll live, die, or share a body with Bonnie Parker forever. Hopefully the ritual at the memorial in the last few seconds will resolve everything the way I want.

Ha! I know Clyde has a different plan for us. One that don't involve you.

"We'll see," I say aloud to the mirror, wishing I could flip a switch and turn her off. As I dry my hands on my skirt, I spy a green disposable lighter on the floor and immediately brighten. Bob from the Half-Dead Society said the woman who claimed to successfully get rid of her spirit, burnt the poem along the Seine River. Yeah, Dad will be mad that I'm burning up seven grand, but compared to the alternative, I know he'll agree. Sliding open the zipper on the inside pocket, I deposit the lighter alongside the slugs and the poem so that everything I need is all in one spot. When there's no telltale *clink!* of plastic against metal, I gasp. Did Clyde take them from me when I was asleep? In a rush of panic, I dig inside. The moment my fingers hit the metal chunks, a blurry picture of Clyde's 1930s face comes roaring into view.

He lies on his side on a wool army blanket facing me. I look down and see a huge scar on my calf—the gnarled yet smooth skin of an intense burn. He hands me a clear bottle of vodka. "Go on, beautiful. Suck down some of that and let's get busy. We got to get back on the road right quick." I reach out and accept the bottle. The sun makes me squint as I tilt the bottle toward the sky and take a sip. Bonnie's annoying giggle-laugh slips from my lips. "Do you love me, Clydehopper?" Clyde nods. "You know I do. Now get over here."

I don't have time to watch any more of this. I fight Bonnie for use of my hand and win.

How'd you like that moving picture? I tole you that Clyde loves me. If you keep flirting with him, maybe I'll kill us both.

Me flirting with *him*? Hardly. But chill out, Bonnie. He'll be all yours very soon.

After witnessing Clyde pledge his love to Bonnie in person, I now know that he either really loved her, or he's a total conniving liar who will say and do anything to get what he wants. Although something about the way he acted with her bothers me, I can't quite put my finger on it.

On the way out of the store, I stuff two cherry Hostess pies into my pocket without paying for them. I hope God, or Fate, or Karma knows I'm only doing it for survival and will forgive me. I hurry to the car, ready to fight with Clyde about driving. As I approach, Clyde hangs the gas hose on the hook and calls out, "Time to prove yourself, Twinkle. Get in the driver's seat and start the engine."

"Yes!" I do a fist-pump in the air before leaping into the driver's seat.

The second I start the car, Clyde hops in and slams the door. "Go, go, go!" He slaps his knees while turning to look out the back window.

I floor it, a little too quickly, sending us both jerking backward. It's been a while since I've driven, but it's quickly coming back to me. As I fly through the gas station, I glance at the rearview mirror and see the old clerk hobble outside, waving his fists. I grimace, wondering if he saw me steal those pies. I roll my eyes, wondering why I even care at this point. My list of crimes is growing by the minute. "I hope he didn't catch our plate number."

"Not to worry." Clyde holds up a license plate. "I took care of that. I switched plates with another car sitting there. Luckily the bolts wasn't rusty like they was on the pickup."

"That's brilliant!" I grin at him admiringly, gliding back onto the highway.

Seconds later, my conscience points out that I'm complimenting the illegal acts of one of the top gangsters who ever lived. I'm really in deep now. Looks like I'm part of the historic Barrow gang now too, I realize with dread. Compared to the guilt I felt after committing my first crime, the rest have been so much easier. Anxiety starts to rear its ugly face, so I push those thoughts out of my mind. I'll have plenty of time in prison to mull over my sins.

Clyde laughs. "I think of everything, Twinkle. Like I tole you, I'm a planner."

"Well, I'm glad you changed your plan and let me drive."

He waves off my concerns. "Eh, that was easy, soon as I heard you promising God that you'd turn yourself in after the deadline. But now that you're driving this stolen buggy, you can add grand theft auto to your rap sheet. You might not want to run so fast to the fuzz now."

My heart sinks. I shoot him a dirty look. "Thanks a lot."

"Hey, you was the one who said you wanted equal rights." He smiles at me but I don't smile back. His tone softens. "Come on now, woman. Don't be sore. I was hoping maybe you'd want to stick around with me after it's all over instead of running to the laws. Maybe we can go hide in a little cabin in the woods until this whole thing blows over. What do you think of that?" He reaches toward me, resting his hand on the seat between us. "Sure wish I could touch you right now. Convincing you might be easier if I could hold your hand and look you in the eye."

"Don't," I warn, looking away from the road a second to eye him sideways.

He reaches up and strokes my thigh for a split-second. My heart skips a beat—his touch sending sparks flying through my body. "Whoops," he says, grinning. "My hand did that all by itself. My apologies, Twinkle."

This time I throw him a look of bemused annoyance. "Not funny, Clyde."

"Okay, okay. But let me ask you this . . . if I *could* touch you without nothing bad happening, would you want me to? Or are you just pretending, hoping to bring Jack Daniel back at the deadline?" He gazes at me with such intensity it takes my breath away. That's when I figure out what was wrong with the last mind movie. Clyde's eyes were hollow, emotionless, even bored, when he declared his love for Bonnie. The opposite of what I see in his eyes now.

My mind reels, wondering what to say to that. "Why are you asking me this?"

"You know why. I'm dizzy over you, Twinkle. You're pretty and smart, and hell, I even like how you're as bossy and demanding as I am. When those gorgeous green eyes of yours look my way, I want to know that they're all mine. Tell me you felt it when we kissed as much as I did. I need to know the truth. Do you like me too?"

I breathe in sharply, not expecting such an honest response. My heart races, remembering our kiss—the way he looked at me, the things he whispered, how kind and loving his touch felt. But I can't tell him that what he guessed is the truth—that when the time comes, I need it to be Jack at the end. I decide to talk about my feelings, but not about my plans. "The truth is, Clyde, I really—" Suddenly, I can't breathe. A soft whimper escapes my lips.

If you say you like him back, I'll choke you. Make you swerve off the road and we'll end it for us both right here and now. I'm letting go now, but I'm listening, so mind what you say.

Her words shatter my thoughts as I breathe deeply, trying to bring air back into my lungs. The anger in her voice makes me believe she'll go through with her threat. Not that I was going to tell him that his kiss sent tingles down my spine, made my knees weak. That he completely intrigues me in some crazy way that I can't even explain to myself, even though in my heart, I know it's true.

"You really what?" he presses.

"I really didn't feel a thing before." I bite the inside of my cheeks to keep from saying anything more. To tell him that Bonnie's threatening to choke me if I tell him my feelings.

"Is that so?"

I hear him unbuckle his seat belt, making my anxiety soar. "What are you doing?"

"I'm gonna see what happens when I come over and kiss that pretty heart birthmark of yours again. Then I'll know for sure. Your pulse, your eyes, your whole body can't lie."

I know exactly what'll happen if he kisses my neck again. Either Bonnie will take my body over or she'll kill us out of jealousy. "No don't, Clyde! It's not the right time." I floor it, bringing the car up to ninety instantly. "You said yourself we only have a few minutes to spare."

"A few minutes is all I need to prove how I feel about you, Twinkle." He gently slides one fingertip down my arm from wrist to elbow. An immense jolt of passion makes me jerk my arm away instinctively.

"Clydehopper!" Bonnie manages to squeal in the few seconds his skin touches mine.

If he touches me again, things are going to go south real fast. She's either going to tell him my plan, close off my air supply, or pull this car over and prove her love for him by getting it on with him on the side of the road.

Part of me—the impulsive, "you only live once!" part, considers letting her do exactly that. The rational part screams, "Think before you act for once in your life!"

He chuckles. "Sounds like Bonnie's raring to go. You sure *you* ain't?" In one quick motion, he leans toward me, so close I can feel the warmth exuding from his chest.

I force anger into my voice. "No, Clyde! Move back. You're making me nervous."

"Nervous I'm going to find out what you really think of me?" Before I know what's happening, he plants a soft kiss on the curve of my neck, his breath warm. I shiver.

"Don't," I plead, my voice softer now.

"Come on. Just one kiss. I'm so mixed up, I don't know which girl to take with me."

He's just toying with you to make you feel good. I know it's me.

His words and hers make me grip the wheel tighter. Fear pricks my heart, eats away at my throat. I keep forgetting that I'm not running the show here, Fate is. I swallow hard. "In the end, if you are the one who gets to choose who to keep, then who are you—" I shrug, not able to finish my sentence. Hell if I'll ever become whiny like Bonnie, pleading for Clyde to choose me.

"I want it to be you, Twinkle. The thought of never hearing your headstrong stories makes my heart hurt. But there ain't no sense in taking you along with me if you don't feel the same way about me." The way he says it, so softly and with conviction, makes me want to believe that somehow, he knows how to control who stays and who goes. My heart races and palms sweat, making me dry them on my skirt.

Take it back, Clyde! Take it all back right now or we're through! Bonnie screams, her words coming in tearful spurts.

I feel horrible for her but can't help enjoying my slight victory. Seems like all I need to do is tell Clyde he's the guy for me and he'll choose me in the end. But telling Clyde I'm falling for him seems wrong, immoral to the core. I adjust my seat belt, waiting for a white SUV to pass me.

I stare straight ahead, trying to concentrate on driving, but I can see my fingers faintly trembling on the steering wheel. "My heart tells me one thing, Clyde, but my head another."

"I ain't thinking with my head right now, Twinkle. I'm going with how I feel. Maybe you should take my advice for once and do the same." Before I can process what is happening, Clyde leans in and softly, sweetly kisses my neck. "See how nice that is?"

While his lips linger a moment, Bonnie cries out, "I hate you, you two-timing bastard!"

"I'm going to block her out for a few seconds, so bear with me." Clyde smiles at me before making a slow circle with his fingertip on my thigh. An alarming warmth spreads through me like a wildfire, heating up sensitive regions of my body I didn't even know existed. I shift in my seat, trying to keep the car on the road. He grins at me with half-lidded eyes, but he's so close I can see the golden flecks reflecting off the dashboard lights. "You're something special, Twinkle. There's a bond between us and you feel it too."

The protective shield around my heart breaks into pieces, as if Clyde wields some sort of magic power. A few more seconds of this and I'll be blurting out how much I like him. But I can't—won't—let myself be swept away by a guy who, if everything works out the way it should, will be gone come daylight. I gently push his hand off my thigh, but Bonnie clamps on and digs my nails into the soft skin on the back of his hand.

Clyde squints at me. "What're you doing, doll?"

"I'm teaching you a lesson," Bonnie wails, but this time, her voice sounds faint, quieter. Like she's whispering. Only I can tell from her tone that she wasn't.

I pull my hand away without any effort, easily resuming control over my mouth. "Huh. That was weird. You-know-who's still there, but she felt weak that time. Like barely there. Unless . . ." I shrug. "Unless maybe she's too sad to fight back."

"Or she's fading away because my feelings for her are fading," Clyde says. "I don't much care how she felt about the kiss, but I'm dying to know what you thought, Twinkle."

Taking a deep breath, I decide I need to test Bonnie's strength before I say anything. Maybe she really is fading away and will perish at the deadline, like Jack's been saying all along. Clyde too, and then it won't matter what I say. But maybe she's bluffing, hoping I'll touch him so that she can clamp on and not let go until after the deadline passes.

Time to find out.

I reach out a tentative hand and place it on top of Clyde's. No reaction from Bonnie. I grin, excited to finally say whatever I want without Bonnie's interference. "I might be stupid for telling you this, but I liked kissing you, Clyde. Something about you drives me crazy."

He picks up my hand and kisses it several times, his grin lighting up his entire face. "So you're crazy about me, huh, Twinkle? I knew it!" He caresses my hand, softly massaging my fingers. "You ain't gonna regret it neither. I'm gonna make you the happiest gal that ever—"

He suddenly yanks my hand, pulling it hard before letting go. I glance over and see Clyde's body jerk and contort involuntarily—the same way Jack's did when Clyde took him over on the bus. My fear skyrockets in direct proportion to my heart plummeting.

"What's going on? What's happening to you?" I glance at the road and then back at him in quick intervals.

No, please not yet. It's too soon.

"Succumbing to my weakness," he whispers, his eyes linking with mine.

One final shudder later, my world crumbles as my biggest liability resurfaces.

Jack.

CHAPTER 26

Monday, May 23rd // 5:18 A.M.

Clyde

The second Twinkle pledged her feelings for me, I lost control of my mind and Jack Daniel took over. As mad as I am for not controlling myself, of letting my feelings show, I'm out-of-my-mind, over-the-top happy that the wildest, purdiest girl in the world is dizzy about me. Me—Clyde Champion Barrow—born nearly a century ago. Hell if that don't prove I still has what it takes to make a girl swoon.

I watch out of Jack's eyes, my heart breaking as Twinkle turns as white as one of Mama's freshly laundered bed sheets when she realizes Jack Daniel has shifted into my place. I see her pleading with him like crazy, her face all wrinkled up tight like the skin on a busted balloon. Wish I could hear what they's talking about, but I can tell it ain't puppies and roses, that's for sure. Jack Daniel's waving his arms like he's a goddam baton twirler in a parade, but Twinkle's giving it right back to him in spades, the anger in her face showing she don't care what he thinks.

My guess is that Big Crybaby prolly wants to drive himself right to the feds. With Twinkle behind the wheel though, the only way that's happening is if he leaps into her lap and overtakes her. We all know *that* ain't possible. Ole Chickenshit can't even fight a little water on the road, much less a bearcat like Twinkle for control of the car. After what seems like eons, the fuming and shouting seem to give way to talking. Twinkle hands him the flask, but he don't take it. What a teetotaler. She leaves it on the seat and shrugs, before concentrating on the road.

Chickenshit huffs on the window, making a steam circle with his breath. He writes, "Fuck you, Clyde." Next thing I know, he grabs the flask and starts drinking all my hooch. Staring and drinking. No more talking. When he finally closes his eyes, I figure I must have worn out his body and broke his heart when he watched me steal his woman right from under his nose.

If that don't make me the wiliest thief that ever lived, I don't know what else I got to do.

The way I figure it, we got less than four hours until Fate lets her intentions be known. Hope Jack Daniel don't sleep too long cuz I need him to catch a fright. Then I'll take over and he can sleep until the end of time, while Twinkle and I will go on to make history ourselves.

Unless she's the best actress that ever lived and she's actually lying through her teeth. Then I'll plug a hole in her head the size of a dime and send her down the riverbank.

Even thinking that makes my blood boil. No, I ain't getting my ire up about her intentions. My fine-tuned instincts tell me she's giving it to me straight. I have faith that when the time comes, if I haven't busted back on my own, Twinkle will find a way to fetch me.

When the deadline's all said and done, I'll live up to my word, too. I'll do whatever it takes to keep her safe and by my side—'til death do us part.

However long, or short, that parting comes.

CHAPTER 27

Monday, May 23rd // 6:18 A.M.

Monroe

I breathe out a huge sigh of relief when Jack finally falls asleep. The strain between us was excruciating. Took me almost forty minutes of arguing to convince him to stick it out for a few more hours and stop fighting me on this. That he had nothing to lose by going to Gibsland but everything to lose if he didn't. He finally drank himself into a coma and passed out. Makes me wonder if the two minds are blending into one—Clyde's strong will to survive meshing with Jack's desire to have a jail-free future. Could be the perfect combination.

When I see the time, I jam the gas pedal to the floor. I have a long stretch of straight highway ahead of me, and I have to just hope that no cops are hiding out, waiting for a speeder. With slightly less than three-quarters of a tank left to burn, I pray this car can make it all the way to Bonnie and Clyde's death memorial because there isn't time to stop. I made sure I haven't had much to eat or drink so I won't have to use the bathroom. If Jack wakes up and has to pee, as gross as it sounds, he'll have to use the coffee cup I saw in the back seat.

With Jack passed out, I finally have time to mull things over—like how and why did Jack take over, right in the middle of Clyde and I talking about our feelings? As soon as I told him that I liked his kisses too, he mumbled, "succumbing to my weakness" and vanished. Was he trying to tell me that his weakness is being in love? Betraying Bonnie? Me?

I wait for Bonnie to set me straight, to bitch about what a two-timing cow turd Clyde is, or to remind me how she's going to take over my body at the end. Or to say that Clyde still loves her and he's only saying these things to trick me. But to my shock and my delight, she stays quiet.

Hello? Are you in there, Bonnie? What's going on?

When she doesn't answer, a tiny flicker of hope surfaces that she's gone. If Clyde wasn't lying and he does have feelings for me, maybe she up and went back to limbo. If she had hoped to spend forever with him and he doesn't want to, maybe she saw the futility in sticking around.

Of course, it might just be that she's depressed. Seeing the guy you love, the man who you thought was your soulmate—the guy you died for!—pledge his love to another girl right in front of your eyes is enough to shut anyone up for a good long time.

Even that sentiment brings no response.

While I do feel sorry for her, I can't say I'm sorry to see her go. *Buh-buh-bye, Bonnie! Have fun in Limbo!* My mood brightens considerably at the thought that she could be gone for good, even though I know I still need to complete the journey for Jack's sake. I quietly rotate through the limited number of radio stations, looking for any song from the last decade that I recognize. No luck. It seems every song that plays in these little rural towns is a country song about being in love, falling out of love, or pride in America.

Soon I'm lulled by the sounds of the car's tires on the highway. I'm making good time but the monotony of driving along a pitch-black road begins to wear on my alertness. Minutes later, I get a burst of energy when a song my mom loved comes on, "Don't Forget to Remember Me." Hearing it reminds me how she used to tune her little transistor next to the stove and sing along with all the hokey country songs while she made dinner. I quietly sing what few words I remember, when it hits me hard that the song is about an eighteen-year-old girl moving out and her mom telling her how proud she is of her, reminding her daughter not to forget her.

A searing pain erupts deep in my chest. Tears lick at the edges of my eyes as I realize that, unlike the mom in the song, mine would definitely *not* be proud of how I turned out. She must be sad that I'm such a loser. I keep complaining about how rough things are for me, and how unlucky I am to have gotten busted three times, how much probation sucks. But this time around, it wasn't Fate who was driving this train wreck, it was me. How could I have been so blind, so stupid, so completely immature as to tempt Fate yet again?

And like Jack so gruffly pointed out, maybe it's time I did something about it.

If I get out of this mess alive and in my own body, I am going to turn myself in to the police. I'm not going to keep running like Bonnie and Clyde did. No one's going to rush in and rescue me this time. I'll tell the cops that I alone stole the cars, and that I threatened Jack with a wrench to come with me. There's nothing I can do about Clyde clubbing that woman, but hopefully her injuries aren't too bad and he'll get a lighter sentence since it was his first arrest.

Turning myself in means the district attorneys will officially enter a felony conviction for vandalism in my name, along with new charges for auto and retail theft, aiding and abetting a fugitive, and driving a stolen vehicle across state lines.

How did things get this bad?

Goodbye to my scholarship, goodbye to NYU, goodbye to believing that bad things only happen to other people, that somehow I can fix whatever it is I ruined with my impulsivity. Tears start streaming down my face then, too fast for me to wipe them away. One small act triggered a whole lot of other illegal acts, and now I'm going to jail. Whoever said that things always turn out okay in the end was wrong. This time, things will not turn out okay, no matter how hard I wish they would. How could I have been so naive to think I was magically protected?

Of course, if I'm still on Earth and in my own body in a few hours—with or without Bonnie inside of me—I suppose one could argue that things did turn out okay.

Jack stirs, making me freeze. I hold back a sniffle, holding my breath, trying to stay perfectly still so as not to wake him. The longer he sleeps, the less time I have to worry about him sabotaging my plan. After a few seconds, he smacks his lips and resumes sleeping.

It hits me then that Clyde's parting words to me might very well be the last words he'll ever speak. Even though he makes my pulse race and we have some odd across-the-century connection, I can't—won't—help him come back again. I take a deep breath, feeling sad that I'll miss him, but happy knowing I'm doing the right thing.

As I drive along and the sun begins to rise, optimism starts to slip between the cracks. I'm young, I'll serve my time, and hopefully be out in a year or two, and then I can start over fresh. Not sure I can get into college when I'm out, but maybe there are online schools for film production. Hell, maybe I can take college classes in prison, who knows? I try not to think about my future because it makes my stomach ache. I had everything and I threw it away. Again.

When I finally hit the Louisiana state line two hours later, Jack continues to sleep deeply. All the whiskey and the events of the day must have really worn him out, thank God. I follow the signs for Highway 167 and continue on our way, running into only a minimum of morning traffic. As I head south, the sky becomes a beautiful blend of bright pink and purple swirls. Maybe things will go my way today.

I check the clock. It's 8:04 A.M. An hour to the deadline. I ride the gas pedal even harder when I see the flat barren landscape of Missouri give way to heavy pines as we pass through the outskirts of the Ouchita National Forest. When the radio becomes more static than country music, I turn it off, letting Jack rest in peace.

Whoops. I did not just think that.

Let Jack sleep peacefully, I mentally edit.

I sure don't need him going crazy and panicking, so the longer he sleeps, the better. Twenty minutes pass, then thirty. 8:37. We should be getting close, but I haven't seen any road signs in over five miles.

Where the hell are the signs for Gibsland? I memorized the set of directions I gave to Clyde, but none of these road names sound familiar. I can't wait any longer. I take a deep breath and hope for the best. "Jack! Wake up! I need your help."

There's a sign showing a fork in the road coming up ahead, but I don't recognize either of the highway names. Athens Avenue? Horseshoe Road? Where's Route 154?

There's a sharp intake of breath as Jack awakens. "What time is it?" He sits up, rubbing his eyes.

"It's 8:40. There's a fork coming up and I need—"

"What?! Why'd you let me sleep so long?" he barks, staring at me.

"What does it matter?" I glare at him, pissed that he's been awake three seconds and he's already arguing with me. "We're looking for Route 154, but I don't see—"

"Look out!" Jack shouts, pointing to my left.

A brown blur zooming into my vision makes me slam on the brakes. I swerve to my right, then to my left, but I don't know where the deer begins and the road ends. My screams are barely audible over the squealing tires, breaking glass, and horrendous thud as we hit the broad side of a massive white-tailed deer.

"Noooooo!" I scream. One ear-shattering second later, the bulk of the deer flies up over the hood and hits the windshield, cracking it in several places. I raise my forearm to block my face from shattering glass, doing my best to steer through a foggy distortion of brown fur, horns, and an ungodly amount of blood. The death stare of the frightened buck sears into my brain like a branding iron before the weighty mass slides off the car. We come to rest five frightening seconds later in a drainage ditch, ten yards off the road.

"Ohmigod, ohmigod." A sharp stabbing pain, along with liquid warmth, engulfs my forehead. I reach up and extract a shard of glass embedded into my skin, tossing it on the floor. Jack slumps sideways toward me, his seat belt holding him up. "Jack!" I scream, trying to rouse him with my voice as I undo my seat belt. "Jack! Wake up!"

When he doesn't respond, I pause only a second before checking for a pulse. My hand shakes as I try to locate the correct spot on his neck. For a few frightening seconds, I feel nothing. Panic claws at my throat, my neck, my heart—making it hard to breathe. Stop and get yourself together, Monroe! I scream in my head.

I close my eyes and concentrate on feeling a beat. An infinitesimal *bumpthump* grazes my fingertip, and I sigh with relief. When I try to remove my hand, a sudden twitch makes my left shoulder jerk, and I grip Jack's shoulder harder. Bonnie!

"Not now, Bonnie!" I screech. "Go away!"

No! You go away! Bonnie wails, the first I've heard from her in hours. *Sugar? Wake up, baby! Is that you?*

In my fright, I hadn't even considered that Jack could have gotten so scared by the accident that Clyde took over. Only . . . it doesn't seem like Clyde would be the type who would, I don't know, *allow* himself to become unconscious. With his eyes closed, I don't have a clue which guy is next to me. All I know is that I need to get us to the death memorial and I don't have much time to do it.

I strain to pull my hand away, but Bonnie fights back. I use my other hand and lift, finger by finger, until I pry my hand from his shoulder.

You might have won that victory, but this war isn't over.

Perhaps, but I won't be making that mistake again.

I'm about to ask her why she's been hiding when Jack gasps for air. I wait, hoping he'll snap out of it. When he doesn't, I let out my breath, not realizing I'd been holding it. I shake a few broken glass shards off my t-shirt and glance at the clock. 8:43.

I lunge for the door handle, ramming the door with my shoulder at the same time. The door doesn't move. My side of the car must have been pushed in from the weight of the deer. I try again, heaving all my weight against the door, but still it doesn't budge. "Noooo!" I shove and push frantically, bruising my shoulder and clawing at the handle, trying to get free.

There's a knock on my window, making me jump. A huge bearded guy peers in at me, his body taking up the entire width of the window. "Y'all okay in there?" he asks, his drawl thick as lard.

My body is catapulted into action. "I am, but my friend needs help!" I swipe away my tears and plead, "Please sir, get us out of here. We need to get out right away!"

Mountain Man attempts to open my door but he can't do it, either. "Hold on, sweetheart."

I push Jack's shoulder with my fist in gunfire bursts, doing my best to prevent Bonnie from latching on. "Jack! Wake up! Wake up NOW!" I shout, hoping the volume of my voice will rouse him. This is no time to be unconscious.

Mountain Man plants his feet and pulls with all his might, producing a ghastly grinding of steel. Unbelievably, the door cracks opens and he pops his head into the car. "There you go, little lady." His breath reeks like yesterday's booze, his face hasn't seen a razor in decades, and there are several gaps in places where there should be teeth. But to me, in this moment, he's a freaking superhero.

"Ohmigod, thank you! Can you please help us?" I beg. "We need a lift to Gibsland."

Mountain Man wipes crumbs from the sides of his mouth. "Don't you think you oughta go to the hospital? The closest one's ten miles up the road, in Monroe."

I'm stunned at the crazy coincidence, but we don't have time for small talk. "There's no time! I mean, we're heading to my mom's, and she's a doctor," I add, pulling that out of my ass. "It'll be cheaper and quicker if we just go there."

Mountain Man's face erodes into a mass of concentration, scratching his chin through his beard. "I don't know. Gas costs money, you know."

A greedy Good Samaritan? "Look, I don't have any money on me, but there's an expensive watch in the gym bag back there." I look around in desperation, trying to find other things to bribe him with. "Just drive us to my mom's house and you can have it. And the gym bag too, if you want."

His eyes narrow into slits. "What's your ma's name and where does she live?"

I know enough about small towns to realize he'd know in an instant if I lie. "She's not from around here. She's visiting a friend who lives near the Bonnie and Clyde memorial. Do you know where that is?" I bite my lip, praying that he knows and that I haven't veered off track.

Mountain Man nods. "Course I do. Everyone does. It's a few miles up the road."

I clutch my heart. "Thank God! Can you take us?"

"Hmmm . . . I don't know." Mountain Man frowns.

I think about kicking him in the balls and running to steal his rusty old shitbox, but quickly reconsider. Even if I did, I still wouldn't know where to go.

Stop thinking and move, girl!

Bonnie's urging pushes me into gear. I turn and kneel on the seat, grabbing the gym bag.

Mountain Man whistles. "Niiice."

Pig. Must have been looking at my ass. I swallow the taste of bile in my mouth and hold out the bag. "So here. Will you do it?"

"Yup. On one condition." He picks something out of his teeth with a dirt-embedded fingernail, staring at my chest.

I pause, not liking where this is heading. "Name it."

"I want the deer." He nods toward the front of the truck.

Relieved it wasn't some foul sexual favor, I look toward the bloody pile of intestines lying next to a hoof. "Deal! Drop us off and it's yours!"

"First I got to load this sucker onto my car. If we leave it, someone else will come and take it." He pinches one nostril and leans over, blowing snot out the other with a repulsive snort.

I can't believe my fate is in the hands of this moron. "I'll leave a note! Will that work?"

He thinks about it, nodding slowly. "I guess so. Okay." Fast as an arthritic mule, Mountain Man strolls into action. I follow him to the passenger side and wait while he hoists Jack over his shoulder like he's a feed sack. "The name's Thorp. Write down 'This here is Rufus Thorp's deer.'"

"Got it!" I flip open the glove compartment, hesitating only for a second before tossing the gun in my purse. I scrawl the message on an old envelope and glance at the clock.

8:49.

I run to the front of the car, slipping once as I step into a slew of blood and ooze. I shove the envelope into the dead deer's mouth, wondering if its painful grimace matches the one on my own face. Racing to Rufus's car, I arrive just as he tucks Jack's leg into the front seat. He shuts the door and I hop in back. "Floor it!" I shout.

Rufus nods and pats his pocket for his keys. He touches his flannel shirt pocket and looks around. "Let's see once . . . they gotta be here somewheres."

"You're kidding me, right?" I stand and lean forward over the bench seat, my face between the two guys. I scan the seat, filled with tons of junk, but I don't see his car keys. "Look in all your pockets again!" I start whipping all his crap onto the floor—doughnut bags, coffee-stained Styrofoam cups, a half-empty roll of toilet paper, and a sticky *Playboy* magazine. Gross! "Where else could they be?" I screech, my heart pounding.

Rufus dangles the keys in the air. He licks his lips, looks at my cleavage. "How bad you want to get there, honey?"

The Hostess cherry pie I ate hours ago threatens to come back up. I glare at him. "We already made a deal for the deer!"

"I ain't driving 'til I see your bosom," he says, staring at my chest.

My ears burn with fury. I reach inside my purse and grab the gun, leveling it at his face. "How do you like this view? Now drive the car or I'll blow your redneck head off."

The smile drops off his face and he holds his hands up. "Whoa. I was just having some fun, is all." He fumbles to get the key into the ignition, his hands shaking badly.

"Faster!" I wave the gun, but aim it toward the roof in case it's loaded. Don't need first-degree manslaughter on my rap sheet, on top of everything else.

"I'm going fast as I can." Rufus gets the car going and pulls back onto the highway, spitting up gravel.

"And don't try anything sneaky. I'm watching you." One glance at the clock and I nearly burst an artery. 8:52. "You got three minutes to get me there, or I'm shooting one body part for each minute you're over."

Rufus sits up and presses the accelerator, wiping sweat off his forehead with an old rag. "No need for that. It might be more like five miles, I don't know for sure."

"Three minutes," I repeat.

He pats the dashboard and starts pushing his chest forward and back, as if trying to make the car go faster. "Come on, Bertha. Move it, girl." The car chugs and chokes its way to sixty.

I start jiggling my knees, going over my plan of what I'll do when I get there.

First thing is finding out which guy is next to you, you man-stealing hussy.

Relax already, Bonnie. No matter what Clyde's feelings are for me, in a few minutes, I'm going to do my best to grant your wish to be with him forever—in limbo, of course.

Then you'd better find out now. Go on. Test it. Touch him. I can only use your mouth when you're touching something that belongs to me, remember? If Clyde's in charge, I'll be able to talk because he's mine. If I can't, it's your fella at the helm.

Good idea.

I'm an inch away from touching his shoulder when I stop. What if she grabs on to him and I can't let go? Then she'd have complete control of me and could do any ritual she pleased. How could I have come so close to blowing the whole thing only minutes away from the finish line? I look out the window and see rows of trees with no end in sight.

Nice try, Bonnie, but forget it. I'll drag whichever guy is here to the memorial and hope for the best.

As if on cue, Jack or Clyde groans and moves his head. His eyes flutter, trying to open against the bright morning sun. "Jack! Clyde! Wake up!" I push his shoulder with a closed fist, hoping to make it harder for Bonnie to grab a hold of him. "We were in a car accident, but you're going to be okay. We're almost to Bonnie and Clyde's memorial!"

"Okay," he says groggily, not clear enough for me to figure out which guy it is.

"Good thing he's awake." Rufus glances nervously at me in the rearview mirror.

8:56.

"It's been four minutes. Which body part you want to lose first?" I hold up the gun.

"No, please don't! I ain't good at math. We's almost there. One more mile, two at the most!" Rufus wipes a line of sweat off the side of his face with the toilet paper roll.

If he's messing with me, Bonnie's going to stay inside of me for the rest of my life. I refuse to even consider the other alternative—trading places. "It better be." I hold the gun up. "It's a matter of life and death. Yours."

He starts patting the dashboard again. "Give it all you got, Bertha."

Jack coughs then, a deathly gurgling cough from deep in his lungs. He puffs up his cheeks and looks around, panic in his eyes.

Rufus points. "Spit that gunk out the winda. Mind the upholstery now."

Jack leans out the window and spits. A mouthful of globby red saliva flies past me, specks of it sticking to the window. He wipes his lips with the back of his hand. "Sorry," he grumbles.

"Are you okay?" I need him to answer or look at me so I can see which guy it is.

Please be Jack, I beg. It'll make things way easier in the end.

Please be Clyde, Bonnie murmurs simultaneously.

He coughs and holds up a finger, wincing in pain.

I stare at the side of his face, waiting for him to look at me. If it's Clyde, I'll know by the way his golden eyes stare into mine with that penetrating, lovesick puppy gaze.

Rufus bops the wheel with his palm, making me look at him. "Dagnabbit! I hear sirens. Someone musta called for an ambulance when they seen you on the side of the road. I bet you a hundred bucks that them docs are gonna steal my deer."

If an ambulance is on its way, how soon until the police follow? Terror starts up deep in my chest as I do a final check for the ritual. I slide open the side pocket and see the poem, the slugs, and the lighter—everything I need—except the identity of the guy in the passenger seat.

I hold my breath, waiting for his response. "Jack, Clyde, answer me."

"It's me, Jack." Jack glances briefly at me before coughing again.

I nod, trying not to think about Clyde and how much I'll miss meeting him. Kissing him. No matter how wrong it was for me to have any feelings for him, I can't deny they were there. And worst of all, how horribly, stupidly ironic it is that the first guy I truly connect with and who seemed to really like me back is a half-dead ghost that will be gone forever in a few minutes' time. I've got no one to blame but myself.

Hurry! Do something to make Clyde come back!

Do you think I'm stupid? If Clyde is here, you're going to try to call out to him or trick me somehow so that you can stick around. But you and Clyde had your chance and you blew it. Jack and I deserve to live our lives—without half-dead spirits inside of us. Hopefully your final chapter will be swift and painless, which you'll have to admit is considerably better than the first time you two went down together.

You need him here or the ritual won't work.

For a second, I'm fraught with alarm, thinking Bonnie knows something that I don't. But then I realize she's going to say and do anything she can to stick around.

Getting greedy now, huh Bonnie? I thought all you wanted was to be with Clyde forever. If everything works out according to the plan, once I do my ritual, you and Clyde will be together forever and Jack and I will head to jail. Then you'll be glad you're not inside of me, right?

Well . . . I'd rather be here than the waiting place, but as you'll soon find out, the waiting place is better than jail. But as long as Chestnut's by my side, I can be happy anywhere. Don't do anything sneaky now, like trying to bring Clyde back at the last second.

You don't have to worry about that. He's all yours.

I take a deep breath, ready to do what we came here for. "We're a minute away from the memorial, Jack. So the second we stop, we need to run for it, okay?"

Jack nods, but starts hacking away, holding his chest. Another blood-stained stream of saliva leaks out of his mouth. "I . . . I . . ."

Rufus holds up a hand. "You prolly punctured a lung. Don't try and talk, or it'll make it worse, y'hear?" Rufus licks his fingers and rubs the unkempt beard hairs alongside his mouth. "Same thing happened to my brother once. He jumped off the plow trying to save his dadburned cow from—"

"Ohmigod—just shut up and drive, will ya?" I watch as the clock turns to 9:03. "Where the hell is this place anyway? You said two miles!" If we don't arrive in the next minute, I won't be able to perform the ritual before the deadline hits. Despite the heat, thinking about sharing my body with Bonnie makes me shiver.

"See those people up ahead a piece? That's the spot you want." Rufus slows the truck.

"Wait. Why are they here?" My voice sounds high and whiny, not like my own.

Rufus scratches his neck. "Lots of people come by this here rock—some shoot at it, some cuss, some even screw alongside it at night." He smiles, revealing his rotting brown teeth. "Is that why you two is in such a hurry? You feeling frisky this morning?"

"Pull over!" I bark. "Now!"

He stops on the side of the road, ten yards past the shoddy-looking memorial. I knew from the picture that it wasn't much, but the blob of cement two feet wide by five feet high riddled with bullet holes is even less impressive than what I remember.

I glance at Rufus's clock one last time. 9:04. I bolt out of the car and whip open Jack's door. "Hurry! We only have a few minutes!"

As Jack stumbles out of the car, Rufus says, "You two mind if I watch?"

"Go get your fricking deer!" I slam the door and give him the finger, then turn my attention to Jack.

"Can you run?" I want to link arms with him and sprint to the death rock, but I don't trust that Bonnie won't try latching on to him.

He nods, glancing at me for only a second before starting to jog toward the rock.

My heart stops. Was that Clyde's soft hazelnut ones staring back at me? I stand frozen to the spot for a moment as he shuffles past me, holding on to his chest, coughing. "Come on . . . Monroe."

Relief floods through me. Clyde doesn't even know my real name. The gold flecks must have been sunlight or maybe a reflection. Still. I need to double-check one last time before the ritual's done.

When we get to the memorial, two couples roughly our age are there, along with a ton of empty Lone Star beer cans by their feet. Sitting on top of the rock is a guy in an army jacket who has his arm slung around a black-haired girl who has a half-sleeve of tats, their legs dangling off the sides. The other couple, a body builder with an LSU t-shirt and a blonde bimbo, stand a foot away talking.

"Y'all here for the Bonnie and Clyde reunion party?" the army guy asks, handing the tattoo girl a fat blunt.

"Yep." I kneel on the ground in front of the memorial, reaching into my purse to find something I can dig with. I think about using the butt of the gun but decide on the hairbrush. Would be just my luck to accidentally kill myself. I jab the handle of the brush into the gravelly ground again and again, not making much progress. I start pounding it into the ground as hard as I can, little clods of dirt flying up.

LSU guy steps forward, standing only a few feet away from my meager hole. "Why are you digging?"

It's not a deep hole, but it'll have to do. I almost say, "none of your business," but don't want to start a fight. "It's for a love ritual, that's all. We'll be gone in a few minutes."

I reach into my purse and grab the folded poem. An electrifying zing travels up my arm, making me drop it onto the ground. I'd forgotten Bonnie's ability to control me any time she's touching something that belonged to her. I'm about to reach in and grab the slugs when I stop. I can't afford to lose precious time hypnotized by a two-minute mind movie.

Jack has his arms crossed in front of him, but at least he's not making a run for the police station. "Jack, you need to grab the slugs out of my purse—quick!" I hold my open purse out to him. "They're in the side pocket."

I hope you know what you're doing, because I don't feel Clyde's spirit here.

Just hang on, you will in a minute.

Jack reaches in and pulls the slugs out, brushing my arm. I wince, expecting Bonnie to yelp or grab on, but she does nothing. Jack holds the slugs out in his open palm while I remain in control of all my limbs.

Touch him again! I could have sworn it was Clyde.

I ignore her, not falling for any more of her tricks. Pushing my hair behind my ear, my hand trembling, I glance at Jack. "Now drop the slugs right there and I'll read the poem."

Jack nods and tosses them into the hole.

LSU guy steps closer. "Hey, what are you doing? You're making me nervous."

"Like I said before," I say, fighting to keep my tone even, "we're trying to reunite Bonnie and Clyde. You know, for their anniversary gift."

I grab the poem from off the ground as another icy sensation races up my arm. Fighting nausea as I unfold the paper, Bonnie competes with me for use of my arm muscles. I grip the paper tightly between my fingers, my hands shaking as I try to lay it flat on the ground. But when I try to release the paper, she won't let go.

Stop it, Bonnie! We need to read this so you can be reunited with Clyde.

Fine. I'll read it.

Bonnie starts reading aloud, *"You've read the story of Jesse James/ of how he lived and died./ If you're still in need;/ of something to read,/ here's the story of Bonnie and Clyde."*

"That's the poem!" The tattooed girl looks at her friend. "The one I told you about!"

"You like it? I wrote it!" Bonnie drawls.

"Funny." The stoned blonde girl erupts in giggles at the thought.

"No, it's not. It's a dedication to my true love. *My* true love," Bonnie barks before resuming use of my vocal chords. *"Now Bonnie and Clyde are the Barrow gang,/ I'm sure you all have read/ How they rob and steal;/ and those who squeal,/ are usually found dying or dead."*

Fighting to get control of my fingers back, I concentrate on pulling my elbows apart, hoping she'll drop the paper, but Bonnie grips it even tighter.

Damn you, Bonnie! You agreed to this—to being with Clyde in the waiting place.

I'm trying something else.

LSU takes a swig of his beer. "Read it louder," he commands. "I like it."

Bonnie continues reading—louder, faster. I pray she'll finish it before the time ticks even another minute.

"Anyone want a hit?" Army Dude holds in a lungful of smoke.

Jack shakes his head, his jaw set tight.

Bonnie rushes through the middle stanzas. She must be too delighted with revisiting one of her beloved poems to realize this ritual could mean the end of her, or else she doesn't really care about being with Clyde after all. *"If a policeman is killed in Dallas/ and they have no clue or guide./ If they can't find a fiend,/ they just wipe their slate clean/ and hang it on Bonnie and Clyde."*

"If they can't find a what? Let me see that." LSU reaches out to snatch it from me.

Bonnie pulls it out of his reach and continues reading, louder, faster.

Jack steps between us. "Leave . . . her . . . alone," he hacks out.

I attempt to scream, "Grab it, Jack! Take it from me!" but Bonnie won't allow me to speak. The closer we get to the deadline, the stronger she's becoming.

LSU laughs. "What are you going to do if I don't? Cough on me?"

Holding his side and wincing in pain, Jack reaches into my purse and pulls out the gun. "Or kill you."

LSU's eyes bug out of his head. "Whoa! What the hell, dude? Put that away."

I watch in total shock as Jack takes a fast step forward, jutting out his chin in a threatening gesture. "Leave!"

Clyde must have totally worn off on him, I think. Unless . . . oh my God. No.

Army Dude and his date slide off the rock in a hurry. "Man, total buzz kill."

I keep stealing glances at Jack whenever I can, desperately needing to get a good look at his eyes or see some other telltale sign that will confirm which guy this is in front of me. But he stands with hands in fists staring at the four stumbling off toward their car, swearing and complaining.

A horrible, gut-wrenching thought occurs to me: Could *Bonnie* be trying to do a ritual to get rid of *me* instead of the other way around?

Bonnie laughs. *Who's the stupid cluck now?*

Jack leans against the rock and casually crosses his ankles. The whole trip he was trying to run to the police, but now that I need him to pay attention and see what's going on, he's completely oblivious. What the hell? I try to stand up so I can kick Jack or do something to alert him, but the moment I do, Bonnie keeps my knees bent and starts reading even faster.

Stop this, Bonnie! This is *my* body, *my* life!

Not for long it ain't. Buh-buh-bye! Have fun in Limbo! Isn't that what you told me?

274

She shouts the final stanza, as if to drown out my screaming pleas, as she digs out the lighter. *"Some day they'll go down together/ they'll bury them side by side./ To few it'll be grief,/ to the law a relief/ but it's death for Bonnie and Clyde."*

She thumbs the wheel of the lighter, igniting the flame. She lights the edge of her poem. I watch the flames race up the sides.

Bonnie cackles. *Rest in peace, you little tramp,* and sets the poem into the hole.

The second her fingers—no, *my* fingers—are no longer touching something that belonged to her, I leap to my feet and reclaim my body, gloriously happy to be back in charge of my own limbs. "Goodbye, Bonnie Parker!" Making fists, I raise my arms up in a V. "Rot in Limbo, you annoying Clyde Barrow groupie."

Whatever that is, you are one, too. But since Clyde's coming with me, it looks like I win after all.

Thinking of Clyde makes my heart heavy. In a way, she's absolutely right—but for the wrong reasons. While she liked the rush of loving a badass gangster who robbed banks for a living, I fell for the kind, non-criminal side of Clyde Barrow. He's probably pissed as hell that I betrayed him, not to mention completely freaked out as he watches his second chance burn to a crisp through Jack's eyes.

Clyde, where are you? Bonnie wails, frantic. *Come with me now!*

He'll join you in the waiting place in one second, I reassure her. Together forever, just like you wanted, the moment these final shreds of paper turn to ash. I'm vaguely aware of a car engine starting, followed by an old rap song about Bonnie and Clyde blasting from the windows.

I gather some dirt with my toe, ready push it over the fire and end our ritual. I fold my hands, praying that the wishes of the dead as well as the universe have been satisfied. With only a tiny corner of the poem left to burn, I deliver what I hope is the perfect eulogy. "Bonnie and Clyde, may you now be buried side by side, just like you always wanted."

Jack grabs my arm—hard. "Hold up."

Clyde! Bonnie squeals with delight. *There you are!*

I feel a combined rush of sadness and guilt, knowing Clyde is heading to meet her at that moment. Goodbye, Clyde, I whisper. It was cool getting to meet you. You're not as horrible as everyone thinks.

Jack seizes his chest. "Lord, grant his final request." He leans over and spits a bloody mass into the hole. "Find it in your heart to let Jack Daniel . . . reside in heaven forever and ever."

And with that, the last of the poem burns completely and he pushes the dirt over the hole with his toe. "Amen."

"Yes! We did it!" I squeal, hugging myself.

Wait.

He said Jack Daniel.

I'm caught off-guard, zapped into the twilight zone. I can barely breathe as I turn toward the guy next to me, looking for a retraction. What I see is Clyde's golden eyes gazing back at me. "Clyde?" I whisper.

He nods, grimacing in pain. "You got that right." He gives me a lop-sided smile, a bit of red saliva glistening on his lips. "It's me and you from now on, Twinkle."

My head spins, blackness flitters at my consciousness. It can't be! How did I screw this up? I swallow hard. "Is Jack gone?" I lick my lips but my tongue is dry.

"As soon as the deadline hits, he will be. I did a ritual granting what I figured was his last request—going to Heaven." He smiles, holding his chest. "Ain't that grand?" He looks to the sky and shouts, "Thank you, Lord!"

"I . . . I'm confused." I rake my fingers through my hair as it all becomes clear. How could I have been so blind? So dumb? Jack would never have picked up that gun, would not have been brave enough to get rid of the stoners.

Clyde shrugs. "Let me help you out. Bonnie's last wish was to be buried together, but mine was to live forever." He smiles at me. "Thanks for granting my wish."

"Bonnie?" I call out. "Are you still here?"

Yes, but where's Clyde? she wails, her voice filled with anguish.

A better question is . . . where's Jack? Can he see through Clyde's eyes right now? Is he screaming my name, cursing me? This can't be happening!

Clyde's expression darkens. "What's wrong? Ain't that what you wanted? You and me together?" He fights to speak between short gasps for air.

"Yes, but . . ." I can't admit I was betraying him. My knees wobble, threatening to give out on me. I back up, holding on to the rock for support.

"You're whiter than an Easter lily, woman." He comes closer and presses up against me, caressing my cheek. He places his hands on my waist, gazing into my eyes. "Stop fretting, kitten. This is the way Fate wanted it or it'd be Jack Daniel and Bonnie standing here, not you and me."

Bonnie lets out a loud cry. *What are you saying, Clyde?*

If Bonnie's still in my head, that means I still have a few precious seconds to get this right, or I'll forever live with my mistake.

Hold on a second.

Why didn't she speak aloud?

This proves Clyde had been telling me the truth about how he felt about me. He obviously no longer belonged to Bonnie, or she'd be the one using my voice right now. I get one final, desperate idea.

If my gamble is right—that Clyde's weakness is thinking about the girl he loves—then I might be able to resolve this. I run my hands up the sides of his arms, smiling. "I'm glad it's you and me, Clyde. Let's get out of here and find us a cabin in the woods. Let me show you how I feel."

"Now you're talking." Clyde grins, about to lean in for a kiss, when he backs up, grabbing his chest. His expression on his face turns dark with rage. "You, you . . . tricked . . . me."

His Tequila gold eyes roll back in his head as his body contorts wildly.

I want to hug him, console him in his final seconds, but I can't risk Bonnie's interference. "I'm sorry, Clyde! You and me really were cut from the same cloth, like you said. But you already had a life to live—Jack hasn't."

I'm right here, Clyde! Hold me so we'll be together.

I can barely stand to watch as Clyde writhes, his limbs jerking and twisting in response to Jack rushing forward to take back his body. It's like seeing a dying animal breathe his last.

"It's 9:10!" the blonde girl squeals from the parked car twenty feet away. "Time to make out with your gangster of love so you can live forever like Bonnie and Clyde!"

A river of ice rushes through my veins from my shoulders to my knees, every limb reacting to her exit, making me shiver violently. I hold on to the rock as a scorching sensation rides up my body, from toes to knees to waist to neck—a final shudder leaves me dizzy.

"Bonnie?" My heart beats loudly in my ears. "Are you still here?"

No response.

I lift my hands and move them any way I want. I think she's gone, for real this time. I hold my breath, waiting to see who appears in Jack's body. After a final violent thrust of his chest, he coughs and spits out a bloody gob, wiping his mouth with the back of his hand.

I hold trembling fingers to my lips. "Jack?"

He blinks a few times, nodding. When his eyes meet mine, I see dark chocolate marbles, not caramel-colored irises. I nearly cry with delight. It's true. I clap my hands as tears stream down my face. "The deadline is over, Jack! Bonnie and Clyde are gone. It worked. The ritual worked!"

Jack leans against the rock, glaring at me. "You still think you had something to do with it? You're so conceited! The deadline passed, Monroe. Maybe they left on their own like I said they would. If you would have listened to me, we wouldn't be in all this fricking trouble!"

"Whaaat?" I screech, unable to believe my ears. My heart races out of control, my face burns in anger. "I saved your ass, Jack! I schemed and fought for every single clue to solve this thing. If I didn't get Clyde to drive us to Gibsland, didn't convince him that I was in love with him, let him kiss me, you wouldn't be here right now."

"Yeah, I'd be at home on bail, getting myself a good lawyer." He grits his teeth, coming toward me. I back away, not liking the look on his face. He pushes my shoulders every few words. "You liked every minute of it." *Push.* "Don't act like you were doing me a favor." *Push.*

"Stop it, Jack! You're hurting me!"

"I'm hurting you?" *Push*, harder this time. "How about screwing up my future? Aggravated battery is one thing, but three counts of Grand Theft Auto? You're going to pay for this if it's the last thing I do." Then he does the unthinkable. He spits in my face.

I slap him.

A faint wail of police sirens hits our ears, making Jack and I turn to look up the highway. Tiny blue flashing lights are way off in the distance, heading this way. My heart rate skyrockets. I take a deep breath, closing my eyes. Time to face the music.

"If you're going to run, you'd better do it now," Jack says with a sneer. "Run away like you've been doing for two days."

I look at the cops and then at Jack. I could've run. Three days ago, I would've run. "Despite what you think, I'm not running. I promised my mom that I'd take the blame and that's exactly what I'm going to do."

He lets out a disdainful snort. "A lot of good that'll do me. They have videos of Clyde at the ATM. Nothing you say can help me with that." He stares at me, his words hanging in the air.

I look him straight in the eye. "That's true and I'm really sorry for everything that's happened. I wish I'd never taken those slugs, never went to that party. I can't change what happened, but I can take the sole blame for stealing the vehicles. I'll tell them I threatened you with a wrench and made you do it."

The police cars are less than a mile away now and closing fast. He shrugs. "If you think I'm saying thank you, you're wrong. You got me into this mess and nothing you say will ever make me forgive you." He spits another bloody wad on the ground between us.

I know he's right, but it doesn't make it any easier to hear. "And I guess I wouldn't either if I were in your shoes. But I have one last thing to say to you before the cops arrive. We'll never know for sure whether coming here and doing the ritual was the thing that got rid of them, but I'll always believe in my heart that it was. Bonnie and Clyde were in us and now they're gone."

The police car appears then, kicking up gravel. Two cops exit their vehicle, one balding and middle-aged, the other blond and not much older than us. They stay partially hidden behind their open car doors, guns drawn. "Drop your weapons and put your hands in the air."

My heart pounds, my intestines twist, knowing what I'm about to face. I raise my hands in the air and shout, "There's a gun in my purse on the ground." I indicate where it is with my head.

The older cop walks toward us, his gun aimed at our chests. The young cop goes for my purse. Seconds later, my arms are pulled backward and the bald cop cuffs me—so tight I'm sure he's made a mistake. "You are under arrest," he drawls in the same thick accent as everyone else around here. "You have the right to remain silent. Anything you say . . ." As he finishes reciting both of us our rights, he grabs Jack and I by the elbow, leading us to the squad car.

Intense pain fills my chest, my head, my entire being—knowing how horribly sad my dad will be when he gets this phone call. All my dreams for my future, all his dreams about what I would become, were burned to a crisp right along with Bonnie's poem. That's when I realize with total certainty that if I continue to live by the motto, "You only live once," I might have to die to defend it.

We're placed in the back seat and the cop slams the door. I look at Jack. "What should we tell the cops? Are you going to talk about Bonnie and Clyde invading our bodies?"

Jack scrunches his face in disbelief. "Hell no! I'm going to say I was on drugs and wasn't thinking straight. You can say whatever the hell you want, but you should know that I'll never corroborate your story about Bonnie and Clyde, so good luck with that."

I sigh. Not that anyone would believe me anyway. If I did tell the truth, I'd be spending my time in a mental clinic instead of jail, forever branded as a schizophrenic. No thanks.

The bald cop gets behind the driver's seat and turns on his computer screen. He presses a button on a black box and calls in his location while the blond rookie approaches the police car, my purse in hand. When he sits down, the older cop asks him, "Did you recover the weapon?"

The rookie nods and holds up the gun. "Gun had no ammo, but I found something else that was interesting. I saw some upturned dirt over by the rock, like they buried something, so I dug it up." He opens his palm to reveal the two slugs, alongside a bloody slice on his middle finger. "One of them cut me up like a son of a bitch, but it looks like we got us some evidence."

My mouth drops open in shock and I glance at Jack, who is staring with an equally dumbfounded expression on his face. I whisper, "You don't think that Clyde could have—"

"No." Jack shakes his head. "He's gone. I felt him leave."

The bald cop grabs an evidence baggie and hands it to his partner. "Good work, Hamilton. Seal those slugs up and we'll send them to ballistics when we get back to the station." He starts the car and pulls a U-turn on the highway. As he drives away, he pulls the police radio to his mouth and starts calling in his report.

The rookie cop drops the slugs into the baggie and seals it. "Sounds good to me." He looks over his shoulder at Jack and I. "You two look as scairt as squirrels on a high wire in a storm."

My mouth drops open. No, it can't be. It's just a Southern guy with weird sayings.

The rookie cop laughs. "But not me. I'm free as a bird—a day I been waiting for my whole life. Time to wipe out all the crooked laws, just like God wanted me to, but this time, I got me a badge so I can do it legally."

"Clyde?" I whisper.

He smiles, his golden eyes gazing back at me. "I know I should be madder than a hornet at you, Twinkle. But if you hadn't done what you done, I'd be sitting in the back seat right alongside you. But don't you worry about a thing, you two. I'll get you out of this mess."

Jack stirs. "I don't want your help. Stay out of my life, Asshole. You've done enough."

Clyde tilts his head back and laughs. "You're still stupider than a hunk of coal, Jack Daniel. I was going to get rid of the moving picture for you, but since you ain't enough of a man to watch your tongue, I'm going to enjoy watching the movie I made again and again."

I swallow hard, because the next words I have to say will break both our hearts. "Thanks for trying to help me, Clyde, but I need to pay for my mistakes. I wasn't lying about the way I felt about you, but I need to do things the right way this time—for my mom. You of all people can understand that, right?" I stare at him, pleading with my eyes for him to respect my wishes.

"I knew it!" Jack says, staring at me, his voice filled with disgust. "You're such a—"

"Shut your mouth!" Clyde warns, fury in his eyes.

The cop who's driving gets off the radio. "What's wrong, Hamilton? Is there a problem?"

Clyde glares at Jack for another second before he rubs his chin, looking at me and then at the other cop. "Nope. Ain't no problem except I think I got a bit of a heartache. This gal in the back is a real looker."

"Better get used to it," the cop says. "This might be your first day on the job, but you got a long career ahead of you. You got to learn to harden your heart when you need to."

"I just might do that." Clyde gazes at me. "For now." And with a wink, he turns around.

ACKNOWLEDGMENTS

We've reached the best (and most important) part of writing a novel—thanking all of those who have played a part in making my dream come true. And there are a lot of you.

First and foremost, I have to thank the Big Guy upstairs. As with all my endeavors, it's with His blessing that I am able to do all the things I love. I'll also be forever grateful to my editor, Jacquelyn Mitchard, and all the fabulous people at Merit Press who coached and coaxed my story into a better place. And if it weren't for my genius agent, Eric Myers, who helped fine-tune my novel—especially the 1920s vernacular and culture—this book wouldn't be nearly as historically accurate as I hope it to be. Huge kudos to editorial consultant, Jennifer Rees, who was instrumental in helping me rethink the direction of the novel prior to sending it out on submission. Your advice was invaluable.

For me, belonging to a critique group is both a professional and personal necessity. Not only do these writers look at my story with a critical eye and give expert advice, they have now become my lifelong friends. GIANT hugs of writerly love go out to Cherie Colyer, Katie Sparks, Pippa Bayliss, Terry Flamm, Mike Kelly, Veronica Rundell, Marian Cheatham, Marianne Lurie, Susan Kaye Quinn, Allan Woodrow, John Petit, Terri Murphy, and all the others who I've met both on my online groups and in person. You hold special places in my heart—not only because you've guided my stories, but also because you're fabulous encouragers who still love me despite the mess I send for you to help fix up.

A unique note of appreciation goes out to Ginny Nelson, the warm-hearted person who first encouraged—no, insisted—that I stop talking about writing a book and actually do it. Thanks for the kick in the pants. I also need to give a shout-out to my close friends Jeanette Ruby, Mary Mulholland, and Lori Henkels, who stood with pom-poms on the sideline for years. And I'd be remiss if I also didn't recognize my Facebook friends, work colleagues, SCBWI, CHRP sisters, and all the other fellow authors who help spread the word about my books. Thanks for your support and kindness.

On a more personal level, I must enthusiastically and generously thank my parents, OB and Rita, along with my amazing daughters, Emily, Karly, and Kaitlin, and finally, my wonderful husband, John, for standing by my side and believing in me—even after a loooong wait for the YES to publication. You were my first readers, biggest supporters, and ultimate high-fivers. A special note of thanks to Kaitlin, who always has time to listen to my latest chapter and then succinctly tell me her true thoughts, painful as they sometimes may be. I love you all now and forever. And finally, it is with sincere sympathy that I acknowledge the victims of the Barrow Gang. I extend my condolences to all the families involved. May your loved ones forever rest in peace.

ABOUT THE AUTHOR

When Kym Brunner isn't writing, she's teaching middle school, chatting online, or watching movies. Although she spends a lot of time in fictional worlds, she hopes to someday interact with you in person or on the Internet. She lives in a Chicago suburb with her family and two dogs.